MERCILESS
MATES

BLURB

War is coming. And if I don't break free, my biker family will pay the price.

The Jackals are keeping me hostage. They think I'm a traitor and saboteur. Bait they can use to lure my brother and his club. Payback for stealing their drugs.

But the Wolves aren't coming to my rescue. I'm my brother's pawn to justify a turf war between the clubs.

Wounded and locked in a cell, I can't use the mate bond as leverage to weasel my way out of captivity. My enemies have severed our connection and rejected me as their mate.

My father's murderer remains at large. I have to get out of the Jackals clubhouse, find them and avenge him. No rugged, dangerous bikers tugging at my heart will stop me.

***Merciless Mates** is book 2 in the **Jackals' Wrath MC** series featuring a stubborn, yet strong heroine and four love interests with a guaranteed and rewarding HEA. If you love shifters, fated mates, Egyptian mythology, this is the series for you! This series contains dark elements with trigger warnings, suitable for 18+ readers. There is no bullying from the men to the heroine who treat their woman like a goddess.*

Jackals' Wrath MC is the 3rd series in the Godverse but can be read as a standalone.

Merciless Mates (Jackals' Wrath MC #2) © Copyright 2021 Skyler Andra
Cover art and chapter vector art by Atra Luna Design.

All rights reserved under the International and Pan-American Copyright Conventions. No part of this book may be reproduced or transmitted in any form or by any means, electronic or mechanical, including photocopying, recording, or by any information storage and retrieval system, without permission in writing from the publisher/author.

This is a work of fiction. Names, places, characters and incidents are either the product of the author's imagination or are used fictitiously, and any resemblance to any actual persons, living or dead, organizations, events or locales is entirely coincidental.

Warning: the unauthorized reproduction or distribution of this copyrighted work is illegal. Criminal copyright infringement, including infringement without monetary gain, is investigated by the FBI and is punishable by up to 5 years in prison and a fine of $250,000.

❦ Created with Vellum

GODVERSE

Welcome to the ***Godverse***, where avatars serve the roles of their gods in the Greek and Egyptian pantheons.

Meet:

- Hermes (God of Thieves, Travel & 50 other things) is a slippery and fun ex-thief.
- Eros (God of Love) is a former Phone Sex Worker who runs from love.
- Hades (God of Underworld) is lonely, cold, and hard until he meets Persephone in the bubbly and warm Autumn.
- Osiris (King of Underworld) is an ex cop who joins a motorcycle club to take the law into his own hands.

This isn't a re-telling of the gods' story, this is my unique spin on the mythology.

Gods from different series make an appearance in other books, but you don't have to be read each series to understand them all. You can if you love my books though :)

Here's the list of series:

GODVERSE

OPERATION CUPID
Completed reverse harem mythology romance. First series in the Godverse, but can be read as a standalone.

1. Battlefield Love
2. Quicksilver Love
3. Awakened Love
3.5 Stupid Cupid - a Valentine's short story

Cupid's Surrender - Operation Cupid boxset with bonus Valentine's short story Stupid Cupid

HADES' REDEMPTIOM
Completed Greek mythology romance. Second series in the Godverse, but can be read as a standalone.

1. Lady of the Underworld
2. Lord of the Underworld
3. Rulers of the Underworld
4. Return to the Underworld

JACKALS' WRATH MC
Completed reverse harem paranormal motorcycle club romance with Egyptian shifter gods. Third series in the Godverse, but can be read as a standalone.

0.5 Prophecy of the Gods - prequel exclusive to newsletter subscribers
1. Cursed Mates
2. Merciless Mates
3. Brutal Mates
4. Broken Mates
5. Sinful Mates
6. Festive Mates

7. Vengeful Mates

BLOOD DEBT KINGPIN
Mafia arranged marriage romance. Fourth series in the Godverse, but can be read as a standalone.

1. Married to the Mafia - coming 2023
2. Betrayed by the Mafia - coming 2023

More gods series planned! Stay tuned.

AUTHOR'S NOTES

Just a heads up:
1. This book contains alternating points of views between the heroine and her four men.

2. This book contains **3 x trigger warnings**:

Chapter 13 - dark and distressing scenes

Chapter 30 - scenes contain memories of child loss and an actual beating

Chapter 38 - violent torture

No need for hate mail in this book. There's no cliffhanger, but a nice 'lil surprise that'll make up for the end of book #1 :)

GRAB A FREE BOOK

One last thing before you jump into the book. Sign up to my newsletter here to grab an exclusive *reader's only* ebook copy of the prequel if you haven't already got it, ***Prophecy of the Gods***.

https://dl.bookfunnel.com/1hwipcn67p

CHAPTER 1

Slade - Jackal's Wrath MC President & Avatar of Set

"Shut the fuck up." The edge in my voice silenced the twenty Jackals in the room. "Church is in session."

What I was about to tell the club was critical for our future, and I wanted them to listen to every fucking word and get it through their thick skulls. I swallowed a finger of whisky to settle my nerves and wet my dry throat to deliver the shitty news.

Filled with too much pent-up energy to sit, I stood at the head of the table, knees bouncing, cracking my knuckles. "The club is under threat on several fronts, and we need to deal with it immediately."

Murmurs swept through the meeting room. Members glanced at one another. Jaxx shrank in his seat, twitchy, edgy. Prick fucking should be. Fucker failed me on our last ride. Scoped out Reg's delivery warehouse, told me everything was a-o-fucking-k when the Wolves were lying in wait.

One stern look from me reinstated the silence for me to speak. "The Wolves ambushed our delivery of Pharaoh yesterday. We don't know why yet." Speaking the words slow calmed my storming pulse. "But we suspect they stole our last delivery to sell it off, test it, and have someone come up with a cheap knock-off. We believe they want to get that shit to market to undercut our business."

Uproar erupted in the room, men hollering threats, some kicking away their chairs, fists thudding against palms. Testosterone, outrage, and lust for revenge swarmed my senses, making them throb with power, willing to exact justice. Clubs didn't brazenly attack another unless they wanted a war. Before old Heller's death, we had no dispute with the Wolves, and kept out of their business. These bullshit murder charges gave Danny license for vengeance.

Set was the god of fucking vengeance and with his power, molten fire in my veins, I'd not sit idle and let an attack go unanswered. Once I confirmed the Wolves were behind the stolen shipment, and slicing up my distributor Joey, I'd meet every strike from Danny fucking Heller with the smash of a sledgehammer.

No one went up against the Jackals, not since the Winter's Devil's attack on our club two years ago, burning most of it to the ground. Those fuckers caused the death of my former mate and lost us a crucial business partner. We killed every last one of them for their intrusion in our territory and raid on our clubhouse. Victorious, we claimed their territory in Newcastle, a thriving port north of Sydney where plenty of product could be shipped nationally to Queensland or south to Victoria. From then on, we controlled anything going north of Sydney, and all approvals filtered through us. Important and valuable territory to acquire. I'd not lose that if the Wolves wanted to play dirty and attempt to steal it.

In fact, their territory was on my radar. If we acquired

everything from Katoomba in the Blue Mountains, the Jackals would own everything in the Central West, the largest territory within the state, and everything east to Sydney.

"Here's where we're fucked up the ass, boys." Silence lingered in the room, thickening with every word I damn well uttered. "We have thirty days to pay our suppliers, and we don't have that cash. We'll have to liquidate some of our assets to get the debt off our backs. Good suppliers are hard to come by in our world." I let that sink in before delivering the worst blow. "If we don't pay our suppliers, they might storm the club and our businesses. We can't risk the safety of our members, our staff or the girls in the shelter."

"Fuck, no." Tank flew to his feet. "I say we go in and smash the Wolves. Put those dirty dogs down."

A move I was all up for, but Zethan and Castor would block it. Fuckers were sensible versus my tendency for blood-soaked demise. One of the reasons I promoted my VP up to his rank. Without him, I'd be mowing down my competitors without a second thought, going against the biker code.

Hands splayed on the table, I leaned forward, bringing everyone's attention back to me. They shifted in their seats, throats bobbing nervously, swallowing too much of their drinks. Scared. Anxious. They had every right to be. Our club was on the line. Their home and families. I wasn't the sort of man to be fucked with, and at the helm of the Jackals, we weren't the club to screw over, either. And when I got like this, I was a storm in a fucking teacup that couldn't be contained.

"Fuck, no." I clenched my jaw and reminded myself to breathe. It did fuck all to steady me. Fire had been lit on this fuse and it was only a matter of time before I went off.

"Here's what we're going to do. Everyone is going to keep his nose clean and stay out of trouble. Hear me?"

A chorus of *'Yes, President,'* went around the room.

I cracked my knuckles again to relieve the building pressure that wanted to rain chaos on the Wolves and whoever else fucked with my club. "By now, you've all heard about the cops planting speed on Alaric and arresting him. With the cops trying to charge me for old Heller's murder, we can't risk any more attention from the law. They're out for blood, and I won't give it to them, unless it's their own. And not until I'm done with the Wolves first."

Silence mounted, each member hanging on my every word.

Time to solve another problem. I had to get to the bottom of who stole our product. "Castor, I want you to track the missing shipment of Pharaoh. I suspect the Wolves played a part in this, but I need a smoking gun before I charge in there to waste them."

"Yes, President." Castor was more than happy to oblige. The incident left him pissed and embarrassed that it had gone under his radar. Piss off the smartest god of the Egyptian pantheon and his avatar and expect retribution.

I risked a look at Zethan, and he nodded. My rock within the room, the one to lower my temper from molten lava to tepid room temperature. "For now, all manufacture of Pharaoh is canned until further notice."

Glances shot between the members. A risky move that would cut into our income and hurt the club, but it had to be done. The cops were practically salivating for our demise, and I couldn't afford for the whole club to be arrested and sentenced for manufacture, distribution, and sale of prohibited drugs. Death was not coming to Jackal's Wrath MC.

"Alaric, I want you to scope out the Wolves and watch them, gather intel," I said. "I want to know who they're trading with and if any of our connections have fucked us over."

"You got it, sir." Fucking sir. I'd constantly told him to stop calling me that. I would have torn him a new one, but he was still edgy after his arrest. Being locked up behind bars reminded him of a dark time in his life that he wished to forget but couldn't because it was seared into his mind, heart, and soul. Scarred his body in more ways than one.

Two matters down and countless more to go on my never-ending list. The next problem made my blood boil because someone had murdered our product delivery guy, Joey. Cut his body up into pieces, shot up his staff, and left them for us to find. Joey was part of our extended family, had been close with my dad for fifteen years, and I took his death personally. That affront to the club would not go unpunished, either. Some cunt had sabotaged our club by destroying a trusted business partner and stolen a very valuable drug product from us. Whoever that person was, they'd die slowly, painfully, and I'd let Zethan bring them back from the dead and torture them all over again. Repeat at least a hundred times until we let them descend into the Underworld. Then, they'd burn in Hell for eternity. Zethan would make sure of it with his influence with other Underworld gods.

My VP rubbed at his permanently creased forehead.

"Zethan, I want you to find out what asshole knocked off Joey, and I want you to cut him up slow, finger by finger, toe by toe ..." Blood tasted on my tongue, and my Jackal relished it.

"All right." Zethan raised a hand. "I fucking get it. Move on."

Squeamish. Touchy. Pussy. The sight of blood was getting to him more and more. He'd seen a lot in his time. Dead bodies, beat up women and kids, innocent people caught in the wrong place. Enough to fuck a good man up. I shut the fuck up for my best friend's sake, but the carnage continued inside my head, and I lapped it up.

The next was a delicate situation that I wanted to handle personally. Marcus, one of our five cop informants, had stabbed us in the back. Arrested our fall guy prematurely, then had the fucking nerve to plant shit on him and make him provide false statements to the police about us hiring him for the drug shipment. We'd paid that dirty prick well over the years, but at his unreliability and insatiable greed, we'd backed away. A move that put us in his crosshairs, and I'd not let the fucker drag the club down. I had to be strategic how I handled this. Wait to clear my name first then take out old Marcus.

Armed with my deadliest expression, I said, "I'll handle that dirty cunt, Marcus, for double-crossing us."

The Jackals chuckled, throwing smiles around the room. Some of them had run-ins with him in the past, requiring us to pay him off, and they were more than happy to see the asshole go down.

"Fucking cunt." Tank slammed a fist on the table. "We've paid that dick thousands, and this is what he does." He didn't need to tell me.

Brix piped in too, "Smoke the bastard."

Not an option. Too many eyes on the club. A move like that would draw the spotlight on us.

I raised a palm. "We'll deal with him when the time comes. For now, we sit tight and wait to collect evidence. When the smoke clears, we'll teach old Marcus a lesson for fucking with the Jackals."

Hoots went around the room, fists raised, bottles of beer or whisky tumblers clinking in cheer.

Something told me Marcus knew the club was in a tight spot and that this wouldn't be the last we heard of him.

MERCILESS MATES

Blackmail and intimidation were his style within the police force. Declaring us enemies wouldn't end well for him. Fucker better enjoy the last few months of his life. Live it up while he could, enjoy his strippers, gambling, and trips to the pubs with his cop buddies, because all that was about to end soon.

"What about the Wolf captives and that bitch in the cell?" Rusty's question set my body alight for referring to my mate that way.

What the fuck? I caught my thought, rolled it back. After exposing her identity, I'd dulled the mate bond's hold and lure on me, leaving me susceptible to about twenty percent of its full effect. That traitor was not my mate. The sooner Castor broke the curse, the better, because I didn't want another thing to do with Aaliyah fucking Heller.

My hands curled, and I planted them by my side to keep my cool. "Zethan, I also want you to track down the dealer who hired the mugger. Find out if they have ties to Danny Heller." I only trusted my inner circle with this. Plus, it was god-related business, and I only wanted the four of us to handle it. "The rest of you, reach out to your contacts for information. I don't care how small or insignificant. Rumor or whisper, I want to know it. Got it?"

I poured myself a double shot of whisky.

"Yep, Prez," Rusty hollered.

"No problem, Prez." Slim skulled the last of his bourbon and Coke.

This whole time, Jaxx hadn't said a damned word, staring at the church table, not meeting anyone's gaze. I'd keep an eye on him and have Castor pay him a visit for his fuck-up yesterday.

"Church dismissed." A gulp of my whisky calmed the flames within.

I eyed Zethan, Castor, and Alaric, signaling for them to

hang back. *'God talk'* was in session. Everyone except them cleared out. It was time to confront our traitorous mate. Alaric poured a larger than usual tumbler of whisky. He had a lot on his mind with his hearing in three days. Castor sat in his chair, back stiff, drumming his fingers on the table, showing off his skull ring with jeweled ruby eyes. Zethan looked pissy and moody, and I was about to find out why.

CHAPTER 2

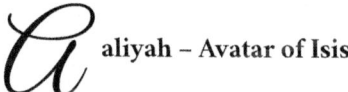

aliyah – Avatar of Isis

THERE CAME a time in everyone's life when they realized they were in deep shit. I knew it the moment I woke up in a cool, dark, musty room, groggy from anesthesia and painkillers.

Fog clouded my memory, a distant dream close. My brother and I playing in a field, chasing each other, him showing me a spider, him tucking my head in the crook of his elbow, smiling, promising to protect his younger sister. With each passing moment awakening from my recovery, my mind cleared more of the haze away.

Pieces of the puzzle I struggled to fit before everything went to hell in a handbasket snapped together with ease. Mugged and beaten up by a junkie. Rescued by two of my enemies and taken to their women's shelter. My escape, being kidnapped by my brother, and thrown back into the thick of it. Taking a damn bullet for Slade fucking Vincent and waking up here. Ending with the grand finale of being kept as his prisoner. Thrust into this mess against my damn will.

I groaned as I took stock of my surroundings. Light filtered through a single window to my left. The only other source was an old fluorescent bulb in the ceiling. An empty chair situated across from my cell suggested someone had been stationed there to watch me recently. All suspicion pointed to me being kept underground by my Jackals jailers.

More memory drifted back into my reach. The last time I'd spoken to the Jackal's president, I'd barely come out of surgery, and he'd accused me of infiltrating his club and letting my brother beat me up. Both lies. Danny betrayed me and threw me into the Jackal's world.

Everywhere ached with a dull heat, but not as bad as the bullet wound, and my internal organs, torn up from Danny's bullet. I groaned and glanced at the medicine, needing a slightly higher dose to ease the pain. A drip connected me to painkillers—fentanyl or morphine, perhaps. My hand skimmed over the bandages wound around my waist and torso. Movement stung as the canula in my wrist bit into me. Stitches prickled against my skin with every flex of my core muscles, scratching me and making me itch.

At least Dr. Shriver had removed the bullet fragment from my abdomen. Ironically, my gunshot wound took my mind off the rest of my problems, of which many clouded my judgment.

I'd dipped in and out of consciousness for hours to days at a time, and I didn't know the day, month or time, or if this was my version of hell. After taking the bullet, I had no memory of being transported to the hospital, only of waking to Slade's wrath.

My brother betrayed his club, our father's memory, and what little morality he held onto while he presided over the motorcycle club. Barely six months passed since we buried dad, and Danny had pursued revenue sources that broke every one of his rules. Absolute disgrace. The knowledge of what my brother did burned more than my bullet wound.

Danny used me to get an inside track on the Jackals, and I used him as an opportunity to get the concrete proof the police needed to arrest my father's killer. My, how the tables had turned. Slade was the prime suspect in dad's homicide investigation. After he showed up flying colors at my father's funeral, I was convinced of Slade's guilt. Now, not so much. But the Jackal's president wasn't the one stuck in a cell.

I tested my strength and pushed off the rickety cot my jailers were kind enough to provide. The worn-out and rusted springs squeaked in protest to the amount of support they gave. Blood and other bodily secretions stained the floor, but the Jackals had been kind enough to provide me clean sheets and blankets. Woozy and weak, I didn't have the strength to cross the small cell to reach the cell door.

I called out instead. "Hello?" My vocal cords scratched together like two pieces of sandpaper. "Is anyone there? Can anyone hear me?" I clutched my sore throat.

No one answered my pleas for help. Apart from the sounds of a bush tapping against the window or the wind howling at the joints, everything was suspiciously quiet. I wished I could have said the same about my mind. One thought circled the others, all of them involving my brother.

Slade's warning sat heavy on my mind. *"You're staying here until we decide what to do with you."*

Unbearable panic crawled along my skin, a prickling, burning sensation that spread like wildfire. I wasn't getting out of here alive. Slade would kill me as soon as he extracted information from me. Fearful for my life, I prayed to Isis for guidance, but she remained silent and unhelpful.

Anger surged above my sickening heartache. My life, my career, all of it down the fucking toilet. I'd worked my ass off to get out of and stay away from the biker life. Left the Wolves, and in part, my family behind too when I went off to college. Kept my nose buried in textbooks to maintain my grades and grant eligibility to accept my diploma with a clear conscience. The eight and a half by eleven slip of paper framed on my bedroom wall wasn't tainted by drug or illegal gun money. It belonged to me, when before, everything belonged to my father and the club. Independence and freedom were the sole reasons I'd left. Jimmy's death and the aftermath had contributed too. I clutched my belly with one hand and rubbed it with another.

The road to hell wasn't just paved with good intentions, it was paved with bad decisions and blood. A saying that rang true for members of an MC. From the moment we buried my father, I made one bad decision after another. I chose the wrong side and would pay for it. After seven years of studying, internships, and caffeine-fueled double shifts in the ER, I ended up right where I started. Neck deep in biker bullshit.

Slade and the rest of the Jackals loved to tell the fated mates' story, that our avatars were bound to one another, and they were my destiny as much as I was theirs. It was why they were so quick to fall for my ruse of an innocent woman beaten by a junkie mugger. That lie made my treachery that much worse. The easiest lies to tell were the ones wrapped around a core of truth.

I thought about my dream again, how sweet my brother was as a boy, and where it all went wrong. Somewhere along the way, something had tarnished his soul, turned him dark. Danny was dangerous. Quick-tempered, prone to violence and made good on his threats. I found myself on the receiving end of that anger on more than one occasion.

But I couldn't blame my predicament just on my brother when I bore the brunt of responsibility. I kept up the lie to stay in the Jackals and gain their trust. Time to face what I'd done and tell the men who had been so eager to devote their lives to me the truth. The chances of salvaging any sort of relationship with the Jackals were slim to none, but I had to try.

By the thump of feet above, the squeak and protest of hinges in desperate need of oiling, it sounded like I was about to get that chance. Wooden treads creaked under the weight of boot-clad feet and lumbering steps. One of the Jackals made his way down the shoddy staircase. The dim lighting made it difficult to tell which of my fated mates it was until he reached the desk.

I caught his smoky, whisky, and molten steel scent before he appeared. Anger replaced the passion and promise of things to come that simmered in his eyes whenever he looked at me. Tension and a glacial demeanor replaced the playful banter, the easy way we had about us, the fight for dominance. The president of the Jackals MC stared me down from the other side of the metal bars, no longer the overconfident, flirty, possessive potential mate. Ready to handle his business the moment I ceased being his mate and became a threat to his club.

"Aaliyah." His clipped greeting and arctic indigo glare were enough to make me want to heave my guts. My injury and frazzled nerves contributed too.

"Slade, I can explain." I gripped my blanket as much from desperation as my need for support.

Slade's bear-like muscles and overall body posture relaxed when the groan I'd been holding slipped out from behind my gritted teeth. The mask of anger he wore fell enough for me to see the concern in his eyes. He still cared, and I had a glimmer of hope. But I wouldn't play him anymore. I couldn't.

He speared a large hand through his Mohican-style blonde hair as if to stop himself from coming to my side.

SKYLER ANDRA

"You're healing faster than I expected." He cleared his throat and turned his back to me while he took a moment to recover, and the faint hint along our bond told me he made sure his emotional mask was firmly put in place before he turned to face me again.

"Not fast enough. I wish I could heal myself the way I heal others." I tried to break through the wall he built between us with a gentle reminder of how I helped people, helped him and the women in Zethan's shelter. It didn't work, and that hard, vicious edge returned to his almond-colored jaw.

"I'm going to wait for the rest of the guys to come down before I hear your confession." Slade hooked a boot around the leg of the chair and dragged it out before sitting backward on it across from me as if he were about to interrogate a convict.

The irony of being inside a cell when a person who ran guns and drugs for a living was free to come and go as he pleased wasn't lost on me. Normally, I would have a fiery response for him to put him in his place. My guilty conscience tamped down my ire, kept my tongue in check, and the situation from going from bad to worse. I had to handle this carefully, not push him over the edge and drive him to unleash that chaos and destroy me.

The rest of the Jackals weren't far behind. Zethan, Castor, and Alaric marched down the stairs single file. Zethan in his classic red plaid and jeans, making me doubt he wore anything else, even in summer. His piercing green eyes dove into my soul for a different reason today. Tattoos on his scarred neck twitched with impatience to get this over and done with, arrest me, throw me in front of the judge, and hold me in the cell.

Castor wore his Calvin Klein jeans, scratched at the knees, and a Tommy Hilfiger shirt. He smelled delicious with his aftershave and hair product styling his curled, shoulder-length dark locks. He stood silent like a judge deliberating on his verdict, and I braced for the gavel to pound at the delivery of my sentencing.

Alaric wore his scowl like a badge of honor. His gray and golden eye trained on me, absorbing every movement, devising a plan to tear apart his prey and enemy like the hawk of his god. Both he and Castor hadn't shaved, which was unusual for them. But Alaric wore freshly pressed clothes, a white shirt beneath his cut with jeans and polished boots.

Slade was the president, the Alpha of their club, and they knew their rank and flanked him accordingly. Castor and Alaric stood on either side of their president with their arms folded across their chests, nodding their agreement with his desire to enact their revenge for the attack on the club.

"Now that we're all here, let's get started." Slade rested his elbows on the back of the chair and leaned forward. "What are you really doing here, Aaliyah? Because you sure as fuck aren't innocent."

Snitches get stitches, and traitors get killed. My father's warning rang truer than ever, and my gut churned.

I answered with a question of my own. Something to put my mind at ease. Only then would I tell him what he needed to know. "What happened to Danny?" The tremor in my voice had little to do with the possible loss of a family member. I was past that. Danny needed to act like my brother before I could mourn him like one. The only thing that would comfort me was knowing whether my brother was dead from the four bullets Slade put in his back.

"Dead and buried, hopefully," Slade answered, cold and hard, like the bite of a steel blade.

I didn't even react. Had no emotion about it but anger and betrayal.

"Your coward brother managed to slip away from us."

Slade spared a glance over his shoulder at the three-man wall behind him. "Won't happen again, will it, boys?"

The knife of betrayal stabbed deeper, and I groaned, fingers digging deeper into the blanket at how my brother used me, shot me, then left me for dead, like I meant nothing to him.

"Fuck, no, it won't." Zethan spat on the cement floor, his green eyes dark with disgust. "The best he can hope for is that Alaric gets to him before I do. At least he'll make it quick."

Slade adjusted his position, stretching his long, thick legs in front of him. "I told you what happened to that piece of shit brother of yours." His expression said cool and calm, but the muscle twitch along his jaw said otherwise. "Your turn. How long have you been working with the Wolves?"

Going over old ground. Again. Time to remind him and this time convince him. "I told you I left the club seven years ago. After Jimmy—" My voice broke, and I glanced down at my belly, stroking it. I didn't just lose him that day. Using all my strength, I leveled my gaze at Slade and cleared my throat. "After Jimmy died. I went to college and became a nurse. I didn't have a lot of time for running guns, and the only drugs I handled were prescribed." My tone made my feelings on biker's illegal activities crystal clear.

"Who the fuck is Jimmy?" Slade's growl rang with the same possession pinching the mate bond. Only the sense was fainter this time. Distant. Harder for me to reach and read.

"My ex-boyfriend, and the ..." I couldn't say the rest. The words dried in my throat. That was none of Slade's business.

I dug through the clearing fog in my mind for more information, some nugget that might buy me a lifeline. A recent conversation with my mother came up, and I focused hard to recall it. The Wolves' involvement in prostitution and pornography against my father's and senior members' wishes. My brother had ambitions, but it was a shame his desire for evil dwarfed his potential for good.

If the last two weeks with the Jackals taught me anything, it was *better the devil you know*. My father's murder got more complicated, the players murkier, the hows and whys still at large. But in my heart, I knew this sticky web had my brother's signature all over it. I didn't need fingerprints or eyewitness testimony to prove Danny was responsible. He didn't send me to the Jackals for revenge, justice for the loss of our father. His motives had everything to do with expanding the family business he inherited. That greedy bastard's treachery knew no bounds, and he yanked the net out from under me. If I was right, I owed Slade a damn apology.

Thinking about it made my stomach heave and roll. My poor father. The deceived Wolves who served him. Worst of all, my devastated mother, having to reconcile with her worm of a son. Fuck, I'd been so blind, miscalculating how deep Danny's love of money and power ran. I paid the price for my ignorance, and it cost me everything.

"I guess you cleared your calendar, because you seem to have time for Wolf business now." Slade took a deep breath and likely counted to ten before he lost his cool and said or did something he'd regret. I felt his betrayal, disappointment, and hatred simmer along the mate bond. "Tell us what you know about their operations, who they work with, where their stashes are kept."

"You think my brother shared his business plans with me?" I scoffed. "Danny is a master manipulator. I refused his order, and next thing I knew, I was attacked in my work parking lot, carried into a van by Alaric, and driven back to Zethan's shelter. I didn't ask for this."

Distraught and wanting out of my confines, I dipped my chin to my chest and stared at the floor. I closed my eyes and took a deep breath. When I found the courage to raise my head and look at him again, my eyes burned with the anger and determination of a patsy arguing her case.

Slade crossed his legs at the ankles. "What *do you* know, Aaliyah?"

I ran my hand over my stomach. "Danny and I have very different ideas of what justice is. I didn't come here to destroy the Jackals. I could have run if I wanted to." I stared the president down. "But I stayed to find out who killed my father and collect evidence to put that person away for good."

My fingers ached from gripping the blanket so tight. My lifeline.

The more time I spent with the Jackals, the less convinced I was about their involvement in my father's death. But I was in too deep now and couldn't see a way out. Danny signed my death warrant, and Slade Vincent would carry it out.

I wanted answers as much as Slade did. I also had to prove I wasn't guilty here, otherwise I was dead. "Did you kill my father, Slade?"

The four men bristled at my question. Tension rolled off them down to me. Their anger fueled mine, fed my avatar, and the storms Slade manifested. Through the bond, I sensed the combined emotions of the four of them helped him bring an F-one up to an F-four tornado. But rather than release the energy like normal, he absorbed it. The last thing he needed was to unleash a natural disaster.

"Do you really think I killed him?" He held my gaze. "I didn't kill your father. He was my rival, not my enemy."

"That's the same thing." I wanted to believe him more than anything. Just let my father rest and release my soul from this burden.

"You still have a lot to learn about our organization, so I'm going to lay it out for you." Slade's chair creaked under his massive weight. "The Jackals don't go around killing people and destroying families to get ahead. We won't start the fight, but we sure as fuck will finish it. Your father knew that. The same way I knew it about him. We had mutual respect. He stayed out of our territory, and we did the same."

"So how did the cigarette butt with your DNA wind up at my father's crime scene?" I choked back a sob.

Up until this point, Castor remained silent, stoic, assessing. Probably using his years as a prosecutor to form an opinion, a legal argument to condemn or absolve me. Instead, he rested a hand on Slade's shoulder in a show of support.

"The question you should be asking is, who put the cigarette there?" He spent as much time defending the accused as he did prosecuting them before reaching his avatar status.

I think I already knew the answer to that question and so did they. Now it was a matter of proving it. But the Jackals wouldn't let me out of this cage to help them do that when I was their prisoner and prime suspect. No avatar or fated mate bond would see me through this. The gods saw fit to toss me into the Jackal's world. How I got out of it was up to me.

CHAPTER 3

Alaric - Jackal's Wrath Road Captain & Avatar of Horus

IT TOOK everything I had not to rip the bars from their hinges to free Aaliyah. She wasn't just ripped up by a bullet, she hurt physically and emotionally. Betrayal from her brother. Shock from Slade locking her up. Fear of what would happen. I wanted to take away her pain, to soothe and comfort her while she recovered from her wound and whatever bullshit was going on with her family. We all did. Our desire flexed through the bond like a muscle working to lift her out of the bed into our arms.

Fucking mate bond.

It clouded our judgment and left us weak and susceptible to her charms. The last time I'd trusted someone, I'd lost my damn eye. Never again. We had to be wary of our connection, not let her sway us with excuses. Guilty as hell was stamped on her forehead and flashed like a neon sign. I resisted the undeniable attraction through the mate bond.

Traitor had tricked me into believing she cared for me and wanted to help me. I rubbed at my temple. Fuck, I thought she was the one, but I was wrong about her.

Aaliyah slumped into her pillows, her caramel skin, aqua eyes, and crimson lips a few shades paler from blood loss and the ordeal her body went through. Her dark mahogany hair was sweaty and disheveled from sleep. Even from ten-feet away, I detected the change in her scent, from vanilla and cherries to iodine surgery disinfectant, ammonia antiseptic, citrus cleaner, and salty sweat.

The thing that pissed me off the most was that we'd seen parts of the real Aaliyah. She was a nurse, a healer. She genuinely cared about the women from the shelter and what happened to them. Sharp-witted, strong-willed, feisty, and independent, the woman could give any of us avatars a run for our money. She soothed the savage beast within me with just a touch. Had we met under different circumstances, we could have been good together. Shame the situation weren't different.

Shitty as they were, this was the hand we were dealt, and we had to play it out. I didn't know what that meant for the curse or the bond, and for the time being, I didn't care. We had to see this through. Play it out to the end, or the gods wouldn't regenerate Isis into a new avatar. Based on how things were going, we needed a replacement. Aaliyah went from our most prized possession to prisoner of war overnight.

Because of her, I failed the damn club and let my president down. I deserved punishment for fucking up, but Slade had seen mercy, leaving my ass alone. I should have known to look deeper when I couldn't read her. True to my suspicions, she'd been hiding something, and boy, was she hiding a fucking doozy. Got me damn well arrested and a criminal record. Had the club ambushed, my president and enforcer almost killed.

All because of her dirty, rotten brother. She was loyal to her family, something I never understood. Not until Zethan, Slade, and Castor stormed into my life. I would do anything to protect my brothers and anyone within our circle. Aaliyah was supposed to be in that circle. Supposed to break the curse, but now the cycle was doomed for failure, just like all the others.

I used all my strength to shift my focus from her and the nagging mate bond back to the conversation. Castor's last question regarding who had put the cigarette with Slade's DNA at Alexander Heller's crime scene dangled in the air, waiting for an answer.

"The Wolves have as many if not more cops in their pocket as we do." Slade scratched the stubble along his jaw.

Under normal circumstances, a punch from Castor preceded his questions for occupants in that cell. But Slade never hit a woman and wasn't about to start, no matter how much her betrayal hurt. It was up to me to wade through the bullshit without violence, even though I felt his desperation for it raging within him.

"We know someone in the department planted it," my president said. "We're still working on the how and the who."

That someone had that dirty cop Marcus' name written all over it. Castor met with our bagman to pay him for a stunt man for our last delivery of Pharaoh. Instead of nabbing the fall guy for a petty crime, diverting the cop's eyes off the club while we conducted business, that dirty fucker arrested our stunt guy. Squeezed him for a 'so-called' confession. More like coerced him into an admission that the Jackals hired him for a delivery run of drugs. Warrant for the Bathurst Police to arrest me and plant drugs on me. Motherfuckers would get whacked when the time was right.

For now, a red target burned into my back, and it was just a matter of time before the cops returned to get Castor, Zethan, and the rest of the Jackals. My hands curled into fists, cutting off my circulation.

A hint of a smile formed at the corner of Aaliyah's mouth, and it was enough to melt through a layer of ice around my heart. "You said it's been a year since you quit smoking, right?" Clever. Cunning. Just like her goddess.

"That's why you asked to bum a smoke from me at the shelter? I knew there was something off." Slade chuckled and shook his head, probably amused that she managed to infiltrate us so easily when she had zero undercover skills. "I never pegged you for a smoker."

"I smoked a lot when I was a Wolf. A few times in college, mostly during exam times, when I was stressed." Aaliyah said with a shrug. "I had to give up because of …" She stopped mid-sentence, arousing alarm, and my eyes didn't leave her. From the wince of pain that followed her next shrug, it was obvious her pain meds wore off, and she regretted the casual gesture.

I had to hold back, cement my feet to the floor, refuse the urge to go to her. Castor rocked on his feet beside me. Zethan flexed his massive, ripped forearms, undulating his navy plaid shirt. Slade gripped the back of the chair tighter. We all fought the mate bond. None of us would give in to this traitor.

"That wasn't quite the confession I was looking for. I answered your question. Time for you to give me something," Slade prodded with a less acidic tone than he'd used with her before.

"You're looking for specifics, and I don't have them." Aaliyah's pallor took on a sickly greenish-white hue as she leaned back into the cot. "Danny wants to take the Jackals out, but you don't need me to tell you that."

"Yeah, we pretty much figured that out when the Wolves ambushed us in Sydney," Castor chimed in from his position flanking our president to my side. "Funny how you showed up, huh?" I liked his line of questioning. Direct and to the point.

"Once you left for your *business*, I left the shelter in Zethan's van." Aaliyah's expression softened along with her posture as if a weight had been lifted from her shoulders with every word she spoke. "I'm sorry. I think it's still at my mom's place … maybe not anymore." She tapped her sweet, voluptuous lips. "When I was about to leave and return to the shelter to tell you what Mom said, someone grabbed me and injected me with a sedative. They might have stolen your van … Shit. Really sorry. I'll pay you back if I can."

Bullshit. She snitched and ran. Had no intention of returning to warn us. All an act to stimulate sympathy to get her freed.

"Fuck, that's my collection van." Zethan wiped a palm over his eye.

She went to apologize again, but Slade's chair scraped along the ground, and I flinched. My hawk screeched with alarm. Sudden and unexpected motion set us both off.

"Someone injected you with a sedative?" he growled.

"She was pretty groggy at the ambush," Castor backed her up, and Slade's jaw hardened further.

"Who?" he demanded, inching closer to Aaliyah's cell.

"I don't know. I never saw him. I woke up in the middle of a gun fight." She hunched over and used the hem of her shirt to blot the beads of sweat from her forehead. "Where I took a bullet for you, Slade."

Four pairs of eyes zoned in on the caramel flesh of her belly, peeking underneath her bandages. Worry rang along the bond like swords raised, ready to defend our mate. Slade growled at us through the link, and we settled back into place. She never noticed, taking a long pull from the bottle of water on the floor beside the cot.

He scraped his large hand over his chin, thinking. "What were you doing at your mother's?"

Slade's question put Aaliyah on the defensive, and she shook her head and sighed, staring at him as if he were thick. "You kidnapped me, held me for almost two weeks with no contact. I visited her. She was worried sick and hadn't been sleeping well since losing her husband. I worry about her after Dad ... died." The last word came out choked, and my chest pulled with longing to sweep her into my arms to brush her hair and kiss her forehead. "Alexander Heller was a bad man, a terrible husband, but a good father. My mother worshiped him. Six months ago, she buried him, and I didn't want to cause her more pain or stress."

Fuck, every moment we stayed down in the basement, we risked losing ourselves to her, getting swept up in her story and her wily ways. Falling under the bond's spell again.

Stay strong, I sent the reminder across the bond, and it tensed with resistance from my three brothers.

Slade prowled closer, his jackal doing the same beneath the surface, growling, teeth bared. "What did you tell her?"

"Everything." Aaliyah closed her eyes, her lips pressing together tightly. "I thought I was free of it all. Of you four. Until the gods threw me into your bullshit again."

I wanted to take her dirty mouth with mine and feast on it. Slide my cock between her damn traitorous lips. Fuck it until she couldn't take any more. Punish her for what she'd done to me. I wasn't the only one. Slade wanted to do worse, and I felt his hunger, his dominance, and fury a tight ball, ready to explode and pounce if she so much as groaned again.

"Fuck. You told your mother about the shelter?" Zethan paced along the wall, cupping his mouth and jaw. Danger to women or his shelter set him off. "Do you know how much shit that could put the women in?"

"I'm sorry, I didn't know it was such a secret." Zethan's comment got her back up, and that feisty streak of hers rose in the link. "I suppose I should also admit I didn't do your reputation any favors by telling my mother about the good work you did."

"This isn't fucking funny, Aaliyah." Zethan crossed his huge arms over his chest. "We don't need any weaknesses used as leverage against us."

Aaliyah scoffed at him. "Guess you should have thought about that before opening the shelter." Her top lip arched with her moan of pain.

Her torment was agony to us all, like a beacon guiding my plane to land on the air strip.

"My mother is a fierce woman," Aaliyah said between gritted teeth, her voice wavering, lips wobbling. "Believe it or not, she had a much bigger impact on the way my father ran his club than you might think. I don't think she'll say a word to Danny. She doesn't trust him anymore."

Her emotional dam burst and the tears she held back streamed down her cheeks. Watching her collapse on the cot, her body wracked with sobs as she broke down damn near broke me. I pulled on the bond with my brothers, relying on their borrowed strength to see me through. Even without our connection, she affected us, her effortless and unintentional influence a natural gravitational pull we couldn't resist.

From her outburst, I expected her to close herself off from the attachment and put an end to the conversation by refusing to answer any more of our questions. But the woman surprised us all, pulled herself together, and dropped a fucking bombshell.

"Danny's expanding my father's business ventures." She

sniffed, shuddered, and tucked an errant strand of hair behind her ear. "According to my mother and senior club members, he's not interested in monopolizing the gun or drug markets. He found a much more lucrative franchise."

I ran my hand over my face and let out a deep breath in anticipation of what she was about to say. Admission that her brother had stolen our drugs and tried to seize a second shipment. Confirmation that Danny was making a play for our business, our territory, and finally, our lives.

"Pornography and prostitution have a lower risk and higher return on investment." What came from her lips backed up what her uncle told Castor.

The instant Aaliyah started crying again, Slade went to the bars, gripping them tight. Muscles in his back swelled as if he tried lifting the iron from its foundations to get to her.

I fought my desire and shoved it down.

"My father would be disgusted if he knew what my brother was doing to the Wolves." She wiped snot from her nose. "It's breaking my mother's heart. Destroying the club."

"Aaliyah." Slade's voice broke, and he wavered on a knife's edge of his decision to enter the cell and hold her. Backed by a god of pure passion, destruction, and chaos, it made sense for him to struggle with his desire for vengeance versus his need for his mate. Weakness he tried to shield himself from but lost the war.

Castor's god, Thoth, embodied knowledge and truth, so he held firm. Composed and calm, assessing the situation and formulating his verdict. Zethan's god, Osiris, represented wisdom and leadership, and our VP didn't let emotions sway his analysis and opinion.

My god, Horus, on the other hand, sought retribution and justice against Slade's god for taking his eye in battle, so I empathized with his urges. On the personal front, I clashed with longing for my mate and believing her when my trust had been shattered, and I didn't let people in easily. Once bitten, definitely not twice shy. If someone betrayed me, they were dead to me, and there was no way to convince me otherwise.

Aaliyah didn't notice and went on, "Mom said Danny tried to convince Dad it was good business to expand the club, except my father shut him down every time. Then he winds up dead, and I end up here." Her furious, red eyes hit my president like a laser beam seeking its target. She wiped away the tears running down her cheeks.

Slade pressed his forehead to the bars, the back of his neck red and bulging like the furious muscles in his shoulders.

Zethan stepped forward about to deliver one of his pearls of wisdom. "If there's one thing I've learned in my life, it's that good people do bad things and bad people do good things. Even the worst of us are capable of drawing lines in the sand."

If she could resolve that, maybe she could come to terms with who we were and what we represented. But my brothers were a long way off from trusting her. I know I'd never trust her again.

What she said about her brother raised many red flags about the new nature of the Wolves' business. Seriously bad shit. Stuff that went against everything the Jackals worked for. We helped women, empowered them with stability and independence while that dirty fuck Danny exploited them.

The women in the shelter and their kids depended on us to get them somewhere safe and ensure they stayed that way. Actions that didn't come cheap. Cold, hard cash made these women disappear and set them up with a new life. That money had to come from somewhere, and it sure as hell wasn't from pencil-pushing office jobs. All the good we did to balance the bad shit would come to a screeching halt if the

Wolves continued to fuck with our operations. But Slade wouldn't let that happen on his fucking watch. If we disobeyed our gods and used our powers just to get ahead, to abuse others, the gods would make us pay. Strip us of our magick and destroy us.

"I'm not saying another word." Aaliyah shuddered, and we all heard the call, her scream for comfort and ease to her pain. "I'm tired, in pain, and hungry. I need rest. Please."

Slade wasn't having any of it. He unlocked the cell door, yanked it open and entered. Towering over her, he jerked out his phone and tossed it on her bed. She held his gaze the whole time. This woman wasn't frightened of him. Frightened of what he'd do to her. A list a mile long. But more frightened of what he made her feel.

"Call your brother or one of the Wolves," he ordered her, voice hard and steely. "See if he's still alive."

"I can't, Slade." Her eyes watered up again. "Please don't make me." The agony in her voice ripped me to pieces.

Suddenly, Aaliyah was overwhelmed with emotions at odds with previous sentiments conveyed through our link. Guilty was her verdict for Danny, ninety percent assumed from the series of events he dragged her through. The nurse and scientist in her needed the remaining ten percent to convince her of his crimes. Only she didn't have the heart to ask him if he did all this and smoked her dad.

Once, they'd been close and loved each other, yet they grew apart over the years. She didn't understand how he evolved into such a greedy and heartless bastard. Discovering the truth about him, about her father's demise, would destroy her and everything she viewed as good in this world.

Fuck. Tightness wrenched my chest. Everything good in my world had been stolen from me *that day*. She was our captive, but I was captive to my past and the demons that haunted me nightly.

If Slade made her do this, she'd be just like me. Dead inside and unable to come back from it. My heart pleaded for me to tell Slade no, but my mind and mouth, the military man, the one who obeyed and followed orders, stayed clamped shut. The enemy had come into our camp and set our hearts and club on fire. For that, she had to pay.

"Don't you want to know who smoked your dad?" Slade collected his cell and shoved it in her face. "Prove it. Call them. Get it straight." He rolled his shoulders at her thickening sobs and pleas.

"No, please." Aaliyah shook her head. Her face went red, eyes swelling, nose running. Fuck, it was hell to watch her. My brothers stiffened by my side.

"Do it." Slade pried open her hand and jammed it in her palm, wrapping her fingers over it. "This shit has gone on for too long."

She narrowed her eyes at him. "Fuck you, Slade. Stop toying with me. Just kill me and be done with it."

"You, of all people, know when a patient is lying, and you'll know if your brother is too." In a moment of weakness, he stroked her face, then quickly recovered and snapped his hand tight to his side.

She shook as she stared at his cell's screen. A waterfall ran down her cheeks as she dialed a number. Slade grabbed the phone and activated the speaker function.

Someone answered in five rings. "Yeah." Croaky and groggy. "Who the fuck is this?"

Aaliyah's mouth opened but no words came.

"I thought you said no communications," Danny rasped.

What the fuck did that mean?

"Danny?" Aaliyah's angelic voice had adopted a fraught edge.

"Aaliyah." Her brother's voice darkened with disappointment. "Where the fuck are you?"

Her eyes slammed closed, and she refused to speak.

Slade said her piece for her. "I think you know where she is."

"Slade." Danny sounded as if he smiled. "Didn't do your job very well, did you? Still alive and kicking, you cunt. And I'll be sure to pump you full of double the bullets you smoked me with when I'm better."

Rage exploded down the mate bond. Nuclear-level clouds. Gunpowder-fed fire. Lava spitting from a volcano. Slade was losing it.

"Danny," Aaliyah coughed out, reaching forward to place a hand on Slade's leg, and wrap her fingers over it. "Did you do it?" Slade's attention went from the phone to her grasp. "Did you fucking kill Dad?"

"Sweet sister," Danny mocked her. "You picked the wrong side, and I'll be sure to put you down like the other Jackals."

Slade snatched the phone back and yelled into the speaker, "Listen here, you dirty mutt!"

Danny laughed then coughed for a few moments. "I want her back within forty-eight hours. Or I'm coming for you, desert vulture."

"She's in no shape for travel."

"I don't give a fuck. We'll take care of her." The line went dead, and my president crushed the phone to fucking dust.

Danny had the means and motive out of all the people responsible for Alexander Heller's death. Based on that call, his culpability just solidified in my mind. As for Aaliyah, she had assisted him, and blame lay at her feet too. Something she'd not be forgiven for.

Zethan removed Slade from the cell before he crushed something else.

"We have forty-eight hours to decide what to do." Aaliyah jolted as Zethan locked her back up.

I watched Aaliyah for a reaction, ignoring the ache in my

heart when she nodded as if accepting her fate when we turned her over to the Wolves.

"Danny won't be healed by then to lead his men in an attack," Castor argued, rolling a ball of dark magick over his fingers.

"His VP could do the dirty work," Zethan said over his shoulder, leading Slade away from the cell.

"I'm not fucking handing her over." Slade smashed his fist into the wall by the stairs, crushing the brick. "She's dead if I do, and she's still our mate, and we have to protect her."

Whatever we did, the clock was ticking for all of us.

CHAPTER 4

Aaliyah

I COLLAPSED ON THE COT, emotionally spent from Slade's interrogation and being pushed over the edge with the phone call. If I wasn't injured, I'd have gone another round with Slade and still had energy for a third. He might be able to overpower me with strength but not will, and I had that in spades.

Darkness settled over the room as the sunlight waned. The wind hadn't eased up and whistled at the window jambs. Cold draped the room, and I sank deeper under my blankets, my body starting to shiver. These wouldn't do and I would freeze down here.

My throat had dried from all the conversation and crying, and I leaned to the side to retrieve my bottle of water. Pain gripped my wound, and I whimpered. Whatever post-op pain meds I was given had started to wear off. I glanced up at the drip connected to me, wondering if I should up the dosage. Without knowing what they put in there, I didn't touch it. I could do more harm than good. Frustrated, I finished the rest of my water and tossed the empty plastic bottle on the floor.

My accommodations lacked an adjoining bathroom. At some point I would need to use the facilities but I was still dehydrated from the blood loss, and my body retained what little water I supplied it. Did the Jackals expect me to piss on the floor?

Falling asleep wasn't a problem since I was exhausted. Staying asleep, on the other hand, proved damn near impossible with the constant throb in my abdomen. Normally, I slept on my side, curled up, hugging a pillow, but with the location of my injury, I was forced to lay on my back. Constant shifting failed to provide comfort.

Eyes closed, I prayed to the gods for grace and mercy. Isis answered by blessing me with a rush of healing energy. Warmth spread over my body, easing the pain, and soothing my mind.

Thank the goddess, I thought to myself, finally drifting off into a nightmare-plagued sleep.

The events of my injury replayed over in my dreams. In one, a demon chased me, capturing me, letting Danny shoot me. In another, Slade held me in front of my brother, and the bullets tore into me. In the third, I couldn't bear the pain of losing Slade, and I threw myself in front of him, taking the hit and protecting my Alpha. I woke with a start at the last one, covered in sweat.

Night bathed the room, and silence clung to the late hour. Chilled to the bone yet shivering as my body fought infection, I clutched my blanket tighter. Dr. Shriver, the Jackal's medic, removed the bullet and patched me up. Roughly, might I add. The guy was a general practitioner not a surgeon, his wound care needed some improvement, but he was the best I had on offer.

Something moved on the edge of the bed, and I gasped.

"It's just me." Castor's hand found my calf and squeezed.

Feeling vulnerable, I pulled the blanket over my chest, my body tensing. There could only be two reasons he visited my cell in the middle of the night. And in the dark. Slade had changed his mind and ordered me a grisly death, or he permitted his men to abuse me for their pleasure. I'd not let the Jackals do that. My mind went into overdrive with ways to defend myself and my muscles primed with what little strength I had.

"What ... what are you doing?" I stammered, reaching out across the mate bond for his emotion, finding a murkiness with a dull pulse of desire.

"Don't worry. I'm just here to deliver dinner and let you freshen up." Reassurance streamed down the mate bond. A single blast, no more. Castor shut himself off to me ever since the ambush. The harsh snap, like he'd broken his connection to our link, echoed in my mind whenever I looked at him. We were back to the old mystery.

Judging by the duller sensations coming from my other avatar mates, they'd done something similar. Although, I got more feeling from them, especially Slade, who lost hold of his emotions easily, sensations streaming through from him.

My eyes adjusted to the dimness, making out Castor's broad shape at the end of my cot. A candle flickered to life at my side, and I flinched, then blinked, squinting until my eyes adjusted. The cell door hung wide open. Two more blankets rested at my feet, supporting two books. A tray rested on his lap, hosting two bottles of water, a plate of bacon and eggs, and a small bowl with a hand towel. The crispy, salty scent of bacon made my stomach rumble. Dinner. Better than the canned crap they'd previously provided. The hollow ache in my stomach suggested it had been a day or two since eating.

"I've blocked the mate bond with a little help from my magick." Castor sat on the edge of the bed, as handsome as ever. "Can't let you play mind tricks on me."

Darker, dominant, and mysterious. Long, inky hair pulled back, scented with a wax that blended with his aftershave, an irresistible spice and cinnamon combination that lit up my senses. The pale light turned his maple eyes a deep, rich amber, almost supernatural in their vividness like a wolf shifter from a movie. He wished. Unlucky bastard got a lame-ass ibis shifter from his god.

Thank fuck he didn't want to rape me. For a moment there, I thought I'd have to use some moves to disarm him, then choke him with the IV line. Relief washed through my tight, sore body, and I slumped into the pillow.

Goddess, he thought me a sly, clever manipulator who played him to gain the Jackal's secrets. Guilty as charged. Loyal, strong, independent, caring, and honest described my true identity. Anybody would change their behavior to survive this fucked-up situation. Anyone. And I dared him to prove me wrong.

I picked at the fuzz balls on my blanket, unable to meet his gaze, demanding answers. "Castor, I know it looks bad. I was thrown into an impossible situation and did what I thought was best. That's not who I am."

He nodded, absorbing every word, contemplating them, the faintest hint of his analysis pumping through our link.

"I've laid everything bare now. No secrets or lies." My voice came out hoarse and strangled. "Maybe we can clean the slate and start again? Get to know each other?"

"I'll take that onboard." His grip on the tray tightened. No commitment. No indication of how he felt. Closed off to me. Blocked by a wall of steel warded with magick.

"Okay." I guess that was the best I could hope for from him.

His dark pink lips curled upward, chasing away the chill in my bones. "Is that how you'd make your escape? Knock me out with the IV line? No attempt at magick?" At least we hadn't lost the natural playfulness we had between us. "I'm disappointed in your cunning, dark sorceress."

Oh, goddess. The nickname and flirting. His deep, dark voice, reached cold places inside of me in desperate need of his fire. Syrupy warmth soaked into my muscles and made me giddy and soft. The spark was still there between us, even brighter despite him dialing back our connection.

My mind quickly recovered and returned to his question about how I'd escape. How the fuck did he know that? I thought emotion was transmitted along the mate bond, not thought or intentions. Fuck, I had to shield my thoughts like he did. Some things had to remain private between the five of us.

I changed the topic quickly. "What time is it?" I adjusted my back and wiped sweat from my forehead with the back of my hand.

"A little after seven." Castor passed the tray to me by shifting it across the blanket. Tempting, but another bodily function needed addressing.

"I ... ugh ... have to use the bathroom first." In the hospital, I wouldn't have batted an eyelid about a patient with a bedpan or taking them for their business, but with him, I suddenly went shy. And I'd never been shy with him.

"Umm." Castor's gaze flicked from me to the empty space in the cell opposite the cot and back again. At least he had the decency to look embarrassed. "The holding cells aren't really set up for long-term use."

I knew too well what went on within these walls. Beatings, interrogations, torture, and murder. Shivers ripped through me, and I clutched my blanket tighter. "Cells? As in plural?"

"We've had instances arise where we needed more than one." Castor shrugged my question off and set the tray he carried on the space beside him. "Jerry, Sonny, and Tex are next door."

Uncle Jerry. I flung off my thin blanket and draped my legs over the side of the cot. Dizziness hit, and I sympathized with all surgery patients.

"Easy." Castor stopped me, catching me with both hands on my upper arms. Comforting warmth seeped into me, making me relax. The mate bond flared with a low, burning need. Mine. I detected a faint flicker of his reciprocal response. "Don't exert yourself."

"Is Jerry okay?" I didn't know the other two well. Met them a few times at Christmas and other holiday events.

"He's faring better than the other two." I closed my eyes at Castor's response. Translation—he'd beaten them to extract information.

Uneasiness gripped me, and I groped for Castor's wrist, catching it, squeezing. "Did you hurt him?"

Strong as an ox at sixty years of age ... like my father would have been if he had lived ... Jerry was getting on. Palms burning, I let go of Castor, horrified that he'd hurt my uncle by name, but not by relation. He was family, and we'd depended on each other. Jerry had been there for every Christmas, birthday, and anniversary. A man I had the highest regard for and utmost love. The thought of Castor harming Jerry left me with an unbearable chest ache.

"I didn't need to." Castor dabbed at my forehead with the wet cloth. "He gave me everything I needed willingly. He also offered to defect."

Jerry was loyal as they came. For him to do that, things must be seriously bad in the Wolves.

"What?" I sighed. Fucking sighed from each gentle dab cooling my skin. "Jerry's the vice president."

"Not anymore." Castor cleaned all the sweat from my face and neck, leaving me burning for a completely different reason. "He was demoted and replaced for not supporting your brother's new politics."

Fuck. Danny had no loyalty or respect whatsoever. He sounded more and more like a damn dictator with every fresh piece of information to my ears.

"I'll take you up to the bathroom, Aaliyah." Castor leaned into me, stoking the low burning fire between us, filling my senses with his overwhelming scent. "But first, I need you to promise me you aren't going to try to run."

I snorted. Like this? Haphazardly patched up by an unqualified doctor, aching, exhausted, weak, and dizzy. News flash ... I wouldn't get very far. About as far as some of the elderly patients got when they snuck out of their rooms to sneak a sweet treat because the hospital food tasted like shit. Two hundred feet max before I passed out.

"I'm a little disappointed that the avatar of knowledge and science doesn't know more about surgery, medicine, and healing from gunshot wounds." It came out flirty and teasing. *Oh, well.* Too late to recall it now. "Because if you did, you'd know I'm not really feeling up to a marathon right now."

Through the mate bond, I sent him an image of me punching his arm, because I couldn't do it for real without hurting myself.

"I'm serious, dark sorceress." His voice thickened from my nickname. "Promise me you won't magick me and gangrene my dick."

Yeah, 'cause I was up for that too. I searched for my

magick, but everything was dark, distant, and unable to grasp.

"Thanks for the tip. Didn't know I had that ability." I smiled, and he cursed under his breath. I lifted my hand in front of my chest, the absence of my magick troubling. "I can't feel her in the darkness."

"It's because the cell's warded." Castor scanned the ceiling then the iron bars and sigils glimmered, responding to his magick. "I had to stop you from getting out and hurting us."

I snorted at his joke, even though that troubled me. "Probably won't be up for any gangrene attacks or smiting for a few days."

Be smart, Aaliyah, my mind warned.

I know, I shouldn't have joked with him, not in such dire circumstances. But he brought it out in me, lightened and cleared my mind, giving me clarity. I didn't want to think about consequences with him. Couldn't a girl get a moment's peace? Away from my brother, my father's murder, my uncertain future, and the threat of the Jackals.

Castor's eyes darkened, and his eyebrows scaled his forehead. He wanted me to promise him. Word to the avatar of Thoth was a sacred vow he valued above all else.

I let out an exasperated sigh because my bladder had reached critical status, and I wasn't up for playing games. "Castor, I promise I won't try to run or use magick on you." Goddess, he made me feel like a schoolgirl promising not to hit Mandy for stealing my *Play Doh*. "Now can you let me out before my bacon goes cold and my bladder bursts and I have to lie in my piss?" Flattering. But I had to get my point across and fast.

Castor seemed to have the most compassion and empathy toward my situation. He held the key, literally and figuratively to my freedom. All I had to do was convince him to let me out and let me go home

"That's better." He stood up, closed the distance between us, and lifted me into his arms. A dull heat banked between us. I'd missed being close to him, in his arms, his body pressed to mine. My lips tingled with the memory of his curious, exploratory, and assertive kisses. But his next words killed all feeling in my body. "I'm on high alert with you, dark sorceress. One move and I will hurt you."

CHAPTER 5

Castor - Jackal's Wrath Enforcer & Avatar of Thoth

AALIYAH SHIVERED with both trepidation and excitement at my warning, and it shot straight to my damn cock, waking him like never before. I wanted to sink into this woman, meld our bodies together, fuck her until she screamed my name, but she was injured and in pain. I'd not touch her until she was ready. Until I was ready. And I was quite a way off from that. I hitched her tighter into my arms, and she whimpered as she tried to hook her arms around my neck. She rested her head on my shoulder and clutched my arm.

I'd been burned before. Dissolved my marriage, split our assets, and broken up our home, friendship, and partnership. It damn well destroyed me. All my fault for spending too much time in the office, working late on cases, remembering my speech to the magistrate. In hindsight, we were young and dumb high school sweethearts who changed along the way. Introspection didn't make it easier, even after four years.

Liz had brought me back from the year of hell. Clearly, after all that time, I still wasn't over it and guarded my heart. Placed impenetrable and unscalable walls around it.

Aaliyah had broken my trust and confidence with secrets I'd shared with her, and from now on, I'd be wary and careful. It paid to be cautious even against my mate, which was a sad and depressing thought.

I carried her up the staircase, into a hallway, and came to a stop outside one of the club's three bathrooms. In total, we had five bathrooms, another two in Slade and Zethan's private quarters. Out of respect for the club's leaders, we didn't touch their reserved rooms. Believe me, when the club was packed with family for celebrations, those three bathrooms were kept busy.

"There's no shower facilities in these bathrooms." I managed to twist the door handle and fling the door open with her in my arms, revealing the toilet and utility sink.

Carefully and slowly, I set her down on the floor, and she leaned on me, gripped my arms, pressing her head to my chest. Pain coursed through her wound and surrounding tissue, making me bite back my temptation to go and kill her brother myself for what he'd done to her.

I stroked her silky hair, wanting it wrapped over my fingers, pulled taut as I dove into her from behind. "Can you manage, or do you need help?" I croaked, fighting my arousal. This wasn't the fucking time or place.

"I'll try." Her short nails dug into me. The slightest movement cost her. Unavoidable since her torn stomach muscles worked with just about every motion of the human body.

The scientist in me knew its way around anatomy and medicine, but something told me my little nurse could teach me a thing or two. Fuck, I realized my mistake and wound it back, like a sailor withdrawing an anchor from the sea's floor. She wasn't mine and might never be.

Reluctantly, I let her go, and she shuffled into the small cubicle.

"There's toilet paper." She sounded grateful for such a trivial blessing. "It might as well be a suite at the Hilton after where I've been staying."

Pressure squeezed my lungs. I didn't like leaving her down in that dank, cold cell, but an order was an order.

When she tried to close the door, I thumped a hand on it, resisting. "Leave it open."

She blushed and glanced away, surprising me at her embarrassment, considering she dealt with this sort of bodily function every day. Being a gentleman, I afforded her the decency and privacy of facing away. No more leniency than that. She'd not get out of my sight. Slade would have my balls for it. Every bit of trust between us had been eroded from her actions.

Although I put a lot of stock into her confession, her testimony corroborated what Jerry had told me about Danny's new business operations. Aaliyah's reaction to them, her flashed teeth, arched lip, and the disgust tightening our attachment, said she spoke some truth. How much, was still up for debate. We'd find out soon, though.

I let my mind wander to my latest finding while she did her business. A new lead in the curse. Ingredients I had to track down to perform a ritual and spell. Looked promising, but I wouldn't get my hopes up.

The commode flushed as Aaliyah concluded her business. I almost spun around and caught her when she whimpered upon standing. Unclothed, her pants down, I might not be able to resist. Eyes closed, I bit the inside of my cheek, holding back going to her.

Water trickled as she washed her hands at the sink.

Cleanliness. As a nurse she valued it. The reason I had mercy and brought the bowl of water and washcloth down to the cell. An opportunity to cleanse her body and freshen up. Nothing worse than feeling dirty and disgusting when your body ached all over after surgery.

"Thanks again, Castor." Aaliyah wiped her hands on her gray sweatpants for lack of anything to dry them with in the bathroom.

"Shit. No one replaced the hand towel." I shook my head.

Men, especially my brothers, weren't the cleanest of guys, a hand towel the last thing on their mind. They thought things like that were a woman's job, something their wife made them do when they were content to flick their hands and let them dry naturally or wipe them down their jeans. I prided myself on being well kept and presentable, and that included a fucking hand towel. Assholes.

"Let's get you back to your accommodations." I offered a meager smile as I picked her up again.

Back in the cell, she picked at her meal. "The bacon looks good. Thank you for bringing it down."

It was probably cold by now, but better than nothing. All we had upstairs after my brothers wolfed everything down. She shoved a piece in her mouth, moaning as she chewed, bringing on a fresh onslaught of longing. I wanted to feed her. Lift the crunchy, oily, salty meat to her lips, brush them and let her eat, then lick and kiss her mouth clean afterward. I put aside that thought as she made quick work of the rest of the food on her tray. Hungry little thing. Not surprising, since she was in the cell for three days sleeping off her surgery.

Pain meds had kept her sleeping for most of the day after she woke from surgery and had a brief chat with Slade. We'd kept a constant vigil since Doc Shriver patched her up, taking turns for four-hour shifts, twenty-four-seven.

Checked her temperature, fed her water, even helped her with the bedpan. I didn't think she remembered that from her drug-heavy fog.

No one was getting close to our avatar mate and finding out what she could do. Slade didn't want anyone harming her when he had an itch that a mole hid inside the club. In addition, Danny Heller was salivating for war, and his sister's death would be the catalyst for it.

When she finished, we came to the even stickier end of my visit and shift to watch and guard her. Cleaning herself of blood and freshening up.

"I thought you might want to take a bath." I pointed toward the bowl of water and washcloth untouched on the tray. "Dr. Shriver's technique is okay, but he's not the most sterile guy. Fixed us up before you came along, and none of us are dead. We just can't take the chance. If the lifestyle doesn't kill you, a staph infection just might," I teased as I dipped the washcloth in the cool water and wrung it out.

My words hung in the air, tense, thick, and edging toward my thirst. I didn't need to spell out the rest. Despite being a traitor and liar, she was still precious to us and our gods, and we had to obey their laws or suffer the consequences. Slade thought it best to honor our patrons and keep her safe for whatever promise from Set that we needed Aaliyah for what was to come.

Her eyes didn't leave mine. She worried about being naked in front of me and giving me the wrong impression with an unintentional peep show. As a nurse, Aaliyah had seen more than her fair share of bodies and learned how to shut the hormones down and differentiate between naked and *naked*. Consoling, considering I worried about losing it if she took her top off to clean her armpits or her pants off for ... fuck, I'd leave it there.

"I can turn my back if you'd like." I used my best soothing

voice, the one that coaxed a witness into revealing evidence. False promises were nothing to me. Blood was everything. Honor and oaths, truth. I didn't entirely believe her assurance before when she'd laid everything bare.

Bare. Fuck. I didn't want to think of that word. I scratched my stubbled jaw, unshaven since her injury. At the moment, her welfare and safety were more important than inconsequential crap like my appearance. I got out of the cell before I snatched the bowl of water and did the deed my damn self.

While I repositioned myself outside the cell, Aaliyah scrubbed her face, sucking in a breath when she rubbed the terrycloth against a tender part of her scalp near her left temple. I glanced over at her, and she smiled, reassuring me she was fine. Rusty, dried blood coated the cloth as she prodded her sore spot. A decent-sized gash cut into her scalp, and blood matted the hair around it. The bowl of water and small cloth seemed grossly inadequate when she needed and probably longed for a hot shower. Not going there. She'd probably need me to hold her upright. I appreciated that she didn't complain or look a gift horse in the mouth since I was the only one to go out of my way to make her accommodations tolerable. An admirable quality. I might like to look and smell good, wear expensive clothes, ride a classic bike, but I fucking hated princesses.

"Why are you being so nice to me?" she asked, tempting me to glance over my shoulder, cast my eyes over her beautiful body.

"Being cruel doesn't do any good." I crushed my hands to my side, fighting the pull of attraction between us, less intense since I'd dialed back the bond but no less enticing.

With my advanced hearing, I heard her tug at the hem of her shirt and pull it off. Searing pain shot through her arm and across her chest when she tried to raise it above her head. I hesitated and was at the cell door, lingering, unsure whether to help her. Fuck it. I gave in, moved inside, and hoisted her shirt off. Bashful and modest, she grabbed her shirt and covered her bralette with it, but it did nothing to conceal the generous cleavage swelling beneath. Bad idea. I shouldn't have stepped inside because now the urgency to touch her reached fever pitch. My palms and fingers burned to hold her perfect breasts, squeeze and caress them.

"Thank you." She clutched the t-shirt in both hands. "I should be able to manage from here."

We both knew it was a lie. Overdoing it in her condition could be detrimental. She craved to be touched as much as I wanted to touch. Beyond the desire and longing, I needed to help her as much as she needed my help.

"Let me help you," I rasped, throat dry, tongue thick. I reached for the washcloth and dipped it in the water bowl.

"Nurses make for horrible patients." She smiled and tried to make light of it. Didn't help one bit. She turned to give me better access to the wound and the flakes of dried blood on her skin.

"I bet." I sucked in a sharp breath and held it as I lightly brushed her gorgeous, honey skin. "Too much pressure?"

"No, it's fine." More than fine by the uncertain smile she gave me.

I gnawed on my bottom lip to keep from leaning in to kiss her. My tender strokes were enough to buckle her knees. She tilted her head back, exposing the length of her neck as I wiped along her collarbone. Soft, silky, and I couldn't help myself, letting my pinky skim over her. Muscles in her neck flexed then loosened, there for the taking.

"I'll change your bandage after this." If I didn't explode in my fucking pants before then. Holding my breath again, I dipped the washcloth in the bowl and swished it around a few times before wringing it out, leaving a muddy, reddish-brown cloud of blood in the water.

Through the bond, I spied on her, turning the tables. Magick spells allowed me to feel her but conceal myself, like a hunter stalking its prey. She focused on the blood settling to the bottom of the bowl, comparing it to her situation. The woman she used to be had settled into the recesses of her mind and spirit. Everything spiraled out of control the moment her father died, and brother inherited the Wolves. She fought for every inch of independence, for a life outside of the motorcycle club, and still ended up shot and held behind enemy lines. Except we weren't her enemy. The Jackals were the only thing that made any damned sense in this messed up situation. That made her want to crunch into a ball and cry into a pillow.

I leisurely stroked her hair to show her I understood her sorrow and confusion, even though she interpreted it as a sly touch from her mate still interested and showing his claim on her. She was right. The woman never stopped being my mate. The last vestige of me that respected rule and law hoped that she was innocent until proven guilty, and this was all a big misunderstanding. I didn't want to consider the alternative when it hurt too badly. Losing a wife and a mate was unbearable, and I'd not add a third to the damn list.

Her grip on her shirt loosened, and my eyes trailed to her nearly bare chest. I cleared my quickly thickening throat. "Do you want me to clean you everywhere?" *Say yes. Fucking say yes.* I wanted to drag the cloth over her goddamn nipples and then drop my mouth to them.

"Armpits will do, and I can do the rest." Fuck. Probably for the best. I was quickly spiraling out of control. "Will Slade hand me over in forty-eight hours or go to war with the Wolves?"

Danny's ultimatum. Coldest shower *ever*. Dick shrinkage guaranteed.

"My president said he wouldn't." I cleaned her where she asked.

"He could change his mind to protect the club."

She took me aback by that. "You think handing you over is going to help us? You dying doesn't help any of us. Trust me."

"Will Danny kill me?" Her voice shook. Deep down she knew the answer and I didn't have to point it out to her.

"Yeah, and make it look like we did it to justify a territory war." My strokes turned harder, rougher, and she winced. "Someone already set up Slade for your father's murder. They laid out the blueprint, and Danny's going to follow it."

Her hands grabbed mine, squeezing. "Castor, please. I have to fix this. I have to know who killed my father and make this right."

What if one of my brothers had killed old Heller? Then what? Let her kill them? Didn't work that way. I'd fucking beat the shit out of them even if it was Slade for putting us into this shit. Risk my membership in the club for laying a hand on the president. But I knew deep in my soul he didn't do this.

I cupped her hands and warmed them. "I'll run a plan past Slade for when you're better. See if he's willing to let you stay upstairs and work in the shelter. That's the best I can do."

"Thank you." She choked back a sob before collapsing on the cot.

With her clean, I took the bowl of dirty water and washrag out of the cell and set them on the chair. "You should rest. You need your strength."

"Strength for what?" that sassy mouth of hers scoffed. "To sit in this cell and do nothing?"

"Think of me. Of riding bitch with me when we go to kill

your brother." She winced at my words, showing she didn't have the heart to pump a bullet through her brother's heart. Not a problem. We'd do it for her.

"You can ride bitch with me." She smiled, trying to hide her conflict between family and justice. Everything was screwed up, and the one person who she could have turned to for advice was dead. Through our connection, I felt her heart crack, missing her father more than ever.

I had to leave, otherwise I wouldn't ever be able to. Slade would kill me for leaving my post, but I just couldn't do it, couldn't stay there.

"Good night, dark sorceress." I resisted the urge to go over and kiss her.

I remembered the last time our mouths met. She let me have a little taste to tide me over until after I returned from the ride to Sydney, but it wasn't enough. Now that need was about to break, and I hurried up the stairs with the bowl before she caught me in her clutches again.

CHAPTER 6

Slade

"What's up, Prez?" Castor started. "You look tense." Smartass was one to talk, with his shoulders curled almost up to his damn ears.

I sat on the edge of the table. He smelled of her. Had touched her, the scent thick on his skin. Asshole had gone against my order.

"I don't want any of you going near *her*." My growl came out like a distant rumble of thunder. "Do not talk to her. Do not tap into the mate bond to check on her. Switch that shit off, *now*. That's an order."

We had the ability to dull it so we weren't as weak to it and couldn't feel as much emotion communicated through it. I didn't want her to manipulate us further using one of her many powers over us. I had the club's safety and future to think of, and the lives of my men and our family.

Zethan raised two palms, and I knew I was up for an argument. With all the shit we were juggling, I was not in the fucking mood when all I wanted to do was raise hell. "Hold on. You can't tell us to stay away from our mate."

I jabbed a finger at the polished wood in front of him. "That traitor is not our fucking mate anymore—"

Zethan, the prick, cut me off, and I growled. "Slade, you're being reactionary and not thinking this through." Cop talk. Collect evidence. Connect dots. Find the suspect. I knew his drill. He always said I led with my emotions and not my head. Bastard was right.

I burned too hot to bring it down. "She's a goddamn spy and saboteur who lied to save her ass. I want nothing more to do with her." Once someone fucked me over, they were dead to me. I was an unforgiving prick and as punishing as my god. "Once we off Danny and destroy the Wolves, we send her packing on a one-way trip to the Underworld."

Zethan rested his flanneled arm on the table and leaned into me, his eyes wild and dark with annoyance. "We're not fucking killing her."

Heat waves rippled between us, hot and cold going toe to toe.

"That's a big accusation, Prez." *Here we go.* Castor, big, hot-shot lawyer, throwing his opinion around. Innocent until proven guilty. Backing up Zethan like he always did. "She explained everything, and it makes sense."

Fuck that. It was pretty clear Aaliyah wasn't innocent. Let her brother beat the shit out of her to get us to pick her up and take her to our shelter. Lied to us about who she was for starters. Drilled my men for information on their roles in the club when we weren't supposed to talk club business with our old lady. Witnessed Alaric's route-planning maps. Could have listened to our conversations and gathered intel for her brother. Don't get me fucking started on the phone call she made to Danny. Escaped the shelter and then happened to be kidnapped and thrown into the ambush fray. Everything seemed too coincidental for my liking.

I was fucking president, and they had to obey my orders. If they didn't like it, they knew where the door was, and they could leave the club. Decision was simple. They could choose loyalty, brotherhood, and trust over deceit, betrayal, lies, and that fucking curse tricking us into loving an evil witch.

"For starters, Aaliyah saw Alaric's map, but the destination wasn't marked." Zethan, tag-teaming it with Castor, fucking WWE style. Boom. One hit. Castor's turn. Slam. "How did she know where we were going?"

We didn't mark shipments on our maps or put anything to paper. No evidence for the cops to be used against us if they raided us.

I squeezed my tumbler, creating a crack in the thick, expensive, and hearty glass. Any more pressure and I'd smash it to smithereens. "She fucking told her brother and did a runner! Makes her plenty guilty in my eyes."

"We brought her to the club without investigating her," Castor threw in. Those two always challenged me on decisions. Called me a hot head and themselves the rhyme and reason. "That's our fault."

Zethan had a reputation for being cool and collected, which was why I put him as second in charge. Where I was passion, fire, and emotion, he was logic and analysis, assessing every detail until he came to a conclusion. And right now, I needed every bit of rationale he had to offer when my rage blinded me. His cool head, analytic mind, and incredible sense of justice were some of the reasons Osiris chose him to rule the Underworld and help judge souls. Fuck, could you imagine someone like Set or me on the throne? We'd send every bastard to the pits of hell to burn.

"I checked the phone records." Castor twisted his dry whisky glass. "No calls were made from the shelter to Danny's phone after her initial contact. In fact, no calls were made to him in the last two days. On the eve of a big ambush like that? How the fuck would they have mobilized so fast if she somehow called him the night before? That's a big job. Nothing makes sense, and something isn't right, Prez. Give me some time to look into it."

He had a point. My god senses were tingling with suspicion. If that were me conducting the raid, I'd have been on the phone, doing last minute checks with all parties involved.

"Fine. Look into it." I waved an approving hand at him.

"What about that dickhead, Jaxx?" Zethan threw in, like a wrestling elbow to the jaw. "He scoped out Reg's warehouse." He did the fucking quote fingers, and I wanted to snap them off and shove them up his ass. "Didn't see a single damn bike or the employees acting funny. Where the fuck did they hide twenty bikes?"

Fuck, another point he had me on. Assholes. I hated being wrong and growled at him. Jaxx's fuck-up pissed me off, and I'd grill that dick later. Right now, I had bigger shit to deal with. Aaliyah Heller was an immediate priority.

"Danny Heller wants his sister back within forty-eight hours." I scratched at my beard. "We're not giving her back." My chest thundered with rage at the way he'd hit, swore at, and disrespected his sister and my ... no ... she wasn't that anymore. "He doesn't give two shits about her. As soon as he gets his hands on her, he'll put a bullet in her brain, blame us, then use it as justification for war. She's staying here until the threat is neutralized."

Three nods returned at my suggestion. Finally, we agreed on something. My temper scaled down a bar. I didn't want to fight with my brothers when we needed to band together, defend our club and family against that ballsy cunt, Heller.

We couldn't afford a gang war with the cops breathing down our goddamn necks. I was not living in a three-walled cell behind bars for ten years for murder. Probably double that to life if the cops tried to pin old Heller's murder on me too.

Alaric remained silent throughout this. I felt his conflict tremble down the mate bond. He didn't want to believe that our mate could deceive us when Liz had been loyal to the core. But all his faith in people had been stolen from him long ago, and he found it difficult to trust when someone hurt him. Forgiveness sat black and heavy in his heart.

I swiveled on the table to face him. "What do you think about all this, Hawk Boy?"

He scratched at his freshly clean-shaven chin. "I hate to say it, sir." My jaw twitched at the word. He knew how much I hated it and said it to piss me off for calling him Hawk Boy. "But I think they're right. I don't trust her at all, but I think we owe her the decency of investigating her claims first." Fuck, not him too. "Ultimately, I'll do whatever you say, just give me the order."

Order? I rubbed at my exhausted eyes. I didn't know what to do now. Those bastards used their reasoning powers on me, and I was tired, confused, and grumpy as fuck. Finding out about Aaliyah hit me hard. Like a rocket launcher to the damn gut hard.

Liz's death had crushed me, and I spent the last seven hundred-and-fifty-two days longing for my mate. Then the nurse crashed into our lives and had me hoping again. Hope that she'd smashed, crushed to dust, and flitted in the wind. How could I trust another mate after her? Trust her even if Zethan and Castor proved her innocent? I'd been hurt like that three times in my life. When the Wayward Eagles killed my mother. Again, when the Winter's Devils took Liz away from us. And now with Aaliyah. Except her betrayal stung more, like a thousand knives to my heart.

"Fuck." Everyone was against me, and I was in the minority vote. "Fine. Cozy up to her. Get information from her like she did to us. Prove she's not guilty. You have two days to do it, or else she or we are dead."

CHAPTER 7

Aaliyah

Twenty-four hours down. Another day to go until the Wolves declared war on the Jackals. No one had said a thing to me and kept me in the dark, figuratively and literally.

I relied on the sole window and Castor bringing me meals at regular intervals to tell time. By now, he should have returned with another tray of food. Biker meals consisted mainly of sandwiches, chips, and bottled water. Ready-made. The shelter had been better stocked than the clubhouse, and part of me wished I was kept there instead of this miserable place. Castor made delicious food for us every night, and I craved something better than what came out of a can. Or the bacon he brought me the previous night. The Jackals had more important matters to deal with, like defending their clubhouse and preparing for an attack.

Time was relative when being held prisoner. Spans of isolation dragged on for eternity, and I missed visits from my compassionate jailer. A man who enforced the Jackal's rules and hurt people that didn't. Juxtaposition I couldn't marry up. At work, the bustling vibe of the ER kept me busy, and I hated long periods of silence and quiet when it made me think. I'd done a lot of that since landing down here.

Familiar footfalls on the tread sounded upstairs at the door to the basement. I'd studied them all and matched their voices to the gaits. Nothing better to do in this damn cell. The first one was Castor's. Steady and even-paced stride was like his bird, an ibis searching for bugs and aquatic animals among the reeds. Slade and Zethan walked with heavy, determined strides, like prowling jackals. Alaric, light and stealthy like his damn bird of prey. But Slade and Alaric hadn't visited since our interrogation, and Zethan once, when Castor couldn't make it.

Dinnertime and companionship were on the way. Excited, I sat up, my stomach burbling. Last time he'd brought me bacon. Castor descended the stairs, balancing a tray of food, bandages, cleaning wipes, water bowl, a bundle of clothes. My heart kicked up a beat, and I leaned forward.

"You look much better since breakfast." The mate bond betrayed his real feelings, the words stunning despite the circumstances, sliding through. "He set the items on the seat ten feet from my cell and dug the cell key out of his pocket. "How are you feeling?"

"Do you really want me to answer that?" I arched a quizzical brow as he opened the door and entered. "My hair has gone rogue and taken on a life of its own." I finger combed the errant hairs back into place.

"Sassy, are we?" He deposited the clothes and bandages at my feet, and laid the tray across my lap. Campbell's chicken soup. Food for a university student barely scraping by on her scholarship. The smell of it made my stomach roll, and I slumped in the bed, disappointed.

"No gourmet food today?" I pushed aside the tray of slop, unable to stomach it. "You're the studious one. Patient enough to scour old tomes for information on a centuries-old curse. But not for a decent, healthy recipe?"

Castor grinned. "You're definitely on the mend."

"Mended enough to get out of here?" Worth a try. The tilt of his head and sharp eyebrow told me that was a big no.

Castor's personality made him the most appealing mate of the four. In tune with my feelings, what I needed and when, showing me mercy were qualities I looked for. Looking like an Arabian prince was high on the list, too.

All four of the jackals were blessed in the appearance department, but that didn't mean I wanted to be their mate, yet or ever. When Slade first told me about the mate bond, I thought he was joking, until the feels hit me. Intense waves of emotion shared between the four of us. The thought of losing them, or the future I never knew I wanted, broke something inside me, and I slumped back into my pillow.

"They'll come around, Aaliyah." Castor stroked my unruly hair and tucked a strand behind my ear. "Slade and the others feel betrayed. They understand the reason why you lied to them, but their trust is hard won."

"I hope you're right, Castor." My life and freedom depended on it, as well as that of Jerry's and the other two captive Wolves. "So, we're stuck down here until that happens."

"Slade will come around on that front too." Castor nestled the bandages and change of clothes by my leg. "He's worried about the safe house and the women staying there right now. We tried setting up a rush transit, but these things aren't always easy to coordinate when manufactured documents are involved."

"I understand," I told him, but we both recognized it for the lie it was. The longer I stayed down here, the more I resented the situation and that I'd done it to myself. Lie after lie, compounded for the sake of finding my father's murderer, and everything blew up in my face.

"Focus on recovering and let me handle things with Slade and the guys." Castor broke the plastic on the bandage and gestured for me to lift my shirt so he could cleanse it.

"Who's the nurse and patient here?" I grumbled, shifting the blanket back, shuffling down the bed to lie flat on my back.

"Fiery and sassy." Castor beamed as he peeled back my shirt. A flicker of desire shot through our tie, fueling mine, and my breath quickened.

"We're running out of time before my brother comes to get me." Poor attempt at a cold shower.

"That's not going to happen." Castor tore open a steri-wipe, peeled back my used bandage, making me hiss when he brushed the cold alcohol over my sensitive flesh. "I promise."

"You shouldn't make promises you can't keep." I cautioned.

"I don't." Castor's tone brooked no argument. I almost believed him.

Goosebumps sprouted over the area of my wound where he thoroughly cleaned and replaced the bandage.

Castor circled the back of his head and looked up at me under his lashes. Shy. The man never seemed shy about anything. He said and took what he wanted. Had claimed me in two kisses. Yet something had sparked the cutest blush to spread across his cheeks.

"What?" I laughed.

"Your lady parts."

I crushed my thighs together.

"You're uh … coming into heat soon and will need products for it. I'll have to give you iron, spinach, greens, and be careful because of your blood loss."

I blinked, shocked at the way he came out with it. Suddenly he cared about my nutrient intake after filling me with enough salt and sugar ready-made products to give me a heart attack?

"My heat?" I chuckled and shook my head. "I'm not a dog, and we're not in high school. You can call it a period."

His blush deepened, and he waved a finger at me to take my top off to wash me.

"Aw, look at you ... big, bad enforcer, going red at the mention of blood." I pinched his cheeks. Couldn't help myself. If I was going to die, might as well go out having some fun. Life was short when you lived on the road. Even shorter when you got caught up with bikers ... and gods, it seemed.

His husky chuckle kindled the fire in me, and I warmed below. "You're a shifter like us and can go in heat." Fuck, would that make the Jackals go wild and descend on me to mate?

I didn't make a move to undress, so Castor did the honors, and my eyelids fluttered as his knuckles ghosted my stomach and sides.

Trying to control myself under his heated, amber gaze, I grabbed my shirt and covered my breasts. "I think I would know if I shifted."

"Don't get all scoffy with me, dark sorceress."

The old vagina recovered like a pro and steamed up again. "You're a book worm and probably a Scrabble genius. But even I know there's no such word as *scoffy*."

He tickled my sides, and I almost dropped the shirt, lowering it enough to expose the top of my full breasts. His gaze went there, and he licked those damn perfect lips of his.

I bit my lip as he purposely feathered across my skin with every brush of the wet cloth. "Believe me, the word *scoffy* is definitely in the English language. Just not in the context I used."

"You're a bullshitter." I hit him in the chest, regretting it when the pain gripped my entire left side in a stinging cramp.

He captured my hand, rubbing his thumb over it, dulling my pain. "If I'm right, I get a kiss."

I barked out a pained laugh. "I know better than to go up against the god of Writing and Knowledge on a Scrabble challenge."

He traced my chin with a finger. "And I know better than to go up against you, dark sorceress."

He really should stop calling me that. The power in those words, the seductive way he whispered it had me losing my grip again, and my heart holding my brain in a chokehold.

I cleared my throat, but it still came out rough. "I want proof of my shifting abilities and *supposed* heat."

"In Egyptian Mythology, the gods use their shape-shifting power to perform their duties, attack enemies or defend followers." The side of his finger trailed down my arm, and full-body shivers ripped through me. He knew the effect he had on me and pushed me to the edge. The damn edge where I lay back on the bed while he buried himself in my eager and waiting pussy. "Isis sprouted wings to fly over her people."

I tried to dislodge the lust wedged in my throat. "I bet an Ibis god was pretty lethal." I nudged him with my fisted knuckles.

"Fuck, not you, too!" He chuckled and shook his head, telling me he copped a bit of teasing from the other avatars about his bird shifter. "Thoth might have a long beak, but he's also well-equipped and knows how to use it. Some might say, the longest of the pantheon."

I giggled. "Something tells me we're not talking about birds anymore."

His dark, delicious smile swept me under his spell again.

"Like you can talk, anyway." He made two devil horns on his head with his fingers. "Isis wears cow horns. When you turn into a heifer, this lame-ass ibis will ride your back."

Banter and chemistry came easy for us, and I could easily see myself falling for a guy like him. It made my days in this prison less lonely, and I looked forward to the times he came to visit and tend me.

"Take backsies!" I hit him in the arm but it hurt, and I crunched my hands into fists.

He drew me in for a blazing, dominant hug, rubbing to the side of my wound, easing my discomfort. "No can do, cowgirl."

Cowgirl. Did he have to mention a sex position? It set my body alight even more than it was and I struggled to contain the bonfire growing into a wildfire.

"When you shift is up to you. Our previous mate, Liz—" His voice hitched on her name, and I detected a sad ending that I wanted to know about. He took a moment to compose himself. Talking about his ex did wonders to douse the fire within my body. "She sprouted wings at twenty-five after being fired." He adopted a devilish grin. "But you might be lucky to get the wings as well as the body, cowgirl."

I tucked my head on his chest and smiled. "Oh, God, we have lame shifter animals, don't we?"

He stroked my hair, and I closed my eyes, falling into his dark web of intrigue. "We do."

This man could teach me a lot about my avatar abilities, about magick, and my goddess' secrets. It felt incredible to have someone to share my secret world with after being unable to confide in anyone about what I was or who I represented. Though, trusting the Jackals and their intentions was difficult when I didn't know if they wanted to keep me a prisoner or kill me. Something told me Castor might not be so forthcoming with my yearning for answers with the tension between the other Jackals and me.

His hands moved to the space between my neck and shoulders, and I clutched him tighter. I felt his need, dark, possessive, and longing when he touched me. My body responded at every brush of my skin, the knot in my throat thickening. When his teeth grazed the shell of my ear, his tongue swiping over the sensitive skin on my earlobe, I knew I was a goner. Every part of me clenched with needy anticipation. My pussy ached for his touch.

Fuck, he was right. I was going into heat. No wonder I was drenched below and smelled like it too. I clenched my thighs together, pulling the blanket over me tightly. But then my heart intervened, spreading them.

Goddess, my body refused to obey instruction after that. I almost replied in a husky voice of my own, "You sure you don't want to stay?"

Sense finally reasserted itself with my brain wrangled out of my heart's clutches and stuffed its opponent down where it belonged in my chest. *Hell no, Aaliyah. You're healing from a gunshot wound, and this man is keeping you prisoner. Do not fall for his devilish charms. He'll only bring you heartache. The four of them, pain and ruin.*

Startled by the reminder, I pushed off him and brushed my silky hair away from my burning body. I wanted to clothe myself and hide from his hungry gaze. If we kept going like this, we'd end up having sex, and I couldn't go there again. Not after Slade. Not with my injury.

"You better go." I pulled the blanket over my entire body, and disappointment flashed in his eyes. "They might think I've kidnapped you or used my wily ways on you."

He hid it behind a cocky smile. "When do I get my kiss for being right, cowgirl?" Typical Castor, bargaining for a kiss.

I tucked the blanket under my armpits. "Teach me how to

sprout wings, and I'll give it to you." A promise I shouldn't have made, but I wanted him out of here, to breathe and calm down my out-of-control hormones and emotions of the mate bond wrecking me.

"Deal." He backed away as if he intended to leave, and loneliness tapped the bond. I reached out, capturing his hand. For several moments, he studied my hand as if it were a precious artifact he wished to examine. His thumb strokes increased in pressure and heat, sending pulses of desire through us both.

Goddess, what was wrong with me? Wanting to get rid of him one minute, then desperate for him to stay the next.

"Aaliyah," he breathed, throaty and hoarse, and I trembled.

"Yes?" I grabbed his strong hand, encouraging it to circle my stomach, and brush my voluptuous curves.

"Stop." He pressed his lips to my hair and inhaled deeply through his nose. Control quickly slipped from his grasp too.

Our breath came faster, his chest pumped more rapidly against mine, his fingers tightening on my arm. We were both charged up and on edge. Swiftly, he released my arms, circled me, and leaned back to sweep his dark gaze over me. Modest all of a sudden, I covered my breasts, leaving the rest of me exposed. The pulse point of his neck thumped in time to my heartbeat. His lips were so close to mine. Close enough to take in mine and suck on. My breath caught as I waited for him to kiss me again like he had in Zethan's office. Commanding, unbendable, and hypnotizing. I couldn't control the whimper that flung free when he grazed the bottom of my breasts. Wetness drenched me below and I smelled like it too.

That man had no right to do what he did to me, but as my fated mate, he had every right. Every dutiful caress and longing gaze weakened my resistance, shooting me headfirst into dangerous territory. The more time I spent with this man, the less I cared about what he might do to me, and the more I cared what I wanted him to do to me. Lusty currents swept me away, lost forever from the girl who protested and guarded herself.

"I better go," he rasped, thick and husky. "I can smell your heat and it's driving me crazy. If I stay any longer, I'm going to tear off your sweatpants and bury my face between your legs."

Panting, he snapped back and collected the water bowl and washcloth, leaving the cell and locking it behind him. As he disappeared up the stairs, his boots thumped in time to my disappointed heart.

I threw my shirt back on, gasping at the pain.

"Aaliyah?" he called out, worried.

"I'm fine." I didn't want him to come back down here. Next time, I might not be strong enough to resist him. "It just hurt to get into my shirt."

"Want some help?" He wanted any excuse to stay and so did I.

"No!" I said too quickly.

He paused for a beat. "Good night, dark sorceress." His footsteps continued, and light illuminated the stairs as he opened the door and closed it.

CHAPTER 8

Zethan – Jackal's Wrath MC Vice President & Avatar of Osiris

THE LAST TIME I'd seen *him*, things hadn't ended well. Prick had tried to kill a soul from my pantheon, and Underworld magick called me away in the middle of a firefight with the Wolves. He had every right to demand vengeance for an injustice—hell, I would have demanded it too, if my wife was kidnapped twice. But I drew a hard line at crushing the offender's soul, ending their cycle of reincarnation.

The only reason I visited my counterpart was because he owed me a favor and I was calling it in. Last place I wanted to be, if I were honest. Regret dragged across my skin like claws, adding yet another scar to my body.

Osiris ruled over and judged the dead souls. Newcomers were arbitrated in the *Hall of Two Truths*, where their hearts were weighed against the feather. My heart sat heavy, like a lead weight, aching in my chest. Triggered by my past, pure hatred of abusive men, I'd acted on emotion and fucking killed the junkie for beating up Aaliyah. Only to discover she'd possibly stabbed us in the back and initiated a war with a rival club, which was the worst kind of betrayal. Jury was still out on that front, and I'd reserve judgment until I had all the puzzle pieces. Still, it didn't ease the guilty vise around my throat.

Green magick shimmered at my arrival at the gates of his realm. A crook and flail appeared in my hands, tools carried when on Underworld business. An opal river flowed deeper into the kingdom, where a lone boat and ferryman navigated the waters. Souls screamed from the depths, begging me to save them from their drowning pit of hell.

Sorry, not my domain. I couldn't interfere here.

A three-headed hellhound that came to my chest stood guard at the gate. At my appearance, it lowered its body, snarling deep and menacing, threatening to tear me apart if I took another step. Sharp teeth gnashed at the air as jaws snapped and spittle flew. Good thing I wore my trusted flannel jacket and jeans. Some protection if I got bitten.

"Summon your master." I tapped the tip of my crook in my hand, warning the beast I was in no mood to go up against it.

The three heads released a long, deep howl that hit every bone in my body. Underworld magick differed between the pantheons and customs, but ultimately came from the same heavenly source, and that power echoed through me.

They appeared moments later. *Him* dressed in dark, pronged armor and a Greek skirt, clutching his bident. *Her* in a beautiful purple gown fit for a queen, high pumps and straps winding up to her knees. A stunning couple, more like statues than humans, because they'd both merged with their gods.

"What are you doing here?" *He* growled at me, eyes dark with displeasure.

Feeling was mutual. I wanted to be here as much as I wanted a bullet in my brain. But I was the only one who could do this.

"Relax, *Hades*." My voice came out as tight as his. "I'm not here to hurt anyone."

"What do you want, *outlaw*?" Hades' bident prongs found the space over my heart.

I laughed at his insult. Heard worse. Deserved worse.

Adamantine prongs bit into my chest, Hades' judgment tool declaring my heart guilty. *Impulsive. Murderer. Deserving.* Fuck, I was as bad as Slade and Set, taking that man's life before I deliberated on the facts.

Hades' nymph-like wife, Autumn, put her hand on his chest to hold him back. "Let him speak, my love. I'm sure Zethan is here for valid reasons. Like apologizing for saving Colton Raine."

"I don't speak for that asshole." Apologies were not on the agenda. Period.

"Language in front of my wife," Hades growled.

Autumn smirked, linking her elbow with his, keeping his temper down. "Good to see you've got pants this time, Zethan." She always lightened the mood with her grumpy-ass husband.

It took me a moment to work out what she meant. Fuck, the shendyt. Standard Egyptian uniform that I had to wear in the Underworld. A thin, pale, cotton skirt that hid nothing when going commando. Unfortunately, she and Hades dropped in during a lull, when I'd taken a nap on my throne, old legs parted and all. I didn't give a fuck, though.

Her joke eased the tension for a few seconds, and I chuckled, glancing at the flannel covering my scars. Denim and boots were my MC uniform, and I felt more comfortable in them. "I can change if you want."

Autumn hid her smile behind her hand when Hades growled.

Old and familiar sensations thrummed in my chest. Undying, passionate, all-consuming love. Exactly what I wanted back in my life. Heartache stung my chest. I missed my former mate and wanted her back. But she was gone, replaced by another. One I didn't entirely trust, but wanted to learn more about.

The gods were cruel if they dropped our enemy into our lap to ruin the club, us, and break our hearts. But not as cruel as whoever placed the curse between her and me, and the five of us. Not being able to be near my fated mate, have her in my arms, watching her with the others, them touching her, Slade marking her... fuck, that was the definition of agony.

Enough about her. Fists jammed tightly to my side, I called upon all my strength to push my thoughts of her down.

I straightened and stiffened, letting the prongs prick me. "I've come to call in that favor you owe me, Hades. For letting your wife meet with her mother."

"All deals were null and void when your colleague kidnapped my wife." Hades flashed plenty of white teeth. Lots of bark, but no bite. Understandable for someone who inherited the kingdom of the Greek Underworld without control over death. Grumpy asshole couldn't do half the shit I could.

"I had nothing to do with that." I kept my cool. No point goading him when he was quick to temper like Slade. Places to be and all that shit.

The whole tension with Hades came about because of Colton fucking Raine, avatar of Anubis, royal pain in my ass, and my unfortunate colleague in the Underworld. Always armed with a snippy remark. *Wake up, you big lug. Stop sleeping on the job.* Excuse me if I worked tirelessly night and day at the club and shelter, then fucking ran the Underworld in my sleep. Cockhead kidnapped Autumn twice because of some deal with Zeus and put me in the shitter with Hades.

Hades' weapon cut through my shirt. My favorite fucking red and black shirt. "Get out of my realm before I throw you out."

Short on time and patience, I yanked his weapon away, throwing it prongs-first into the fertile banks of the River Styx. "Give me the soul of the man who beat *my mate*." The last two words came out as natural as night and day, and I couldn't recall them.

Fuck, why did I say that? I didn't know what she was to me anymore. Confusion had me caught up in a tempest of emotions. The logical side of me said give her the benefit of the doubt. Same argument I'd used with Slade. Yet, the heartbroken side of me screamed that she deceived us. The scales of Maat in the Underworld wobbled all over the place with my emotions, unsure which side to sway to.

Autumn winced at the mention of my hurt ... mate? Traitor? I didn't know what to call her. Soft heart that Autumn, not into violence. Strange for a Lady of Death.

She grabbed Hades' shoulder and jerked him back. "What do you want with him? You sent him here before his time. Why should we allow it?"

"Allow it?" Hades puffed at the preposterous notion. His wife wore the pants here.

"I need to find out who hired him," I said as honestly as I could. "Then I'm gone, and our arrangement is concluded." Didn't need the reminder of what I'd done or the guilty fucking conscience weighing me down. Had enough of my own shit to deal with.

"Only if you permit another visit with my mother," she bargained, "and let me take her granddaughter."

My eyebrows shot up at her request. I liked her! Expert level negotiator. Far from the frightened woman I'd encountered when I'd saved Coltan from certain death at Hades' hand. Hades was known for making bargains, not his wife, but she'd impressed me. This woman had a way to drag me from the bad mood clouding my day.

"Then we're square?" I wanted this matter with Colton settled ... and the matter with the junkie, Aaliyah, and the fucking Wolves, come to think of it. "No hard feelings against me for the Colton mess?"

"Not agreed," Hades grumbled. This was the reason I hated dealing with him. Next time, I'd go through his pleasant and cooperative wife. If there was a next time. There always was with Underworld business.

"Agreed." Autumn side-eyed her husband, telling me there were a lot of disagreements in their household and probably a lot of hot make-up sex too.

"Deal." I reached out a hand, and she shook it.

"Never send another here before their time." Autumn waved her hand, summoning the soul I'd prematurely sent to their realm.

Prick deserved it for touching my ... I bit back the word. It slipped out whenever I thought of Aaliyah. She was no mate of ours, not until we got to the bottom of this complicated mess of who sabotaged us and why. I thought my sister's death hurt, but this cut deeper, right through my heart, slicing it in two with no chance of repair.

It took me a few seconds to summon the courage to look at the soul I'd hastily and possibly unfairly sent here. He looked healthier than the last time we'd met despite the pale green outline of Greek Underworld magick over his skin. Scratch marks from the meth addiction plus the bags under his eyes, wide pupils, and lanky, oily hair had all disappeared. Souls were their most beautiful in death.

"He … he…" The soul stepped away from me and towards its master. Rightfully so, and the hand on my throat tightened. "Make him leave."

"You will tell him what he wants to know." Autumn's voice came out part human, part goddess, and the soul shrank before her.

"Yes, gr … great lady." The soul cowered before her.

Great Lady. Wanky title. Didn't do them. But whatever floated her boat.

An impression hit me of his ultimate resting place. The Crag, a region within the Greek Underworld reserved for multiple offenders but not the demons of human society.

Three slow and hesitant steps carried me to the soul. Looking at him sparked memories of his shitty and cowardly act. Regardless of Aaliyah's guilt, no man should ever touch a weaker and more fragile female. Anger surged, tempting me to kill him all over again, but I crushed it with the squeeze of my hands.

"Tell me the name of your dealer," I bit out.

He looked at me, gaze pitiful, remorseful. "I'm sorry for what I did to her."

Too little, too late. Fury snapped inside me, and I lashed out, belting him across the face with my crook. "I don't give a shit about your penance." That was Hades' and Autumn's task to deal with. "Give me the name."

Hades caught my wrist and it cracked as he crushed it under his punishing grip. "Do not touch my souls."

My body trembled as I calmed the rage as Hades let go of me, and I let my arm and crook fall to my side. This wasn't me. I didn't lose control like this. Aaliyah had me in a spin.

"Give me the name," I repeated as steadily as I could manage.

"Garry Young," the man stuttered.

That name didn't resonate with me as he didn't belong to

my realm. Keen to know the Underworld he belonged to, I searched my soul directory, finding him in the Romanian afterlife. The origin of a soul, their very first life, directed them to their hereafter, not their heritage in this current life. Reincarnation and all that shit, and I didn't want to get into the complexities of it as it did my head in.

"That his real name or dealer name?" I asked.

The dead junkie scratched the crook of his elbow absently. A habit from his last life when it itched on meth withdrawals. "I ... I don't know."

Didn't matter, Castor would find him through messages from junkies and users. Garry Young couldn't hide forever. I was coming for him once I had the final piece of information I needed. Prick was taking a one-way trip to the afterlife. "Where do I find him?"

"By the wharf in Sydney." The man's wary gaze flicked to mine for a second before returning to the ground. This soul was a worm from the inside out. Hated himself for all his life choices. Regretted the day he picked up a spoon and dissolved Ice on it with a lighter. "Can I go now?"

Not until I performed one last check. An honesty scan with my powers. My magick didn't work as well here as it did in my realm, but after a bit of probing, it told me he spoke the truth. Good.

"Get out of my sight, you piece of shit." I nodded at Autumn and Hades to get rid of him before I punched him one last time for hitting a woman. I didn't care if Aaliyah was innocent or not. No man should raise a fist at a woman. Ever.

Hades glared at me while Autumn sent him back to the Crag.

I opened a portal. "Call my name when you want to visit your mother."

"Wait." Autumn tiptoed toward me in her sexy shoes. She leaned in and kissed my cheek. "Don't try to cheat me, outlaw." She poked me on the nose, and I blinked. "I know where you live." Friendly. Bubbly. I liked her. What the hell did she see in Hades?

I hadn't been touched in over two years. Her kiss on my cheek left a soft glow, not in a sexual way, but in a way that left me longing for another's lips. Lost for words, I stumbled away, leaving them standing on the banks of the River Styx.

Slade was onto me the moment I returned to my clubhouse office. "What'd you find?" He'd waited for me while I was gone, salivating for justice and vengeance. Always looking for a fight, just like his war god.

"Garry Young." I delivered the name he wanted. "Deals by the Sydney wharf."

"Upmarket scumbag, huh?" Slade smiled and clapped me on the shoulder.

"Guess I'll find out."

"You paying him a visit?"

"Not today," I replied. "I'll get Castor to look into him. See if it's a moniker."

"Good work." Slade gave me another clap on the shoulder, a lighter gait in step as he departed.

I went to my desk, everything in order, pens in holders, papers in trays, calculator sitting on the left side. Just the way I liked it. Mess clouded my head, and I hated it when I lost my stationary.

Slade must have left a rectangular parcel in front of my keyboard. Fuck, that came quick. I'd ordered it several days ago before all the shit went down. The packaging came off with one rough tear, and I removed the goods inside. This would do. Bring on phase two.

Pleased, I exited my office and knocked on Castor's door.

"Come in," he muttered like he was in the middle of something.

I entered, bumping into a whiteboard and sidestepping it.

Castor was on the other side of it, drawing a line from a photo of a number plate to a CCTV image of a truck. Leads on the stolen shipment of Pharaoh and the truck.

I studied his handiwork, the three men emerging from a BMW with machine guns and the timestamp. Two climbed into the truck cab. "You going all *Criminal Minds* on me?"

Castor chuckled and clipped the whiteboard marker lid in his mouth to his pen. "I was able to pull security footage from Joey's warehouse transmitted to the security firm servers before it was erased."

"Three men?" I scratched at the image of the BMW. "No bikers?"

"Could be associates or hired guns." Castor stuck another image of the truck caught on a traffic light camera thirty minutes later. At least that gave him a range of where to look. "Whoever they are, they covered their tracks well, and I'm struggling to pull clues together."

Fuck, we couldn't afford a trail to go dead. We were one mill in debt and needed to pay Tony for manufacturing the last batch of Pharaoh.

"On a positive note," I said, trying to stay calm when my mind exploded with debts and figures since I handled the money along with Rusty, who was the club's official treasurer. "Hades gave me a name."

Castor flicked his head up, signaling for me to give it.

"Gary Young. Not sure if it's a legit name or an alias."

Castor lifted his hand and rested it on the top of the whiteboard. "Let me look into it. Want me to come with you if I find him?"

Anger coursed through me at what this fucker had done to Aaliyah. Mate or not, she was a woman, and I hated any man who struck a female ... even if she was connected to it.

I crunched my fist into my palm. "Yeah."

"It might take me a couple of days to get to it." Castor rubbed at his lined forehead. "Slade said this is priority."

We all had our work cut out for us. Too many competing priorities to attend to, and only one hacker for the job.

"Whenever you can, brother." I squeezed his shoulder. "For now, I've got to plan how to get info out of Aaliyah."

CHAPTER 9

Aaliyah

BURY HIS FACE between my legs. *Holy fuckeroony!* Sign me up, my heart said. My head punched my heart in the vagina to shut her up and make her keel over.

Fuck, why'd you let him leave? my heart sassed me. *He was going to kiss you. Care for you. Are you mad?*

Perfectly sane, I argued back. *I'm not doing something I'll regret, no matter how much I want him.*

Fuck, why was I arguing with myself? I shook it off, slowly dressed, and slipped back under the covers, feeling exposed from Castor's bathing. Hungry, I consumed the dinner he brought me, only to give my body the fuel it needed to heal. When I finished, I set aside the tray on the cold stone and winced as I climbed back under the covers.

Alone, bored, and horny as hell from Castor's words, I couldn't stop thinking about him, those maple eyes glowing a darker amber in the dim candlelight. Heat in my belly and core from his hungry gaze persisted. No matter how many mental cold showers I dumped on myself, it burned hotter and brighter.

Goddess, I was in heat.

Shedding my resistance, my fingers skimmed along my stomach, beneath the blankets, under the elastic of my underwear. A wet prize awaited me, and I gasped at my touch, burning, throbbing, just like my clit. Another stroke made my back arch, and I rubbed harder, chasing my release.

The stairs creaked, and I jolted up, listening. Faint murmurs wandered from upstairs, conversations that I couldn't make out words to. Wind whistled and a bush tapped at the basement window, but the stairs went silent.

Relaxing back into my pillow, I continued my sensual descent, moaning at the return of my finger.

A second and third creak, one from the door, made me hit pause, bite my lip, and hold my breath. Light illuminated the staircase as someone entered and descended.

"Castor?" I pulled the blanket tighter.

"Don't stop on my account." His dark, secretive voice prompted my hand back to my pussy. He'd only been gone five, maybe ten minutes. The door clicked closed behind him.

"What are you doing?" I tried to gauge his location on the partially illuminated stairwell or the basement's corner shadows.

"I give the orders down here, dark sorceress." His dark, thirsty voice caressed my ears and belly. "You think that you're going to touch yourself without me? I can smell you from my office." My thigh muscles groaned from clenching them so tightly.

Fuck. Did ibis shifters have a good sense of smell? I guess they did if they detected bugs in the mud.

"Keep touching yourself and think of only me," he

crooned, deploying that convincing voice that would make me sign my soul over to the devil.

Something about him made me want to obey his every command. My core reignited as my finger lowered to my clit. Maple-colored eyes exploded behind my closed lids. I imagined him biting his lip as he watched me from the darkness, taking his thick, long cock in his hand, stroking it, and bringing it to me. The velvet and steel in my palms as I pumped him.

Goddess, what was I thinking? I was injured and shouldn't exert myself. Touching myself like this was inappropriate and wrong.

"I ... I can't do this," I whispered. "I'm healing."

"She's healing you," Castor replied, his ghostlike voice touching me all over, making me light up and blaze. "She needs you. Needs us. That's why she sent you to us. To break the curse."

What the hell? Isis had sent me to my enemies? No.

My body tingled as if Castor had touched my stomach again. I felt his hands all over me. Caressing my neck, my jaw, my shoulders, my breasts. I squirmed at the warmth and adoration. Four sets of hands landed on my fiery skin, worshipping me, massaging me, pleasuring me. A taste of what it would be like if I became the Jackals' mate.

"Take them," she coaxed me, dark, secretive, and beautiful. *"They are yours and you theirs."* A command I wasn't sure if I could obey but wanted to.

In seconds, I was lost to the heat and desire consuming my body, stripping away all pain, worry, and doubt. My period was coming, and with it, a dump of hormones, and according to Castor, a shifter heat. My first. And I couldn't resist it or deny my pleasure.

The buckle on Castor's belt unclipped, followed by the lowering of his jeans zipper. Holy fuck, he was going to touch himself too. A long, deep groan from the back of his throat erupted in the shadows. I heard him spit on his hand and lubricate his cock, and I almost split apart at how hot this was. I'd never masturbated with my boyfriends before, and this was sensual, erotic, and an act of complete trust.

"Keep going, baby." His voice thickened with need. "Touch yourself just for me. Come on that finger and suck it for your *Dark Daddy*."

Lord, the nickname stoked my fire, and I gave myself a single stroke.

"Fuck." My head didn't want to listen to my heart, but my body responded to him, sliding along my wet heat again and again, drawing out a moan. I couldn't believe I let him dominate the play, but I was lost to his dark charms. The dominance and mystery in his voice that took complete control of me. Lost to the will of my goddess and my heat.

"Yeah, like that," he crooned, stroking his cock, softly at first, the sweep of the motions becoming faster, hungry, and urgent.

I rubbed myself harder, desperate for him to watch me, hear me, encourage him out of the shadows to touch me. "Where are you?" I wanted to see his face, his responses to me, the way he stroked himself. Hell, dammit, the size of his fucking cock.

"Never you mind." Always secretive and mysterious, keeping me guessing. Touching myself had drawn him down the steps like a damn ninja. By the sound of his voice, I pinpointed his location to the corner, and I focused my gaze there.

"Come here, touch me." The desperate pleading in my voice made my head cringe, but my heart didn't care. She wanted her mate by her side, his hands all over me like the promise Isis had shown me. Naked, getting to know each other's bodies, caressing, kissing.

"I'm staying right here." His firm command made me sag deeper into the pillow. "Away from you and your dark, alluring tricks."

He thought I did this to manipulate him. Never. That wasn't me. I might have pried him for information about the club, but I would never manipulate his feelings for the sake of escaping. It was clear the Jackals weren't that easy to sway.

"Suit yourself." A girl had to keep an element of control.

"You're so fucking turned on right now." The dominance in his voice deepened and hardened like a blade. "I can smell it. And you're not getting any release without me."

Oh, yes, I could. With or without him. He'd have to come over here to stop me. And I was more than willing to let him.

"Your pussy is aching for me, isn't it?" His growl made the iron of my cell groan as if he squeezed the bars with his magick.

"Yes!" I wanted him more than anything.

"Touch your perfect breasts," Castor ordered me, and my left hand traveled there, squeezing it. "Fuucckk." He let out a long groan that rumbled through me. "I want my cock between your cleavage."

I wanted him there too. Though, he'd have to come near me, and unlike him, I didn't have a single complaint about that. I kept rolling my breast in my palm to coax him. Strong-willed and stubborn, he remained in place, and my enticing smile fell from my lips.

One minute, I was in control of my body, the next, I was a slave to him.

Smiling seductively, I resumed my finger on my clit, the friction making my spine arch, my neck stretch back, and my tits go into the air. My wound complained with a deep throb, but I ignored it, focused only on my pleasure.

"Yes, like that. Good girl." Castor liked to be in complete charge, and I let him, desperate to get off and relieve the pressure of my heat. "Harder, faster, suck that finger deep for me."

I did as he ordered, and I heard him speed up and groan, low and gravelly.

"Who does your pussy belong to?" Castor liked complete control. To own my mind. So different from Slade, who dominated and destroyed my body like a hurricane that left nothing standing.

"You." I needed him kneeling by my bed or on top of me.

"Show me where you like to be touched."

I threw off the blanket, and squeezed my breast again, skimmed over my belly, neck, and legs. Everywhere I could reach.

"Fuck, I want to taste that sweet pussy of yours." His dark, possessive growl made my pleasure heighten. "But not yet."

"I want to see you," I begged again.

"When you're a good girl." Frustrated with his reply, I turned my face away. "Let me see more of that gorgeous, wet, pink flower between your legs."

I did as he ordered, spreading my legs wider to give him a better view, hoping this would draw him from the murk.

"Insert one finger into your pussy," he commanded me, and I cried out from how good it felt to have my pleasure controlled by another. "How does that feel, baby?"

"Good," I ground out, my thighs quaking from holding them wide when they normally relied on the backup of my stomach muscles. Strength that was all shredded, thanks to the bullet.

"Two fingers." I groaned at his order and did as I was told. "Which one do you like better?"

"Yours."

He chuckled darkly, groaned, then repeated the question, harsher, sharper, and it went right to my core.

"Two. Better friction." I let out a little cry to show him. "It's thicker and fills me up."

He cursed at that, and I swore his tempo sped up.

"Use one for both," he growled, totally in control of my actions.

"Fuck!" Half my pleasure receded and slowed my orgasm.

"Spread your legs wider." My need grew at his total display of dominance.

I wanted to completely surrender to him. Be owned. Be his. "Let Dark Daddy see that perfect, pink pussy."

I almost laughed at the way he referred to himself in third person. Instead, I spread myself wider, giving him the access he craved.

Air hissed between his lips. Hungry, honeyed eyes lit up the dark. "Wider."

That move bordered on pain, testing my weakened muscles. "It hurts."

My next swipe made me tremble, jolt and I bit my lower lip to trap my murmur.

"Louder, baby." This was so inappropriate given the circumstances, but I was out of my mind with heat that I couldn't stop myself. As my captor, he kept his distance, his hands to himself, respectful of me. Now his words, the command in them, touched my body, practically drawing the orgasm from me.

"That's it. Good girl." His voice turned wicked and possessive. I whimpered at his praise. He didn't show me any of his body, choosing to remain shrouded in shadow and mystery. The way he kept hidden on the bond.

"Please." Heat coiled at my base, desperate to expand outwards and explode in my neck and head. The start of my orgasm bubbled and would soon boil.

"This good girl deserves her prize." Rewarding me, he partially emerged from the shadows, letting me see his long, hot, iron bar of need. Fisted in his grip, he stroked it, releasing some of his pent-up pressure. "You want this?"

Hell, yes, I craved this man. Needed him. "Yeeesss."

His body tightened, the muscles in his stomach flexing. "You're going to come with me. Give it to me." My head flew back in a sharp snap as my pleasure peaked. "That's right, sweetheart."

I screamed as an ancient power took control of me, mind, body, and soul. Pleasure crashed over me and swept me along for the ride.

Afterward, I needed a minute to come down from our high.

"Suck your finger for me." My final order.

Drawing my dripping finger into my mouth, I gave him his sweet send off. My eyes closed at tasting myself, the pleasure he brought me. My finger came out with a pop, and I lapped at it. Gaze back on him, I smiled and panted.

"Good night, dark sorceress." And that was all I would get from him. No kiss. No touch. Just pure, sweet dominance.

When my hormones and pleasure subsided, my mind took over again, scolding me. *That man is going to break your heart.*

I had no doubt he would. That dominance and confidence to control me said he'd use it as a weapon against me in future. I had to be smarter, stronger, and resist him next time if I was going to get out of here.

CHAPTER 10

Castor

THEY'D HIDDEN FROM ME. No trace of Joey's truck or who had stolen it. Besides a few sightings on CCTV footage, the damn thing had completely vanished after the pricks left the depot. Left me completely blind to find them. Nothing to tie the Wolves to the theft of our drugs and murder of our supplier. I bet whoever stole the shipment had stripped the truck and bundled the goods into a new vehicle. Total chop shop job. Made me look fucking incompetent to my president. But my gut told me it was the Wolves, and in five years prosecuting criminals, I was never wrong.

Slade wouldn't let a slight like this slide. He was out for blood, but we needed proof to justify a war with our rivals. Going in guns blazing would earn us a bad reputation with other clubs we needed on our side to use their territory for transport. Good relations were important for MCs when we relied on crossing through other clubs' territories for business.

After a run-in with the Winter's Devils that killed our former mate, we'd annihilated them and acquired their territory two years ago. Handy ground to have in this line of business. Entry into and out of Sydney, and we used it as our bargaining chip.

Flexing our muscle expanded the Jackals' power, and our operations expanded exponentially, shooting us to the spot of the wealthiest, most powerful, and invincible club in Australia. No one could touch us. Of course, the punks like the Desert Snakes tried. We took them out, too. After that, no one dared fuck with us, and I made sure of that.

Until the Wolves threw their weight around. A minor club with territory bordering on ours.

Irritation growing by the second, I rubbed the creases in my forehead, performing another scan of the minuscule clue I'd gathered from my initial search for the truck. The first two letters of the number plate that had emerged from the last known place the truck had passed. YD. *You're dead*, I like to think it meant. A promise Slade would deliver.

Then the truck disappeared. Not another sight of it. Like it had been switched or rebadged with new plates and stickers.

I need more than that. I couldn't find a damn mention of Joey or a stolen shipment, not even on the damn dark web. Whoever was behind this was smart. Or they knew the Jackals had an avatar like me working behind the scenes. A scenario that crossed my mind more than once.

To make matters worse, I couldn't stop thinking of Aaliyah and what happened last night. Fuck, I hadn't planned that. Drawn to her cell by her heat, I lost damn control and let my guard down when I shouldn't have. I was lucky she was locked in her cage. Without it, she could have used her magick to knock me out and escape. Slade would have my balls if he knew I touched her ... correction, encouraged her to touch herself.

Dark Daddy, my wicked side, emerged and I let him have fun with our mate. I damn well Stockholm Syndromed her. Thinking about it now felt dirty and manipulative, and I brushed my hands along my jeans. As my captive, Aaliyah was helpless and at my mercy. Off fucking limits. What was I? A damn soldier giving women for pleasure as a reward? *Hell, no.* I crossed the line and should have respected her, not given in to my baser needs.

The strain of it all started to pile up, clogging my communication channels, and my desperation for a clue increased by the second. Buckling under pressure, I admitted I couldn't do this alone. I needed help from another like me. Someone not attached to the case. Someone with a clear head. Someone mad enough to take the case.

Praying he agreed, I picked up my phone and dialed his number.

"My brother from another mother," my Greek counterpart answered.

I laughed. "Mads. Been a while."

Mads worked for Hermes over in the Greek pantheon. Hermes and Thoth got confused and worshipped as the same deity somewhere along the line. Definitely two different gods. Where Hermes was slippery and delighted in causing trouble just like Mads, Thoth was intelligent, introspective, and solved problems like me. Thoth was smart enough to keep his nose buried in books and out of the strife of other gods. I sort of followed in his footsteps but joining a motorcycle club threw that out that window.

No regrets, though. Through my role, I got justice for the innocent and trampled on the cruel fucks who delivered injustice. I had a list a mile long of grievances to take care of. Later. When the club wasn't in strife.

"What's up?" Mads asked, sounding too eager to cause friction. "Don't tell me there's been some scandal about me on the dark web that needs erasing. I've been on a Hermes' highway break." He sighed. "Got ordered by the missus. Apparently, I spend too much time on my phone." He used a girly voice to mock his girlfriend, Locke.

Six months back, Mads had called in a favor, and I'd flown to the US to collect Locke as she escaped Hades' realm. Feisty little woman, that thing. Must be a handful for Mads and keep him on his toes. He needed it. Anyway, I'd met her at the secret entrance to the Underworld, which few gods knew about. Most people that dared to escape or enter were confused by mazes and illusions set there by Hades. Still didn't understand how Locke escaped. Power of love, perhaps?

"Listen, brother, thanks for collecting Locke," Mads said. "Appreciate that."

"Anytime." We often worked on cases together, calling each other for advice. "What are pantheon brothers for?"

"Please tell me you've got something for me." He breathed hard, sounding desperate for something to take away his boredom. "I'm going out of my mind here. Locke's out hiking with Rane, and I'm sneaking in this call."

"On that note," I said, "if you're up for a challenge, I have a beauty."

"I'm interested." Mads could never resist a challenge. "For two favors."

"Stiff price." I laughed. That was Mads for you, always squirming for an unsavory and unworthy deal. "As long as I don't have to fly to the US again to rescue your girl, I'll be happy."

I told him about the club's issue and the brick walls I'd hit.

"Haven't heard a peep on my channels, brother." Mads paused for a beat. "Then again, I've been banned this last week. Watched by three avatars. Let me check it out." He went silent for about three minutes then came back. "It's dark. Everywhere. But I managed to find something small."

"Give it to me." I was running out of options, my leads going cold fast.

"I detected a strange code that I traced back to the tower near your rival's clubhouse." My phone beeped as he said that. An email. "Just sent it to you. See if you can decode it. In the meantime, I'll keep my ears out."

I heard a car pull up in the background, and Mads gasped. He fumbled for something, and the TV flicked on and blasted.

"Shit, Locke's back!" Mads shouted down the line. "Gotta go if I want to keep my balls!" He ended the call before I could thank him.

Pussy whipped! Never seen him so willing to comply for a woman. I chuckled and set my phone down on my desk. That would not happen with me. I was the man in the relationship, and I'd ensure my woman didn't come between my godly job and my duty to my club. Not like the last one did.

I opened the email from Mads on my phone, trawling through the code he'd sent me, putting my skills to shame. In fairness, he'd been at this since he was fifteen and had a head start on me. Being too emotionally invested had blinded me. Now I had a lead and I intended to crack it.

It took me about forty minutes to crack the code and finally I had an answer. A truck fitting the dimensions of Joey's fleet, disassembled for pieces, the chassis crushed. Where, I had no clue. I squeezed my phone tight, taking the win, no matter how small.

Eager for more information, I searched for another five minutes, unable to uncover anything. I tapped the desk and wiped my mouth. Another search led me to ten possible truck wrecker sites within a three-hour drive from Joey's warehouse. Distance the truck couldn't have gotten when it disappeared from all traffic cameras. Ten sites could take me a week to investigate. Time we didn't have. I had to shorten the search. Pay a visit to the captive Wolves for more information.

I left my room and made my way downstairs to the second basement to pay Jerry, Aaliyah's uncle, and the two other captive Wolves a visit. I stood in front of the three men bound to chairs by chains. Out of respect for Aaliyah, I hadn't chained them standing up. Their wounds had healed somewhat, bruises yellowing, eyes opening back up, and cuts sealed over with scabs. I'd left Jerry relatively untouched because he gave me the answers I needed, plus, I had morals, and drew the line at hitting an old man. Enemy or not.

Knuckle dusters set over my fingers, I showed the captives what they'd get if they refused to cooperate. They got the job done better than knuckles. Less pain and blood for me. "What can you tell me about the Wolves' chop shop operations for cars and trucks?"

"Fuck off, Jackal," the one on the left spat at my feet.

I swooped in and smashed him in the cheek, feeling metal crunch on bone. One of his cuts reopened and blood seeped from it.

"That's enough, *Enforcer*," Jerry said, voice firm. "We use Blaxland Wreckage. Ask for Roger."

Blaxland was along the Greater Western Highway, forty minutes from the Wolves' clubhouse. Not many cameras along that stretch from Orange to Blaxland. Five, to be exact. Whoever stole the shipment must have switched trucks and dumped Joey's because I found no hint of it along that route.

Unless they took the back roads, which were completely blind to me.

I slid off my knuckle dusters, pocketed them, and turned to leave.

Jerry stopped me with a question. "Is Aaliyah alive? Can I see her?"

"No." My body clenched, but I didn't turn around.

"Enforcer, I'm under no illusions that we're dead once you're done extracting info from us," he said as if he'd already made peace with his impending end. "I just wanna see her before you send me to my maker. Can you arrange it?"

They were family and the deal only seemed fair. But it could be his last opportunity to pass on a code or something. I'd seen every dirty trick in the playbook in my time, and I didn't trust any men except those who wore the same cut as me.

"If this tip works out, I'll see what I can do." No promises. Decision sat with Slade. In his current mood, I doubted he'd show an ounce of kindness.

***

OLD KING of the road maps, Alaric, pulled in ahead of me at the address I'd given him, cutting his engine and sliding off his bike. I parked beside him in the parking lot of Blaxland Wreckage, climbed off, depositing my helmet over my handlebars. We were lucky the gravel was hard packed and not soft, otherwise Alaric would have flicked up stones behind him. He kept my back while I entered the garage where a truck rested on a hoist while a mechanic disassembled a truck axle beneath it.

Place was a damn pigsty; truck chassis, tires, and cargos.

"You think Aaliyah had anything to do with this?" Alaric asked, setting his helmet over his handlebar.

"Could have arranged it before she infiltrated us." Although, I still wasn't sold on the idea of her infiltration. My gut screamed she was innocent, but the skeptical side of me, the solicitor, said to keep digging. "You still think she's guilty?"

"Hell, yeah." Alaric gave an irritated shrug of his shoulder.

"I'm not so sure."

"You're sticking up for her?" Alaric sounded dumbfounded.

"All I'm saying is that I understand where she's coming from." I moved around my bike to pat him on the shoulder. "Put yourself in her shoes."

"I can't believe this." Alaric shook his head.

Out of the four of us, he and Slade would be the hardest for Aaliyah to build trust with again and win over ... if she managed to at all. Break trust with either of them, and you were dead to them. Aaliyah's betrayal was the ultimate deception to them both for different reasons. Alaric valued trust as he needed to feel safe after his time in the military. Trust was a covenant in our club's bible, and Slade demanded it. His mother was killed in front of him, and our previous mate taken from us in a raid on our last clubhouse. Collateral damage that should never have happened.

I grabbed both of Alaric's shoulders. "She was thrown into our club and left to fend for herself amid enemy lines. What would you have done?"

"Left." Alaric huffed like it was that easy.

"Slade wouldn't have let her go that easy, and you know it."

"He would have found out eventually. If we tailed her again."

Alaric had a point. As a lawyer, I had to consider all sides and arguments to form my own and make my case.

Tiring of this conversation and wanting answers to our problem, I said, "Come on," and led Alaric to the steel shed.

Spare parts were tossed haphazardly across the floor, nuts and bolts everywhere, stray wheels leaning against the shed walls, and discarded tins and bottles of oils or lubricants left on benches and the pavement. The shed smelled of grease and oil. Loved that smell. Reminded me of Tank's workshop back at the club.

I cleared my throat above the radio droning in the background to let the man under the truck know he had company. "Is Roger here?"

The man dusted his hands on a rag and slid out on a mechanical wheel bed. His eyes dropped to the patch on our cuts, and he gripped his rag tighter. "Fellas, what can I do for you?"

My hand went to my gun beneath my cut, letting the shape show through the leather. "Any trucks come through your yard in the last week?"

Roger's body went rigid. "Who wants to know?"

"Jackal's Wrath MC," I said.

"We only deal with the Wolves." He climbed off the mechanical wheel to stand. "Jerry's my uncle."

Fuck, that'd be right. Relative of Aaliyah? I'd keep the details of Jerry's captivity and possible death tight to my chest. "One of our shipment trucks was stolen, and we believe it was disassembled and crushed here."

"Nothing like that been through here." The octave leap in his voice said otherwise.

"Really?" I put on my pair of knuckle dusters to show I wasn't kidding. "You better start talking or else I'll have to make you talk."

Palms raised, Roger backed away, stumbling on the mechanical wheel. "Never seen these guys before."

I rubbed at the metal rings over my knuckles. "Gimme names."

"I don't know who they were." He kicked aside the mechanical bed. "I swear on my life. Never dealt with em' before."

I took a step closer. "Sure you're not protecting a member of the Wolves? Cause they've been giving us trouble. And I'd hate to give you trouble, too."

The threat clicked in the man's mind like a gun trigger going off. "No. They weren't Wolves."

Losing patience, I stepped closer again. "Then who the fuck were they?"

"Don't know." The nervous man swallowed. "They wanted it off the books. Paid in cash. Told me to forget the transaction and left."

Fuck, another perpetrator. Who and why? The mystery deepened.

"Enforcer, look at this." Alaric used my club role rather than my name to protect us. Club rules.

Sunshine hit me as I stepped out of the garage. "What?"

"Take a look. He pointed to a security camera above the reception block of the workshop. Nice. I clapped my observant partner on the shoulder. Always good to have a second eye with me.

"I want to take a look at your security footage, Roger." Maybe I could pull a number plate of the car they left in.

"Come with me." Roger moved quick and jittery to the small reception space where his clients paid for their work.

The three of us crammed in the small office, Alaric keeping watch at the door, Roger and me behind the receptionist's desk. Roger fast-forwarded through the footage from seven days ago, stopping when Joey's truck and a dark

BMW pulled into the lot. The same men I'd seen steal the truck on Joey's security camera. Two burly men got out of the cab and conducted business with Roger, and he paid them in cash. I recognized the number plate from Joey's registration papers. Definitely his, all right, and the only one missing from his warehouse. The two men left in the BMW, and Roger paused on the side view of the vehicle's rear. Not a perfect angle, but enough for me to catch the license plate.

Thank you, Mads, for the tip. I'd send him a bottle of champagne when I got back to the club.

"Appreciate your help, Roger." I tucked away my knuckle dusters. "Hope we won't be seeing each other again. But we might if you deal with that crew of scumbags again."

CHAPTER 11

Aaliyah

A GIFT SAT on the end of my cot. Probably from Slade. Definitely ignoring it, then. The man ran as hot as a volcano one minute, then as cold as a glacier then next. But the box in gold tissue paper beeped, and I stared at it. A phone? I picked it up, scratched off the paper, found a cell inside, already put together, the battery intact, glass protection cover on.

Curious, I glanced at the stairs as I twisted the gold-colored phone in my hand. The color reminded my goddess of Egypt, and she smiled, warming me.

When she faded, my gut hardened. This could be from my brother. Someone forewarned my brother where the Jackals would be, and it wasn't me. The Jackals had a rat. Fingers pointed at me until otherwise proven. A mistake I wouldn't make again.

I must have been asleep when whoever delivered it. Time

to find out who left it for me. I activated the phone's power switch and let it boot.

"Hi," the first message on the screen said.

"Don't think that I haven't wanted to come and talk to you," the second one said. "Because I have. Like crazy."

Could be my brother. Doubted he'd talk this that, though. The Jackal's deadline to hand me over was almost up in a few hours. I tensed, suspecting Danny communicated to me about rescuing me.

"Every time I go to talk to you, I turn around." The third message. "It's killing me." A flash of sorrow and regret streaked down the mate bond, twisting in my chest. My heart whimpered, wanting him to come to me, too, and I clutched at my shirt.

I crushed the phone to my chest, wondering who gifted me this and sent these messages. Someone who wanted to contact me in secret by the look of it. Intrigued by the mystery and wanting to uncover it, I kept reading.

Incognito didn't seem Slade's style, and he had no illusions about hiding his interest. Mr. Cocky and Direct came right up to me to tell me what he wanted, and I gritted my teeth, thinking how he'd gotten his way. Besides, he was president, and no one could challenge him if he contacted me.

The voice of the text ruled out Castor too, since we'd been speaking. I smiled and tapped my hip. Although, he might have reached out behind his president's back. Sure hoped so after last night. W-O-W. Needed another night of that ... and more to keep me from getting stuck in my head. The act left me feeling stronger, vibrant, and in less pain. In fact, my wound healed twice as fast.

Alaric kept his distance, ever vigilant and untrusting of me. Something dark had happened to him to make him so hell-bent on uncovering my betrayal. My heart pinched at his accusation and suspicion of me when they were the ones keeping me prisoner.

That left Zethan. Guarded and elusive. Of all four of my supposed mates, he was the one who called to my heart the most, and I wanted to get to know him. A deep part of me secretly hoped he was behind the phone.

Whoever was behind the play, my heart warmed at the sweet gesture, eager to know the identity of the mystery man. Feeling like a giddy schoolgirl, I dropped to my bed, reclining on my pillow to read the last message.

"I don't want to hurt you," it said. Definitely Zethan. Both Slade and Castor had warned me to stay away. And Zethan himself ordered me away from him. I still didn't know the answer to that mystery.

My heart cried out, yearning for him. A cry that would go unanswered since they'd inhibited their ends of the mate bond to block me out.

On the opposite end, my mind warned that this was a play. A trap designed to befriend me, pretend to be nice, and get information from me. Wary but excited, my fingers hovered over the keyboard, keen to reply, but unsure what to say. I typed out three messages, erased them all, then tapped my foot, thinking of something appropriate.

Finally, I went with, *"You won't."*

I paused over the send button, holding my breath. If I replied to him, I opened myself up to more dialogue, and I wasn't sure I wanted to encourage that. I didn't want to get to know the sender when they held me hostage, accused me of acts I'd never done, held me as a bargaining chip in their war, and refused to return me to my family. After two weeks with the Jackals, one week in the shelter, and another recovering, I was done with them. I wanted to go back to my life, Nurse and heal people. Not be stuck as a captive in their clubhouse basement. I didn't want to be stuck here when Danny came for me.

Fuck this curse! Fuck the Jackals! One day Castor would break the bond between us. They wouldn't let me go even if they broke the curse. I was leverage. Slade would end me before he let me walk. If I were in his place, I'd do the same. Couldn't have loose threads undealt with.

Feeling stupid, I set the phone down and clenched my fists, wishing I'd left the shelter when I had the chance. If I had listened to my head, I wouldn't be in this mess.

Despite all my reasoning, my excuses, my heart screamed at me, begging me to stay, win their trust, prove to them I was worthy of being their mate, and them to me. Bitch wanted her happily ever after with these four gorgeous, dangerous, and hard men.

Hell, no.

I didn't have to prove anything to them. The Jackals brought me to their shelter and didn't have to. How dare they question my integrity. Bringing a stranger, a rival into their midst, that was on them. They should have done their homework. I didn't admit who I was out of fear for my life. Any self-respecting person would have done the same. Information I fed my brother was useless because Alaric had interrupted and stopped me. Beyond that, I didn't know anything besides the Jackals made a run to Sydney. But I hadn't had the opportunity to let my brother know. There was nothing to prove on my end besides the identity of my father's murderer.

Fuck, this war between my head and heart was going to ruin me. I gripped my hair, tugging it hard as if that might snap some sense into me.

My fingers twitched, and I picked up the phone, going over the messages, my chest sparkling, chasing away my doubts. Finally, my head said *fuck it*, and I hit send on *you won't*. What was the harm in getting to know the mysterious sender? I was bored and had nothing else to do.

Ultimately, my goal was to establish the identity of my father's killer, and I'd not leave this world until I did. Hopefully this might lead to some clues.

Within seconds, a reply shot back. "What are you wearing?" Wink face. No response to mine, and suspicions needled in the back of my mind that this person befriended me for answers.

Still, I couldn't help but laugh deep in my throat. The sender was cheeky and confident. Reminded me of Castor. He liked to play games. My pussy lit up at the memory of him bathing me. Of him ordering me to pleasure myself.

"Nice try," I bounced back.

"Can't blame a guy for trying."

"What are you doing?" I stroked my lip, smiling. Fucking smiling. Shit, I must be desperate for company and human connection.

"Thinking of you." Fuck, the mystery was killing me. It had to be Castor. This was so his style.

"Hands on your phone I hope." I sent back quickly, my message designed to eliminate my suspect.

"Now that you've said that ... surfing lower ..." Oh God, were we sexting? Already? Jumping the gun. I shook my head, thinking of Slade. He'd brought me the clothes for our date, and this had his fingerprints all over it.

Nope. Not encouraging that. Strictly business. Break the curse and leave this nightmare behind. See if I still had a job and apartment when I returned home.

"Bye, Slade," I replied.

"Don't go." Didn't sound like Slade. He'd burst into my room, goad me into an argument if I ignored him. My mind swung back to Castor again.

"Goodnight, Castor." I texted.

"He has a long beak but not as impressive as what I'm packing..."

I laughed into my hand and blushed at that text. A Slade answer. I wanted to say, *'seen it, and it was damn impressive,'* but something told me the sender toyed with me for answers, pretending to be someone else.

"You have a beak?" I added smiley faces. Fucking smiley emojis.

Goddess. *Don't be cute, Aaliyah. Don't encourage him.*

"No! My shifter is bigger and meaner."

"Slade?"

"Keep guessing." Then who the hell was it? The mystery had me wound up in a ball of suspense and intrigue.

"Wings?" That would be Horus and Alaric.

"No, but you do." Cryptic answer.

Reminded of what Castor told me about my shifter, I searched inside for my goddess' answer. As usual, she remained silent, never giving anything away. Infuriating. I tried to search on Google with the phone, but no internet had been supplied with it. Just text and call by the look of it.

"No internet to research." To this I added a sad face.

"Nope. I want you talking to *ME* only." He didn't accuse me of trying to contact my brother, so I scratched Alaric off the list indefinitely.

Fishing for information, I replied, "Not worried I might try to call the police and claim I've been kidnapped?"

"You don't want to." Pretty bold answer. Something Slade would say. The cocky president struck me as the kind to brag about his dick size, too. But something told me it wasn't him, and the secrecy had me on edge, my nerves about to explode.

"Shame," I replied. "I'd like to confirm the wings thing."

"Nice try." Hah! That was something Castor would say. *Stop trying to use your dark sorceress powers on me.*

"Maybe you can show me in your books sometime?" I

groaned as I added a wink face and hit send. Wink face ... really? To a dangerous biker?

"Still think this is Castor?" Another response.

Yes! He or Slade tricked me. Plucking my lip, I stayed silent, thinking what to say.

Another message vibrated. "The only books I read are the clubs'. Too busy."

Another hint. Couldn't be Slade as he struggled to read the menu on our date. But I didn't know who held the role of secretary within the Jackals.

The next message arrived. "Touch the cell bars. I want to feel you." Games. Lots of them. Tired of them. And how would he feel me through metal anyway?

"No," I texted back. "Tired. Need a rest." Total lie. I wanted to see how the texter would respond.

"Touch the bars." The dominance behind his words had me obeying, and I slipped off the bed, surprised by the lack of pain by small movements. I tiptoed over to the bars, laying a hand on the cast iron. My hand trembled from the magical connection. Beyond the metal, I felt him, his yearning, reluctance, and fear. My soul mate. The one who wouldn't let me near him.

Zethan.

I gasped and pulled away, falling back a few steps.

"Come back," his next text insisted.

His unquenchable craving called to me, and I moved back. This was the closest we'd been since the ladies' room at Carlie's shelter. Ever since, I'd wanted to be near him, but every time he ran away, and I didn't know why.

I wanted answers. The damn truth. "How did you do that?"

"King of the Underworld," he replied. "I feel through everything buried in the Earth. Metals, minerals, it's in my domain, baby." *Baby.* Did he say it as an affectionate term or for emphasis? Fuck, he had me questioning every little detail, and it drove me crazy. I wasn't insecure, but I was stuck in an impossible situation.

Goddess, I had so much to learn from these men. I didn't know how long they'd been avatars, when I was only fresh at coming up on two years.

I typed in the ultimate question lingering on my mind and heart. "Why won't they let me near you?"

"Because I can hurt you and vice versa."

Not good enough. "Why?"

"Our gods are doubly cursed." Meaning we were, too. "Fated mates cockblocked."

I skipped over the fated mates, soul mates or love at first sight part. Absolute crap that my heart subscribed to and had managed to convince my head of. "What does that mean?"

"We can't go near each other without draining each other's life and killing each other. It's why you felt sick on the drive to the shelter and again when we were in the ladies' room." His answer made me think of the suspected food poisoning from Slade's sandwich, my cramping and seizing stomach. But that was a curse?

"What the fuck kind of curse is that?" I echoed that in my next message.

"Don't know," he replied. "Castor's working on it. But I'll kill the bastard who set it up. Torture him for an eternity."

I giggled at that. A glimmer of a smile transmitted through the cell bars, and a faint hint hit the mate bond. My chest tightened at not being able to see him smile. The whole week at the shelter I'd not seen him smile once. Wasn't even sure it was possible for the grim and serious man. Despite the darkness in his soul, it called to me on a deep, aching level, and I couldn't walk away if I wanted to.

"Are you smiling?" A girl needed to know. I bit my lip waiting for his reply.

"Yes, now that I'm talking to you." Goddess, he was sweet too.

I needed proof of this. "Send me a picture."

He sent me one, and my heart fluttered at the gorgeous curve of his pouty mouth. I wanted my lips over his, to encourage that smile wider, his lips to part, to flick our tongues together and get lost in a dizzying kiss, curse be damned.

"Didn't think you could smile," I replied.

He hit me back instantly. "I smile once a year, thank you." I giggled. My phone buzzed again. "Return the favor. Naked and smiling, preferably."

I laughed again, liking him and his surprising sense of humor. My fingers acted on their own accord, activating the camera, taking the snap. In the bright light of the flash, my smile was coy, shy, despite the circumstances. Hell ... I sent it to him and gripped the phone, desperate to know his answer.

"You're the most beautiful woman I've ever seen." His words prompted my heart to crash in my chest, frantic to break down the wall between us, so that no barriers existed. "It kills me that I can't touch you."

The mate bond opened up and flooded with his emotion. Hunger, loneliness, and heartache. It burned in the pit of my stomach with my longing for him.

Before I knew what I was doing, I replied, "Me, too."

Fuck, Aaliyah! That was dangerous territory. But I couldn't help it.

"Well, don't think you're getting a dick pic just for chatting me up!" he said. "That's a fifth date kind of deal."

His humor caught me off guard, and I laughed harder, snorting.

Another bing called me back. "Did you just snort?"

My hand snapped off the bars. Not letting him sense that. "No. I'm a lady."

"You did." I tuned in and felt him lingering in the bond, reading me.

Fuck, I hiccupped laughed. "This is a date?"

"Hell, yeah." Grumpy and gruff no more. Never would have pegged him to make a joke when he came across as serious as death. I'd had him all wrong. His lighter side appealed to me, and this was the kind of guy I'd go for. Goddess, I couldn't believe I admitted I was attracted to a Jackal. Correction: another Jackal besides Castor.

"You probably shouldn't take the Underworld's name in vain," I teased, throwing out all earlier objections and hesitation in talking with him. This dark, grim man called to the depths of my soul, and I couldn't resist him.

"I can when I'm the god of it."

"Ego," I threw back.

"Not as big as Slade's."

I snorted again.

"Snorter." He accompanied his text with an emoji blowing its nose.

I didn't know if he was a shifter, so I just threw it out there. "Bird dick."

The link trembled with his laughter, and I pressed my whole body to the bars, wanting to melt into it and reappear on the other side and march right upstairs to fall into his arms.

"More like hellhound dick. And that talk is reserved for a tenth date. Don't want to scare you off." Hellhound shifter, hey. Made sense since he was the King of the Underworld and Death.

I howled at that and slid down the bars. Surprised, I prodded my wound, feeling a slight tender sting.

"A howler, too? My beast likes you."

Damn mate bond. As treacherous and dangerous as my

heart. Deflecting, I went with, "Is beast a euphemism for cock?"

His laughter, warm and deep, warmed my chest. "Maybe." Wink face.

Goddess, I was loving this. Encouraging it. Basking in the fact that the man who felt so closed off had opened up to me.

He sent me an image of a man riding a bike with the text, "I'd love to take you for one once the curse is gone."

Fuck, I clutched the screen to my chest and held my breath. What was I doing here? Every part of me wanted to reply *I'd like that. Let's fucking go. Now!* But that would be making a promise when I wanted to leave, and I valued my word more than anything.

I twisted it with a flirty joke of my own. "You're riding bitch."

His laugh and heat drifted along our bond. I couldn't have this man, curse or no curse.

"G'nite, Z." My final text.

"Sweet dreams." I almost broke down at the two kisses he dropped at the end. Fucking kisses. I wanted to hate him for keeping me prisoner. For putting my heart through these crazy emotions of hate and attraction.

Deep down, I knew I was his. Eternally. We were bonded whether I liked it or not. I was a tool of the gods, belonged to them, and belonged to him by association. But I didn't want my love life dictated to me by some primordial force. I wanted to be free to choose. I'd break this damn curse if it was the last damn thing I did. *So, help me, goddess.*

CHAPTER 12

*S*lade

NEED to destroy swelled within me so strongly, I struggled to contain it. Wrath ran in my blood like a deep vein of opal through a mine. Vengeance demanded to be exacted, and I craved justice for my club and reputation. Set never had the patience to wait, and neither did I. But we couldn't bust into the Wolves' clubhouse without evidence to pin them to the Jackals' ongoing problems. If Danny was responsible for stealing from my club, wiping out our biggest form of income, and putting us in a dangerous financial situation, I'd fucking kill him.

My phone vibrated for the sixth time in thirty minutes. God dammit, I couldn't get a break, even for a minute. Reports and rumors came in at blinding speed. Nothing concrete. Zethan had gotten a name to investigate, but we waited on Castor to locate the identity of the prick who hired the junkie to beat up Aaliyah.

I fished in my pocket for my phone and took it out. Reg's fake name flashed on the screen. Our idiot salesman who let the Wolves sneak up on him and attack him and us. "Yeah?"

"Slade, hey, man." His teeth rattled with fear. "Heard on the down low that Juicy has been offloaded to Hellfire and sold real cheap. You could pick up a bargain." Code for our stolen shipment of Pharaoh had been accepted by the distributor for the Hellfire MC and sold at undercut prices.

Dirty motherfuckers. Hellfire MC hated us for swooping in on the Winter's Devils' territory. Their headquarters were in Gosford, smack bang between Sydney and Newcastle, so they thought the territory belonged to them. Get fucked. We earned it. Lost a man for it. Had our clubhouse burned down. My goddamn mate taken from me. Those delusional pricks could suck my dick.

My grip on my phone tightened, and the screen cracked. "When'd you hear this?"

"This ... this morning." The sound of his chattering teeth tempted me to pull the phone away from my ear or hang up on him. But I needed more info first.

"You absolutely sure?" The edge in my voice warned Reg not to get this wrong. Barging into the Hellfire MC's turf would be viewed as aggression against the club, and I wanted irrefutable proof before I made another fucking enemy. Resistance stormed in my mind, dulling my godly urge to pay them a visit and just burn the place down, regardless of guilt or innocence. Fuck, Set was a testy bastard sometimes. Then again, so was I.

"Positive." Reg couldn't lie if he tried. The bastard was too honest for his own good. Plus, my avatar senses told me he was right. Set didn't just become a god of War without honing his craft with gods, goddesses, and soldiers.

"You better be right," I snarled, still pissed that Reg's security detail got overwhelmed by the Wolves, allowing them to penetrate his business, take him hostage and ambush us. "Or I'll be looking for a new distributor."

"Slade, please, let me—"

I cut the prick off, not in the mood for excuses. "What's this cunt's name and address?" In the drug trade, you needed your wits about you, security, weapons, an impenetrable business. Things failed Reg me at, we'd not be dealing with him again if it continued.

Reg rattled off a name and address, and I ended the call.

Muscles in my neck and shoulders clenched, and I rolled my arms, trying to release them. Fuck, my back was killing me. Whenever I got tense like this, my old lady massaged my shoulders. Chest tightening at the thought of her, I struggled to contain my heaving emotions. Fat chance of that happening now with that traitor in the basement. Shame, too. She was perfect. Beyond beautiful. My equal in every way, my queen. But the bitch used her charms to fool me, and I'd never forgive her for duping me.

Outrage growing by the second, I marched down the hall to Castor's office, thumped on his door and shouted, "Need you for a minute in Zethan's office." My shifter hearing sensed him scrambling around and getting off his chair.

We burst into Zethan's office without invitation. Time for a little cool-down and chat with my VP and enforcer.

I dialed in Alaric from his position spying on the Wolves. "Yes, sir?"

"Fuck it with the sir crap," I snapped. "Or I'll beat it out of you."

"Yes, sir." I heard the smile in his voice.

"Asshole." I scratched at the irritated twitch beneath my eye. "Hellfire MC's distributor is selling the stolen shipment and undercutting our prices. I think it's high time we had a little chat with them, don't you?"

Zethan shook his head. "Who called it in?"

"Reg." Unable to stay still, I paced the length of my VP's desk.

"You think it's a trap?" Castor rubbed at his palms.

"Won't know until we investigate." I scratched my neck. "Alaric, we'll meet you in Katoomba and travel onto Gosford. I want you to scout."

"Roger that, sir." Asshole hung up before I could tear him a new one.

Zethan coughed to hide a smile, and Castor flat out smirked.

Sighing, I threw my cell, grateful it hit the couch instead of the wall like the last time. "Everything went south as soon as that bitch showed up. She's royally fucked us."

Zethan snapped to his feet. "Don't speak about her like that."

Great. She'd worked her charms on him, too. Put wedges between us. "What the fuck are you defending her for?"

"Don't call her that unless you have proof she's guilty." Fucking Zethan. Innocent until proven guilty, my ass.

Palms outstretched, Castor came between us. "Let's lower the testosterone and animosity and think this through."

"She's ruined us." I dug my chest into his hand. "Made us question our sanity. Doubt her involvement. Fight among ourselves. I won't stand for her destroying our brotherhood."

"Fuck, Slade." Zethan speared a hand through his hair. "Tone it down. She's still our mate, and we have to respect the gods and their reason for choosing her. If she's guilty, go for your fucking life with the insults, okay?"

Someone was a bit pissy and defensive today. I didn't take any offense from it. Never did. Guy needed to get laid. Too serious for his own good. Having the second curse on him couldn't be easy. She was his mate more than ours, and he had to deal with that if she was guilty as I suspected. Not the easiest pill to swallow.

Set rumbled inside my head, his patience losing grip, his agitation like mine, at boiling point. He was pissed that we were behind on breaking the curse. Least of my worries. Jackal's Wrath MC couldn't function without cash. I'd not let my father's or my hard work go down the toilet just because a god wanted freedom from a binding curse.

For now, I'd respect Zethan's wishes and call her by her given name. The instant I proved her guilt, that traitor was dead, executed along with her brother. "Get five men and get your bikes ready to leave."

***

"All clear," Alaric advised as he threw his clothes back on.

His nipples were small and hard, and I remembered times I'd sucked them while fucking him. We'd all shared our bed with Liz and with each other, but never since. Hurt and grief hit me hard, raw as the day we lost her. Liz had been loyal, perfect, sweet, a dream. Taken from us and replaced by that vile creature in the club's basement. After Liz died, Set told me she wasn't our life-long or true mate, and the next one would be. No consolation. Nothing. I'd wanted to kill him for it. But how do you kill a god?

Then Aaliyah entered our life, beautiful, feisty, strong-willed. Woman made me work for it, wasn't afraid to stand up to me, and gave it back to me straight. I fucking loved it. That made what she did even more of a betrayal. Thinking about her made me sick to my stomach.

Alaric caught me admiring his chest and swirled his pink peaks, hurtling me back to the conversation. "Wanna kiss them?"

In all honesty, I wanted to bite them, draw blood, express

my anger. But I slapped him on the side of the ear instead. "Maybe later. Concentrate."

Alaric grinned like a devil. "Could say the same for you, sir."

Smartass. I went to swipe him again, but he ducked, and I couldn't get him with his bike in the way. "Fucker."

Dressed and ready to go, we jumped back on our bikes, him waiting for me. I paused, running my gloved fingers over my handlebars, remembering her on the back of my bike. The press of her body to mine. Her hard nipples grazing my back. Fuck, it felt like I'd lost Liz all over again, having that traitor thrown into my life.

"Slade!" Alaric yelled at me.

I snapped back to attention, motioned for him to take off and trail behind. A crew of four defended us from behind. We tore into the lot at the Gosford address Reg had given us. Set's magic rolled the security fence back, permitting us entry. If I didn't have witnesses, I'd have snapped the damn thing off and flung it free.

Our surprise inspection was the last thing the Hellfire MC's distributor expected, catching everyone inside off guard. They double-timed it inside their warehouse, trying to roll the door closed. I halted it with another show of magick, and they panicked, doubling down their efforts.

First mistake. Sign of guilt. Second mistake was not contacting me the minute they realized our product dropped into their laps. Errors they wouldn't make again if they wanted to live long enough to spend the hefty commission this operation made dealing drugs for Hellfire MC.

The four of us parked in front of the roller door. Tank, Kill Bill, Rusty, and Brix parked out front to trap anyone who tried to escape.

Zethan was off his bike and charging inside before I killed the engine. Bullets snipped at the metal warehouse walls and door. Third and very big fucking mistake. One swipe of his arm killed the triggers on every gun raised by security inside and made the shooting mechanism lock. Alaric was quickly behind him, followed by Castor. I left my dramatic entrance for last.

"Weapons on the ground and kick them away!" Zethan shouted.

Nobody moved. My VP let off a shot that hit a steel column near one of the security teams. Sparks flashed and made the guy flinch. Next time, he wouldn't miss. The guy threw his gun on the ground.

Zethan jerked his Glock at the next detail. "The rest of you, too."

They all lowered their weapons. Guns scattered along the concrete. Time for me to enter properly.

Notes flickered on counting machines. Bitches in their underwear weighed drugs on scales and parceled them in taped bundles. Men packaged the product in plastic bottles, kid's toys, and ice cream tubs to conceal them for drug runs. Security men went for additional guns stored on their bodies.

Blood simmering, I removed a *Rollies* paper, preparing myself a cigarette. "Where's the fucker who runs this place?"

All eyes in the place turned to a fat fuck by a half-packed truck with sweaty armpits, greasy hair, and a pallid, sick complexion.

"What's going on, guys?" he asked with a shaky voice, crossing back to his desk, using it as a shield in case we opened fire.

"Funny, we were going to ask you the same thing." In seconds, I was at his filthy, powder-ridden desk, dropping into the chair opposite his and propped my feet on the desk. I lit up my smoke and sucked down a sweet lungful of hot, tobacco-flavored air.

The anger seething inside me threatened to boil over, and that was never going to work in this guy's favor. Hasty decisions backed with mayhem were my style, and if this cunt had fucked with my business, I'd burn his down.

Zethan hovered at my side, Alaric kept watch by the door, and Castor was behind me to protect my back. All of us ready to unleash some pain if this dipshit didn't tell us what we wanted to know. Namely, who in the hell stole from us.

"Walsh, right?" At least that was the name Reg gave me. The name this fuckwit was known for in the industry.

He gave a sharp nod. "What brings you to my establishment?" The guy uneasily sat at his desk, hands trembling as he pushed aside his computer keyboard. "Looking for a new distributor?"

"I'm here about the shipment." I cracked my knuckles to relieve some of the building tension bursting to get free. "More specifically, the lack thereof."

Walsh's hands trembled as he shuffled a stack of papers, the scrape of drugs on his desk irritating my nerves. "Whoa, hang on a second, guys. We would never fuck the Jackals. You guys are legends."

I sucked my smoke so hard that flames licked at the end. Impossible for a normal smoker, but I wanted to show this asshole we weren't messing around. "Damn straight."

I dropped my feet from the desk and leaned on it, stabbing this prick with my glare. "That so? Cause a week ago, someone stole a shipment of Pharaoh, and we get word you're now dealing it. What are the chances?"

"Let me explain," the pathetic loser attempted, tearing a handkerchief from his pants pocket, and mopping sweat from his brow.

"By all means, Walsh, let's hear it." I crossed my arms over my chest and leaned back in the chair, quickly taking another scan of the warehouse.

Water and rust stains on the roof, steel walls, and floor. Tire skid marks, fuel, and oil stains all over the pavement. Wary security inched closer, setting off my suspicions, and my attention flicked between them and Walsh.

"We had a delivery and were told it was a competitor product." Walsh shrugged, exposing the sweat stains on his shirt under his arms.

"Come on, Walsh." I stood, leaned over the desk, hands splayed. "You run drugs for Hellfire MC, and you expect us to believe that you got tricked, and were dumb enough to sell our shit without a call to me to check?" I glanced over at Zethan. "You buying this shit, man?"

"Nope." Zethan kept one hand on his Glock at all times, his gaze on the men creeping toward their boss. I wasn't worried so long as he maintained control of their guns.

"Not good enough." I shook my head, dabbing out my smoke in the middle of his paper stack, setting it alight.

Walsh jumped away from the flames soaring on his desk as it consumed his paperwork.

Three seconds flat was all it took for me to round on him. "Here's how this is gonna go." I grabbed his neck with my palm. "You're gonna tell me everything I want to know, or my enforcer is going to start breaking fingers."

He gave me a terrified nod. "Hellfire won't be happy about this."

"I don't give a fuck what they think." I tightened my grasp, and he choked. "You accepted stolen merch. On their orders or your own?" I lifted him off the ground, enough to show him what I could do but subtle enough that the other bystanders didn't see.

Walsh gurgled an answer, and I lowered him and relaxed my grip to let him get it out. "I've sold half of it already." Fuck, half our shipment gone. "Take the rest and get the fuck out of here."

I glanced over my shoulder at Zethan, jerking my head, indicating for him to retrieve what remained of our shipment.

My hand clamped around Walsh's throat again. Harder. Merciless. "Greed can creep up on you, Walsh, and the next thing you know, you're ripping off someone you don't want to mess with."

"I'm sorry." Spineless fuck.

"That fear you're feeling?" His windpipe flexed under my grasp. "I want you to remember how scared you are, Walsh, because if this happens again, it will be the last time. Do you understand what I'm saying to you?"

Walsh's eye bulged, and he beat at my wrist.

"I'll take that as a yes." I tossed him at his chair, and he stumbled, tipping it over and toppling backward. "Get our money and take extra as payment for stealing what belongs to us," I ordered Castor, leaving just Alaric to watch my back.

"Hellfire will make sure you pay for that," Walsh rasped at me.

"If Hellfire sanctioned this sale, then they're dead too." I removed my gun, pausing for a moment, remembering that it had been inside of Aaliyah's pussy. After her betrayal, I'd thoroughly cleaned all her scent from it, never wanting to smell her again. My jackal howled for his mate. I quieted him with a bullet to Walsh's brain, and he went down with a thud.

Women screamed and ran for the exit door to the side of the warehouse. Tank, Kill Bill, Rusty, and Brix emerged from outside, joining a blockade with Alaric. The frightened women whimpered and clutched each other, glancing around nervously. They were safe. I wouldn't hurt them when they weren't responsible for the theft. That decision fell to Walsh.

One of the security men approached, palms raised, to inspect Walsh. The guard bent down to close his eyes. I caught the sly move to slide out the dead man's gun, and I ended his life with a clean shot, making the women yelp and huddle closer. Security cleared them out pretty quick.

In twenty minutes, my men had collected and packed our drugs into a truck Slim had confiscated as payment for the missing half of our shipment. Castor and Zethan wheeled their bikes into the cargo hold. Once all my men were ready, I gestured for them to get going, and when the non-avatars took off, I set the place alight, torching the Hellfire MC's drugs, leaving Walsh's men to explain their mistake.

On my way out, I stopped my bike by one of Walsh's men. "We'll be taking the truck as payment for stolen goods as well." I pressed a finger to my forehead in a salute move. "Send my regards to Hellfire."

CHAPTER 13

Alaric

TRIGGER WARNING: dark and distressing scenes.

FUCKING DANNY HELLER. I thought the guy was a piece of shit before he ambushed my club, but now his men led cuffed women from a truck. Dressed as whores in ass-revealing short skirts, pumps, and midriff-baring shirts, they fought their bonds and refused to go with the men. One of the Wolves slapped a woman, and she reeled back. My hands fisted, and I had to hold back from charging down the hill to teach him how to treat a lady. Women were to be cherished and spoiled, not treated like mutton dressed as lamb. I stayed put, though, flat on my belly, elbows propped on the ground as I spied from above.

Two reliable sources indicated Danny ventured into pornography films. Correction—make that one reliable source. Aaliyah might have told us the truth about what her brother was up to, but only after she'd been locked in a cell. Credible as the fake news. Lied about her motives for staying with us, and to my fucking face on more than one occasion. Took advantage of our generosity. Avatars and our predestined mate meant jack shit now. How the fuck were we supposed to break the curse if the woman destined to be ours couldn't be trusted?

Castor and Zethan seemed convinced that Aliyah deserved a second chance after redeeming herself by telling us about Danny's business operations. I agreed wholeheartedly. Only to find out what she damn well did so we could pop her. She did the right thing for the wrong reasons. Saved her own ass. Nothing redeeming about a coward.

A woman's scream brought my attention back to focus on the late-night activities I'd tracked the Wolves to. Three illegal brothels, two dark alley titty bars, and this dirty porno movie set-up. Since Aaliyah's interrogation and our subsequent meeting afterward, I'd been on the case, only returning to the club for supplies and going with Castor to Blaxland. One of the filthy, greasy Wolves dragged the shrieking woman by the hair and threw her inside. I had to use all my self-restraint to remain put. Spy only. Gather intel. Rescuing women in danger was not my order, and I'd not risk pissing Slade off when he was a category seven earthquake waiting to happen.

Not that I could get closer, anyway. Inky shadows throbbed all over the building's walls, like tar leaking from the cement blocks, a slick cancerous mass growing in size. Seen these nasty blobs all over the Wolves' clubhouse and every single building they conducted business in that I'd visited.

Dark fucking magick. We'd encountered the shit two years ago when we lost Liz. Sigils throbbing with menace and darkness weakened us, made us ill and irritable. Markings invisible to human eyes, painted everywhere across the Wolves' territory, prevented me from getting close enough to inspect the buildings without risking harm to myself. The last time Castor touched one of those sigils, he almost lost his stomach's contents and was left drained, forced to draw on the power of Slade and Zethan to scan his magical texts for answers.

Dark whispers called to me. Demons writhing in the oil bubbles, their hands reaching out, groping for me. Wary, I kept a safe distance. Any closer and the magick would impair and affect me.

My hand fumbled for my whiskey flask, pulling it out and lifting it to my lips. Except it was dry. No drinks on a stakeout. Self-imposed rule that spoke volumes when I rarely went without a drink in my hand. My demons chased me down to the bottom of a bottle whenever they could, mainly whenever I closed my eyes. Stakeouts kept me sober and gave me something to focus on besides my trauma, which is why Slade assigned them to me. He got the intel he needed, and I got a little peace and quiet. Except this wasn't a normal stakeout. Tonight, the demons bubbled to the surface, encouraged by the dark magick, sinister chants from some ancient power. Louder than ever, they called to me, raspy whispers promising to hurt me.

Slade and the guys found me at the right time, stopped me from spiraling into the dark abyss of my rage and alcoholism. They gave me a purpose and helped me keep my anger in check. Still working on the alcohol, though. An uphill battle I seemed to be losing.

Hope blossomed in me that Aaliyah might be able to drive away the demons, only to be dashed when I discovered her treachery.

I rubbed hard at my eyes, silencing the demons for the

moment. I could deal with them later. The only thing I cared about was putting an end to the prostitution and Danny Heller and the Wolves. They exploited those women, forced them into servitude, and they needed my help more than I needed whiskey and silence from my demons. Sending them off to a life of degradation and drug abuse. A slow death from abuse—that was something I was all too familiar with. I had to help them with whatever information I could get.

Only one thing was getting me insight about what was occurring inside. My god's eye. With Horus' power, I could penetrate the walls, search the interior, get a bird's eye view, so to speak.

Over the last twenty-four hours, I'd not been able to locate Danny Heller after trailing the Wolves to various locations. Instead, I'd gathered the addresses of ten of their businesses, this one included, and radioed back Castor the details. Emails from him arrived on my phone moments later. Building plans approved by the local council. Layouts that no doubt had changed significantly since the Wolves' occupation. They likely gutted and rearranged rooms to suit their purposes. I hazarded a guess that the basement of this joint was sound-proofed, decked out with lighting, and set up for filming their porn.

Horus' eye would give me a better picture, but I couldn't peek inside for long, otherwise the dark magick could sink its claws into me and poison me. By my estimation, I had two minutes tops and better make the most of it. With the help of *His* eye, I cast my consciousness through the walls, sinking through the pale brick exterior, the timber studs, plasterboard walls into a dimly lit hallway.

Two Wolves smoked, guarding the front door, one forcing one of the women to blow him off, shoving her head down hard. Her long, fake nails dug into his legs as she tried to push off him, but he held her by the hair and back of the neck. The other raped her from behind, and she closed her eyes, brows tight, each thrust tearing her pussy.

Fuck. My body rocked with anger, almost thrusting me out of the building. I held on, maintaining my position, going deeper.

Disturbed, I moved beyond them, down the hall, unable to hear a damn thing. Just sight. Nothing much happened upstairs. Women in a dressing room being made up by makeup and hair attendants. Two more Wolves watched them, eating pizza. Below was where all the action happened. I just felt it.

I drifted into the basement, where two stages had been erected. Lounge, bed, spa, all sets for the porn movie they were shooting where a guy with a fucking gorilla dick pounded the woman's pussy and another shredded her ass, making her bleed over the satin sheets. This was no normal porn. This was dark shit where the men were rough and raped the woman. My grip on *His* eye faltered, and I dug my hands into the ground from my position, holding on.

The other stage contained something far worse, and I almost came out of my skin when *His* eye penetrated the next wall. A woman strapped to a chair, a man hovering over her, forcing her to give him a blow job while another man cut into her, bleeding her. The man pounded into her mouth, and her jaw hung at a funny angle, broken, allowing his thick, horse-length inside her.

Jesus Fucking H Christ.

My connection to *His* eye broke, and I vomited on the ground in front of me and had to take a few moments to compose myself before casting myself back to the disturbing scene. Upon my return, the torturer burned her with a blow torch, and she screamed over the guy's dick, almost passing out. I watched in horror, my own torture brimming to the surface as the guy came, then moved behind her, fucked her in the ass while the torturer marked her stomach. Everywhere shook with fury and revulsion as they hurt her, finally ending her life, slitting her throat before the guy came from behind. Fucking snuff movies.

Breathing hard, I came out of my vision and rolled into a seated position, hands clutching my thighs. I barely held onto my sanity as I remembered everything I'd suffered at the hands of my torturer five years ago. The tanned face, brown lips, dark hair, and eyes that haunted every dream. Fuck, I was sinking into an anxiety attack. I leaned forward on all fours, gulping down air, possibly giving my location away.

"Horus." I scratched my hand down the grass.

"Help them, my child." My god sucked the panic from my body and injected me with a blast of fire that threw me to my feet.

My heart pounded with a mighty terror and rage. I had to help those women. Cross this line, though, and there was no going back. No safety net. No salvation. If I disobeyed this order, crossed Slade and my brothers, it was over. For the first time, I didn't care. What I cared about were the women held captive within that building. I'd not leave them to the same fate I endured.

Unholstering my gun, I descended the slope to the building of Hell. Gaze planted on the front door, I marched with the determination to kill every last motherfucker in that building, reaching the door in record time. Leg raised, I leaned back to kick in the fucking door, when the cold, hard barrel of a gun pressed to the back of my skull. From the click of a hammer pulled back into firing position, I knew it was a revolver, probably with a hair-trigger.

"Drop your gun, now." A Wolf had snuck up on me.

Fuck, I'd played into his damn hands. Didn't do my regular scan of the area. Lost in my thoughts and a red haze of anger, I never heard him coming. Things went from bad to worse in a flash.

"Been a slow night. You must have been bored sitting around here waiting for nothing to happen." He snorted and jabbed his gun harder into my neck. "Stupid ass Jackals. Get up. Real slow." Sure as hell liked to run his mouth. I'd close it for him. Forever.

I tossed my gun to the side, far enough from his reach, using the toss to glance over my shoulder at the jittery asshole behind me. This guy was high on something. First lesson: no drinking or snorting shit when on guard.

"Danny figured one of you would be lurking in the shadows." The gun twitched on my neck. "I was hoping I'd find his pretty little sister with you. We're a couple of girls short on the last order." He used the gun to shove me forward, pressing it harder against my head. "She's a sweet piece of ass. Shame she's wasting herself fucking around with cunts like you when she can do so much better."

My hawk screeched at the derogatory way this asshole referred to our mate. She was precious, ours to protect and defend, and my bird would not leave without scratching his eyes out for that.

"Let me guess... with someone like you, right?" I laughed. "She wouldn't give your greasy ass the time of day."

"Doesn't matter now," he grunted. "I'm not looking for Jackal sloppy seconds. But our clients? They got no qualms about it. No accounting for taste, I guess." He moved the gun and pressed it between my shoulder blades. "I was going to take you in alive, but why bother making a mess back at the clubhouse when I can just do you right here and let you bleed out in the dirt? On your knees, fucker."

He was a cocky son of a bitch. Dumbass should have frisked me. A mistake that would cost him.

"Make up your fucking mind. Get up, kneel down." I

acted like I was getting down on one knee but went for the Sig P226 in my ankle holster and rapid fired two shots between my legs. One in each of his feet. "You talk too much."

I whirled around on him, fired once more and hit him in the arm, disarming him, but not before he managed to get off a shot of his own on his way down. The bullet trajectory hit at a weird angle, impacting just below my left shoulder blade and exiting through my bottom rib. Hurt like a son of a bitch and bled like water through a sieve, but the bullet went clean through and missed anything vital on its way.

Talons extended from my fingers, and I raised my hands, slashed across his face, right through his eyes. He screamed like a bitch and went down to his knees, where I sliced his throat out. Served him right for working for Danny Heller and abusing those women inside.

It wouldn't take the Wolves long to realize they were down a man, and I sure as hell didn't want to be anywhere near their territory when it happened. I'd not be any good to the women inside like this. I had to get to Doc Shriver. Adrenaline worked for and against me, keeping me on my feet, running toward my bike parked a quarter of a mile away and hidden in the darkness. The faster my blood pumped, the faster it leaked out of the gunshot. I pulled off my cut and shirt, tearing it in half, wadding one strip of cotton fabric against the exit wound on my side. The second, I wrapped around my shoulder and held one end with my teeth, tied it off, and crammed the last strip of fabric under the double knot. I prayed to the gods the makeshift bandage was enough to get me back to the clubhouse before I bled out.

My Chieftain wasn't an ideal mode of transportation with a gunshot wound and one good arm. I barely kept both wheels rubber side down. A ride that should have taken an hour and a half turned into almost two. By the time I reached the clubhouse, I'd lost so much blood I saw double and could hardly ride straight, let alone hold the bike steady. Blood loss left me weak and shaking all over. Air wheezed through my punctured lung, and I couldn't seem to get enough. My heart strained to pump my blood, my body worked overtime to repair the damage. Wobbling everywhere, I coasted into the parking lot, crashing into the side of the garage. I slid off, falling to my hands and knees, then braced myself against the shed and climbed to my feet. I didn't bother switching off my bike or kicking the stand down as I stumbled through the front door.

Vision darkened as I called out for my brothers, hoping one of them heard me before I passed out and hit the floor. "Slade? Castor? You here?" My voice came out a wheeze.

Chairs tumbled as I crashed into the table, dropped to my knees, causing the table to tip and smack its top against the rough wooden floor. Everywhere went cold and numb, and I knew this was it for me.

The noise summoned Slade and Castor from their offices.

"What the hell happened?" Slade knelt by my good side and hooked his arm under mine, hoisting me up off the floor. "Call Doc Shriver, now!"

"There's no time. Look at him." Castor helped Slade get me to the office where they laid me on the desk. "He's been shot and lost too much blood."

"Zethan, get your ass in here!" Slade barked, and I groaned at the demons nipping at my soul, ready to drag me down into Hell with them.

Castor peeked behind the wads of cotton that plugged the leak in my side, and I hissed as dried blood ripped at my skin and encouraged more blood to leak. "Aaliyah can heal him."

"We still don't know if we can trust her. The less she sees or hears, the better." Slade said, shutting him down, tearing off his shirt to use it as a bandage. "Besides, she's barely got enough strength to heal herself."

"We don't have a choice." As a cop, Zethan gave Aaliyah the benefit of the doubt like Castor, until all investigations cleared her name. I must have looked pretty fucking bad if he was willing to ask her for a favor.

Cold spread to my fingers and toes, and I trembled uncontrollably. "They were waiting for one of us to show up. Never saw him coming."

I shook my head, disgusted with myself for getting caught in the act. My military training and surveillance work for the Jackals was supposed to give me an edge. Ever since Aaliyah came into my life, I'd been off my game, elated to unite with my mate. Worst decision of my life to bring her home. The shit storm she created. No good deed went unpunished. Still, I needed her help, or the Jackals would be one member short.

I kept my hand pressed against my side to stem the blood flow. We thought the uncle was full of shit, and Aaliyah backed him up to cover the Wolves' lies. Not the fucking case at all.

"It's worse than what Aaliyah and the old man downstairs said," I moaned as Slade lifted me into a seated position to compress his shirt to my wound. "They're making rape porn and snuff films."

Vivid and horrid images flashed in my mind, bringing back the panic attack that Horus had staved off. I gripped the edge of the table and sucked in air that burned as it wheezed through my torn lung.

"Fucking hell." Zethan moved to the wall and smashed it in with his fist. Violence and rape didn't fly with him, and I worried he'd leave the clubhouse and make tracks to the Wolves' studio and burn it to the ground.

"Motherfuckers." Slade scrubbed his light beard with bloodied fingers.

"Slade, he's lost a lot of blood, man," Castor pleaded, the closest thing we had to a doctor with all his knowledge. "We need to get Aaliyah to look at him. She can patch him up enough to hold out for Doc Shriver."

"Goddamn it." Slade tossed his chair against the wall. The veins at his temple pulsed and his hands were clenched into fists at his side. "Fine. We get her to heal him, and nobody says a fucking word about what's going on. Got it?"

"I'll handle it," Zethan ground out through a clenched jaw.

Slade fisted Zethan's cut, and they squared off. "I know exactly how you'll handle it and that's not happening tonight. As your president, I'm telling you right now that if you act without my approval, it'll be your last act. You get me?"

Zethan didn't say a word. His jaw flexed, and he shook Slade off his chest.

"Let me get through one fucking disaster at a time," Slade warned him. "Then we get that bastard Danny and the rest of his pigs, and we fucking spit roast them. Then we save the girls. Got it?"

Zethan gave his president a stiff nod, and the three of them got over their shit and carried me downstairs to Aaliyah's cell.

Finding our mate was supposed to bring us together but it only seemed to tear us apart. I just hoped we could hold our shit together long enough to save the women being mistreated by the Wolves. If we were lucky, maybe we could save ourselves in the process.

CHAPTER 14

Aaliyah

COMMOTION UPSTAIRS HAD me bolting upright. A heavy crash on the floor upstairs sent bits of dirt and dust raining down on my head. Shouting and arguing. My heart pounded. Forty-eight hours had passed, and Danny burst into the club, attacking the Jackals. Next, he'd come for me, and I didn't have a weapon besides my water bottle—hardly deadly—or the drip line to choke him. Locked in the cell, I'd be dead with a bullet to my head before I had the chance.

Footsteps thudded above, boots hitting the floor hard and fast. Seconds later, the door leading to the basement swung open and slammed against the wall. I rolled over the edge of the bed to hide under the cot and make it difficult for Danny to find me. A dull burn seared down my stomach and side, and I pressed a hand to my wound, trying to ease it. I was getting better by the day, but sharp movement hurt.

Several men lumbered down the stairs, struggling with something.

"Where the fuck is Aaliyah?" Zethan's voice, tight and worried.

"I knew it." Alaric. Shallow and strained. "She used her magick to get out."

"Impossible, I warded the iron bars." Castor. Puzzled by all accounts.

Aching like mad, I crawled out slowly from under the cot.

"Fuck, get Doc Shriver down here, now." Slade all fire and fury. "I don't care where he is. Alaric's not gonna bleed out."

Alaric was injured? Fuck, what happened? I hurried the rest of the way out and rested on my shins.

"What's wrong?" My voice came out as a grunt of pain, and I wheezed, holding my belly tight.

"Fuck, Aaliyah," Slade roared, his voice thundering in the confined space. "What the hell were you doing?"

"I thought Danny was coming to collect—" My eyes fell to Alaric, propped in their arms, ashen, lips blue and chest bleeding. "Oh, my gods, what happened to him?" I rushed over to the cell door, pressing my face against the bars for a better look. Walking and moving was easy with my wound healing fast. "Has he been shot?"

"Yes, and you're going to heal him." Slade approached me.

My back straightened from the stubborn column of fire he set off in me, shooting like a rocket launched into the inky night. "You always ask so nicely."

He wasn't giving me a choice, the flames in his indigo gaze telling me he'd kill me if I denied him. Ready to fight him, I backed up from the door to my cell so he could unlock it.

Marching in here to make demands of me to heal Alaric while they kept me prisoner was the last straw and I snapped. "I answered your questions and told you everything

I know. Which, by the way, I'm assuming from Alaric's injuries, you now realize is the truth." Ignoring the slight throb in my abdomen, I rested my arms over my chest and gave him my best glare.

"Don't start on me, woman." Slade dragged me by the arm out of the cell where my magick would work.

I whimpered from the sting of jerking free and from his manhandling me. "I think I've been the model prisoner, yet you storm in here with more demands. Fuck you, Mr. Vincent."

"Aaliyah," Castor said my name in warning not to push his explosive president. He feared that I'd push my luck and not fare so well. His sticky apprehension clung to the bond. The little he showed to me.

Tired of being locked in a cell, locked out of my life, I no longer gave a shit. Time to bargain. Slade Vincent could be worn down. For the most part, he was pushy, possessive, and cocky. But once I'd witnessed him go easy on Slim when his family was sick, letting him stay home to care for them instead of going on their important delivery. I'd have to tap into that same singular reasonable bone in his body.

"I'll cut a deal with you."

"Woman, don't test me."

"I'll heal him, Mr. Vincent." I raised my voice above Slade's. He growled at the use of his full name. Days ago, he'd loved it when I called him that, getting hot all over. "In return, I want out of this shitty cell. Give me a real room with windows and fresh air. And a goddamn bathroom." I tapped my foot against the cement floor.

The others looked on, Castor smirking and impressed, Alaric almost passing out, and Zethan tense and grim.

A quiet storm of rage brewed in Slade's eyes. "Are you seriously trying to cut a deal with me right now?"

"It's called negotiating." I kept my chin up, feigning confidence I didn't feel when this could blow up in my face with everything else. Too late. I'd gone this far and had to see it through. "It's the only thing people like you and my brother seem to respond to. Let me out and I'll heal him, or you take him to a hospital where they'll ask a lot of questions. I doubt you'll find another avatar as accommodating as me. Your choice, Mr. Vincent."

"Aaliyah." Zethan shook his head and gave me a look that said I made a huge mistake.

Fuck him. Fuck them all.

Yes, please! my heart decided it was the right time to chime in.

"Don't *Aaliyah* me, King of the Dead!" I pointed my finger at him, burning up from the frustrated heat pulsing through me. He could butter me up with his text messages, but I wasn't having it. "I want to help him, but you can't keep me hostage in this basement forever. I'm asking you to treat me like a person and not a prisoner. That's all."

They all glanced at one another, narrowed eyes, raised eyebrows, and tight jaws a sign of their silent communications.

"She gets the room upstairs." Slade agreed to my demand, but he didn't sound happy about it. "With a guard around the clock. We take it in shifts." He rubbed his eyes. "Fucking manpower I can't afford to lose. Satisfied?" He glared at me like he wanted to bring the full force of a landslide down on me.

Aaliyah one. Slade zero. And the Jackal's president hated to lose.

"For now." I elbowed him out of the way and knelt in front of Alaric. Hand pressed to his chest, I scanned his body, getting a picture of his wound. A bullet wound similar to the one that had brought Slade Vincent crashing into my life. How fitting. "This is going to hurt."

"More than getting shot?" Alaric scoffed.

Been there, done that. Not pretty. Never again.

He was lucky he was afforded my powers to help him. I got patched up by a dodgy backyard club doctor.

"I have to knit the bone and muscle tissue back together." I gave him a quick biology lesson to distract him while I got down to business. Didn't work.

After removing the t-shirt he used to stop the bleeding, I jammed two fingers into the entrance wound. Alaric's head shot up, and he let out a string of profanity that would have made a sailor blush.

"That's all you got?" I asked. "That's nothing to an ER nurse. Heard it all before." He stuttered a few more words but fell back, wheezing.

Castor chuckled, encouraging Slade and Zethan to give me room to work. "He's in good hands. Give her some space." The president stood tense, refusing to budge. Only Zethan and Castor gave me the space I needed.

I found the entry and exit points within Alaric's body and could start work. With some of my power diverted to heal myself, I wasn't sure I was up for a full Slade-type healing, but I'd give it my best. If I could stop the bleeding and repair the worst of it, Alaric could come back tomorrow for another fix and finish the job.

"Don't worry, Mr. Vincent," I teased. "I promise not to kill him."

Slade bared teeth as he growled, and a thrill of adrenaline hit my blood. I fucking enjoyed riling him up. Shoe was on the other foot now.

Just like I'd done with Slade, I concentrated all my energy into Alaric. Muscle wove back together, nerves reformed, and lung tissue bubbled as it sealed with fresh cells. Exhausted by the process, I hunched over him, arms across his heaving chest, ready to puke or pass out. He wasn't one hundred percent, but this would do. His body could do the rest until he came back for round two.

Alaric brushed my arm away from him, slid out from beneath me, and leaned on the wall to put as much distance between us as possible.

Alone on the cool, damp floor, I braced my hands in front of me. "You're welcome."

"Thank you." Slade kicked Alaric with the side of his boot, telling him to do the same.

"Thanks." Alaric pushed himself up, wobbling, and Slade hoisted him the rest of the way. Sounded as genuine as a politician on a campaign trail.

"I heal you and the best you can do is a half-assed thanks." Rest was required after my taxing exertion. I crawled over to the chair and used it for support, wobbling once I got to my feet, unaided by any of the four men. Castor wouldn't have dared in front of his president.

"What do you want me to do, Aaliyah?" Alaric's harsh snap echoed throughout the cell. "Fall all over you? Shower you with gratitude and my unending devotion?" His bitter laughter hurt my heart. "Did it ever occur to you that I wouldn't have gotten shot in the first place if it weren't for you?"

"That's rich." I folded my arms across my chest. "Considering I wouldn't have gotten shot, locked up in a cell, or forced into a fated mate bond if you hadn't taken me from the hospital parking garage. So, if you're looking for someone to blame, turn that finger around and point it at yourself."

Alaric grappled with a comeback. "You should have been upfront with us from the very beginning. We could have helped you." He shook his head. "But you went and fucked it up instead."

"Oh, yeah, because if I said 'hey, I think your president

killed my dad,' you'd just hand over the evidence I needed to convict him?" It was my turn to laugh.

"We wouldn't have to turn any evidence over to you because Slade didn't kill your father." Alaric shot back, raising his voice to a shout.

Castor got between us, raising two palms that both of us ignored.

Zethan kept quiet in the corner, observing, analyzing every little detail.

Slade just scratched his beard watching it all play out.

"You spied on us, Aaliyah." Alaric stormed over to the stairs, pausing by the wall. "You used the mate bond against us."

I did what now? He was one to talk, laying it on thick to me, too. They all did. Making me swoon over them. I got suckered into kissing Castor … an incredible kiss, by the way. Tricked into throwing myself at Alaric. Overwhelmed by Slade, making me do something I *really* regretted. *Oh, God.* I felt his touch burn my neck and back all over again. I crushed my eyes shut.

"Why? Because I kissed you?" I shouted, about to lose my cool and faint. "How long have you known about the bond? How long have you all had to process its effect? Because I've had two weeks, and I can't help how I feel. Sometimes I feel like kissing you, and other times, like right now, I want to smack you upside the head."

Castor smirked. Even Slade hid his grin behind his fist. Zethan remained unmoved, stoic, and unreadable. Typical cop, giving nothing away.

Annoyed at them all, I pushed over the chair, struggling to stay upright and it was Zethan who caught me, taking me by surprise since he didn't say much. Only when it counted. I remembered our sweet and fun text exchange but was too upset to care and jerked free before the curse kicked in.

Alaric glared at me. "Trust is a big deal with me, and you broke it. Even if, and that's a big fucking *if*, I wanted to fix it, I wouldn't know how. I'm not known for giving second chances. Neither is Slade." Alaric took another step back, distancing himself from me a foot at a time.

"Ironic, considering I just gave you one." I stumbled back to my cell, yanking the cell door, slamming it shut. I'd essentially locked myself in since I couldn't storm off.

That seemed to throw him for a loop. The truth had a way of doing that to people. "I wish I could tell you that I don't care that you lied to us. That your reasons make it okay. It doesn't change anything."

I broke the biker code. To them, I was a traitor. To my brother, also. I knew the possible repercussions of my actions and stayed inside the Jackals' camp anyway. If I had to do it all over, I'd do it again because my father deserved justice.

"Cut the pious act, okay, Alaric?" I matched him decibel for decibel. "You act like you've never made a mistake. Didn't you almost choke me?"

Slade growled and fisted his hands.

Alaric flinched and bowed his head.

"That was low, Aaliyah, even for you," Castor warned, but I was too tired and pissy to care.

"Was it?" I cut Castor down with a scowl. "I forgave Alaric for it and didn't hold it against him. Yet, you can't seem to move forward."

Alaric left me alone in the dark. Literally and figuratively, which was probably for the best. After the way the night had gone, I preferred to be by myself.

"Aaliyah." Slade sighed and pinched the bridge of his nose.

No. I was done.

"Fuck all of you." Losing my balance, I fell back onto my

cot. "Take me to my room as we agreed. I need to rest after saving your man."

Slade rubbed the back of his head. "About that." Here we go. Taking back his promise. More fire ignited within me. "Alaric's going to need to crash in your room tonight, but I can have it ready for you tomorrow."

"Fuck." I rubbed my face.

"You can sleep in my bed if it makes any difference." Slade fucking Vincent offering his bed. Wow. Miracles happened.

"No thanks." I settled under my blankets. "I'd rather sleep here where the filthy traitors belong."

We all knew what would happen if I lay on the same bed as him. Nothing good. And I wanted to be as far away from him as possible. Away from all of them. Where I could think and process everything.

Slade gestured for everyone to get out. "Suit yourself, woman."

CHAPTER 15

Aaliyah

I HISSED as his fingers stroked my wound. The pink skin burned at the doctor's touch, still raw and tender, but healing nicely. Much faster than I'd anticipated, considering I was locked in an iron cage marked with magical runes to prevent my magick healing my body or getting me out. My insides felt pretty much the same but gave me a bit of discomfort when I shifted in the bed to reach for my water, get a book Castor left me, or do my business on the pot that he'd left me. Things could have been a lot worse.

Thank the goddess.

Alaric stumbled forward a few steps. Habit for his mate. His alarm trickled through the bond. It hurt him to see me in pain. Reluctance quickly squashed and replaced his worry, and he moved back into line, watching over me with his keen, suspicious gaze. Deep grooves cut into his mouth and eyes indicated he hadn't slept much since my capture.

Whether it was because of concern for me, or his club, remained a mystery. Though, the way he'd spoken to me yesterday when I patched him up, indicated his worry for his club and his freedom now that the cops had arrested him.

Dr. Shriver took off his glasses and wiped his eyes. Wind had ruffled his gray-tipped brown hair. "This is incredible. I've never seen a patient recover so quickly and miraculously. No infection. Perfect wound closure."

Skin gashes from a gunshot wound in a human sealed shut within ten days. Mine had worked in a matter of days. Each day the red faded from the entry point.

I tensed in my bed. Obviously, the good doctor had never met a shifter with an advanced rate of healing, which confused me since he worked for four avatars.

"God must be smiling down on me." My feeble attempt to explain away the miracle fell flat, and Dr. Shriver's dark eyes narrowed, unconvinced.

"He hasn't struck me down with brimstone for working on the side for a biker gang." Dr. Shriver's lips curled into a cunning smile.

I chuckled and played along. "Lucky you."

He struck me as the kind of man who liked to tempt fate, much like Slade, testing how much he could get away with. Working off the books for a motorcycle club, conducting surgery, performing x-rays, ultrasounds, and other scans without the proper training, credentials or even set-up … well, that was grounds for misconduct and loss of his medical license. If only the good doctor knew that more than one god existed despite his belief in a higher power.

"The next stage will be therapeutic activity." Dr. Shriver packed up his belongings. "Physiotherapy to build up the strength of your stomach muscles."

Tears in the stomach wall from gunshot wounds often led patients through months of physiotherapy to rebuild strength in the core muscles, teaching them to learn basic functions again.

I croaked out a laugh at his irony. "Good one, Doc." I hit him lightly because my strength was rebuilding faster by the day. Revitalized by Castor's visits, renewing my strength and hope. "I'm kept prisoner in a cell by the Jackals. Not much chance of me getting out for some physical therapy." I bent my head, picking at my nail. "Unless they give me the room upstairs they agreed to." The last part I directed at Alaric.

I had a life of my own, a healthy career, friends, a lease on my apartment. Obligations I couldn't leave unattended indefinitely. Disciplinary action was likely to follow if I returned for work after my disappearance. Money talked for expenses, and without employment, I'd lose everything I'd worked so hard to achieve. All because of my fucking brother. Things didn't look too bright for my foreseeable future.

The doctor's hand came down on my shoulder, and I jerked my attention to him. "Slade's given you approval to work in the shelter, dependent on my medical clearance."

"What?" I leaned forward, biting at the dull sting in my abdomen.

Last time I spoke with Slade, he made it clear that I was his hostage, on round-the-clock guard by his men when I got shifted upstairs to my room.

Why the change of heart from Slade? For how long would they let me do that? Castor must have made a case for me. My heart warmed at the considerate gesture, and I made a note to thank him later.

On a related matter, what about the three Wolves captives in the cell in the other basement room? My uncle, Jerry. What did Slade intend for them? They needed exercise and to get sunlight for their health. I doubted the Jackals' president would be as considerate and compassionate to them. Enemies, number one.

Then again, so was I. This didn't make sense. Did I get special privileges because I was their mate? Or was it something more sinister? I rubbed at my goosebumped arms. This didn't feel right. The Jackals were up to something. That something had everything to do with me. They were going to dangle me as bait to lure out Danny, but he wouldn't be that stupid.

Dr. Shriver's voice called me back to the conversation, and I blinked a few times, trying to concentrate on his words. "I don't see any harm in you getting some social interaction and using your nursing talents." I jolted as he clipped the tongue of his leather medical satchel. "But I want you in a wheelchair while you're still recovering and undergoing physical therapy. I'll have one sent to the clubhouse for tomorrow."

I doubted I'd need that. Castor had helped me stand when he bathed me. I'd also managed to walk out of the cell to Alaric last night. No problem there besides a little imbalance and dizziness. Though, I hadn't tested myself with walking, bending or lifting on a longer basis. Actions that the stomach muscles were crucial for.

"Thanks, Doc." I shook his hand, even though I trembled all over. Shock from the news that Slade would let me out of my cell for probably small periods of the day. Apprehension over the Jackals plans for me and for losing grip of my old life, which felt like I had no hope of going back to.

"I'll come back to check on you tomorrow." The doctor patted me on the shoulder.

I set my hand over the doctor's. "Thank you."

He gave Alaric a cursory nod as he climbed the stairs. The Jackal turned to leave me alone, but a stab of worry hit me over his wounds. They needed checking, maybe redressing, and certainly another round of healing.

"Alaric, wait," I called out to him as he ascended the bottom three stairs.

He stopped but didn't turn around.

"How's your wound?" My voice came out quieter than I'd hoped for. "Did Dr. Shriver check it?"

"Fine." He kept on climbing.

"Alaric." I sighed and leaned back on my pillow. "Just let me take a look at it." Pointless calling out to him when he'd made his feelings about me *very* clear. Rejected. Disowned. Mate no more. Just like Slade. But did Alaric discard me to follow his orders or because that was how he felt?

Hunger tore down the mate bond with surprising intensity. The thought of me touching him made his body rock and weakened his will. Barely holding on, Alaric paused, placing a palm on the stone wall, bending his head, sucking in a deep breath. Reluctance wrestled with longing until he got a handle on his sweeping emotions and recalled them quickly. Suppressed the mate bond's allure and slammed the lid back on that box.

My lips burned from our kiss goddess knew how many days ago, when I'd lost count of time from sleeping and recovery. Make that our second kiss, not that I was counting or anything. *I was fucking counting.*

Muscles in his neck strained as he struggled to control himself at my reminder. "Doc Shriver can do that." His voice was heavy with indifference. "I don't need your help."

Fuck. Why did I bother? Loneliness, perhaps. That, mixed with a longing so powerful it consumed me sometimes. Maybe also a sense of obligation to the Jackals because of what my brother had done to them. Logically, I knew I didn't owe them anything when they kidnapped and held me captive, but I couldn't overcome my feeling of responsibility.

"Yes, you do." He jerked his gaze to me when I said that. "I heard your nightmares last night. They're getting worse, aren't they?"

I remembered all too well the way he'd choked and bruised me when he fell under a PTSD anxiety attack and hallucinated his attacker.

"It happens when I'm stressed." He shrugged and pulled out a flask of whisky, throwing his head back for a couple of swallows.

"It doesn't have to be that way," I whispered, touching my neck, the clamp of his hands on me returning, cooling my body.

While I was here, I could make myself useful. Do my part as a nurse and healer. I'd eased the minds of the women at the shelter, and the least I could do was ease his. Especially if he was going to be on guard duty with them. The man was a ticking bomb waiting to go off, and it was only a matter of time until he exploded and hurt someone else, too. Something I had to prevent, even if it was my final legacy on this earth. Then, I could meet my goddess and go to the Underworld with a light heart, knowing I made a difference to a few people. Oaths bound me to protect, treat and heal all those who came for my care, enemy or not, and that extended to damn Alaric.

Alaric spun on me, fast, like a bird swooping and snatching up its prey. "What can you do for me?" His cold gaze was like blades to my heart.

Hatred spat across the mate bond like sparks on a live wire. His emotion fed our connection, pumping it wider for me to interpret his feelings, believing that I broke his heart. Ripped it open again like it had been when he lost his first mate, even though the circumstances were different.

"Liz would never have betrayed us," he spat at me like it

had anything to do with our situation. He took another swig of his flask.

Several words came to mind about him. Damaged. Lost. The nurse in me wanted to pick up all the pieces and glue them back together to make him whole again. But he had to want that, and I couldn't force that upon him. The wild, spirited woman in me hated that I felt compassion toward my enemy when he kept me locked up like this. A part of me I'd left behind so many years before. Buried her with my cut and Jimmy's body.

I rested my head in my hands despite the pain in my belly. "Yeah, so you like to remind me." I sniffed and rubbed my face. "I wish you'd stop comparing me to her. Liz, the *damn* angel! We're different people, and she isn't here anymore."

He jabbed a finger in the air. "Don't you fucking talk about her ever again."

Excuse me? "You brought her up!" I was sick of this. Sick of all of them. "What for? To make me feel like a piece of shit? Well, I don't. I did nothing wrong. You kidnapped me, remember?"

His golden eye glowed, and he tilted his head. "You're hiding something, Aaliyah. I'll find out what it is." What the fuck was he talking about?

"Get the fuck out, Alaric." I leaned over, hissing at the sudden throb down my side as I picked up my book. Brought on from him, no doubt.

His boots thumped down the stairs as he backtracked. "Aaliyah?"

I squeezed the book's spine. "I said get out."

He hesitated for a moment, the mate bond wavering with his indecision to comfort me versus leave. In the end, his spite won out, and he left me there, the door slamming after him, making me flinch.

Fuming, I snapped open the book, trying to concentrate

but no words sunk in. I flicked the page, almost tearing one. Fuck, I couldn't ruin one of Castor's precious tomes. I slammed it shut. Tears bubbled in my eyes. Goddamn Alaric had gotten me all riled up. How dare he compare me to his ex. Did he and the others really expect me to be like her? Delusional.

I didn't have anything to hide. Everything was laid bare through the mate bond if he just looked into it with a rational mind. But was I dealing with someone rational? Something had tainted his body and soul, stripping away his trust, and if I wasn't careful, he might snap and hurt me.

CHAPTER 16

Aaliyah

CASTOR CARRIED me up the stairs, relocating me to another room upstairs in the clubhouse. Better conditions. A window and fresh air. Slade had delivered on his promise, respecting the negotiation terms. I took the small win and accepted it.

At the top of the stairs, Alaric waited, his eyes on me, and not in a good way. Hawk-like. Observant. Sharp. Watching every movement. My own personal guard. Slade kept throwing him in my path. Nothing I said would sway Alaric to my side, and I gave up trying. From now on, we were nothing to each other, and I wasn't sure how I felt about that. Empty and disappointed.

Memories of the moment we shared on Mount Panorama, the kiss and embrace, burned vividly in my mind. That thought traveled along the link, and his stance weakened for a second before stiffening again. He didn't trust me. Frankly, the feeling was mutual.

"This is your room here on the left." Castor led me through the door of the simple room, bland décor, mattress on a frame, a nightstand, and private bathroom. It smelled like stale alcohol and sweat, but someone left me a candle. The black quilt cover with golden lines reminded me of the club's colors. "Slade's and Zethan's rooms are right across the hall. They get their own rooms because of their rank."

The Jackals' clubhouse was larger than the Wolves, but then they didn't have living quarters on site. Just a bunkroom when one of the guys needed a place to crash or to spend *"quality time"* with one of their side girls. Not my idea of quality, and I had no intention of filling that role for the Jackals. I was an all-or-nothing kind of girl, and certainly not for four men who claimed to be my fated mates, yet who held me captive.

A dull ache hit my stomach as Castor set me down on the edge of the bed, and I bit my lip. He crouched beside me, hand on my thigh, the other on the back of my head. The faintest hint of concern crawled along the bond, but it was gone quicker than it came. Castor was a closed book and kept his emotions under lock and key, remaining a mystery. I waved him on to keep going.

"The other two bedrooms, yours included," he said, "are reserved for the two members on duty for the night. We always have two men on shifts to guard the club."

Protection was paramount to an MC. Rivals invaded and stole belongings, money, weapons, drugs, anything on site. They even killed sometimes. The Wolves had fought off two attacks from lower Sydney clubs trying to inch in on their territory.

Castor stroked the quilt dripping off the side of the bed, a whisper away from my calf as if he stopped himself from touching me. "My office is next door if you need me. I sleep on the couch when I'm on duty or take one of these rooms. But with you taking up one, that leaves one less available."

Alaric stood at attention by the door, forever my shadow, eyes glued to me. I'd deceived him in the most unforgivable way, and all signs indicated I couldn't come back from that. My heart shrieked at that while my mind shrugged and said *fuck it*.

Freedom came at a price when Jerry and the other two Wolves were still locked in another cell downstairs. I suspected the Jackals gave me special privileges because of my status as their mate or because they wanted something. Insider knowledge on Danny's operation. Information I couldn't give them. My body remained alert and on edge, knowing my circumstances could turn at any moment, dependent on Slade's whim and giving the Jackals what they wanted. What happened when I couldn't deliver? I swallowed the lump in my throat.

No one had schooled me on my rights now that I was free of my confines, and I ought to clarify since I was still the Jackal's prisoner. "What are the rules of this arrangement?"

Castor's mouth drew into a thinner line. "You're to be guarded at all times. Slade has allowed you to go to the shelter whenever Zethan does, under guard, of course."

I huffed. Of course. "How generous of Slade," I muttered.

"Aaliyah, understand this is a delicate situation." The tips of Castor's fingers found my elbow and I let him hold me, needing someone to steady me. I rocked on the edge of a dark chasm waiting to swallow me. If I fell, I'd never return, and I had to hold on with everything I had. "We're working as fast as we can to resolve it. You're not safe, and neither are we."

Always the lawyer, looking at every side of the situation. I liked that about him, but it pissed me off right now since nothing worked in my favor.

Now to the looming question in my mind, hanging over me like a noose over my neck. "What about when I'm of no more use to you?"

The bond between Alaric and me prickled with tension.

Castor speared a hand through his hair, giving me little, as usual. "We haven't discussed that far ahead yet. The next few days to weeks will be crucial, though."

Dread coiled in my stomach. Everything was uncertain and contingent on the war's outcome with the Wolves. My mother was in danger, and I had no way to warn her. I didn't care about Danny at the moment when every indication drenched him in guilt.

I glanced at Alaric, wary of his history. Shrewd, piercing savvy that made him my biggest threat besides Slade. Military training, deadly combat skills, an efficient killer, capable and willing to end my life whenever his president commanded it. I was living on borrowed time, and Alaric had no hesitation in reminding me of it.

I flinched when Castor stood up.

Protectiveness surged through our connection at my fear, and my eyes went to Alaric. We both fought the need to comfort and stayed away from each other. Mine from a need for survival. His from longing for his mate and the stain of the event that haunted him.

Castor crossed to a small, one-door closet in the corner of the room. "I guessed your size and took the liberty of ordering you some clothes." He opened the door, revealing some shelves and a tight space for hanging clothes. "Nothing fancy, just some everyday stuff like jeans and a few shirts."

He skimmed over the folded shirts, sweaters, and the three pairs of jeans folded over hangers. One in each color. Cute, he'd picked me a variety. Considerate. A small comfort in this dark and uncertain time. At least I'd look good. My chest warmed at his considerate gift.

Castor flicked on the light in the bathroom. "Toiletries are under the sink, and there's towels in the linen closet."

Wow, he really went all out.

"You thought of everything, didn't you?" Exhaustion hit me the moment I laid back on the bed. My shirt hiked up, exposing my belly, and the bond went rigid with desire from both men. Alaric's iced over in point two-three seconds flat ... but, hey, who was counting.

A smile tugged at the corner of Castor's mouth. "We don't know how long you'll be staying." I didn't know if that was a good or bad thing. But given our encounter some nights earlier, still fresh in my mind, I took it as a positive.

More questions remained unanswered that needed addressing. "What do you want with me?"

Castor tsked me and waggled a finger. "I fell for your tricks once, dark sorceress." He probably referred to the time I played judge and solicitor with him to pry info from him. "You're not privy to club business."

"Oh, that's right." I slammed a fist on my bed, setting off the ache in my abdomen, making my back arch and Alaric resist the urge to come for me. "Why don't you get a neon traitor sign and hang it on my door?"

He chuckled, the deep, rich timbre going through every nerve, making them glow and buzz. Fuck, I hated that I wanted and loathed him at the same time.

"Our orders from the gods are not to kill you." Alaric was pure ice. "We need you for what's to come."

Castor shot him a look that could melt that ice and generate steam.

Great. A pawn in the god's and Jackals' game. "Fuck being an avatar. I didn't sign up for this shit." I tried to sit up, but my muscles couldn't hold the weight. Since healing Alaric, my healing had taken a step backward.

Both Castor and Alaric lunged for me, the latter

restraining himself and returning to his position. Castor put his hands beneath my armpits and dragged me back, setting me upright, with pillows behind my back. Considerate for someone who didn't trust me. Unlike his cold friend by the door. The cold friend my heart wanted to warm and melt. Sink into his body, kiss him some more, soothe that haunted soul.

Castor's eyes went round at my desire screaming down our bond, his gaze jumping between us, assessing the dynamic, his need tipping to urgent.

Alaric responded to both triggers, and his dick twitched, boxing to get out of his jeans. Hmm. He liked a bit of ménage action. I imagined myself pressed between their fiery bodies as they made love to me. Castor guarded his heart like a dragon with treasure, and nothing was getting close to that thing without being burned alive. After our heated kisses, he seemed wary of touching me, knowing once he gave in to temptation, he'd not be able to resist.

Alaric shook his head as if that would stop me from getting access to his mind and heart. "Stop it," he growled at me, holding back from looking at me, knowing if he did, he was in trouble, too.

Nice try, buddy. You fuck with me, I fuck with you.

"Why?" I smiled, decided on having fun with my situation rather than worrying about it all the time. If I was going to die, why not enjoy the last days or weeks of my life? "You're such a *good* kisser." My socked foot toyed with the quilt. "Probably the best out of three sampled so far." Gentle, equally giving and taking, designed for pleasure. In stark contrast to Slade's conquering and Castor's mouth domination.

Castor's chest rumbled with jealousy.

Alaric lost control, his gaze flicking to me, his body quivering with barely repressed need. "Don't mess with my head."

"Why?" Yeah, I was being wicked, messing with him. But I was bored, and these four had well and truly fucked up my life. "The real estate agent will soon issue me papers to vacate my apartment for not paying rent in two weeks. I'll probably be put on disciplinary action for failing to turn up to work and not calling to advise of my absence. My mom will be worried sick from not hearing from me."

Steam hissed on the bond as the fire went out. Worry drowned my end of the bond.

"We've taken care of all that," Castor said, rubbing his palms down his thighs, the way he did when he cooled his need. "Paid your rent for the next few months."

Fuck. That was one less worry. But I didn't need their money. "What about my job? My mom?"

Castor went to my nightstand, slid it open and removed the phone Zethan gave to me. "Call your boss and your mother."

I couldn't wrap my head around their sudden and unexpected generosity. They were letting me take care of my affairs. But what the hell would I tell my boss, Barb? By now, she'd have suspected something strange had happened to me. Reliable was my middle name. I never missed a shift except when sick with a cold, and I did every double shift she offered.

As for my poor mom, telling her I was the Jackals' captive would make her worry and break her already fragile state of mind. Danny's behavior with the club already caused her undue stress, and I didn't want to add to it.

I looked at Castor then to Alaric, unable to get his attention. "So, what am I to you, then? Pseudo prisoner? What about Jerry and the two Wolves? Did you let them call their wives who are probably worried sick?"

Castor twisted his Jackal ring on his finger. "You're a special case." Meaning, I could plead for those poor men all I liked. It wouldn't do a damn thing. "We're under higher orders." Godly orders.

I rubbed at my temples. What did the gods want from me?

The more time I spent with the Jackals, the more I questioned who the bad guy was in all of this. Danny was no angel, but neither were the Jackals. Everything was a twisted, fucking mess. Discovering the identity of my father's murderer inched further away, and my chest locked up with grief.

When I first arrived in the Jackal's domain, I expected to find a nest of vipers. Horrible people who killed in cold blood and ruined the lives of innocent people. Except that wasn't the case at all. They gave back to their community, rescued and protected battered women, and that called to me on a deeper level than the bond we shared as avatars. The only community service my family provided was an annual toy drive during the holidays.

"I'll let you get settled in. Make a list of anything you want from the store. This is your home now, Aaliyah." Castor headed for the door. "Get some rest, you look tired."

Home. For how long?

"Tomorrow Zethan will take you to the shelter." Castor held onto the doorway. "He's got a wheelchair if you need it."

I'd test the strength of my legs. Plenty of time alone in my room to do that. In the cell, I'd had some short walks to my potty chamber.

"I'll see you in the morning." Despite his goodbye, Castor made no effort to move.

By the edge of the door, I caught the side of Alaric's arm, indicating his position guarding my door. I wasn't getting out of here without going through him, and he'd be formidable, overpowering me easily. I was weak, my power consumed by healing the both of us, and I couldn't fight him if I tried.

"Hey, Castor," I stifled a yawn. "Thank you." I shouldn't have thanked him really, captivity and all. But the small gesture—the clothes, the room, a personal space—was worthy of one.

He smiled and closed the door. No hiding in the darkness, ordering me to get off. No helping me undress and take a shower. No aiding me to slip into the pajamas left on the pillow beside me. Cute flannel things with a stethoscope on them. Hilarious. Probably ordered by Slade. The joke suited him. Or maybe it was Castor.

Muffled murmurs of conversation drifted from the hallway, then Castor's steady steps retreated to his office. I felt the glaring menace of Alaric through the wall, ready to take me out at his president's will.

Bearing the pain, I slowly slipped out of my clothes and into the pajamas, then sank under the covers. Tomorrow I would take a shower before going to the shelter. My eyes were heavy, and I was sore in places I'd only read about in nursing school. Now that I was free of the cell and the runes, I considered tapping into my magick to speed up my healing, but it required effort, and I was limp and drained. All I wanted to do was sleep. Close my eyes, shut everything out, and drift in a sea of nothingness.

The phone Zethan had given me beeped on the nightstand and I picked it up, finding a message from Zethan. Correction: a picture. Him lying back on his bed, an arm beneath his neck, showing off the massive breadth of his biceps, hidden beneath his plaid. Damn, he was fine. I wanted to know what he hid behind all the red flannel.

Another text beeped. It read, "See you tomorrow at the shelter?"

"Yes," I replied.

"Bright and early? 7AM? Coffee and an egg and roll muffin?"

"Sure."

"You're buying." With a wink face.

"Smartass." Devil face.

"Gnite beautiful." My heart did backward flips at that. Fucking flips.

"Gnite, Hellhound Dick." I felt his instant laughter through the mate bond, and I snuggled deeper, imagining him lying beside me. The weight of his massive arm over my waist, my head on his expansive chest, his breath on the top of my head.

Comforted by his messages, I switched the phone to flight mode and set the alarm for 6:30AM.

Sleep eluded me. When the world was quiet, my mind was at its loudest. Alone with my thoughts, I tried to sort them into order, but they were all over the place. So were my emotions. Everything happened so quickly, and I was left struggling to keep up. I'd been beaten, robbed, and rescued by two dark and sexy men who whisked me off to an undisclosed location. It sounded dangerous and romantic if I thought of it that way, but none of those descriptions were accurate.

There was no one to blame for my situation except myself, and the more I lied, the worse it got. I knew what happened to people who betrayed the club.

Snitches get stitches, princess, my father's voice echoed in my head.

Cuts and bruises on his knuckles flashed in my mind from the times he'd taken care of an informant.

Now I was the informant, and I had no idea what the Jackals or the gods had in store for me.

CHAPTER 17

Zethan

TWO DAYS. Two fucking days Aaliyah had been working at the shelter under my supervision, yet we hadn't said a word besides those exchanged in text. We passed each other in the kitchen to grab a coffee. Bumped into each other in the food pantry. Tended to Jan, the new arrival, and got her settled. Nothing. Not a word. Every damn time I opened my mouth to say something, my mind forced my body in the opposite direction. Felt like a sixteen-year-old boy chasing my high school crush all over again, not a twenty-eight-year-old man. The woman had my heart and mind in a spin, just like Beth Donato had done to me in tenth grade. I had the balls to text Aaliyah every night but couldn't get the fucking courage to speak to her.

She'd noticed, too, her replies taking longer to return, fewer and farther in between. I was losing my mate and had to do something to get her back. Fuck, get intel while I was at it.

Leaning on my office doorway, I observed Aaliyah scowling at me, jerking the sheets she changed on Gracey's bed. Our captive was pissed at Slade for forcing her to stay, at being constantly trailed by one of my brothers, and I took the brunt of it. Every moment of silence dug the hole in my heart deeper. She just wanted to know who killed her father. Determine friend from foe. Alaric and I brought her to the shelter, and whether it was under her brother's orders or not, I had to find out.

The angry fire in her eyes directed my way made her even more beautiful, her pupils darkening to turquoise and her lips pinching. I wanted my fingers in her silky black hair, my lips on her neck, my whisper in her ear to erase the tightness in her jaw and mouth. My hand curled into a fist at not being able to touch her. *Fuck the curse.*

Slade had ordered Castor and me to cozy up to Aaliyah, build trust with her and fish for information. Find out her true motivations and role in the shit show that went down on the club since she arrived. I was doing a crap job of it. Couldn't get my shit together or get the confidence to talk to her besides over a damn cell phone. What happened to Liz really fucked me up, and I didn't want to hurt Aaliyah too.

My cell buzzed in my pocket, and I slid it out. Carlie. For once it wouldn't be a call about her shelter since she was on maternity leave.

I answered. "Hey, sis, how's my new nephew?"

"He's grumpy as fuck and won't eat," Carlie grumbled.

"That's five dollars added to the swear jar," I teased her. She'd milked thousands from me over the years, and now it was time for her to cough up.

"Fuck off, I—"

"Ten dollars." Goading each other was our thing.

Whoever got the better reaction won. We'd done it ever since we were six.

Carlie groaned at the game. Payback for her milking me of thousands for the swear jar. "Just suffered a thirty-hour labor for this little thing and my vagina is stretched to—"

"Jesus, Carlie." I almost hung up on her. Didn't need to hear that shit.

"It's just a pussy, Zethan."

"Fuck, I don't want to have this conversation with you!" At my snap, Aaliyah glanced up from her task. "And that's fifteen bucks."

"Every mother earns the right to swear!" Carlie laughed, and my chest lightened at the sound. I needed anything to take my mind off birthing children, the club's increasing problems, and the distance growing between my mate and me.

Over two days had passed since Danny Heller's deadline and no word. Silence. Castor hadn't picked up a damn thing over his airwaves, and we were like sitting fucking ducks.

My sister and I grew close since Abigail died. Carlie went back to TAFE to study a *Community Services* certificate, then got a job at Veritas House, assisting homeless and foster care youths. When I opened my shelter, we'd partnered with hers as sister organizations. Every six months, the club hosted a fundraiser for 'her shelter,' but raising money for both. We kept ours out of the spotlight for safety reasons, not drawing attention to it, for protection from other clubs. Leave the women out of it.

I hadn't seen Carlie since the birth and ought to get out of the shelter for an hour to visit her. "When can I visit my nephew?"

"Today!" Carlie sounded a little too eager. "Bring Alexa."

Fuck, she didn't know her real name. "Alexa's her middle

name. Call her Aaliyah." And I doubted she'd want to go anywhere with me.

"Whatever," Carlie replied. "Just bring her. You're sweet on her."

My grip on the phone tightened, and I glanced at Aaliyah, catching her watching me. Our eyes lingered for a moment too long. Yeah, I was fucking sweet on her, even when I didn't trust her. Our text sessions had been phenomenal. Flirty, fun banter that I needed in my life. Until they dropped off.

At the shelter and every night in the Underworld, I was surrounded by darkness and depression. No light existed in my world until she entered it. And I clung to hers like it was the lighthouse that guided me out of the treacherous and perilous sea.

Through the texts, our interaction at the shelter, I'd assess her and get to the bottom of whether she was guilty or not. I always did. Before I quit the force, I'd been promoted to detective and on track to make Senior Constable. Aaliyah couldn't hide her secrets from me. If I could just get our little thing back on track. I had an idea.

"Okay, I'll swing by in thirty minutes."

"See you, bro." Carlie hung up.

I tapped my phone on the side of my leg. Invite Aaliyah. If I was to get anything from her, I had to show her I was on her side. Manipulative? Fuck, yeah. Duty to my club warred with my heart, and I had to bury my longing down where I stored my dark rage. Where they'd be safe from the world.

But a part of me also craved to be with my mate. Out of all the men, I spent the least amount of time with her, running away from her rather than to her, and now it was my fucking turn. Break down the mystery surrounding her. Get to know the woman the gods called our mate. Find out if she betrayed us or if she was innocent and thrust into these circumstances like we'd been. So far, our texting had been light and fun, nothing serious. A face-to-face would change that.

I summoned the courage and walked up to her, maintaining a cautious distance. "Aaliyah, got a minute?"

Forehead tight, she excused herself to follow me into the kitchen, where I used the counter as a separator between us.

"What's up, Hellhound Dick? Got another club you want me to infiltrate?" Dry humor. I liked it. Feisty today, too.

I chuckled, and her back straightened, the mate bond going rigid from her paying attention to the sound. Need rippled down the link, and I almost closed my eyes and blocked it out. I needed to remain objective and not let it affect my judgment. That was when I did stupid shit.

Damn this woman. She had a way of reaching into my heart, past the fortress that surrounded it, grabbing it, and not letting go. Although I'd dulled the mate bond, the pull was still there, always present.

If I were in her shoes, held captive, my life under threat, I wouldn't be too cheerful either. But she was lucky enough to get out, unlike her Wolf buddies in our other dungeon. Plenty of people got emotional when the cops showed up, so I'd had enough experience to let her frustration wash off me.

"Your horns are getting too big for your head." I stretched over the counter to tap her head and immediately moved back before the curse symptoms set in.

She touched the spot where we connected. Touched. Lingered. Fuck, she felt it too. The ever-present link between us yearning so strong it was like a damn drug we couldn't give up.

I swallowed the lump of need in my throat. "Thought you could do with some time away from here." *Take it or leave it.* Though I hoped she'd *take it*.

This was my mate and I wanted to get to know her. Good

or bad. The offer showed her I trusted her and allowed me to see how she'd respond. Come and comply or try to escape. Either way, I'd be able to tell a lot about her character.

Her eyebrows shot up. She wasn't expecting the invitation. "Sure. Where?" She shook her palms in the air. "Not another trip to Carlie's shelter, though, I'm not up for that yet."

The last time we'd been, she'd lost a patient, and I had to cart the woman to the Underworld. Least favorite damn job. Depressing.

My throat caught as I swallowed the lump in it. "Carlie gave birth to a little boy and I'm going to visit her in the hospital."

"Congratulations, Uncle Hellhound." Seconds later, her eyebrows came down hard like she suspected a trick. "You're not worried I'll cry foul to the nurses, accuse you of kidnapping me for sex trafficking, and they apprehend you, call the cops and let me do a runner?"

I wanted to tell her that I'd then know if she was guilty if she attempted that, but I stuffed it down with another hard swallow. "You know your emergency procedures, Nurse A." She shuddered at the name. Woman liked it. Hopefully more so from my mouth than Slade's. "Do what you want."

Her face lit up with a raised eyebrow and smile combo that took my breath away. Fuck, this woman owned my heart, especially with that smile.

"I'd love to come with you." Her grin vanished too quickly, replaced with deep brows. "But ... is Slade on board with that? Wouldn't want to get you in trouble." She gave a shit about club rank and order? Or was she playing me? Time would tell which. "I'm waiting for our fifth date and dick pics."

She remembered our texts. Maybe she hadn't gone cold on me. I better make good on my promise. Except my dick was a mangled mess, thanks to being fucking Osiris' avatar. Scars put a lot of chicks off and they wouldn't go down on me. I had to work for the one fucking god who had his dick cut off, didn't I? I was lucky I hadn't lost mine in the accident. Instead, mine magically disappeared occasionally. Ached like Hell. My brothers found my cock, turned into a wooden phallus when separated from my body, and played tricks with it. Last time it came off, Alaric used it to shoot pool. Fuckwit!

My mind went back to my conversation with Aaliyah.

"Fuck, Slade." I scratched at the tip of my nose. "I can do what I want."

She folded her arms across her chest. "With a traitor?" Clever. Not easily tricked. Also gathering dirt on us like we did with her. We'd met our damn match with her.

"Jury's out on that." I threw my coat over my arms. "You coming or not?"

"Sure." Her smile returned, and my heart thumped in my chest.

I smiled, knowing she wouldn't be able to resist the chance to get out of here, and like hell I was leaving her behind. My mate came *with me*. "Come on, then." I handed her one of Carlie's jackets that she'd left at the shelter.

I'd sent two Jackals down to collect my van and return it. We jumped into it, and Aaliyah braved the front seat even though I'd warned her about the curse. The cramps would kick in any moment, and our magick and life would drain from us. Her, worse than me. The same had happened to Liz.

"Have you got a gift for Carlie?" She pulled on her seat belt.

"No." I laughed. "Why?"

"You don't show up to your sister's maternity suite empty handed." She gave me a cute eye roll. "Swing by the florist and then a baby shop."

"What?" Carlie already had everything organized. "Who's in charge here, anyway?

"Trust me." Aaliyah raised her palms again, drawing my attention to her nails, making the need to have her hands all over my body intensify.

"Fuck." I smiled and shook my head, ready to endure the ride and the oncoming pain so long as I got to see that smile and be by her side.

Two shops down, five hundred bucks spent, a dent in my wallet, and an aching head later, we were armed with a bouquet of yellow sunflowers and five bags of gifts. Fuck, babies didn't need so much crap. Towels, face cloths, onesies, tops, shorts, pacifiers, toys, and blankets. My nephew was going to be spoiled.

"Yellow means sunshine and happiness to the ancient Egyptians." Aaliyah lifted the bouquet in her arms to make her point. "I thought it appropriate for bringing a baby into the world."

"Yellow makes my wallet ache." Shopping bags I clutched rustled as I walked. Pussy shit with blue ribbons and balloons tied on the handles. Don't get me started on the cutsie wrapping paper and bows on the gifts within the bags. This was why I didn't do presents and left them to my ex.

"Oh, shut up. You're being such a grouch!" Aaliyah giggled, resting the boxed vase of flowers on her hip. "This is your nephew."

"He doesn't need all this shit." I raised both arms. "My kid got by with—" I reined it in before I finished. Fuck. Didn't want to go there. Hadn't in a long fucking time. Dead and buried, and that was where I liked to keep it.

Aaliyah stopped, pulling me to a halt. "You have a child?"

A topic I didn't like to talk about. "He's gone." I marched away, struggling to get air into my lungs and calm the onslaught of anger that hit me.

"Zethan?" Aaliyah ran to keep up with me. "Are you okay?"

"Fine." Nothing was stopping me. I charged through the front door to the patient ward, asked the receptionist where to go, and got into the elevator.

Heavy and thick silence wrapped around us as we rode the elevator to the second floor.

As it came to a stop and rocked, Aaliyah said, "I'm sorry about your son." Her sadness echoed down the bond, but I blocked it out, unable to feel it.

"Don't wanna talk about it." Being here made the ache in my chest deepen. This was where *he* was born and had died. I'd not let myself think about it in so long, but it all came crashing back to my mind.

I forced a smile when we hit Carlie's room and hugged my brother-in-law. "Hey, Pete. Congratulations, man."

I remember when Amanda had Dylan. Light of my fucking life. His smile and marble blue eyes. Cutest thing on the planet, my little boy. Took him everywhere. Made me smile every day. Pete had that same Daddy glow, and happiness and bitterness pricked my chest as I remembered my little man.

"Thanks, bro." Pete clapped my back. "Come in and meet Dylan."

Dylan. Out of all the fucking names to pick, they had to choose that one. My shaky legs carried me to Carlie's bed. Flower vases crowded all available space on the side table.

Carlie's smile dropped away. "We thought it would honor him, you know?"

Yes, it did. I appreciated it, but now I'd have to swallow this gut-wrenching pain every time I looked at my nephew, every time I heard son's name. Fuck. I rubbed my face.

"Zethan?" Aaliyah's hand swirled on my back, setting off another pain.

I moved to the other side of the bed just to be safe.

"Hey, Aaliyah." Carlie squeezed Dylan to her chest. "Good to see you."

"We brought you some gifts." Aaliyah placed the flowers on the food tray, and I set the five bags at Carlie's feet.

"Oh, you didn't have to, Aaliyah." My sister saw straight through it.

"No, this is from Zethan." Aaliyah flushed a cute pink.

Carlie barked out a laugh and handed the baby to Pete. "Pull the other one. My brother's idea of a gift is a bottle of scotch."

Aaliyah glanced at me and smiled.

I shrugged. It was true.

Carlie waved at me to give her a bag, and I did, letting her unwrap the blanket, an expensive patchwork thing with elephants, bears, and tigers. Boy stuff, Aaliyah told me. We'd used plain, blue wooly blankets with Dylan. Then again, Amanda chewed up most of my wages with heroin.

Carlie held the blanket up for her husband to see. "Oh, Aaliyah, this is beautiful. Thank you." She folded it up and held out her arms to hug Aaliyah. "And thank you for paying, brother." She hit me on the hip.

"Actually, I wanted the big ugly, girly blanket. Zethan picked this out." Aaliyah watched me, biting her lip, letting me take the credit when she was really behind it. But that was what partners did, didn't they?

"Look at you two," Carlie teased. "Buying baby gifts!" God, here she went. "Next time it might be you guys sitting here."

Fuck, it was my turn to go red. "No babies planned for the immediate future, sis." I kissed Carlie's cheek and whispered in her ear, "Shut the fuck up." She smiled sweetly and flicked me the bird as I pulled away.

No kids, not with Aaliyah. Maybe not with anyone. The

pain of losing Dylan was enough to bear. Then Liz on top of it. My sister Abigail starting off the horror show. No fucking thanks. Thinking about them choked me up.

"Excuse me," I croaked, making a run for the men's room, bursting through the door, and hunching over the sink, clutching the edges. I took a few deep breaths, then splashed cold water on my face, rubbing it over my skin.

Few things made me lose my cool. Battered women one of them. But nothing like my dead son or lost mate. They gutted me. I wanted to tear the hand dryer off the wall and smash it on the ground, but I slowly pinched my jaw and rubbed it. Coming here was a mistake. I should have visited Carlie when she returned home from the hospital.

I glanced at myself in the mirror. Ear-length blond hair, darker stubble and eyebrows, tattoos on my neck to cover some of my scars. Sleeves on my red flannel shirt rolled up, exposing some of my disfigurement. The extent I revealed to the world. A daily reminder of the darkest day of my life.

The day I'd got the call from Amanda telling me Dylan's heart had stopped, and I rushed to the hospital on my police bike. Not watching where I was going and speeding contributed to the accident. The car pulled out on me, sideswiped me, knocked me from my bike. Amanda almost lost her child and me on the same damn day.

My phone went off in my pocket and I gasped, wanting to fucking cry. I pulled it out and read the screen. Slade. Doing one of his hourly check-ins to see how Aaliyah was doing. Find out if she'd run for it or stayed. Last person I wanted to talk to right now. I rejected the call and slid my cell in my pocket.

Fuck, I'd left Aaliyah alone. I hurried out of the bathroom and jogged back to Carlie's suite, going over all the scenarios in my head if she'd left. Slade kicking my ass and disciplining me. Me and Alaric being sent out to find her. Breathing hard,

I busted in on the four of them, laughing and sharing the box of chocolates someone had brought Carlie.

What the fuck? Aaliyah hadn't tried to run. Hadn't even thought of it. Shit. Was she playing me, or did she genuinely want to stay? I couldn't work this woman out, and it bothered me. Most people I had figured out within a minute of listening to them speak. But Aaliyah remained a mystery shrouded in a beautiful package. A mystery I wanted to unravel.

"Oh my God." Aaliyah swept Dylan into her arms, and I had visions of her clutching our child like that too. Plush lips curled into a proud, adoring smile. Fingers stroking our child's fluffy hair. Bending down to kiss his head.

I had to shake my head to snap out of the vision. Imagining a future with her was out of the question right now. Not off the cards, though, but pointless fanning those dreams when I didn't know her allegiance. I was beginning to see it but wasn't entirely convinced and needed more evidence. Besides, we might never be able to be intimate with the curse. Why the fuck was I giving these thoughts air, anyway? I clenched my fist. No use staring at what could never be mine.

"Isn't he the most precious little thing?" Aaliyah twisted Dylan upright so I got a good look at my nephew.

Light hair and eyebrows like Carlie. A thick, stubby nose like his dad, Pete. Precious, all right. Just as precious as his namesake.

Aaliyah cuddled him for some minutes before looking up. "You want to hold him?" She tapped Dylan's nose. "Uncle Zethan wants to meet you!"

Fuck, it had been so long, and I didn't know whether I could do this without falling apart.

CHAPTER 18

Aaliyah

I MIGHT HAVE REPRESENTED the goddess of medicine, but I also sensed another deeper pain within Zethan that needed healing. Dark, emotional, tragic, and centering around the loss of his son. It weighed his soul down, and I felt it in the pit of my stomach, sticky like quicksand, dragging him lower into the muck. The pain of his loss was written all over his face as he bundled Dylan into his arms. By the way Zethan had mentioned the child's name, also the name of his son, the loss of his child had scarred him. We were both affected by the same burden.

A smile crept slowly over his lips, and he lovingly lifted his nephew to his face, touching nose to nose. I'd never seen anything so beautiful and haunted in my life, and my throat clogged. It reminded me of the time I held the soft, smooth, sweet skin of my baby in my arms before she was taken from me.

"Hi, there." I never expected to hear a biker coo over a baby. But he did.

Zethan stroked Dylan's cheek and kissed his forehead. Family meant everything to him. It had for me once, too. A long time ago. Maybe that's where we were similar. We'd both been broken by our clubs and lost a child. Except I'd chosen to walk away from that life, and he'd stuck with it.

When Danny had his little girl, he'd been on a two-day bender with his younger Wolf pals and didn't sober up until two days after Jess' birth. For Tom's birth, he made me go into the delivery room for him, too busy with club phone calls and sexting his mistress to welcome his son into the world. Prick.

The more I heard about my brother from my mother, Jerry, even the Jackals, it became more apparent that blood wasn't as thick as water. I was glad I'd walked away from the Wolves. God forbid I was stuck with Danny as my president. I'd rather die than support the shit he sanctioned.

Zethan glanced up at me with an even more gorgeous smile that softened his severe and brutal features. Far from the man I met in the hospital garage who beat the shit out of my mugger. Or the man who stayed outside of Carlie's shelter to deal with a husband who had hurt his wife. If I met him on the street, I'd be wary of those disturbed eyes and grave mouth, knowing the kind of punishment those hands delivered. Not in a million years would I believe the good work he did with the shelter.

Texting me, he was a completely different man, someone lighter, relieved, and unburdened. And something told me I did that to him. It made my heart cry out how much he needed me ... and how much I feared I might need him.

Holding his kin lifted some of the pain that wound around his heart, chaining it to his grief, giving him a moment of peace. The healer within me wanted to give him more.

When he excused himself to get some air, I wanted to make a break for it and leave the Jackals behind forever. Except something stopped me, and it wasn't the mate bond or the shared existence as avatars. No, the power within me recognized that only I could banish the darkness in his soul, and that required more than the application of magick. He needed me to complete his soul, his fated mate by his side, a healing that would grant his soul serenity. The significance of this revelation sent me diving into Carlie's candy, almost devouring it all instead of making a break for it.

Idiot. Crazy. Words my head shouted at me.

Hope. Renewal. Love. Whispers from my heart that I couldn't ignore either. Which was right? I didn't know yet, and I chose to stay to find out.

Zethan had shown me kindness and brought me here to give me respite from the Jackals. Trusted me enough to bring me here, knowing I could have made a run for it. Hell, he'd left me alone in the room, given me a prime opportunity. A test, maybe. But he looked pretty broken up about Carlie naming her son after his, the way he'd choked up and hurried out of the room like it was on fire. I wanted to go after him, check on him, but he seemed like he needed the space to breathe.

Both Zethan and Castor had shown me compassion when their president and road captain showed me nothing but hostility and doubt. Because of the argument Zethan and Castor made on my behalf and the deal I'd brokered with Slade, I was allowed out of my cell, and that was more than I could say for Jerry and the other two Wolves I didn't know. Freedom I wouldn't have been given if I wasn't the Jackals' mate or an avatar like them. For the moment, I took the wins, however small, where I could get them.

My mind wandered back to the words from my heart. *Whoa, Aaliyah! Long way off from the L-word, girl.* Screw that! I'd fight it until the last drop of blood in my body. My feelings were a confused jumble thanks to the mate bond and this damn curse. Deeper than that, I knew that Zethan and I were destined to be something. Friends. Lovers. Clubmates. Who knew? All I knew for certain was that I played a part in his recovery, and the selfless part of me stopped me from running out of this room.

Fuck, I was so messed up.

After allowing him a tender five minutes to whisper to his nephew, Carlie outstretched her arms. "Okay, gimme my kid back, you hog!"

Zethan chuckled as he carefully set the baby back with his mother. "No swearing in front of Dylan, remember?"

She laughed and thumped her brother in the hip. "Momma's gotta set a good example since Uncle Zethan will teach him all the bad things, won't he?"

This engaging interaction told me Carlie knew of Zethan's career, didn't care, and she teased him about it. It made me wonder if his sister knew about his other job in the Underworld. Part of me wished I had a close relationship with Danny. Reality punched the dreamer aside and asserted sense. Recent events told me my brother would only use my gifts to his advantage and abuse them.

The way Carlie tickled her son's cheek made me long for little Mia, the baby girl I'd adopted out seven years ago.

Jimmy died, leaving me pregnant and without a father for my baby. I didn't want that life for my child and ran away. If my father knew about her, he would have kept her, brainwashed her, trapping her in his world the same as he did to me. I enrolled myself in college, studied hard, gave birth to her, and gave her to a loving family. Gave her a better opportunity in life. My throat burned, and I clutched it. Depressed,

I snatched another candy, shoving it in my mouth, drawing Zethan's gaze to my lips.

Fuck. I didn't need him to look at me like he wanted to kiss me and swirl his tongue with the chocolate melting in my mouth.

Carlie removed her breast from her gown to feed her son, and Zethan coughed into his hand and turned away.

"You can't handle a boob?" Carlie mocked him, and I smiled. Seen plenty of boobs in the hospital. No big deal. Weird for a sibling, though. "Just look away, geez."

"All right, we're out of here!" Zethan came around the other side of the bed, grabbed my hand and dragged me out. "Bye, Carlie and Pete."

Intense heat circled in my palm, winding its way along my forearm up to my shoulder, binding me to him. His calloused hand fit perfectly in mine, and I squeezed it, wanting to lock it there forever. For this lost and broken man to bare his soul to me more. For the damn curse to be broken forever.

"Come back tomorrow!" Carlie shouted as we reached the door. "I miss my big brother."

"Bye, Carlie!" I managed to get in before Zethan pushed me out of the room and into the corridor.

Cramps started in my sides, and I pinched the left. Goddamn this curse gave me grief, setting off the pain in my gunshot wound. Immediately Zethan released me, stepping to the side a few feet, and my body cooled from his distance and the loss of his heat.

"I had a good time," I told him, massaging my obliques to release the ache. "Thank you for taking me. Trusting me."

"Any time." He jerked his head and started down the hall, leaving me to hurry to catch up with him. At six foot five, he was a big guy, muscled to the hilt, like a damn bouncer at a nightclub, with a hard face to match.

"Want to grab a drink?" I asked when we emerged from the hospital.

One, I wasn't ready to be confined to the shelter just yet. The drive, shopping with him, and the short visit enabled me an edge of freedom I wasn't willing to give up. No clouds overhead, shining sun, a perfect winter's day. I wanted to stretch my legs, maybe walk in the park across the road. And two, Zethan seemed like he needed to talk, or at least have some company before he dove back into shelter business.

"At eleven a.m. in the morning?" Zethan scoffed, glancing at me with a grin. "You're a bad influence, Aaliyah. I ought to warn Dylan about you."

I loved that this closed-off, guarded man had a sense of humor. His comment left me with a sense of longevity and the assumption that he expected me to stick around. I hadn't felt like texting him much the last two nights. Hadn't been in the mood. Especially when he ignored me all day, then wanted to text at night, in secret. Slept across the damn hall from me and could have come across to visit but didn't want anyone to know. I wasn't a fucking leper! I craved human interaction, not to be shunned and followed around the club.

"Bad influence is when I con you into a drinking challenge and drink you under the table." Smiling, I nudged him with my elbow.

He tucked his arms tight to his body. "You wouldn't win." Back to solemn Zethan. He switched so quickly.

"Oh, yeah? Put your money on it." I thrust out my hand to shake, but he jumped away as if I'd pulled a knife on him. I wiped my hand on my jeans, feeling dirty and disappointed because of the curse.

Zethan stopped beside his van and fished for his keys. "Remember, that's dangerous."

"Didn't die." I wiggled my fingers to show him. "Can't we touch for a little bit before the symptoms kick in?"

He scratched at his stubble, and I wanted to be the bristles on his chin just to have his calloused fingers on me. "It's best not to." He left me to open the driver's side door of his van.

"So, it's just sexting and dick pics then and the occasional no-touch excursion?" I yanked open my door and stood there for a moment.

Zethan leaned his massive forearm on the door. "This is serious shit, Aaliyah. I accidentally killed our last mate because of it."

I fiddled with my hands and stared at them. "I'm sorry you lost your mate."

He scratched at his pale eyebrow with his thumb. "The clubhouse got raided. The Winter's Devils tied us up together, and I couldn't break us apart."

"That's awful." I leaned in the van's doorway. "How come it didn't kill you?"

"Don't know." He glanced down the hospital's parking lot. "The symptoms weren't as bad for me, but they're getting worse with you." He hopped into the van, and I took that as my cue to do the same. Frustrated, I blew out a hard sigh and flung myself into the cabin.

Now I understood why he didn't want me to ride in the front of the van. Why he pushed me away at the *Willow & Reed* baby clothes shop and stood on the other side of his sister's bed. Before he'd told me about the curse between Isis and Osiris' avatar, I'd thought I smelled or that he was a vampire and wanted to drink my blood. I almost laughed with irony.

I clicked my seatbelt. "Is Castor working on that too?"

"Yes." Zethan cranked the engine to life as if to silence me.

Hope of freedom and my old life back bloomed in my chest as I stared out the window. "We won't always be fated mates, then?"

In the window's reflection, he leaned his arms on the

steering wheel. "You and the four of us, no. But you and I, that was always in the cards."

Really? Of all the people. No wonder I was drawn to him so strongly. I followed the damn sexy man around like a puppy trying to get his praise and attention. Fuck. Embarrassing. I rubbed my forehead feeling foolish. It was all just because of magick and avatars.

"No chance of getting out of that one, huh?" I made light of it.

"Do you want to?" Disappointment weaved into his words.

"I don't believe that someone's meant for me," I admitted, and that was the truth. "I believe in free will and choice."

Zethan forced his van to tear out of the parking lot. "There's no such thing when we work for gods, Aaliyah."

Good point. But I had an element of choice in this. I didn't have to like him or the Jackals. That decision rested on me, not the gods or the damn curse.

"With or without the curse, *you will* choose us." The assurance in his voice swirled my stomach with butterflies. I didn't know if he meant romantically or choosing their side, club-wise, god-wise. Either way, I'd have to find out.

CHAPTER 19

*S*lade

WHENEVER ALARIC STOOD to attention in front of my desk, I knew I was in for bad news. Trick to soften the blow or habit, I didn't know. Pissed me off either way. The club might be strict like the military with rules and all that shit, but I didn't make my men stand like a bunch of stiffs.

"Fuck. Sit down, would you?" I gestured at him to take a load off after a two-day scouting mission that left him looking worse for wear than when he returned all shot up. I hadn't wanted to let him go after being shot, but he insisted, wanting to get away from Aaliyah. I couldn't deny him that request. "You're making me tense when you stand like that."

I removed my cigarette paper and tobacco, needing a hit.

My fucking back ached after receiving another payment notice from Tony. We'd *never* been late before. Never. The club was down five hundred grand, and what we took from that fucker distributor that stole from us didn't cover our costs. We hadn't been able to offload the truck yet, either, and I was getting antsy to get my hands on the cold, hard cash. Our distributor hadn't coughed up a damn cent for the retrieved product we delivered to him. Something was wrong, and I sensed another ass fuck from him.

"Force of habit, sir." Alaric grinned, slumping into a seat, eyes sunken, his jaw unshaven.

"Fuck it with the sir shit." We both smiled. I kinda liked it, and so did he.

Reminded me of the times we had sexy role play games with Liz. She wasn't really into anything kinky, but occasionally, she unleashed her inner vixen and performed some role play on our birthdays or anniversaries. Nurse-doctor, naughty schoolgirl to teacher, or military superior and inferior. That kind of shit. Better than nothing. Alaric and I got into the General and Lieutenant act, and I'd fuck him so hard for disobedience. Liz enjoyed it when all her courtesans were with her in the bedroom. Only she never let us do anal or anything dirty like sex toys with her. Something I imagined Aaliyah might be into.

Fuck, why was I thinking about her?

Erase that thought.

"Hurry up and deliver your intel so you can get some rest." I lit up a smoke. Hell, I felt like smoking three cigarettes at once. Couldn't get enough nicotine to calm the constant adrenaline rush.

"Prez, I hate to be the bearer of bad news." Alaric rubbed his worn face, his voice as ragged as he looked.

"Fuck." I inhaled deeply, the smoke doing little to calm the growing wave of anger headed for me like a tsunami. "Hit me." The water turned red with the blood of my enemies.

"I saw a rider meet with Danny and his VP." Alaric got up and helped himself to my bottle of whiskey and brought back two tumblers.

Hell, yeah. I needed one too. My nerves were ablaze.

Motherfucking cockroach had emerged from hiding.

"That fucker should be dead." I drew down half my smoke because I needed the fire burning my lungs fueling my rage.

"The mysterious rider didn't wear a cut or anything to identify him or his bike." Brown liquid trickled into the tumblers as he poured, filling my senses with smoky whiskey. "I swooped in and caught part of the conversation."

The clench in my gut said no amount of nicotine or whiskey would ease the pain. My jackal prowled beneath the surface, calling for blood and vengeance. I couldn't get a word past the wedge in my throat. Me, fucking Slade Vincent lost for words. Never happened before. My club and all our hard work were on the brink of being wiped out by an unknown—but suspected—enemy, and I was losing grip on my business faster than I could hold onto it. I'd never been scared before in my life, but the tides were changing fast, and everything slipped from my grasp.

"I only caught the end of the discussion about the halted progress of Pharaoh." Alaric threw back his whole finger of drink.

Fuck, we had a mole. I suspected it but didn't dare think any of my brothers were rats. Now I knew otherwise. Time to smoke that bastard out and execute him. I gulped down my whiskey and hissed.

Alaric poured himself a double shot and tensed before speaking. "Danny was pleased and said they could move into the market."

"Fuck that!" I slammed my tumbler down and smashed it. Glass shards flew everywhere, and I didn't blink. Alaric reacted with a jolt, not because he was scared of me, but because fast movements triggered him. "Danny is kidding himself if he thinks he's cutting in on our market share. I'll kill him before he does. Who the fuck does that cunt think he is?" I jabbed my smoke out on my desk, burning a deep hole in the polished, grained wood, rich and dark. Just the way I liked it.

Alaric poured himself a triple shot this time and slid me the remainder of the bottle, which I swiped and guzzled. "One good thing to come out of this is that we know what he's up to now."

I swiped at the liquid dribbling down my chin. "Yeah, but we need solid proof. We can't justify a war on intel obtained by a spying hawk, can we?"

Fuck. I speared a hand through my hair, messing it up further. Blood boiled in my veins. Any minute that heat would transfer to an explosion. I needed a release. First, the identity of our mole now so I could burn that cunt to a crisp ... once I'd executed him in front of the club. There'd be nothing left for his family to bury. Nothing. Next, Danny Heller. I'd make his death slow and painful for muscling in on my territory.

Flames and electricity danced over my hand, and I jabbed a fiery finger at my road captain. "Scan every single Jackal and find me that mole." One more problem to solve. But I had several tricks to remedy this one. "Call an emergency church. I'm gonna smoke this prick out. Fuck sleep. We can do that when we die." And I didn't plan on failing my god and meeting my maker any time soon.

"Yes, President." Alaric slowly rose from his chair, his body stiff and exhausted. "I'll get everyone here within the hour."

My phone pulsed in my pocket at the exact moment I waved him away, excusing him. *Fuck. What next?* I hesitated before removing my cell. A name flashed on my screen, but I couldn't make out the letters.

"Reg calling," my phone spoke aloud for me. The Jackals' Pharaoh salesman. Not another fucking drama. After his major fuck-up, I was sick of all this bullshit and would fly off my handle.

"Yeah?" I answered, my voice like steel.

"Hey, Slade, got an update." Reg sounded nervous, and it set me on edge. I didn't like surprises and I sure as shit hated bad news. Things had gone too smoothly this last two years as the Jackals rose the rank of clubs. We'd probably done more bad than good, and the gods paid us back in bad karma.

I leaned my head in my hands and rubbed my forehead. "What the fuck is it now?"

"Fuck, Slade, I'm sorry," he paused for a beat, making the lava in my veins go nuclear. "The buyers won't take the merchandise because they've heard they can get it cheaper."

Was he fucking kidding? We went to all that effort to retrieve the damn Pharaoh and now it was worthless. Fucking Danny Heller did this. Soon he wouldn't be a problem. Instead of offloading four bullets into his back, I'd empty them in his brain, then cut off his damn head, burn his body, leaving no way for him to live. Unless his damn sister resurrected him. I'd not give her the chance. Danny would be dead and buried, and so would she if she tried to save him.

"Tell them we'll go elsewhere then and they won't get another drop of it!" I hung up and tossed my phone aside.

I went to my alcohol cart and cracked open another whisky, sloshing half of it down, trying to calm the tension and rage within me. It worked for a little bit. Where the fuck was my VP when I needed to discuss this shit with him? I checked throughout the clubhouse, not finding him, realizing he was probably at the shelter.

I gave him a call. "Where are ya'?" I asked when he answered. "I want to catch up before I call an emergency church. I think we've got a goddamn rat."

"Out with Aaliyah."

He what? Taking her out was dangerous when she could try to escape or run to the cops.

"Why?" Smoke and pressure built within, and I had to hold it back. My grip crushed the phone and it creaked, bordering on breaking. "Where?"

"Took her to see my nephew." Short. Snappy. Moody again. Goddamn broody asshole.

"Carlie gave birth?" First I heard about this. "You didn't tell me, asshole." We usually shared everything. Until Aaliyah came along.

"Been busy." He was always busy.

Prick better be busy drilling Aaliyah for information, or I'd do it myself. I tired of doing it their way. Slow as fuck. Pain and torture got answers and fast, but damn Set wouldn't let me touch her, and it was probably for the best I let Castor and Zethan handle it. Temper might get the better of me, and I could hurt her. Doing that would see me punished by the gods, and not just by Set. I'd always been a slave to my emotions. Captive to my anger and bloodlust. But when I came onboard as Set's mortal avatar, it scaled up a thousand-fold.

My grip on the phone relaxed thinking about her. "Get your ass back here for church in an hour."

"Can you dial me in?" Zethan dug his heels in, using his clout as VP to get out of his duty. Fuck that.

I didn't have to put up with this shit from my VP. "What the hell are you doing that you can't make it to church?"

"Just do it, Slade." Zethan didn't get pissy at me unless something went wrong. Another woman must have keeled it at the shelter. I was in no mood for consoling my best friend when I had someone to catch and kill. I needed him here with the club, not drowning his sorrows. The club came first.

"What's up your ass?" I asked. "*She* pissing you off? Someone in the shelter not make it?" I softened the last question. For the goddamn avatar of death, he didn't appreciate the mention of it when it came to his shelter.

"They called him Dylan." Those four words shut me the hell up.

Fuck. His son's name. Explained his grumpy ass. I didn't want to rub salt into that wound, but I also didn't want to show favor to any of my members. Church was essential, no excuses. Rank didn't mean they got out of punishment.

"You're on cleaning duty all this week for skipping church," I barked. "Next time, get your ass down here."

"Fine." I pictured Zethan gritting his teeth and seething at me, the way he often got with me. History between our gods flared up tension between us.

Liz used to have a way of soothing us when situations got tense. We needed that again. Pity about this Heller woman. She could have been good for us. I hoped she worked her soothing charms on Zethan and brought him back to the club levelheaded.

Temperature in my body scaled down at the thought of my little nurse. Truth was, I missed our playful banter and tense, flirty, goading exchanges. Before everything came crashing down for us, the woman got me hot, and I know I did the same to her. Set burned brighter and hotter than the fucking sun, and so did I. Things had cooled between Aaliyah and me since all the shit went down. Loneliness settled in hard, making me miss Liz and want to talk to Aaliyah to fill that void. Call it a moment of weakness, but I damn well wanted to know how she was.

"Put her on," I said. "I wanna talk to her."

"Why?"

"Just put her on."

"Good luck with that." The phone rustled as my VP passed it over to her. "He wants to talk to you."

CHAPTER 20

Aliyah

CHOOSE THEM. *All of them.* Zethan's statement sat heavy in my mind as I settled into a seat at a raised wooden table at the *King's Hotel*. Cocky much? Slade, I figured for overconfident, but not Zethan. Such finality to his claim shook me to the core.

Why me? Avatar or not, curse or not, he didn't know me. Didn't know whether we'd get along or if we'd drive each other crazy. Yet he was just as adamant as Slade that we'd end up together. I obeyed my heart, not the tricks played on me by the mate bond and curse. Thankfully, the sway of the mate bond had subsided since the men turned it down, allowing me time to process this mess on my terms.

Zethan ordered us drinks at the bar. Music chimed and lights flashed from the slot machines. A fake wood fire burned behind me, warming my back. A man watching rugby on the overhead screens cheered and sloshed his drink on the dark blue carpet. The burgundy walls made Zethan's cut look darker, his golden hair brighter, and his cheery red flannel blend into the background.

Studying him, I noticed how different he was from Castor. Laid back dress sense in jeans and crimson plaid, a plaited leather bracelet, and a Jackal ring on his right forefinger. Tattoos covered some of the exposed skin on his neck and arms, a hint of scars evident. I wanted to touch them and find out their meaning. Wild blond hair to his ears, thick stubble bordering on a beard, and haunted green eyes. Smelled like oil and metal. Pure man. Guarded, but in a different way than Castor. Where Thoth's avatar was all secrets, Zethan guarded his heart because he'd been hurt. Beyond that, I got the impression he wasn't comfortable in his own skin, and I didn't get it when he was so rugged, strong, and brutal.

Zethan returned with a beer in one hand and a lemon, lime, and bitters in the other. I wasn't allowed to have alcohol after the painkillers, so I settled for a standard drink. He handed me my drink, sat opposite me, and swallowed some of his beer. God, why was I jealous that I wasn't the cold, malty liquid flowing down his throat?

He released a hiss after downing the cold brew and set his frothy glass on our table. "That's twice I've left you, and you haven't escaped."

"Aren't you lucky?" I batted my eyelashes at him and gave him sexy eyes over the rim of my glass.

Fuck, Aaliyah. This was a losing battle. Maybe he was right, and I'd be theirs. In a way, he felt like home and comfort, warmth and protection, and I longed for that after two weeks away from my apartment. Wanted him to be close enough to run the side of his hands along the outside of my arms. I needed to be touched. His hands all over me, especially in my hair. Damn Castor had left me high and dry after bathing me. Then that night in the cell. *Fucking hell.* The old hormones had settled down a bit, which was one positive. Maybe Castor had been wrong about my heat.

Being with the Jackals quickly drove me to madness. Goddess, why was I longing for this disturbed guy? We weren't right for each other, yet I couldn't help but be drawn to him, and my resistance only made it worse.

"Testing me?" I leaned back in my chair and sipped at my drink. Wrapped my lips around that straw and sucked. Hard, flirty, and seductive.

Damn mate bond!

His gaze went there. Zeroed in on my mouth like prey viewed a target. "You got me, Nurse A." He held up two palms and smiled the most adorable, sunny smile for such a dark, serious guy. "Arrest me. I'm guilty."

I played with my straw, lifting it up and down, twirling it to mix the red of the bitters into my drink. "So, Slade put you up to it?"

Why should I be surprised? The Jackals' president thought me a threat. A threat he used for information. Sorry to disappoint, but I didn't have any.

Zethan's next smile tried to hide it, make it out to just be a joke, but I'd heard every excuse, every stutter, seen every blink and twitch when a patient concealed the truth about how they hurt themselves. Recognized a bluff when I saw it. Made sense. If I were in Slade's position, I would have questioned me too, sidled up to me and made friends. Still hurt, like a knife slicing deep in my heart. All this time, I'd believed Zethan showed me compassion and kindness as he did with the women at the shelter. But I was collateral to him.

"Played the whole time." I pushed aside my drink, not thirsty. Certainly not for anything he bought me. I rubbed at my face, loneliness sinking its teeth back into me. "I thought the phone was because you were being kind. Fuck. For a second there, you had me fooled."

"Come on, Aaliyah, cut me some slack." He leaned forward in his chair, and the ache in my side returned. "I've got my orders and you have yours."

"I don't have any orders besides those given by my goddess." It came out as a harsh hiss that distracted the football viewers from their match, earning me a glare. "And she sure as shit didn't send me here." The honesty in my words shot down the mate bond like a bullet fired from a gun.

"Sure about that?" Zethan cocked a sexy eyebrow. Goddammit. "Your goddess wants out of this curse as much as the other gods." He paused as if the truth in my statement hit him through our link, and he slackened his tense posture.

"If she did, she never said anything about it." I wanted to say more, but a waitress delivered a steaming bowl of thick fries with ketchup and aioli sauce. Fuck, it was hard to stay mad at a man who knew the way to my heart. I snatched a fry, dipped it, and crunched on it. Still pissed. Still upset.

Zethan selected a fry too. No condiments for him, though. Maybe he feared he'd get contaminated from me if he did. "The phone was from me. *Just me.* I wanted to get to know my mate. Good or bad."

Mate. The word made my blood heat up by a degree. Made my chest go all fuzzy and my heart did a little happy pump. This time it wasn't caused by the mate bond, and that worried me. Was this how it would be between us, even once Castor broke the curse? The ever-burning flame between us?

On the other hand, my mind had hit her limit. "I don't have anything to hide, Zethan." I rubbed my face again. "I'm tired of this."

"Your brother cost our club a lot of dough." He jabbed his next fry in the air. "One million in stolen shipments."

"What?" I stopped chewing. Serious money. Danny had

lowered himself to stealing on top of ambushing. He was asking for a war. Chilled all of a sudden, I pulled my sweater tighter to my body. "My father would never have stolen from another club. He was an honorable man."

"So are we ... to an extent." Zethan bit into a fry. "We were on good terms with your father before his death."

That was the impression I had, too. What changed? Only one variable. Dad's death and Danny's succession. Sickened to the stomach, I sipped my drink.

"We can't work out if you sent Danny after us." Detective Zethan on the case.

I snapped a fry. "I don't know anything about your damn business and don't care to. I left that life behind a long time ago and don't want back into it. You and Alaric dragged me back into it!"

"Were you spying and listening in?"

"Fuck! An interrogation? Really? No, Officer *Don't-know-your-last-name.*"

"Force of habit." He smiled and leaned back. "And it's Officer Stone."

Zethan Stone. Goddess, even his name was hard and sexy like him.

I threw a chip at him. "What else do you want to know, *Officer Stone*? That I keep a spare set of clothes and underwear in my trunk? I have a crowbar underneath my spare tire to break into the clubhouse. Sex toys in my glove compartment beside my gun, license, and registration?"

"You keep sex toys in your glove compartment?"

"Hypothetically."

"What for? Beat a traffic cop over the head with a dildo to escape a ticket?"

I threw another French fry at him, and he caught it and ate it. Okay, he wasn't worried about contamination. "Who would have guessed you're funny when you're such a grumpy ass."

That one might have been aimed as a compliment. I'd enjoyed our exchange of messages and didn't want it to stop. At first, texting had broken up my boredom, then it grew to something more, and I started to like him. But now it felt like a trap, and my arms felt thick and sticky.

But now it felt like a trap, and my arms felt thick and sticky.

I tapped the sides of my glass, staring at him. "Do you think I'm guilty?"

"I'm not convinced either way yet," he replied. "But the series of events certainly looks bad."

I sighed and slumped in my chair. "VP has to uphold club law and all." I couldn't meet his eyes for a moment. "I never wanted any of this. The mate bond, the beating, delivery to the shelter, the kidnapping and shooting." My voice trembled, and I felt the tug on the mate bond, him resisting the urge to reach out and set his hand over mine despite the danger to us both. "I just want my life back. But as a servant to a goddess, I don't have a say any more than you do, and it pisses me off that I have no control."

He stretched across the table, lifting my chin with a finger. "Aaliyah, regardless of whether you're innocent, that life doesn't exist for you anymore." Flames set alight across my body at the nerve of him to say that.

"How long will you keep me?" I ground out.

"So long as your brother's alive, you're in danger. Whether he's alive or dead, I *won't let* my mate go." The possessive edge in his voice made the fire in my chest burn hotter and brighter, and goddammit it, I'd go to Hell for wanting to encourage it. I already had a one-way trip from fucking Slade.

"Even if I'm a traitor?"

"There are ways to be redeemed."

I didn't know what he meant by that, whether he intended for me to prospect with them or slowly build trust to have a functioning relationship. Jury was out on whether I wanted that. All I knew was that the mate bond connected us, and I was bound to them whether I liked it or not. And if I were being honest, some deep part of me liked the fact we were bound together.

Tiring of this conversation, I switched gears, intent on finding out more about this guarded and closed man hiding a deep pain. If he was going to grill me for information, then I'd return the same. I wanted to get to the bottom of the darkness, brutality, and rage that I'd witnessed when he collected me and when he defended Carlie's shelter from the intruding husband.

I broke a fry in half and played with it. "What happened to Dylan?"

Zethan's fingers curled into a tight fist that made his skin whiten, highlighting the fair scars on his wrist. He took a ragged breath before speaking. "He was born prematurely, underweight, and with a heart defect."

I'd seen a lot of babies suffering from congenital malformations at the hospital, not as many as a neonatal nurse had. The parent's agony, fear and suffering as they cried and watched their beautiful little babies in incubators. Many babies struggled to hold on as their hearts beat irregularly and blood couldn't flow through the hole.

Zethan withdrew along the mate bond further than he had before, his pain crashing into him like hammered blows. Feeling the same in my chest, I stretched out to reach him, making him retreat again and shield his emotions. Closed off like a brick wall. Not impenetrable but wanting space.

"I'm so sorry, Zethan." Nothing I could say or do would ease his pain. But I gave him the opportunity to talk about it if he wanted to. Years of experience told me that many people felt better when they offloaded. Better than medicine sometimes.

"My ex was taking heroin behind my back." He gritted his teeth.

Fuck. Heroin and other opioid usage during pregnancy caused Ventricle Septal Defects, which I suspected his son succumbed to.

"He died three years ago." His words had me rooted to the spot. "I nearly killed the bitch when I found out what she'd done to our son. What she'd done to me. Done to her fucking self."

Scorching anger vaporized the mate bond.

"Fuck, Zethan. That's vicious." I rubbed my forehead.

His eyes glistened when he looked at me. "Do you know how many babies I have to carry to the Underworld? How many times I have to relive that?"

Oh, goddess. Heart fucking breaking. Now I understood the tragic darkness shrouding his soul. Caged so long that it couldn't be contained anymore, and it unleashed in a heat of wrath.

Ignoring the danger to myself or him, I reached over the table, clasping his hand tightly. Lost and broken, I hoped to give him the peace he yearned for but refused to accept. "It wasn't your fault."

He yanked away from me, and I almost cried at the torment shredding him to pieces. "Yes, it was. I worked too much. Long hours on the road with the club. Left her alone while I was on rides or at the clubhouse. It was too late when I discovered her secret. She was already six months pregnant."

Fuck, no wonder he blamed himself and carried so much pain.

I'd always been the type of nurse to sit with patients,

guiding them through their grief and heartache with soothing words and a hand of consolation. Rather than move onto the next patient, earn the next dollar for the hospital, like a goddamn takeout restaurant. Corporate nursing wasn't who I was. When I'd left the Wolves to study my degree, I wanted everything that came with it. Good, bad, and ugly, even if it meant seeing people at their worst and weakest. Nursing—the word—meant taking care of the sick, and I didn't just deliver them medications and treatment as ordered by the doctor. Comfort to ease their pain and suffering was my job too, and to hell with what my bosses or the corporation said.

My grief swelled beneath the surface, and suddenly I felt the need for a fucking confession to get my heartache and guilt off my chest. It probably wasn't the right time and definitely the wrong thing to say, but I wanted him to know of the burden I carried. The same pain, just different. Maybe it would ease his mind. Let him know he wasn't alone and didn't have to carry the weight by himself.

I stroked my hands absently. "I had a child once."

Zethan's gaze snapped up to me. "Did you lose it too?"

"In a way." My voice came out soft and trailing away. "I gave her away." I rubbed at my arms and cradled my aching chest. "I lost my baby daddy to an accident and couldn't look after her. Couldn't look into her eyes, his eyes … knowing that I'd killed him."

"You said it was an accident." Zethan was engrossed in my tale, his pain ebbing but still throbbing beneath his skin.

At four months pregnant, Jimmy and I had gone for a long ride, had a picnic, then driven back at sunset and stopped off for a drink. While I selected a song to dance to on the jukebox, some asshole cornered me and harassed me. Jimmy had jumped in to teach him not to grab a woman's ass. He'd scurried away, then returned with his buddies, who jumped Jimmy and fucking hit him in the back of his head. My boyfriend went down, his head hitting the table, injuring his brain.

Months later, I'd given birth to Mia. At just eighteen years of age, studying for my degree with no help from my family, I'd given her up for adoption. She'd reminded me of my old life, and I'd let all of it go to move on. Hated myself every day for what I'd done. More so now that I'd heard Zethan's tragedy.

My fingers clawed my upper arms. "Jimmy would still be alive if I hadn't joined the Wolves. And I wouldn't have abandoned my baby." I crushed my arms across my chest and cut off my air.

Zethan slid to his knees before me, taking my hand, risking the effects of the curse. My body shook with sobs and his burned with darkness. And what did I do? I fucking sang. Belted out David Bowie's *Magic Dance* from the *Labyrinth* movie. The dark man before me blinked and squeezed me tighter.

Dad and I used to watch the movie when I was a kid, and he bought me the soundtrack for Christmas. The song comforted me when I lost Mia, and I sang it over and over to remember her.

Zethan drew me in for a surprisingly soft and deep kiss that drowned out my terrible singing. His lips worked over mine, guarded and wary, but wanting to give me more. Give me everything but holding back. I linked my arms around his neck, drawing him closer, not caring that my stomach began to ache. Right then, I needed him and he needed me, and I wasn't letting go. Otherwise, I'd drown under the weight of my regret. When his tongue parted my lips to explore my mouth, I discovered a tongue bar rolling over my burning flesh, making the kiss that more enjoyable. I hadn't noticed it all this time.

A phone rang, and Zethan pushed off me, jamming his hands in his pocket and removing his phone. "Fuck, it's Slade."

Slade. Ruining a beautiful and soothing moment. One of the men burned into my heart, leaving it craving him despite his suspicion of me and misgivings. When Zethan answered the phone, Slade's loneliness cut the mate bond like a sword, pricking my chest. I didn't hear a word of their conversation, just Slade's resounding longing singing to me, calling me like a siren's song.

Zethan nudged me and held out the phone. "He wants to talk to you."

"What?" Slade was the last person I wanted to talk to when I felt raw and bruised. I groaned, promising that if he got on my case about some club bullshit I had nothing to do with, I'd shred him with my words.

CHAPTER 21

Slade

AALIYAH GROANED, and I imagined her snatching the phone from my VP, scowling at him, looking hot AF all riled up. She sniffed and paused before she spoke. "Aaliyah left the building and did a runner." Her sass fired my chest with a sweet warmth, like a campfire. As much as I wanted to be angry with her and the damn mate bond, hell, even she worked her magick to soften me. "Please leave a message. Beep."

I croaked out a laugh. "Did you just beep me?" First time for everything.

"Leave a message. Beep," she replied, sounding a bit broken, and my jackal responded, desperate to nudge her and put his chin on her shoulder.

"Have it your way, sasshole," I gave it back to her, using the joke to soothe her discomfort. "Nurse A, it's me. The dark, sexy one." She laughed at that, but I kept up her game.

"My gun hasn't been the same without you. It wants another rematch."

Fuck. The words came out before I could catch them. Flirting with her was the last thing I should be doing, but it came naturally between us, and I'd longed for it back. Damn woman hooked her claws into me even though I stayed away. I wanted her in my bed to punish her in other ways.

"Smartass," she shot at me. "Your gun won't get another rematch. Ever."

I leaned back in my chair, falling back into our pattern of working each other up and enjoying it. "Forever's a long time, Nurse A." Nostalgic, I set my gun on my desk, skimming my finger over the butt, remembering where it had been. Touching it made me feel closer to her even though we were miles apart and far from forgiveness or trust. "What are you up to?"

"Drinking with Zethan." Her voice lost some of its sass. "Don't worry your dark, sexy ass. Your VP isn't skipping church for fun. He's getting dirt on me."

"Really?" I played cool, not biting, not giving her any ammo.

"You'll be pleased to know that I had two opportunities to run and didn't."

"You're fiery today, Nurse A. Tense. Hostile. I think you need a massage," I teased, unable to help myself when I was with her. "Swing by when you get back to the club, and I'll arrange it." Fuck, I couldn't believe I made that invitation. I had to shut down this conversation before it got out of hand. Set's powers were uncontrollable, and so was my fucking mouth.

"Don't flirt with me, Mr. Vincent." Her voice adopted a bored tone, and I'd wake her up if she was with me, setting her over my lap, slapping her ass until she lost that spunk. "Not interested in your hot and cold game."

Shot down. Ouch. But I didn't give up. Once I found out which side she was on—hopefully my side—I'd have her again, mark my words.

Zethan chuckled in the background. Asshole.

"Tell my VP to go fuck himself," I growled.

"He already is. We're sexting at night, bish." Double ouch. They were fucking sexting. Since when? I'd allow it because I trusted my VP to gather information.

Still, I didn't like being left out. "I need this number to get in on the action."

"Sure." Aaliyah paused. "The number's 1-800-G-O-F-U-K-U-R-S-E-L-F." Vixen hung up on me, depriving me of a witty comeback, and the mate bond howled with the misery of my jackal.

The fire was still there between us. It roared in the mate bond, but I'd not fall for it. Not until I knew her real motivations. Which side she was on. Team Wolves equaled death.

Straight away, I said, "Phone, text Zethan." The screen flickered with a blue light signaling it was ready. "Gimme her damn number, asshole."

I tapped my fingers on the desk, waiting for the reply and it came back a few minutes later.

"Phone save number under Nurse A."

"Completed," the phone told me.

"Phone, send Nurse A a message." The phone flickered and a text message box opened. "Shame you didn't want a massage. I have big hands and a strong grip." I hit the send button.

The door to my office flung open, and Alaric shoved his head in. "Everyone's gathered except Zethan."

"He's not coming," I grunted as I got to my feet. "Got personal business." He owed me for that lie. I wasn't one to give a pass for missing church.

"Okay." Alaric didn't even question it, and I liked that about him when I got debated by Castor and Zethan.

Everyone in the meeting room went silent as I entered, nodding at me or muttering, "President."

I took my position at the head of the table. "Thanks for coming on short notice. I won't take up much of your time."

Everyone grunted, a few lighting up cigarettes, some slamming down a drink, the rest listening intently.

"Zethan can't make it," I announced. "He's out on club business."

Alaric shot me a look for changing my story, but I ignored it.

Castor sat quietly, leaning back in his chair, studying everyone.

I rubbed my palms together. "Got some good news, fellas."

Every back in the room straightened, eyes lightening.

I hated being a dog and lying to the men in my club. But this was the only way to unearth the traitorous rat. "We sold all the Pharaoh we recovered from the Hellfire MC's distributor and have recouped our costs." Pretending to be pleased, I pressed my palms together.

Every Jackal cheered, some raising a fist, some less enthusiastic than others, and I took note. Benny, Jaxx, and Brix. Three men now on my radar.

Alaric's magical eye zoomed in and out, scanning the members, one by one. He'd have an answer for me, hopefully by the end of the meeting.

"We're able to pay off our debt with our manufacturer and get back into production." I moved to the lectern, holding the edges to still my warring mind.

Howls and whistles echoed through the room, and I waited for it to still before finishing.

"We're fucking back, boys!" I threw up a fake fist. "No one

sabotages the Jackals!" My fist fell to my side, still clenched, ready to lay into the prick within these walls who betrayed us. I eyed every one of them.

Taking a deep breath, I prepared to deliver the final lie to my crew, hoping the snitch would take it back to Danny Heller. This time, we'd be ready and waiting for him, and we wouldn't fail. There'd be no way our rival would come back from the dead. I'd make fucking sure of that.

"Let's prepare for a run for the end of this month to get us back into business as usual." My throat dried, and my voice came out a harsh croak.

"Fuck, yeah!" Tank shouted and raised his beer.

"Jackals forever!" Rusty slammed his fists over and over on the table like war drums that beat in time with my heart.

"Church dismissed." I picked up my gavel and slammed it on the lectern. The noise sounded hollow to my ears, just like my lie, and I shook my head.

I studied each man as he departed, my body primed for any nervous tic or behavior. Those same three men caught my eye. Benny, Jaxx, and Brix. The first and last had no obvious motive for revenge on me or the club, although Jaxx had plenty. His brother Mac had died of an overdose at the Winter's Devils' stripper bar and he had plenty of reason to hate me.

Fuck. Listen to me. I rubbed at my tight jaw. This shit had cast doubt over every single brother, and I hated that I distrusted them. They were family to me. Men I'd rode with since I was a boy. Some I'd known my whole life, others who joined me along the way. Every one of them had pledged their allegiance. Even that meant nothing to them. My chest went rigid from the betrayal. Whoever knew of our plans betrayed them to the Wolves, and if that someone was a Jackal, he didn't deserve to wear our cut. When I found who that someone was, I'd burn his cut then burn him to the ground too.

Maybe I'd had my sights on the wrong person all along. That Heller woman might be innocent after all, and if she was, I owed her an apology. And I didn't apologize. The idea twisted me up inside.

Then what? Where to from there? We'd have to sort out the mate bond and our feelings. A sticky situation. Not something so easy to come back from, even if we wanted to. Flirting and teasing was all good and well, but no amount of gifts or groveling would get me back in her good graces or convince her to become mine. I might have really fucked up here and lost my mate. Again. That shit stung and burned a black trail down the bond.

My jackal howled with regret, and I slammed my eyes shut, fighting the pain tearing me up. Once again, I'd let my emotions get the better of me.

"Prez?" A voice called me back. Castor. "You okay?"

He and Alaric remained in their seats.

I almost spilled my guts about the mole, but I decided to keep my trap shut. Anyone could be a traitor, avatar included, and I kicked myself for telling Zethan. Should have kept it just between Alaric and me. My road captain wouldn't speak a word of it … unless he was the double agent. I doubted it. Liz would have sensed that darkness in his heart. Castor, too. But I couldn't be careless until the mole's identity was revealed.

"Fine." I rubbed at my aching temples. "Headache."

"I'll get you some aspirin." Castor got out of his seat, clapped me on the shoulder, and I nodded.

When he left the room, closing the door after him, I turned to Alaric. "What'd you get?"

Alaric covered his upper lip with his forefinger and thumb. "Three men hiding something."

Three men. Exactly what I'd picked up too. The god of War and Destruction didn't miss much and neither did I. "Benny, Jaxx, and Brix?"

My road captain nodded. "Their heart rates increased, muscles contracted, and they were sweating. I couldn't get more of a read because I didn't have enough time." Didn't matter. That was plenty and confirmed my suspicions.

"Keep on them." I jabbed a finger at him. "Don't stop until you get something. And keep this between us for now."

"Yes, President." Alaric got out of his chair, pushed it in, neat and tidy, then departed.

I stabbed a hand through my hair. The Jackals never had a problem until I took over. Until we expanded our territory and business ventures. Gaining more power naturally acquired more enemies. I just never thought I'd live to see the day where one of our enemies would come from within.

A car rolled into the driveway, crunching on gravel, and I crossed to the window. Zethan's van. Aaliyah and my VP climbed out and came inside. She looked smoking in her skin-tight jeans, knee-high boots, and sweater. Ebony hair flowed down to the curve in her lower back. Bright blue eyes caught the winter sunlight. Lips as rosy as I bet her nipples were. My dick hardened at the need to touch and suck them.

I scrubbed my jaw, resisting the urge to talk to her, flirt up a damn storm, light up the old fire between us. Fuck this mate bond and the effect on me. Sometimes I wished to be free of it and not have it drag me down. It was incredible knowing the feelings of the other person and having no secrets between us. But then there were times where I didn't understand a woman when she said one thing and meant another. Aaliyah, a prime example, refusing to go on a date with me, then agreeing. I knew why now. To gain information from me. Sly little thing. She proved the mate bond could be tricked, and lived up to the cunning of her goddess, the true mistress of magick.

Isis had pulled the wool over Set's eyes a few times, but I wouldn't be so blind next time. I had her in my sights and wouldn't let go. I'd find the traitor in my club, and if it was her, I'd afford her the same execution intended for a Jackal. Fuck what Set said. If it saved my club, that was all I cared about.

My cell throbbed in my pocket, and I checked my phone, instructing it, "Read message, phone."

"Reply from Nurse A," the phone said. My dick went rock-hard in anticipation of her feisty reply, hoping she took me up on my offer for a massage with my hard grip and big hands. I could do with one too, so long as she didn't pull a knife on me. "Must make wanking that much better."

I barked out a laugh and pocketed my phone, smiling. Still playing hard to get. This woman would never let me conquer and own her, which drove me insane, as I belonged to the god of War. She might be a traitor and my captive, but generals always took spoils of war. Maybe I'd take mine.

CHAPTER 22

Aaliyah

I KEPT GLANCING AT IT, biting my nail, wondering whether to use it. Why not? Zethan had given me call and text access for a reason. I picked up my gold phone, tapping it against my palm. Zethan tested me by taking me to the hospital to see if I'd run, and this could be another trap. The Jackals monitoring my phone activity to test my loyalty.

Activating the screen, I opened the call function. My fingers hovered over the numbers. Mom would be worried sick, and I had to warn her of Danny's actions, encourage her to go into hiding. Barb, my boss and best friend, would be out of her mind and probably already told the police I was missing. I owed them both a call to explain everything and hold onto a semblance of my life. Maybe Barb could put me on stress leave or vacation until this shit blew over, to save my ass and my job. The Jackals might be paying for my apartment lease and car, but that didn't guarantee me a job once this was all over.

Dad taught me early in my pseudo-membership of the Wolves to memorize numbers, just in case.

"You never know when you might get into trouble, baby girl," he'd said to me. *"No phone to rely on. No address book to look up."* Locked up and arrested by the cops was familiar to him for failure to obey road rules or disorderly conduct.

Thinking about calling Barb made me nervous. How would I explain my two-week absence from work? Excuses pricked my mind. Stress leave. Depression. Another death in the family. None of them would explain why I hadn't picked up the phone and called her, when I was the most responsible person she knew. I needed something to cover me and provide leeway to stay away longer. Who knew how long the Jackals intended to keep me? My past with my father's club remained sealed in a vault, just like my secret identity as an avatar. I worried what Barb might think, how she might view me, once I confessed the truth. MC connections scared many people, and I didn't want to chase away my best friend. Truth was best after all the shit that went down with the Jackals. Lies just got me into trouble. Fuck. I rubbed my eyes, a nervous feeling pushing against my bladder. First, I needed to go to the bathroom.

I met Brix in the hall, guarding my room, throwing out an arm when I tried to pass. "Where are you going?" Dude took his job a little too seriously. Asked me questions about every little thing. Didn't respect personal space, either.

"To the bathroom." I bypassed him, and he followed after me. When I went to close the door, his hand thumped on the exterior. "Can't a girl get some privacy?" I glared at Brix, getting more pissed off by the second.

Everywhere I went, I had a shadow, Alaric always on my tail. Since our little spat down in the cell, he'd kept his distance, watching from afar, his eyes never far from my location, burning holes into my back.

"President's orders to watch you at all times." Brix made a point to touch his gun to intimidate me. *Dick.*

Good thing I didn't do intimidation. Egotistical doctors at North Shore Hospital often threw their weight around, trying to overwhelm me with their medical specialty knowledge. Wankers enjoyed putting me down and embarrassing me in front of patients or interns. They didn't know I had the goddess of Medicine in my freaking head, and I could always put them in their damn place.

I crossed my arms over my chest, ready to have it out with this cockhead, Brix. "Even when I pee?"

"Yep." Okay, he asked for it.

I yanked down my jeans, leaving my underwear in place, making him sweat, his eyes dart down, then up my body. "Slade will kill you for looking at me." I smiled and dropped my panties. "And I'll tell him you did."

"Bitch." Brix cleared out, giving me privacy.

I'd give him bitch. Fuck him. Every person had basic human rights to freedom, personal choice, and privacy, the last one critical for medicine. I made sure I farted and made a lot of noise just to make him move further down the hallway. When I finished, I flushed twice, just to annoy the dick, and took a long time washing my hands three times.

"Finished." I smiled and waltzed back into my room, slamming the door in his face.

Castor waited for me inside, twisting his Jackal's Wrath MC ring on his finger. "You make your goddess proud, cunning little thing." Fuck. He'd heard the whole thing, fart included. Not sexy. My cheeks heated up. Oh, well, maybe he could tell Slade to go easier on the heavies guarding me.

"What do you want?" I paced my room, yanking my sweater sleeves up and down. "I'm salty."

"And breathing fire." Castor's attempt to be funny earned him a speared glance as I kept pacing. He invited himself to sit on the bed. I ignored the thickness of his thighs, the tightness of his jeans ... and damn, could that man stop wearing such fitted shirts that showed off every hard plane of his chest and arms. Criminal.

Of course, I was pissed. I had no freedom or rights. Couldn't go anywhere without eyes on me. The forty-eight-hour deadline had well and truly passed, and no one said jack shit to me. I'd worn the floorboards down from pacing. Most of all, I'd sat alone in my room, gripping my phone, riddled with guilt about making contact with my family and warning my mom. She deserved to know what her son was capable of.

"Aaliyah?" Castor reached for me, catching my arm, dragging me between his legs. His maple eyes drank me in, flashing with heat.

No. Absolutely not. I retreated three paces. He hadn't come to see me the last few nights after I healed Alaric. No food, no books, no company. Alone. Empty. Cold. After I'd saved his damn brother. I was more than pissed. Five nights earlier, he'd coaxed me into masturbating with him ... then nothing. No mention of it. Was that why he was here now? Making up for lost time? Getting in a sneaky kiss when his president wasn't here. *Fuck that!*

That wasn't my biggest concern. Danny's forty-eight-hour deadline passed loomed large in my mind.

"What's going on?" I bit my lip. "Danny's deadline's gone by, and no one's telling me a thing. I'm worried about my mom's safety."

Castor brushed his dark, curly locks off his face. Sexy. Irresistible. Mysterious. "Aaliyah, if I tell you something, do you swear not to say a word to Slade?" His deep cadence made my knees buckle from desire and worry. This man rarely gave me a glimpse behind the dark curtain shrouding him, and I wanted more than anything to see what he hid from me.

"I swear." My hand went to my churning gut, still tender but aching less by the day. Coming along even better since I got out of the cell and restrictions of Castor's magical runes preventing my magic speeding up the process.

"Alaric's intel is bad, Aaliyah. Worse than what you or Jerry told us."

Acid exploded in my gut, and I rubbed harder. "Tell me." I had to know.

"Your brother is making rape porn and snuff movies." Every word hit like a hammer to my kneecaps.

Reality buckled and shifted, throwing me to my knees, on the side of my thighs, two arms bracing me partially upright. My stomach pitched, and I vomited all over the hardwood. This couldn't be true. How could he do that? *Oh, fuck.* I didn't know my brother anymore. He was a stranger to me. Possessed by a fucking demon. A sick fucker that had to be stopped. Prick had no hesitation shooting me. Certainty built within, pointing to his guilt for capping my dad in the back, too. Fuck, my mom was in danger, and I had to contact her, warn her to go into hiding.

"Aaliyah?" Castor fell to the floor beside me, tucking my hair behind my back, stroking my lower spine.

Sobs fought for freedom, and I heaved them up with a fresh batch of bile. I gasped for air, unable to get enough to fill my lungs and flush away the burn in them. "Oh, goddess." I wiped the puke from my mouth.

Castor drew me into his arms, holding me tight and protective. "I won't let him touch you. He'll die if he tries."

I kept my sticky hands by my side, not wanting to contaminate his *Tommy Hilfiger* t-shirt and *Calvin Klein* jeans. "I need to warn my mother."

"That's not wise." Castor brushed my hair, and fuck, it

was the sweetest sensation, stripping away the need to heave again.

My body shook, and he clutched me tighter. "She's in danger." I scrambled to get out of his grasp, reaching for the gold phone on my bed, seizing it.

Castor grabbed me by the waist, dragging me back. "Don't. They're watching." He pried the cell from my grasp and threw it on the bed.

So, the phone was a trap set up by Zethan. My stomach muscles cramped again, pushing me back to the verge of vomiting. Castor set his warm hand to my belly, sending a pulse of magick deep into my flesh, prompting me to relax.

Confused, I set my hand over his. "Why are you watching out for me?"

"I'll call her. What's her number?" Good old Castor, tight-lipped and never giving anything away.

Secrecy wasn't an attractive quality in a potential mate, and I pushed away from him, slumping against my bed and resting my head back. I gave him the damn number and he dialed it, activating the speaker function.

"Mrs. Heller," he said when my mom answered.

"Who's this?" she replied, and I clutched my thighs, drawing my legs close to my body.

"A concerned friend."

"What do you want?"

I couldn't hold back any longer. "You need to get out of town, Mom."

"Aaliyah. Where are you?" My mom's pitch scaled a few octaves.

Castor pressed me back hard into the mattress. "You're in trouble, Mrs. Heller. You need to skip town. Come to the Jackals' territory straight away."

"Jackals? I'd rather die than seek *their* help." My mom's voice tightened. "Aaliyah, are you with them?"

"Mom, please." That was all I got out before Castor's hold on my chest and lungs cut off my air.

"Suit yourself," Castor said. "Danny's into some dark business. Rape porn and snuff films. The men he's dealing with are not to be trifled with."

"Oh, God." My mom whimpered, and my heart smashed to pieces, imagining what she was going through, discovering the perversion and depravity of her baby boy. "Your poor father."

"Mom, please come here." I cried out when Castor twisted and cupped my mouth, his eyes warning me to shut the fuck up.

"Aaliyah?" That was all my mom got out before Castor ended the connection. I hit him in the arm and clambered away.

Emotions hit me with such force that I struggled to cope. Shock, betrayal, fear, denial. I pressed my hands to my stomach. There was no doubt in my mind that Danny was behind my father's murder. Fuck proof. Fuck clearing Slade's name. I wanted a bullet with Danny's name on it. Unlike Slade, I wouldn't miss with my shot right through my brother's brain.

Castor climbed to his feet, went to my closet, collected some fresh clothes and tossed them on my bed. "Take a shower, get changed, and I'll clean up the mess."

Tears blurred my vision as I watched him. "Thank you."

Moments later, I'd freshened up and changed into clean clothes, and Castor had done as promised. But I was wild, livid, and numb. I snatched up my phone and barged out of my room, marching past Brix, straight into Zethan's office. His head snapped up from a book he wrote in. Numbers and calculations.

The phone thudded on his desk as I slammed it. "You can

shove this up your ass. I've got nothing to hide, and I don't want your damn gifts if you're going to spy on me."

"Aaliyah." Castor's harsh caution from behind.

Hands wide, I leaned over Zethan's desk. "Gimme a gun. I'm going after him, ending this."

"What the fuck are you talking about?" Zethan rolled his chair back and stood, piercing green eyes burying to the depths of my soul.

"Aaliyah," Castor growled, harsher, reminding me of my promise.

Fuck, he'd shown me mercy by calling my mother, and I owed him my silence. "Nothing." I wiped my face and left the room, bumping into Slade's massive chest on the way out. The sheer size of him muscled me back inside.

"What the fuck are you carrying on about?" He kept his voice low, simmering with an unbridled impatience. "Shouting down the whole damn clubhouse."

"What's going on with Danny's ultimatum?"

Slade inched closer, trying to intimidate with his sheer size. "You're not privy to club business."

I didn't budge. Lifted my fist and struck his chest. "I have every damn right when it concerns my safety and future."

Slade grabbed me by the back of the neck. "This is your first and last warning. Don't ever hit me." Rage flooded his veins and scorched the mate bond. He didn't frighten me. I didn't fear death.

I hit him again. "Tell me what the hell is going on."

His grip pinched my wrist so hard I whimpered and scratched at him.

"Slade." Zethan approached, the threat in his voice clear. *Let her go or I'll make you.*

Slade didn't relent but eased his grip. "We're not agreeing to Danny's demands. You stay with us, and that's final."

I hit him again, not caring what he did, wanting to get out of his grip. "He killed my father, I want vengeance."

Slade leaned down and brought me close to his face. Nicotine, smoke, and whiskey hit my nose, intoxicating and alluring. Except this time, other new scents teased my nose. Molten steel, lightning charging the air, furious wind and rain, blistering snow. "I'm not letting you within a hundred yards of your brother." His eyes burned like hot coals.

Because of my promise to Castor, I couldn't say what needed to be said. To ask Slade to rescue those poor women and capture my brother, bring him back for interrogation, and get us all the answers we sought. If Danny was guilty, for Slade to put him down for sinking so low.

Everything tipped me over the edge. Castor's news. Fear for my family. My brother's sickening business operations. Losing my job and the life I'd carved out for myself. Being left nothing but tears and guilt for the women my brother abused. Possibly losing my mother if I wasn't careful.

"What about my life?" I broke down and cried, no longer caring about showing weakness to the Jackals' president. "My family? You've fucked everything for me. I'll lose my job." The thick stream of tears blurred my vision. I lashed out, thumping Slade's chest, a hard wall of muscle, begging to be beaten.

Alaric had just enough room to slide in behind Slade, catching my wrist, stopping me from hitting his president. He glared at me like I'd broken the most sacred of laws.

The Jackals' president caught the other fist, squeezing and lowering it.

I wrestled against their hold. "I can't even go to the toilet without some pervert watching me."

"What pervert?" Slade glared at Alaric with the intensity of a punishing blizzard.

Alaric protested with a raised palm. "Wasn't me, I'm a gentleman."

"Fucking, Brix." Slade's growl thundered through me, clashing with my own storm of upheaval.

I wrestled them both for release. "Let me fucking go, you assholes."

Slade brushed off Alaric and swept me into his arms, crushing me to his thickly corded chest, smothering me. "Fuck, woman. Don't cry."

Fuck him. Still pissed. Still broken. Still craving justice. "My name's not woman."

His chest rumbled with a laugh. "You're a pain in the ass, Aaliyah." He stroked my hair, shushed my ear, kissed my forehead until I stopped crying into his hard pectoral.

I shoved at him for all the good it did. "You're a pain in mine."

He leaned back, and I looked up at him. "We'll keep you alive and deliver you your father's murderer." He stroked my face, and I closed my eyes, comforted by it. "Then we'll sort out all the other shit. Castor, take care of her employer, will you?"

What the hell? Slade Vincent was taking care of my affairs. Looking after me. It didn't make sense when he considered me a traitor and liar. Not even the mighty Jackals' president could guarantee I'd have a job to go back to. Hopefully Barb would give me a good reference.

I gripped both his hands, bringing them to my cheeks, his heat burning away my doubt. "Why are you doing this?"

"We both have a mutual goal here." Slade squeezed me tighter. "Clear my name of murder and find your father's murderer. We can all help each other here." He made his case, a very good one at that.

The man wouldn't let a slight like blame for a murder of a

fellow president go unchallenged. He was out for blood, but he needed proof to justify a war with his rivals. Attacking another club would earn the Jackals a bad reputation with other clubs they needed to keep on their side to use their territory for transport. Good relations were important for MCs.

"I want that too." I rubbed my thumbs over his hand.

Slade bowed his head. "What you did was unforgivable, Aaliyah." His end of the mate bond trembled with barely contained chaos. "Trust is everything to members of an MC. You know that."

Yes, I did. All too well. But I had no allegiance to him back then. Still didn't. The only thing tying us together was the curse on our gods and the bond ... and maybe my slowly growing feelings for Castor. Things with Zethan were brought to a halt, and I didn't know if we could work through it, build trust. That didn't mean I wanted to stay with them or owe them anything. Four men, one woman? That shit was weird, and I wasn't sold on the idea and might never be.

"We protect each other," he said. "Care for each other. Defend our woman." I noticed he used the singular and plural. Did he refer to me or the old ladies in general? "If you're as innocent as you profess, then we have some shit to work out, don't we? Like hell I'm going to let you go, then. You're mine. Theirs. Our mate."

I rubbed at my temples. Everything was a twisted fucking mess.

Slade's fingers weaved through my hair, gripping it. "Do you still want to leave at the end of this?"

Confusion played on the bond. I wanted my old life back, my freedom, but a part of me knew that wasn't possible. The moment Slade Vincent strode into the ER, my life changed irrevocably. For better or worse was yet to be determined. Nothing would be the same. Ever.

"I don't know." I stared into the pools of his indigo eyes and felt the sting at my words through our link.

Fuck, admitting it turned me into a damn emotional mess, and I couldn't think straight. Something told me the Jackals were my future, and I belonged with them, and this decision was coming sooner than I liked.

CHAPTER 23

Alaric

"How does your client plead?" The magistrate droned in long, drawn-out words like he was ready for a goddamn nap.

Bored summed him up. Chin in his hand, eyes distant, posture sagging in his chair. Understandable I guess, since I was the last case for the day. But I demanded the same fairness as every accused person. Innocent until proven guilty. Except the odds were stacked against me when I belonged to an outlaw biker gang, reducing my chances of a fair hearing.

"Not guilty, your honor," my solicitor, Barry, declared on my behalf from his seat behind me. He looked crisp in his dark Burberry suit, hair slicked back, schoolboy style.

I leaned back in my chair, my fingers splayed and jammed together.

Two of the arresting officers sat in the docks with smug smirks on their faces. Fuckers. When I cleared my name and record, I'd wipe the expressions from their faces. I prided myself on honor and integrity. Sure, I worked for a fucking MC, which technically made me a criminal, but I always followed orders, and never dishonored my club or self.

"Not guilty?" The judge sat up, his hand leaving his chin. "Your client was caught in possession of a trafficable quantity of a Schedule One drug under the *Drug Misuse and Trafficking Act of 1995.*"

Fucking solicitors and judges throwing around their big terms and laws.

According to the law, it was up to the police to prove I had custody or control of the drugs found on my bike and prove I had knowledge of them. Six sworn statements from officers added weight to the police's case and didn't look good for me.

I was looking at a two-year sentence for possessing a prohibited drug, and I couldn't be locked up. Not after what had happened to me. Four months of my life lost, my humanity stolen from me, my eye taken. But the cops were gunning for me.

Barry kept his cool, gaze flicking to Marcus and the other prick present during my interview. "Planted by the arresting officers that pulled my client over on the Greater Western Highway."

The magistrate's eyebrows almost jumped off his face. "That's an outlandish accusation against the *New South Wales Police*, Counsel." He glanced over his half square glasses. "You better have the evidence to corroborate that allegation."

"We do, your honor." Fuck, why was Barry saying that when we didn't? Making such a bold statement could fuck my case. "It's not the first time I've been involved in a case where the police have acted above the law and fabricated evidence to convict an innocent victim."

By innocent, he meant Slade. Barry was the go-to man for

many criminals in the Central West. Worth every damn dime.

The magistrate cocked his head and scratched his eyelid. "I look forward to you presenting it." He scanned down the book in front of him. "Court is adjourned until October. That gives you three months to prepare your defense and gather this so-called evidence."

Great. The magistrate already didn't believe Barry. Impatient and wanting to get home, probably for his one-hundred-dollar dinner, charged to the taxpayers, he scribbled something in his book and slammed it shut.

"The honorable Judge McKenzie," the bailiff announced as the magistrate descended his bench and wandered out of the courtroom.

When the magistrate and bailiff cleared the room, the two cops stood, one adjusted his tie, Marcus removed his wallet, flicking through his cash. He tipped up his wallet, made a sad clown-face, then chuckled like it was fucking funny and sauntered out of the place like he owned it.

"Too big for his boots," I muttered, snatching up copies of my paperwork that I had to present to the court for my hearing.

In no uncertain terms they'd told me at my arrest that they were coming for the club and going to destroy us. The Jackals were going to be run out of town or disbanded. The Bathurst branch of police were going to prove the Jackals manufactured and distributed synthetic drugs under the *Poisons and Therapeutic Goods Act*. All production of Pharaoh had halted for the time being while the heat was on the club. Which fucked us royally since we owed Tony, our manufacturer, one million for the extra batch. Delay in payment could break our business arrangement.

The rest of the club didn't need to know that while Slade and I sniffed out the mole in our ranks.

Fucking Aaliyah Heller did this to me. I was certain of it. Bitch squeaked to her brother, and he paid off the cops to arrest me. Heat from the cops landed on us ever since the Winter's Devils attacked and burned our clubhouse down. Bathurst Police didn't want a turf war close to their territory to deal with, and they'd trailed us, spied on us, put plants in our network. Anything to take us down. Slade and Zethan had always been too clever and sniffed them out before they got close. My little god's eye gift might have helped with that, too.

"Be careful of that one," Barry warned as he tossed his notes into his briefcase and closed it. "He set up three of my clients for similar felonies."

I flicked my finger at him, not wanting to discuss anything inside the courtroom. The cops could have set up hidden microphones to record our every word for use against me. Evidence not admissible in court, but it could give them leads to follow. Paranoid? Yes, but I had to be in this digital age. Plus, I wouldn't put it past the dirty cops to throw more mud at me. The things Castor detected in his searches were more than enough to bribe cops and people to bend to our will. No wonder we had so many enemies in this region.

Outside, I squinted into the midday glare, performing a scan of my surroundings. Colored flowers bloomed in *King's Parade Park* opposite the courthouse despite the briskness of the Bathurst winter. The *Carillion War Memorial* scaled one hundred feet into the air, equally as tall as the hundred-year-old trees. A mother chased her child along the stone park path. Children licked at ice cream from *Annie's Ice Creamery*. Tourists took photos of the *Evans Memorial* commemorating the founder of Bathurst in 1813.

My eyes honed in on the man sitting at a park bench in front of the war memorial, talking on a cell phone and sipping his coffee. When our gaze met, he quickly looked away and ducked his head. Another man in jeans and a button shirt strode past the park, talking into a radio device on his arm. Assholes were as obvious as an oil leak from a bike. *Undercover cops.*

A third man, dressed in a *Bathurst Regional Council* yellow safety vest, mowed the grass at the courthouse … if he even worked for the Council or was another cop.

Eyes sharp on him, I waited for him to pass before speaking to my solicitor. "Don't look, there's two undercover cops in the park. A possible third cutting the grass."

Barry coolly slid on his sunglasses, blocking out the winter glare, and using it as a perfect cover to scan the area. "They've been parked outside of my office every day since your arrest." He positioned his briefcase over his abdomen and crown jewels as if he worried the cops might shoot him there. "As your solicitor, I advise you and members of your club to stay clean, Mr. Hawk. Don't give the police any reason to investigate or charge you. But I guess you already know that."

Fuck, the cops were putting pressure on everyone.

"I'll take it under advisement." Unfortunately, I only had so much control to be on my best behavior. If my president ordered me to attack the Wolves, I was duty-bound to obey unless I wanted my ass out on the street. Things could change on a dime with Slade when he ran high on passion and emotion. I tried to stay confident, knowing he'd kept his ass clean since the Heller murder charge.

"I apologize for not warning you or Slade sooner about Officer Marcus." Barry gripped his briefcase handles tighter. "I had my people look into him, and it seems he is in a bit of financial trouble. Gambling debts with a local bookie that extend to a gang in Cowra."

Fuck, why hadn't Castor seen this? In fairness, he was

busy with other shit, like tracking down the missing shipment, following leads. Regardless, this new piece of evidence was handy information to take to Castor to put more pressure on old Marcus and fuck him over like he'd done to me. Find out if anyone made any payments to him in cash.

"I'll look into it." I thrust my hand out. "See you next month, Barry."

My solicitor shook my hand. "I'll be in touch to discuss your case and the evidence, Mr. Hawk. We'll meet in a crowded place. No phones. No security cameras."

"Make copies and send them to a safe place to protect your ass." I didn't trust the cops wouldn't raid his office in the meantime and arrest him for aiding and abetting criminals.

"I always do. Pleasure doing business with you, Mr. Hawk." Barry nodded. "Good day."

I nodded at him and headed north, away from my bike, destined for the warehouse behind the pub to pay a certain someone a visit. He stayed there every time he did his country rounds every six weeks. Time to have this case thrown out of court.

"Whatever you do," Barry warned me from behind, solemn and stern. "Don't pay him a visit. It won't look good with the police watching you."

Fuck, that was all I had to make this bullshit, false charge go away.

Zethan always set aside money in the club's budget for legal defenses. Whatever wasn't used rolled over into the next year's budget. This year's budget got quickly chewed up by mine and Slade's cases. We were fucked if the cops pursued Castor and Zethan too, or any of the other Jackals. Slade put everyone on their best damn behavior to piss off the cops. Hopefully, if they couldn't get us for anything, they'd give up. But I doubted it when they'd gone to extreme lengths to arrest me and plant shit on me. They'd have to get really creative to come up with other charges for the rest of the members, unless they pinned the club with a major charge for producing Pharaoh.

I smiled at Barry. "What if I use some of the club's legal defense fund?"

"He's not that kind of judge."

No, but he deceived his wife. Photos and videos I'd collected revealed his nightly visits from hookers. Fucker screwed around when away from her. Bribes would ensure a favorable result in my case, in exchange for not telling his wife about his work travel arrangements. Something to keep in my back pocket for now.

CHAPTER 24

Castor

"Where are we going?" Aaliyah paused, holding her helmet in front of her stomach.

"Getting the fuck out of here for a bit." I rolled my bike past her out of the garage, inserting the key into the ignition. "De-escalate the tension and get you in a better headspace."

She sidled up to me. Close. Too close. I lost my breath. "What do you have in mind?" Images of a picnic or a ride around the Mount flashed in the bond. Anything to take her mind off what she discovered about her brother and father's club.

That shit couldn't have been easy to hear. Shock, disgust, and despair had soured our link, and she couldn't fake that kind of response. Deep grooves in her forehead, glassy eyes, the vomit, and conviction in her voice when she demanded to kill her brother convinced the hell out of me. Legal matters and court hearings revealed the worst in people, and I'd seen one too many liars, and learned to sniff them out. If she still lied, she was to be crowned the queen of fucking liars.

I moved away to get space and clear my head. The same stunt I'd pulled after I'd commanded her to masturbate in front of me. Space I'd needed to clear my head and think straight. The woman got me so twisted with desire that I wanted to go to her room every single night.

Hurt at my retreat, she rubbed her arm. "You never give anything away, do you?"

Clever. Intuitive. Aaliyah knew that I kept my distance and gave her little information. It stung when she felt she'd shared with the avatars and me her motives, reasons, and even a piece of herself when I visited her cell. I wanted to open up, I really did. But I couldn't.

"It's just into town to get a few ingredients." Several nights ago, I'd found a new spell in Thoth's library, and I needed materials before starting the ritual.

After losing my tight grip on control two nights ago in Aaliyah's cell, I'd thought it best to stay away, bury myself in the only thing that made sense to me besides the club. Magick and spell books.

I flicked the choke on, pressed the clutch and the decompression lever, and kick-started the engine. It purred, soft at first, growing louder like a damn pleased cat.

Jaxx leaned on the support column on the porch, smoking a cigarette. I gave him a nod, and he returned the gesture, looking away, minding his own business. He was still on Slade's shit list for fucking up and failing to spy the Wolves before their ambush. Wanker had pulled his head in and laid low.

Aaliyah stood a few feet away staring at me, her look torn between confusion and admiration. "I hope this isn't another test. I'm sick of them."

Grim-faced, she went to put her helmet on, but I caught her before she did, pulling her to me, locking her in my arms, her helmet at her side. I leaned down to lower a kiss on her nose. She tilted her face up to meet me, and heck, I wanted to lay one on her. BAD. *Hold the fucking line, Castor.*

I gave an inch, letting her in a little deeper, exposing my side of the bond. She'd never trust me if I didn't give her something. And vice versa. Otherwise, I'd never learn if she was my true mate or not.

"Thank you for what you did with my mom." She toyed with my hair, waking the big guy, and he thickened, nudging against her. "I'm sorry I almost betrayed your confidence." She glanced down at my chest.

Close call. Woman almost spilled everything to Zethan.

"Don't do it again, my dark sorceress." The possessive word slipped out.

Her eyebrows arched. *"My?"*

Shit. I didn't want to give her the wrong impression. "Don't read into it."

"Oh, I'm reading into it." She nudged my groin, making my dick kick into a higher gear and rev like a biker in a rally race. This woman was a pure weapon, slicing through my defenses, bit by bit, breaking me down.

Nervous, I laughed and slapped her ass, shifting back a step. "Get on the bike before I throw you on."

"Promises." Her smile buried beneath the helmet she slid over her face.

Garrisons defended the walls around my heart. Soon Aaliyah would bypass my fortress, capture my heart, and not let go. Then I was fucked. Things between us were burgeoning in a comfortable and steady rhythm, and it was easy to imagine us falling into that routine. Flirting, teasing, playful. I'd not repeat the mistakes of the past, not fall for her tricks so easily, and be lulled into a false sense of security. Been there, done that.

I threw a leg over my bike and cranked the throttle, warming the engine, letting Aaliyah slide on behind me. Her warmth was like a brushfire on my back, her body soft, arms cuddled across my waist and stomach. More than anything, my body craved to let go, sink into her.

Red-hot pokers sank into my chest. My ex-wife broke my heart and turned my world upside down. Cheated on me with my best friend and our neighbor. Took our fucking dog with her. My *damn* dog. Bled me for most of my assets and furniture, then took the *Enfield Classic Bullet* motorbike my grandfather left me in his will. Fucking bitch cleaned me out and left me with nothing but a few cooking pots, utensils, and my car. Belongings I could replace, but the heart, the trust, the hope—they weren't easily rebuilt and not easily won.

Aaliyah broke a cardinal rule with me, and I'd always remain on guard with her, no matter how intense the draw to her, the whole destiny bullshit or the way she felt like home. My ex felt like that at one stage, too, and look what happened. For now, Aaliyah and I could fool around, and that was it. Period.

Resolved to keep it cool between us, I took off along the clubhouse driveway. In the rearview, I caught Jaxx removing his cell and texting someone. We all had our eye on him since the ambush.

I pushed my bike onto the dirt road and into town. A ten-minute ride brought us to my destination on George Street, a little shop tucked between the Karate instruction dojo and a restaurant. Bewitched, owned by a practitioner like myself versed in light and dark magick. My kinda shop.

Aaliyah removed her helmet, shook her long, onyx hair,

and combed it with her fingers. Fuck me, she was beautiful. All mine if I wanted to tap that well.

Hell, no.

We left our helmets hanging from my handlebars and entered. The bell on the door tinkled as I held the door open for her.

"Castor, my man." Gable leaned over the counter with an outstretched hand, exposing the dark serpent tattoo on his wrist, symbolizing of his former allegiance. His raven hair had grown out and he styled it swept over one side of his face and shaved underneath.

I took his hand and shook it, making his gray eyes crinkle. "Gable."

This edgy, handsome warlock was my man if I wanted rare and hard to get magical ingredients. No other shop could get the stock he did and at such good prices. His shop made other Wicca shops look like amateur dabblers.

I hadn't been down here for a while. Didn't need to. But since we found our new mate and all the shit went down, Slade bumped up the priority of breaking the curse to get rid of the traitor, Aaliyah. Verdict was still out on that front. After his earlier display of compassion, the indecisiveness on his end of the bond, things might be changing. Until he said otherwise, I'd obey my president.

Aaliyah wandered around the shop, studying the various jars on shelves containing dried herbs, salts, crystals, leaves, bark, and other ingredients for spell work. My gaze went to her perky, round ass, and I imagined my hands on it.

"Who's your friend?" Gable jerked his head in her direction, distracting me. "She's powerful." Pale green magick crackled over his hands. He commanded power from the spell books and amulet he wore around his neck, but he wasn't naturally gifted with it.

Aaliyah glanced over her shoulder, adopting her sassy side. "The name's Aaliyah, and who are you?"

Gable stepped out from behind the counter to approach her slowly, cautiously, like a hungry cat would a new owner. "The name's Gable, love. I'm your man for anything magical. And I can tell you'll be needing a lot of my products in the near future." He produced a business card from out of nowhere and slid it into her palm, pressing her fingers over it, lingering a little too long for my liking. Touchy feely was his thing, and I didn't like it.

I broke apart their connection by grabbing her wrist and holding it close to my thigh. "Hands to yourself, asshole."

Gable smiled wickedly and stuffed his hands under his armpits. Flirt did it for a rise. Always got me without fail.

"Where's Luna?" I purposefully reminded him of his girlfriend, who sometimes worked in the shop with him.

Gable sighed and scratched his dark stubble. "The Shadows." His stiff tone expressed his displeasure.

The Guild of Shadows, a secret organization that protected Earth from supernatural creatures. We'd crossed paths a few times, and they'd tried to take my avatar brothers and I for questioning, but Slade shut that conversation down *real* quick.

"We're not your goddamn lab rats," he told them. *"Stick to your lane and we'll stick to ours."* They never bothered us after that unless they needed our help, which was rare.

Gable, on the other hand, got an up close and personal study of me, and we'd worked together on a few projects. Genius worked out what we were pretty quick, but he kept our secret, and I his, and that was the way it would stay. Leverage worked wonders these days.

Gable smirked and withdrew to lean on his glass top counter. "What do you need, Castor?"

"Black sage, myrrh, frankincense, and juniper," I reeled

off some ingredients, watching Aaliyah flick through a beginner's magical text. I huffed. I could teach her much better magick. Ancient. Powerful. Far beyond anything published by a stupid modern publisher. Not yet. Not until I trusted she wouldn't wield it against my brothers or me. As both enforcer and sergeant in arms, it came down to me to protect the club.

"Coming right up, my friend." Gable got to work collecting my order, selecting items, wrapping them in wax-paper gift bags.

Two bundles of cotton string, cassia, and senna rounded out my purchase, and I piled everything on the counter. Discounted candles sat in a heap on a tray and added two from the impulse display.

A lapis lazuli amulet caught my eye inside the countertop. Ancient Egyptians revered the gemstone, using it in jewelry to symbolize status and wealth and worship of the sky, the water, and afterlife. They crushed it to powder and made pigments from it for makeup to paint. I tapped my fingers on the glass, imagining it dangling from Aaliyah's neck, the smile on her sensuous lips as she stroked it, putting her warmth and power into the gemstone. The symbol of Isis carved into the semi-precious stone sealed the deal, and when Gable returned with my order, I pointed to it, and he smirked again, adding it to my gift bag.

In my world, there was no such thing as coincidence, and everything happened the way it was meant to. Just like I was meant to stop at my favorite apothecary for a re-supply, I was meant to find that amulet for Aaliyah. We were all together, a complete circle, but not entirely whole. Our full potential wouldn't be unlocked until I broke the curse, and we sorted through the confusion of the last few weeks. All I had to do was decipher centuries-old text and find the missing pages to the Book of the Dead. No pressure or anything.

Gable rang up the order on the payment terminal and slid the bag across the counter as I swiped my card.

I picked up the bag. "You haven't heard of other copies of the Book of the Dead, have you?"

Intrigued, Gable leaned on the counter, his gray eyes adopting that wicked gleam. "I might know how to locate one. Why?"

I rubbed a finger along the brass countertop rim. "My copy has pages missing."

Gable nodded, his smile falling. "I'll see what I can do." I shook his hand.

Eager to get back and start the spell, I snagged Aaliyah's hand, prompting her to slam shut the book and return it to the shelf.

"Nice to meet you, love!" Gable called out before the door closed.

"You, too." She smiled as I dragged her with me, tucking my order into my saddle bag, wanting her all to myself.

CHAPTER 25

Castor

"Get what you need?" Aaliyah eyed *Crema*, the local hole-in-the-wall coffee joint, and the mate bond went stiff with longing for caffeine. Still fishing for information, she was desperate to know me.

My hand lingered on my bike's compartment, and I contemplated giving her the necklace now or later. Fuck it. I slipped it free of the bag and handed her the paper.

She twisted it back and forth, studying me. "What is it?"

"Something little for you." My chest pricked, remembering the time I gave my ex a gift, the twinkle in her eye, the curl of her mouth. The same expression on Aaliyah's face.

Rusted spikes drove through my heart, and I recoiled. Detecting the change in me, she probed the bond for answers, testing the dark spots that I shielded behind to conceal my emotions. Each day her power strengthened, and soon I wouldn't be a match for her. She'd be my equal. Thoth urged me to teach and mentor her in the ways of magick, but I wasn't ready to share that side of me yet.

"Fine. Hide from me." Frustrated, she sighed and tore off the paper. She let out the sexiest gasp at the dark blue stone amulet flecked with fool's gold. "Goddess, it's beautiful." She held it out for me, suggesting I put it on for her.

Shit. That would require getting close, brushing her neck. I hadn't thought of that when I purchased it. I just knew it was for her. Tensing, I took the necklace and moved behind her, lowering it over her long, elegant neck. Soft, honey flesh tempted me, and I couldn't help myself, ghosting it with my knuckle after hinging it. A shudder tore through her. She lowered her chin, stroking the necklace, spinning to me.

"Does it have a secret recording device?" She lifted the amulet to her mouth and spoke into it like a microphone. "Hello. Slade, if you're listening, you should know, although you think your *sandwiches* are impressive, Castor here gives you a run for your money in the *cooking* department."

I laughed and slapped her ass. "Smartass."

Remarkable, more like it. Time away from the club had done her good. Taken her mind off the shit storm we were all caught in. Strong, slim arms linked behind my neck, sending my lust into a sharp spike, and making my body strum with pleasure. I wanted this woman like no one before her. She was the light I needed to clear away the darkness that had hung over me for too long. A dark cloud of gloom and misery.

"I love it." She kept touching it, then her fingers found my jaw, sliding away some of my doubt. "Thank you."

"You're welcome." Before common sense righted me, I leaned down and took her mouth with mine. The kiss was everything. Sweet, soft, and growing harder with reciprocal need. My heart thumped as I jerked back and panted, stopping it from getting out of control and leading to a repeat of two nights ago. "We better get back."

Her arms lingered around my neck, reluctant to let me go. She fingered my curls, tugging them, and my dick begged to bury in her pussy in front of everyone on the main drag of Bathurst. "Why are you running from me?"

"Stop, dark sorceress." I hated that she had power over me. Weakness. Vulnerability. Things I'd vowed to never let a woman have over me again. Never let a woman take everything from me and devastate me.

"What if I don't want to?" Fuck, she had to say that, didn't she?

That was all it took for my control to snap. I lashed out and seized the back of her neck and roughly pulled her to me. Our mouths sizzled as they crashed together in a deep, fiery kiss. Tongues clashed and flicked, encouraging my dick to harden and pulse with urgency to get inside her. I cupped her ass and squeezed, wanting to feel her everywhere, my hands on her generous breasts, tweaking her perfect little rosebud nipples. Her fingers twined in my hair and tugged harder this time, and I grunted.

Fuck, bathing her had been torture, her body so close and there for the taking. At my damn command, she'd given in and let me dominate her body. Let me control her pleasure. I wanted to do that again, only this time, I'd deny her orgasm over and over. Punish her for deceiving me and coaxing me to reveal intel. Only when she begged for forgiveness would I permit her to cum. She'd crash so hard, like the full force of an avalanche cascading down a mountain, annihilating everything in its path and slamming into the valley below. Fucking me would be like nothing she'd ever experienced before. I'd have her every which way of the *Kama Sutra* and every other sexual text ever written. Her body would be my temple to pleasure. And pleasure her, I would.

Remembering what she did to me, making me lose control, my promise to remain vigilant, I broke away, leaving her gasping. Her hands fell away from my hair, sliding along my neck, down my shoulders, stopping on my chest. Fisting my shirt tight, she jerked, begging for more.

"That's all you're getting. Until you're a *good girl.*" Dark Daddy had spoken. Law and order. Pleasure and pain. Darkness and light.

She snorted and shoved me. "Good girl, my ass."

I needed a woman like her in my life. Obedient and respectful, yet also assertive, taking what she wanted, and fighting me when the time was right. Turned me on like all hell. My dick fought to claim her. Fuck, we weren't making it back to the clubhouse without an outbreak of wildfire. My cock was hard and primed, my body taut and ready. She'd pushed me too far. My body craved hers behind me, her breasts to my back, her pussy grinding me, one hand on my cock, the other on my chest.

I'd never jumped on my bike and started it so damn fast. "Get your ass on that bike and your hand on my cock."

"Yes, *Dark Daddy.*" I groaned at her sensual words, the way her lips pressed together, how she eye-fucked me. Nothing pretend or cunning about her.

We were on the bike and tearing out of the city center in no time, on the back roads, heading northeast to the clubhouse. One hand massaged my chest, while her fingers crept down my torso, flicking open my jeans button, tugging at my zipper and freeing my throbbing cock. Gods, I needed her to touch me. It had been too long since someone had held me there. I needed my fucking mate, and I didn't care about recent events or repercussions. Only her hand pumping my molten steel mattered.

She worked my length the way I thought she would, alternating between rough, fast pumps with steady, slow strokes.

I didn't give a damn who saw or what they thought. Twists of my head had me crawling out of my damn skin. She massaged my dick in my precum, and it wasn't enough but would have to do. Dry and wild was all I was getting until we hit the rural limits of town, where I'd pull over, bend her over my bike, and rub my cock in her juices. Lick her pussy dry until she squirted on my face. Fuck her until she screamed.

"Oh, fuck that's good." She couldn't hear me, but I sent the words down the bond, and she responded, hers flaring with heady need. She needed to be touched and comforted as much as I did.

This time, she wouldn't deny me, leave me high and dry, desperate, and waiting for her kisses like she'd done in the shelter. This time I'd make her mine and seal the mate bond between us.

Liz's death had cast my heart into a perpetual dark winter. Frozen and lost, I'd wandered, searching for her. Splinters formed in the ice encasing me when I met Aaliyah, and they continued to crack and melt with every moment I spent with her. My past had held me captive, and I'd wandered too long in the cold and needed to be rescued.

Sensing my desperate need to get off, my ache to penetrate her, she worked me harder, and I bit back at the sensitivity of the dry hand job. I shot magick to my cock to numb the sensation, heightening my pleasure instead, and I groaned, making the bike wobble and her yelp. Letting go of one handle, I locked her hand over my dick, showing her how I liked it. A mixture like before, and fuck, did she give it to me. My body trembled like the bike's engine as she brought me home. *Come to fucking daddy!* I spilled over and shot my load onto the gas tank of my bike, but I didn't give a shit. Hungry for more, I hit the throttle, roaring for the countryside to give her what she'd given to me.

As we hit Mount Rankin, two bikes appeared in my rearview, capturing my attention. No one owned a bike down these parts but us. Cautious, I kept my attention between the road and them. Another two un-patched bikers were waiting when we hit a T-intersection, and I knew we rode into trouble.

"Hold on," I shouted to Aaliyah through the mate bond.

Her physical and mental grip on me tightened. "Who the fuck are they?" She shoved my cock back in my pants and did my jeans up.

Whoever they were, they had balls for coming this close to our clubhouse. Doing so uninvited and without permission breached MC code and could get them executed by Slade. One name rang the loudest in my head. The Wolves, minus their cuts, come to collect Aaliyah. They weren't fucking getting her. I'd kill them before they stole her from me.

"One guess," I replied. "Hold on, baby." At my command, her grip tightened, almost cutting off my air. I didn't care though. So long as she stayed safe, that was all I worried about.

Two riders lagged behind us while the ones in waiting roared up beside us. I twisted the throttle, but my Chieftain was old and classic, not built for the speed these new road bikes were capable of. One swerved at me, forcing me left, and my front guard collided with the other bike. Aaliyah screamed as we wobbled and straightened. She hugged me tighter, bracing for the next impact. Scrapes along the side of my mudguard wouldn't kill us. Another dirty move like that might, though.

"Get the fuck down here!" I shouted along the bond to my three brothers. *"We're under attack!"*

I could handle myself, but Slade and Zethan were more experienced riders, growing up around bikes and the club. If one of my brothers were here, they'd strike back with aggressive countermoves, but I wasn't taking the risk with my mate on back. Unlike them, I was cautious and played it safe, my head full of accident statistics. Pretty sure Aaliyah would agree with me on that one. Magick was an absolute last resort to call on, but I might need it if these pricks didn't ease up.

The prick on the left came at us this time, smashing us side-on, crushing our legs. Pain scorched down my bruised leg. My mate's pain shredded my insides, and I fucking snapped. Full of rage, I threw the bike in a hard left, hitting him in the back tire. Taken by surprise, he careened into the ditch and hit it, falling off. One down, three to go.

His buddy glanced over his shoulder, then straight at me. Pissed, he attacked, ramming my back tire in the same way, and we skidded along the road. Another of those moves and we'd tip sideways. Fuck, we weren't going to make it at this rate, and definitely not before my brothers arrived. *If* they arrived. I'd not put Aaliyah's safety in jeopardy.

Charging up my magick, I blasted the pavement one hundred feet in front of us, cracking open a wide pothole. The rider hit it with such force his bike twisted. With a little help, I magically jerked his bike sideways, flinging him off. He bounced along the road, his gear protecting him from road rash, but not the crunch of bone I heard at impact.

Rising to the challenge, the last two riders roared their engines, pushing forward to meet us. I swung a thick, heavy, fallen tree branch from the side of the road into his path. One hit it and went over his bike, flying through the air.

I didn't get a chance to get the last guy as he rammed me from behind. My bike jerked and lost balance, tipping over. Aaliyah and I flew off together, headed for disaster. Her scream tore me in two.

Take him, a dark and ancient voice coaxed me. *Save yourselves. Leave no casualties in war.*

God, Thoth sounded like the damn war god now. I'd never heard him so deep, so vicious and intent on destruction. Smart and wise, he believed in diplomacy and benevolence. Piss him off, unjustly provoke him, and you wouldn't live to tell the tale. Eye for an eye existed between the gods, and even the god of Knowledge wasn't below a good battle. Not when he could really put his magick to the test.

I surrounded Aaliyah and me in a bubble of protective magick that we bounced inside of like we were in a large, plastic air ball. When we stopped springing, I lowered us to the ground and popped the damn thing.

The rider rounded on us, tires screeching on pavement as he spun in a circle and corrected the hard wobble of his front wheel. Revving his bike, he prepared to take us out. Fucker was about to die. I pulled out my gun and squeezed the trigger, firing bullet after bullet until I hit him. The bike went out from under him, grating along the road, him underneath it. Bones crunched and crushed under its weight and the impact. When he came to a stop, I went up to him, removed his helmet, and stomped on his head.

Some hundred feet back, one of the riders crawled along the ground. I changed clips from inside my cut and ran to him, putting two more rounds through his helmet. I reached out with my magick for a heartbeat. Nothing. I kicked him and moved on down the road, doing the same to the last two riders, ending them.

Bikes roared in the distance. My brothers. Too late.

I hurried back to Aaliyah, who stood frozen, clutching her arms. "You killed them."

I crushed her in my embrace, unable to get her close enough, protected enough. "Of course, I did. They fucking tried to kill us." Fatalistic acceptance. No more. No less.

She trembled so violently it made my teeth rattle. "I don't do that. I ... I save people." Horror pinched the bond tight like the skin over a drum.

Two of my brothers screeched to a halt, and Slade was off his bike without setting the kickstand down, making it fall over.

"What the fuck happened? Who the fuck were they?" He'd gathered enough from the bond to put a picture together but still wanted more.

Possessive and protective, he pried my arms off Aaliyah and stole her from me. Losing his mother to a rival club and our previous mate to another made him lose his mind. Muscled arms caged her, powerful and lethal. Dick wouldn't let her go to give her back to me.

Power ebbed and throbbed within me. She was mine to protect. Mine to claim the glory from, and he deprived me of that. He was the Alpha, though, and if I kept this shit up, I'd have a challenge on my hands.

"Wolves probably." I kicked at the nearby bike.

At the mention of their name, Slade stiffened and squeezed Aaliyah tighter. "Check 'em out, Zethan."

Zethan approached the first man, crouching beside him to unzip his jacket and yank it off. From there, he checked all pockets then his jeans. "Nothing."

"Fuck." Slade swiped at the corners of his mouth. He pressed a finger to Aaliyah's chin to lift it. "Do you recognize any of these men?"

She glanced over at him, her eyes slamming shut, and she shook her head. He tucked her head to his chest and stroked her. My ibis cawed, jealous of his attentions.

"Why the fuck were you out on your bike?" Slade's voice hardened like lava turning into stone.

I stood my ground. "Went for a ride into town to grab some spell ingredients."

"On whose fucking orders?" His body quaked with barely controlled rage. "You took her out and risked her safety?"

He let Aaliyah go and sidestepped her. Excessive caution prevented him from ever putting our mate in harm's way. Me, I hadn't anticipated the ambush, and thought it safe to venture into our goddamn town. The look in Slade's eyes, cruel, cold, ice splintering, told me I would be punished severely for this mistake. I didn't run as he advanced to me. If I raised a fist, it could be viewed as insubordination, leading to demotion, a harsh beatdown or being kicked out of the club. Whatever he gave me, I'd take it for her. Fist rearing back, he punched me in the nose, making me stumble back.

I clutched my bleeding, probably broken nose. "Fuck, Slade. I was trying to cool things down. Give us all some space. I didn't think we'd get chased in our territory."

My president's pupils dilated, and his nostrils flared. A wave of red swept over his neck and face. He came at me again and I let him hit me, over and over until Zethan dragged him back. Even Aaliyah got into the fray, kicking his legs, thumping his back, screaming at Slade to stop. It was of little use when he was lost to his inner turmoil and rage. Pure destruction and emotion blinded him to logic.

Restrained, he kicked and raged, spitting and hissing like a damn jackal. "Don't you ever do something so fucking stupid again. Don't get her hurt!"

"Cool it, Slade." Zethan breathed his dark, icy breath over our leader, freezing him in place. Struck by the death breath, our president glared at his VP, refusing to calm down. Slade could breathe, his basic survival operations intact, his eyes the only thing to move and express emotion. "I'll let you go if you calm down."

CHAPTER 26

*A*laric

BACK AT THE CLUB, I heard the argument before I walked into it. Moving down the hall, I searched for Slade, wanting to discuss the hearing with him. Heated, raised voices drew me into Castor's office, where Zethan and Slade huddled around a bruised and bloody Castor cradling a scraped Aaliyah on his lap. She buried her crimson-tainted face in his shirt and bunched his jacket in her fists while they argued. Some shit had gone down, and I stayed back, away from *her*, taking in the commotion.

"You fucking broke his nose!" Aaliyah, voice shrill. "This wasn't his fault."

Slade's voice rose above the rest of the arguing men like a damn bear. "She's not going out again."

Zethan hovered by his side, his shadow, his restrainer in case our president lost his shit. By the sound of it, Slade had lost it.

"You can't keep me locked up like this," Aaliyah protested, and I struggled to keep my gaze off her. Was she bleeding or was that Castor's blood? Swollen, purple eyes said his nose had been broken. I wanted to blurt out *'what the fuck happened,'* but I stayed silent out of respect for my president.

"You're our fucking prisoner." Slade wasn't giving her an inch. "You do as I say. It's for your own good."

"Then kill me. I'd rather be dead than denied my freedom." Getting more worked up by the minute, she yanked at her shirt, ripping it, exposing her chest, and pointing to her heart. That drew my gaze like a laser target. "Do it. Kill me. One clean shot to the heart and I won't be your problem anymore."

"You're our problem whether we like it or not." Slade leaned over her, his gaze as fiery and unbending as hers. "I can't kill you. The gods won't let me. They'll end the four of us if I try."

"Rein it in, the both of you." Zethan. Always the calm in the storm. With his eyes closed, he looked dead on his feet, but he was very much alive. Hell, working days with us and nights watching the Underworld, the man never slept. I felt sorry for him that he tirelessly worked round the clock.

Aaliyah mustn't have heard him or chose to ignore him. "Fuck, I'm going crazy in here." Shy all of a sudden, she pulled her shirt tighter to cover her exposed bra, and I fought the urge to grab her and tear the cotton from her body, baring the rest of her. "I need my goddamn space. Air to breathe."

She wasn't the only one going crazy. We all were fighting this damn mate bond. Dulling it did jack shit to calm its effect. One look at her chest, and I was lost to her damn charms.

"*Castor* gave you some air, and look what happened," Slade growled, and I didn't miss the way his voice sharpened on Castor's name. "I won't have my men gunned down for you."

My head hurt from the stress of my earlier hearing, now this, and I rubbed at my forehead, struggling to follow what was going on. Castor was beaten up or had an accident. I didn't interrupt my president while he dealt with his business. Respect was everything. Chain of command.

"I wish I never met you!" Aaliyah shouted up at him, and he recoiled as if she'd slapped him. "Wish I'd gotten another nurse to tend to your wounds that night." She covered her eyes with her hands and shook her head. "I'm such an idiot. I should have run from the shelter when I got the chance."

Things were getting heated fast, and needed to be brought down a level. Slade and Liz had notorious fights over their relationship because he tried to control and dominate her when she'd been accustomed to her independence. Aaliyah was no different in that respect. Except, Liz's hadn't been under threat until we met the Winter's Devils.

Aaliyah sniffed and wiped at her nose, blood smearing her fingers.

My protective instincts kicked in, and I was by her side in three steps, bent down on my knees besides Castor's chair. "What happened? Why are you bleeding?"

Wind-blown streaks of hair concealed some of Aaliyah's face. Castor brushed a long, dark lock away from her face, and I felt a stab of jealousy that she wasn't in my arms. She took one look at me before burying her head again, still mad at me. I deserved it. I'd said some pretty shitty stuff to her.

My bird fluttered inside of me, scratching its claws, pecking to get at her. Hold her and shield her under its wing. Nuzzle her with the tip of its beak. Caw and coo at her and comfort her. And that wasn't the damn mate bond talking. Aaliyah was strong, fierce, caring, and independent. Yet I'd only chosen to see the bad, cunning, lying side to her. Just like I chose to see the darkness in all people because of what had been done to me.

Castor wiped his bloody hand, smearing it over his cheek. "I took Aaliyah for a ride into town, and on the way back, riders chased us and tried to make us crash. They slammed into us, got our legs, made us fly off the bike."

A ride? No wonder Slade was all stormy. Castor put both their lives in danger. I'd lost one mate to a rival club, and I *would not* go through it again. I hadn't claimed Aaliyah yet, and might not ever after the shit she pulled, but it would hurt just as much to lose her as it did Liz. Traitor or not.

Uncontrollable anger surged in me that Castor had been so reckless and stupid. Of all the Jackals, he was the smartest, cautious like Zethan, always thinking things through before deciding. With Aaliyah, that all went out the window.

"You what?" I stretched up on my knees and grabbed him by the collar of his jacket, prompting Zethan to defend him and shove me back.

Aaliyah struck fast, placing a palm on my chest, dousing the fire inside me. "It's not his fault. If you want to blame anyone, blame me. I was going stir-crazy in here and wanted out. I didn't mean to put Castor in danger."

"Aaliyah, don't lie for me." Castor squeezed her. "This is club business. I accept the blame and punishment."

Fuck, she even stood up for us. Took heat for him. What any man or woman in the service of their country would do. Respect and admiration bloomed in my chest.

"Do you think the riders were Wolves?" My gaze darted between my brothers. "Are they watching us?"

"I took them to the Underworld for torture and they squealed pretty damn fast," Zethan said. "Guns for hire. They knew the location of our secret club. Said the Wolves are camped out somewhere close."

Fuck. My daily reconnaissance had fallen flat, and I'd failed the club.

Zethan had given her a damn phone against my argument. Means to communicate with Danny. What if she sent the encrypted message to her brother and framed my brother, Jaxx?

Suspicion darkened my judgment, and I jerked Aaliyah's hand off me. "Did you contact your brother? Try to stage a rescue?"

How else did they know where our out-of-town club was? The place in town was for show, where we conducted business with other clubs and business partners. We built a second location for safety and shelter after the Winter's Devils raided our last one and burned it down.

I had to be careful of her. Careful of falling back under her spell. I'd guard my heart as closely as I protected my club. Never let her destroy my brothers and me.

Hurt shifted behind her eyes. Her palm came up fast and hard, hitting my face. "Fuck you, Alaric! I'm sick of your accusations. I've got nothing to do with my brother or his club. He fucking murders women, and I want no part in that!"

Heat stung my cheek, flowing to my head, down my neck. I rubbed at the sting. She had a pretty mean palm.

"How the fuck does she know about that?" Slade growled, murderous eyes jumping between Castor, Zethan, and me.

"Hey, bring it down a notch!" Castor dragged her back onto his lap when she went to slap me again, his arms around her waist, pinning her arms to her sides.

I still didn't believe she was innocent in this. Too many coincidences. The Wolves territory stretched from Katoomba to Penrith. What did they want out this far west? In our space? They weren't welcome. Riding into our territory begged for trouble and would just infuriate Slade and the rest of the Jackals.

Nothing added up, either. As road captain, our contacts called me if other clubs rolled into town. There was no way for them to sneak into the back of Bathurst without notice. Daily checks from the sky, me in hawk form, or me looking through the eyes of other hawks let me scan for danger. The past few days, I conducted them like clockwork, every hour, on the hour. Nothing. Not a damn thing. She had to be behind this. I knew it. The riders only came after she was let out of the cell, free from the runes that prevented her from using her magick. With the gifts of Isis, she'd tracked our location.

"Fuck, I let the club down, sir," I told Slade, gaze on his boots. "I've been too busy with my own shit to notice this morning." Confused, I slid out my phone to check for missed calls, finding none recorded. "Why didn't anyone report this to me? I could have scoped it out."

Slade shook me by the shoulders, forcing my piercing gaze up at him. "Don't fucking call me sir." Then he clapped me on the side of my arms. "No one could have predicted this. It's the second time we've been played in as many weeks. The Wolves are fucking with us. Danny and whoever he's working with don't care how many people die in the crossfire, and I intend to handle it." He sighed and rubbed his face.

Zethan poured a drink and handed it to me to soothe my burning nerves. "You were dealing with other matters." Normally he was the quiet one.

I appreciated that they'd given me space from my duties, but charge or no charge, it was still my responsibility to protect the club.

Uncomfortable that we discussed club business in front of Aaliyah, I tugged at the sleeves of my suit. Victim or not, I didn't like her involved in this. Let us handle it while she remained in the background. I stared at her, those heated eyes full of revulsion and passion dueling together. The same emotions tearing at my heart.

"This is retaliation for not handing over Aaliyah," Zethan added, "and for you killing their man. Plain and simple."

"Fuck, this is my fault." I clamped my hands to my side and bowed my head at Slade. "I lost sight of my mission, antagonized the Wolves and killed one of their men. I disobeyed your order and accept whatever punishment you deliver." Head low, I waited for his move. For him to hit me. Scream at me.

Discomfort writhed deep within my president, and I used my god's eye to investigate inside his heart. He blamed himself for this going wrong. An argument sat heavy on his chest. Mind and heart warred for dominance, but he couldn't let his heart and the bond sway him when he had to protect the club first and foremost. Aaliyah penetrated the wall he'd put up between them, and nothing he did shielded him from her, and it left him vulnerable. Something he'd never admit to her or us. He hated that his mate didn't want him. Hated that she betrayed him. Hated that her allegiance wasn't with us, her mates.

I probed deeper for more information about the argument. Her needing space and going crazy being locked up and watched. Castor taking her out for space. On the way back, they were attacked by riders, him defending her. Slade lost his shit and punching Castor when he found out. Things got heated between Slade and Aaliyah to the point where she wanted to kill him just so the Jackals would take her out and free her from us.

"The fucking Wolves are getting more brazen in their attacks." Zethan scratched at his stubbled chin. "They've got balls, I'll give them that. For how much longer is debatable, though."

"We've gotta hit back." Slade crunched his knuckles. "I won't stand for this bullshit. Get me answers, Castor. I want to know who stole our shipment and who whacked Joey."

"No." I gripped my two-way, clinging to the edge of madness, the demons in my soul whispering to me again to take lives. "Barry's got cops trailing him, and today when we came out of court, I spotted two undercover dicks in *Kings Parade*." I pinched the corner of my dried lips. "He warned us to stay out of trouble while I've got my hearing."

"Fuck. They've got us backed into a corner, and they fucking know it." Slade's glare rolled over Aaliyah, and the heat rose in her eyes again, ready to lash out at him and start another blaze.

Zethan rubbed at the bunched lines in his forehead. "We all need to keep our ears to the ground, our eyes on our enemies, and our asses out of trouble, Slade. I mean it."

Our president hooked his thumbs in his jean belt loops. "I'd say something sinister, but I won't do it in front of a lady."

"Don't hold back on my account," Aaliyah sassed back, causing Castor to clutch her tightly, cooling her fire. "I'm no petal."

Slade huffed a laugh. "No. You're not."

Castor remained silent since Aaliyah slapped me, but he spoke up now. "What if the Wolves have an insider?" Everyone's gaze snapped to him. "Someone who told them where to find us. They were waiting for us at the bend at the end of the clubhouse's road."

Silence strangled the room like a cobra had wound around and squeezed the air from our lungs and deprived us of getting more.

"Jaxx saw Aaliyah and me leave." Castor's gaze darted between us all. "He texted someone as I left. I can't find any trace of that message." What the hell? He deciphered all messages. "All I could find was code sent from the tower closest to the clubhouse. The same code I detected that led me to find Joey's crushed and chop-shopped truck."

"Motherfucker." Slade's fist curled, and a tornado swept through him, growing into something the world had never witnessed that would destroy the Central West region if unleashed. "Watch him, Alaric. Don't let that piece of shit out of your sight. If he's the mole, I'll make a damn example out of him."

I nodded, my attention shifting to Aaliyah. Determination rose in me to prove that she had something to do with this. She might not have used the Zethan gave her, but she could have used her magick somehow, and I *would* find out how.

Aaliyah prickled as she sensed my suspicion and the full force of my god's eye on her. Her gaze hardened, and she pried free of Castor's grip, stumbled to her feet, rubbing at her bruised leg where the attacking bike must have hit her. My bird screeched, piercing and pained. Face taut with strain, she grabbed his hand and tugged.

"Come on, Castor. I'll clean and heal your nose. Maybe stab *you* in the back when you're not looking." Heat rolled off her gaze, body, and voice as she said that to me.

Regret flashed in Slade's bond as they both hobbled away. He'd struck Castor. Because of her. Fuck. We were losing our cool over this woman. Old habits died hard when it came to the gods.

CHAPTER 27

*A*aliyah

"Take it easy." Castor's large, coppery hand clamped down over mine, squeezing, halting the trembling in my body.

Seriously? We'd just been attacked by hired guns and almost killed. Rammed by one of them, our legs crushed and bruised, and my leg ached like a mother. Slade snapped and broke Castor's nose for putting me in danger. To top it off, Alaric had me extremely worked up. Accusations against my integrity got old real fast and I was tired of them. Sure, I was no angel. I came to the Jackals under false pretenses, concealed my identity, but I never lied to them. Hiding information was a different story, and I did that to protect my safety. I resented having to defend myself against constant allegations.

"Why are you soothing me?" Ignoring my pain, because Castor's would be that much worse, I brushed the sides of his face. Smooth, round planes of his cheekbones. I had to consciously avoid the ugly bump of his nose punched out of alignment. "You're the one with the nasal fracture."

I couldn't heal an injury like this until I calmed my raging pulse and fiery spirit. A few deep breaths and strokes on my shoulder from Caster did the trick to bring me back from the heart of a volcano.

Slade seemed to have eased up a little after our earlier fight. I felt his push and pull, how all this shit tore him up inside. Allegiance to his club and me, his mate. Loneliness from missing his previous mate destroyed him from the inside. Our trust had been critically eroded, but a deeper part of him wished to rebuild it. I'd be lying if I said I didn't want that too. He called to my soul in a wild, chaotic way that I wanted to sweep me away and turn me to ash.

Then, my brother wanted to hurt me, kidnap, or kill me. I was fighting a war on both fronts, and I wasn't sure I could win either. Nowhere was safe, and I rubbed at my arms.

Blood on Castor's neck brought me back from my disturbed thoughts. Shit, I had to pull it together. My first duty was to heal him, then myself, and think about my situation later. Lost and confused, I rubbed at my forehead, trying to collect my thoughts into a cohesive, linear trail. What did I have to do first? I massaged my temples to stimulate the answer. Jumbled thoughts hit me, and I struggled to sort through them.

Straighten his broken nose, my goddess counseled me. *Disinfect the cuts. Apply ointment to the bruises.*

Thank fuck for her! Wait. Ointment? I didn't have any.

He does, she added, receding into the depths of my mind.

Hands cupped to his face, I applied my magick, letting it work to straighten and realign the damaged cartilage and nasal septum. Bones and tissue crunched back into place with a rough jolt that made his eyes water. He blinked and sniffed. The simple procedure weakened me as I hadn't fully recovered from healing Alaric days ago and wasn't completely restored of my gunshot injury. Soft pules of the same power flowed through me, clearing away the inflamed, bruised cells, restoring the tissue of my leg. I moved back to give Castor space, and he touched his nose, sniffed, pressed one nostril, breathed in, snorted, tested it. He repeated this on the other side.

"How does that feel?" I leaned down to examine the cuts on his lip and forehead where Slade's massive fist had connected.

"Pain's gone." Castor pinched his nose and wriggled it. "It's still a bit stiff and tender."

"It might be uncomfortable for a few days." I patted around a deep gash on his lips. Slade had a pretty mean hook. "Sorry. I'm off my game. Alaric's wound took it out of me. I don't think I've got enough juice to fix the rest of your cuts."

"I can handle those." Castor took my hand, lifting it to his lips and kissing my knuckles. His touch, the intensity in his eyes, the prick of longing getting past his defenses made me tremble.

I wanted to kiss him, but I held back. He was a cold-blooded killer who had efficiently dealt with a threat to our lives. I had pledged my life to saving others. If I kissed him, I worried I'd be accepting the lifestyle I ran so far from and vowed never to return to.

"Um …" Words evaporated from my tongue. I pinched the bridge of my nose, trying to recall them. "Have you got medical supplies?" His cuts needed disinfecting, stitching up, and bandaging.

"Here." Castor led me to a small closet in the hall packed full of bandages, stitches, cleaning solutions, even painkillers. He removed the materials we needed, clearly versed in first aid, and patching up superficial wounds.

My eyes went to the illegal stock of *prescription only* painkillers. Opioids, Demerol, Oxycontin, Vicodin, and more. A stash that would have cost a fortune on the black market. Money the Jackals could easily afford. Back in the day, the Wolves were lucky to stock codeine and morphine. A situation that changed with new management.

"Gonna pretend I didn't see that pharmacy of meds you're packing." I smiled, selecting steri-wipes, a saline disinfectant bottle from the next shelf, and a packet of butterfly stitches. "You could be in trouble for storing these in the clubhouse."

"You can see them?" Castor's eyebrows shot up. He was more concerned that I'd seen them than the club stocking them. Dangerous if the cops raided them. "You don't see shock blankets?" The man never gave me an inch, keeping everything locked up behind his secretive wall.

"What?" I half laughed at his surprise. "They're right there on the third shelf." I snorted, nudging him to move so I could close the door, but he was solid and steady as a boulder.

"They're under Castor lock and key." A ball of browny-red magic, the color of leather hide books, rolled over his hand. "No one but me can see them. I'm the sergeant in arms, too, and I protect it."

I picked up a bottle of Oxycontin and twisted it. "Very much visible."

"Your power is getting stronger if you can see past my illusions." Castor scratched at his bloodied chin.

"Maybe you're losing touch, old man." I nudged him with my hip. Wrong move. Fire chipped at the ice over his gaze and the hold on his bond. Water dripped as it melted and cracked. Finally, it shattered, and he burst free from his confines.

Wild with desire, he pinned me flat against the closet shelves, and my body temperature scaled. "You're one to watch, dark sorceress." The nickname trickled down my spine as if his fingers had teased me, and I squirmed at the pleasure of it.

"How come I can see it?" I squeaked at the fingers that skimmed my arms, trying to redirect the conversation and where this was headed.

He didn't frighten me for what he could do to me physically. He frightened me for what he could do to my heart.

"Your goddess is well versed in magic," he crooned in my ear, wiping aside the hair cascading over it to feather his lips along the edge. "My guess is she can see through my spell."

I needed him to move away, stat. The proximity had my heart firing too fast, desire spiking in my blood, my body weakening its defenses.

"Castor," I breathed heavy, pushing at his solid chest.

He wrapped his big arms around me and drew me into his warm, steady body. "I'm not moving, baby, until I get a thank you kiss for saving your sexy ass."

Fuck. He deserved it. Those riders could have killed me or kidnapped me. Castor had defended me regardless of whether he thought me a traitor. I was his mate, and he would die to protect what was his. Period. And as much as he tried to hide from me, I knew that one fact to be true, and he could deny it all he wanted. Obligated to him, I gave him a quick peck on the cheek and pulled away, discouraging anything more.

He laughed, deep, throaty, sexy, and my core pulsed with wild need. "You call that a kiss? After the way you touched my cock?"

Shit. Another mistake. I squirmed in his embrace. "I'm healing your ass as thanks, too. You're always trying to steal a kiss out of me." I snorted and shoved at him, weakly, because I'd lost some fight from using magick and facing off with Alaric and somewhat Slade.

Castor's throaty rumble set me alight, restoring some of

my energy, waking me from my fatigue. "I kiss my grandma like that." His gaze zeroed in on my lips. "Let me show you how you ought to thank me."

He grabbed me by the throat, firm, but not hard, pushing my head against the doorway. His mouth crashed to mine, hungry and dominant, taking what he wanted and giving everything in return. My body swooned, and my hands went around his neck, wanting every part of his body lined up with mine.

"Do you want me to stop?" His hot breath fanned my lips, weakening any objection.

Dark Daddy could have just owned me and taken what he wanted like he did in the cell. Yet, this dominant, sexy, mysterious man gave me a choice. Take it or leave it. Right now, I needed to take it. Every last drop. Dissolve into the pleasure he promised and forget the shit we'd just been through.

I crushed my mouth to his, showing him what I wanted. At first, he was gentle, thankful for what I'd done to repair his face. Grateful that we were alive and pleased that he'd protected me. All that mingled with a little jealousy that Slade had stolen me from him, when Castor had been the one to save me.

Each brush of our mouths stirred more heat, brighter, hotter, whiter. Dominance deepened in his movements, leading the way. For Castor, intimacy was reciprocal pleasure rather than possession and ownership like Slade. Both different in their approaches, neither any better than the other, giving me what I wanted in diverse ways.

"Now that's more like it." Castor slapped me on the bottom. "Don't give me any more of those granny kisses."

I giggled, touching my throbbing lips, wanting his back on mine. Wanting his thick, hot length in my hand. Inside me. Fucking me to oblivion.

He bundled my arms with supplies, clasped my hand, and drew me out of the closet and closed the door.

"Come bandage me up, and then maybe you'll be lucky to get another kiss and touch my dick again." He walked backward, leading me into his office.

I laughed again, the tension washing off me like the blood I was about to rinse from his face. "Lucky?" I threw a bandage at him, and he caught it. "I ought to give you double the stitches for that."

He sat on the edge of his desk and bundled me into his arms. "Totally worth it if I get another kiss like that. Wipe my mind of that peck …"

I raised the saline solution and twisted it. "Distractions won't get your handsome face mended."

"I think I'd look tough with a few scars." Castor stroked one cheek then the other like a damn model from a shaving cream ad. Sexy AF. "What do you think?" I wanted my hand over his face, that was what I thought.

The banter between us relaxed my tense mind. "I'll rinse and clean them and leave them open then. They're only superficial, not deep, but will add character."

He pulled me between his legs, awakening memories of being in the same position a week ago. "Damn. I'll get Slade to punch me harder next time."

I groaned as I removed the cap and rinsed the blood from his wound. "Not funny. That was hard to watch."

Castor's hands knew exactly the right place to touch as if they were tension-seeking pads sent to break up my nerves. "You jumped into the fray to defend me." His eyes sparked with a honeyed admiration. "My brave little thing."

"There you go with the *my* thing again." I followed up the saline solution with a dab of steri-wipes, and he winced at the sting of alcohol on this open flesh. "Don't fall under my spell."

Castor pulled me roughly to him. "What if I want to?" The dark spots he hid behind on the mate bond lightened, revealing a shadowed outline concealed behind it.

"No, you don't. You're scared to." I played with his hair to avoid his face. "And so am I." There. I said it. Truth was out in the open.

His end of the link breathed out so long and hard it was like a god awakening from a long slumber. "What if I'm reconsidering?"

"You don't trust me." Unable to meet his hungry gaze, I removed the adhesive side of the butterfly stitch. "And I don't trust myself around you, either." I firmly applied the stitch up his first cut.

He placed a hand over mine. "What if I want to trust you?"

I rubbed the stitch to ensure it all stuck to his skin. "Then show me."

CHAPTER 28

Slade

WHAT THE FUCK was I doing here? Standing outside her door, hand raised, reconsidering my decision. This was a mistake after what went down earlier today. I'd fucking broken Castor's nose, and she hated me for it. Aching loneliness brought me here, my skin starved for contact, my mind in need of distraction. Showing vulnerability and uncertainty chased me away, and I took a step back. Being here broke my own damn rule and I should have walked the fuck away to drink by myself. Clawing hunger prompted me to rap on the door, drawing her to answer, wearing an excited smile that quickly faded.

Sensation poured through me at her bare and beautiful face. Dressed in her pajamas, cute little things with cows on them. Fucking cows. Like her goddess. *Good one, Castor.*

"Slade, hi." Surprise in her tone told me I wasn't who she

expected or hoped to find at her doorway. Castor burned bright along the link.

Sucker punch me in the gut, why don't you.

Jealousy snapped through me that she wanted him, not me. Heat whisked over me like a desert breeze. Things were tense between us, but I expected a better reaction than this. A smile, a witty line. Hell, a sassy Mr. Vincent. Anything but her disappointment.

Curiosity burning down the bond stopped me from leaving. She wanted to know why I'd come. Her mind wasn't far from the comfort I offered after the rider attack this afternoon. Aqua ponds in her eyes studied me. Devilishly handsome yet troubled, according to her assessment. I'd take that.

I lifted the bottle of scotch I clutched in one hand and the two tumblers in another. Peace offering. Closest thing to an apology as she'd get from me.

"Thought you could do with a drink after today's …" I ground my teeth, flexing the sharp, tight muscles of my jaw. "*Incident.*"

Today was a shitty day for more than one reason. None of the guys broached it with me because they feared my reaction. I was on edge for more reasons than one. Our argument with her this morning had shaken her and left me unraveled. Her disastrous outing with Castor just topped it off.

"I don't drink much because of my work at the hospital." Playing hard to get as usual, she leaned in her doorway, blocking it, folding her arms over her chest. My jackal prowled under my skin, rising to the occasion.

Images flickered along our connection like a movie, getting stronger by the day when she opened up to us, hiding nothing. Horror stories from her service in the ER. Patients in car crashes from drunk driving, knocked off their bicycle by over the limit speeders, and more. Every patient put her off wanting another drop. That and she drank almost enough to kill her liver when she was a Wolf. Isis' powers had restored her toxic and poisoned organ.

I probed harder into the bond, finding she wasn't feeling very talkative, friendly, or in the mood for company from anyone besides Castor. They formed a tight little bond. He showed her some trust, and she reciprocated. Something she felt I hadn't afforded her. Not true. I sent Alaric out to check her and Jerry's leads on Danny's new business ventures. If I didn't have an ounce of trust in her, I wouldn't have let her out of the cell.

I could take the hint. Shame, because I came here hoping for some flirty, witty banter. Set was the king of disorder and turmoil, and my whole world had been thrown into upheaval since she arrived. I needed one moment of calm to ease my mind of all the shit and the anniversary that hit today. The tranquility offered by my mate. Liz always had a soothing effect on my chaotic mind, caging the destructive beast in me, and I'd hoped Aaliyah would too. Because I really fucking needed a break from it all.

"Goodnight, Nurse A." I cupped the scotch under my arm and moved back.

"Slade, wait." My name, not Mr. Vincent. Spoken softly and respectfully, without her normal feisty edge.

I turned around, and she moved aside, gesturing for me to come in. My heart screamed at me to enter, and my head said otherwise. Bad move. Being near her left me susceptible to her charms. To hell with it. I really needed her. Against my better judgment, I thumped inside her room, set the scotch and tumblers on her nightstand. Exhausted, I collapsed onto her bed, causing it to bounce. Making myself at home, I reclined on the bed like a damn relaxing jackal, legs raised, boots on my damn bed. Fuck it. This was my club, my room, my rules.

"Make yourself at home." Aaliyah closed the door, standing at the foot of the bed, arms crossed.

I twisted open the bottle and poured us both a generous finger of scotch. "Take a load off, Nurse A." I patted the bed, coaxing her closer. Her standing by the bed wouldn't do when I needed her by my side.

Wary, she accepted the glass I offered, examining the light reflecting through the crystal and the dark, honey-colored contents. She closed her eyes and inhaled its malty scent, remembering her father and his preference for scotch, too.

The gold phone Zethan had bought her buzzed on her nightstand. She didn't so much as glance at it.

I pointed my glass at it. "You're not going to get that?"

"Not interested." She twisted the tumbler back and forth, producing a rainbow kaleidoscope across her beautiful caramel face. Still pissed at Zethan for extracting information from her.

"Don't break his heart." I stared into my tumbler. "He's been through a lot."

We all fucking had. Zethan lost his sister, his baby boy, his ex-partner, and mate in the space of a few years. Fate was cruel. Scarred his body in an accident that nearly took his life, too. Left him disfigured, insecure and awkward in his body. With a dick that fucking went wandering because of his affiliation to Osiris. Asshole buried himself in work and barely let a woman near him. If Aaliyah rejected him, as I'd done to her, it could wreck him. And I'd not let him go through that again.

I swallowed more liquid to wet my dry throat. "He and Castor stood up for you, you know?"

That brought my nurse's gaze to mine. Steely and unforgiving. Her heart had been burned by us, him especially, and my words did little to foster any compassion.

Out of all my men, the three avatars were the most

damaged in my club. I loved them like blood brothers. Protected them, their lives my responsibility.

"This reminds me of home," she murmured, ignoring my comment. Fire in my heart crackled, spitting embers. My mate was home to me.

It'd take time for her to forgive Zethan. Forgive us all. Except for Castor, the lucky prick.

"Dad and I used to drink this every Christmas Eve and New Year's." Her voice wobbled as she fought her grief. I knew that feeling all too well.

Dad and I used to settle back for a drink every night. Same time. Celebrate we were still alive and kicking. Admire the club and its achievements. Father to son. President to vice president.

I leaned back on her pillow, gulped down my whole drink and hissed. Liquid malt warmed my throat all the way to my stomach as I swallowed it. "Your dad was a good man. Tough, but honorable." Like my old man. I'd lost him a few years back to cancer.

Wish I could say the same about myself. Sometimes I skirted the lines of ruthless, but it was in my blood, and one of many reasons my god chose me.

"Dad used to get every club member a bottle of Macallan Single Malt for Christmas." Pricey. One g a pop. Generous of old Heller. I gave my men something similar, a fat bonus, vouchers for a holiday.

"I had no grievance with your father, you know that, Aaliyah?" God, why the fuck had I turned confessional all of a sudden? Maybe it was the weight in my heart.

"Danny said you had a disagreement with Dad weeks before his death."

Vehement, I shook my head. "A lie."

Lost in her memories, she cupped her drink to her chest. She needed my arm over her shoulder to snuggle into my side and hold me. I needed the light pressure of her body to mine, the softness of her caramel skin, to breathe in her vanilla and cherry scent.

"Sit. Drink. Warm up your old man." The nickname came out. Blunt. Weighty. Longing. Emotion ruled me, not logic, and I was too fucked up, too desperate for her by my side to care.

It wasn't the command that brought her to rest on the edge of the bed. Heaviness in my voice, the exhaustion, and something else she couldn't identify persuaded her to fall beside me. Inches apart. Far enough away that I couldn't use my oozing sex appeal to get her naked and on her back. Despite everything, my rugged, chaotic wildness called to her, and she hated that alluring charm about me. Ditto. I hated the calming effect she had on me. Hated that I needed it and relied on her.

I hadn't forgotten when I'd taken her to dinner, the way I broke her reserves down, gotten under her skin. The way I'd brushed her arm and set her body on fire. Set my own on damn fire, too. The kiss I left on the shell of her ear made her beg for more. Feeding her cheesecake seductively, turning her on, making her lose control. She thought me devious like the devil, working my beguiling ways to seduce and trick her. Tonight, there was no trick, and definitely no seducing happening. Just companionship and talking.

"I'm not in the mood for your flirting bullshit tonight," she started, and I snorted, my gaze sharpening on her.

My back straightened, and she set my jackal off. Woman was blunt as fuck, her words knives to my chest. "Tell it like it is, Aaliyah. I like that about you."

"Don't get me started, Slade. I'm spent from healing what you did to Castor. So, if you're going to start on me, you can fuck off." The barb in her words pricked my skin like thousands of rose thorns stabbing me.

"Not my proudest moment." I twisted my glass, staring at it. "Sometimes I can't control my reactions."

"You need to rein that shit in." God, she sounded like Liz. We had many arguments over this. For the most part, I was a fair leader, but sometimes I lost my cool, and she hated it when I got violent. Duty of the job. No way around it.

I rubbed at a fingerprint on the crystal. "Liz used to say I was too overprotective. Too smothering and possessive." I smiled, grim, humorless, pining to have her back with us. My jackal whined for its fallen mate. "Habit from losing my mom and my woman. The barrel of a gun won't stop me from protecting what's mine."

There. Laid it bare for Aaliyah. She had to understand where I came from, why I acted the way I did. I'd not lose another mate. Ever. Set had told me after Liz died that my next mate was my true mate. My lifetime companion. Imagine my shock and fucking surprise when she turned out to be a rival and traitor. Bitter damn pill to swallow. This was me giving her another chance. The only one she'd get, so she better make the most of it. I sent her that thought.

Aaliyah rolled her shoulders and downed her whole drink, uncomfortable at the direction of the conversation going to my ex. Couldn't help it. One of the reasons I came here. I poured us both another drink.

She took an awkward sip, letting the drink warm her tired, aching, and cold body. "Liz sounds like an amazing woman."

I wanted to comfort her and tell her we didn't expect her to be the same. No one wanted a carbon copy of her. We just missed her. I couldn't find the words to tell her.

Aaliyah shifted on the bed, one leg folding over the other, the tension in her muscles evident. "We all know what happened to me today. So, what was so shitty about your day?" Topic change.

Fuck, where did I start? She knew about the incident today. No point in burdening her with club business. Not when she wasn't a patched member. So, I led with the heaviest thing on my mind. "It's her birthday today. She would have been forty-seven." The words came out dark and hard like wrought iron. I should have left the conversation at that, taking the hint that Aaliyah didn't want to talk about it, but she had to know. Had to know what fate might be in store for her if she became our mate.

I kicked off my boots and twisted the crystal glass, staring at it like it contained something so precious that I'd never let it go.

"What happened to Liz?" From Aaliyah's end, I gathered she already knew some details from Zethan.

I might have dialed back my end of the bond and revealed as little as I could, but that wasn't in my nature. I was passion and pain personified. Every little emotion multiplied times a thousand. The way of my god. That was why I hit Castor and felt guilty for it now. Why I came to her door. I fought a losing battle to resist her. The curse said she was mine. My heart said she was mine. Once it convinced my head, it would make her mine.

"A deal to pass through territory for a shipment went south." My throat developed a hard, painful lump. "Fucked our relationship with a previous business partner." I threw back my drink.

She swallowed thickly and stared at her empty glass, prompting me to refill it, the sound of the running liquid echoing the molten lava flowing in my veins.

"The club sought revenge, raided our clubhouse, gassed us unconscious, tied Liz up behind Zethan and the curse killed her." I was barely able to pour myself a double the way I shook. "Needless to say, I'm extra cautious when a rival arrives in my midst. I've had everything taken from me twice, and I'm not about to let it happen again. No limits will stop me from protecting my club or territory."

She nodded and tapped the glass. If Set was right, if Aaliyah was my true mate, she needed to hear this. Needed to know that she wouldn't live if she fucked me over again. God or no gods, the club came first. Women second. If she joined us as our prospect and medic, it would be a different story.

"I'm not a threat to your club, Slade. Not anymore." She set her drink down on the nightstand, telling me my time here was coming to an end. "If I was, I could have snatched one of the attacker's guns and popped Castor in the back. But I didn't. How many times do I have to prove it to you?"

True. She also hadn't called anyone on the phone Zethan gave her. Didn't run away when he took her to the hospital or bar for a drink. Didn't slide away into another shop when Castor took her into town today. Still, I couldn't eliminate that niggling doubt. Couldn't help but wonder if she worked in cahoots with the mole in our ranks. Until the threat of the mole and danger to our business was dealt with, she'd remain a suspect. But I owed her a bit of reinforcement to acknowledge her efforts.

"No, you've saved my man, patched me up. I owe you my thanks." I clapped my hand on her thigh and squeezed.

She lifted her chin, pleased at my acknowledgment. "Can we talk about something else? I'm not in the mood to talk about how perfect your ex was or how I'm a traitorous mate. This isn't a touching way to remember her." The last couple of days left us both emotional and fiery, and I'd clearly come at the wrong damn time for conciliatory drinks.

Harsh words thumped in her head. The cruel things Alaric and I had said and done to her. Untrue accusations and unkind names. Caged her in our basement for a crime she didn't believe she committed.

I was wrong to come here and put this on her. I came

seeking sympathy, compassion, a damn ear and shoulder, but after everything, she had nothing for me. She had a heart, to an extent, and me showing her how much I missed Liz and wished she was still alive pushed Aaliyah over the edge. I'd been unfair to her, and it gutted me.

Drink and tumbler in hand, I labored off the bed. "I knew it was a mistake coming here." Sand blocked my throat, abrading it, red, raw, and stinging.

She held out her tumbler for me, but I didn't take it. "Then why did you?"

A choked cry throbbed down the link. Pain and torment. Grief and blame. As president, I took responsibility, and the fault lay with me even though I didn't kill Liz. In my mind, I might as well have, and that sat heavy on my heart, like a weight slowly suffocating and crushing me. I also bore the brunt of Castor and Aaliyah being hurt today and almost killed.

"Slade—" Aaliyah pinched her brow.

"No." The harsh snap in my voice called her attention up to me. "Don't fucking say it. Don't pity me." I didn't want her apology for losing my mate. I wanted the dam gods to apologize for tormenting all of us.

"I thought I could find some relief, a moment of stillness, where I don't have to think about Liz, the club, or this bullshit with your brother." My croaking voice broke down my hostility, and this time she took pity on me. "I just need a moment of fucking peace." We'd both lost someone we loved. Weeks ago, she'd concluded that I'd taken her father from her. I had morals and rules. Act only in retaliation. And I had no reason to gun down Alexander Heller.

CHAPTER 29

Aaliyah

THE EXPRESSION of longing on his face made me soften and go easy on him. I moved to him, sweeping a hand through the blond hair that had fallen across his forehead. For a moment, he leaned into me, nuzzling me, his stubble bristling as it scraped my skin, leaving it tingling.

But then he came to his senses and jerked away. "Don't. It's best if you don't." I'd never seen the flirty devil so serious. So haunted by a memory. Genuinely in love with someone other than himself.

Underneath all his gruff and danger, he was a lonely man, wanting to share his life with his mate. Couldn't blame him for wanting happiness and love. Basic human need.

"I thought if I came here, I might soothe the chaos inside me." He cradled the scotch like he would her in his arms.

His previous mate had given him solace.

"I'm not her and I don't want to replace her or be her," I

said softly, bristling at being compared to her, at him wishing for her when I was here instead.

"No, but you're my mate." He looked up from the bottle to me. "And I wanted the solace and company of that. There's more to me than just fire, temper, and passion, Nurse A. Give me a chance to show it to you."

"I let you into my room, didn't I? Let you get off what was on your chest." Seriously? This guy was a hypocrite. I never got such comforts when I was locked in his basement. "Where was my comfort and solace when I woke from surgery, frightened and scared, and your men threw me into the cell? The only Jackal who showed me an ounce of compassion was Castor!"

Slade smiled. Not the cocky dimpled smile that always got me. A brittle smile that said he knew he wouldn't win with me. And I bet not many people went up against him and beat him. Few lived to tell the tale. I might have signed my death warrant for it.

"None of my men touched you, tortured you, made you bleed like your uncle," he growled. "You're a spoil of war, Aaliyah, and we could have had our way with you. But we didn't."

Fucking asshole. He could change from kind to cruel in the blink of an eye. I brought my hand crashing to his cheek, like stone, hard and unmoving. Pink spread across his jaw, prompting him to smirk and his dimples to dig in, weakening me.

I went to do it again, but he caught my arm, his grip tight and unbreakable. "Do it again. I like it. *Harder.*"

I bet he did. His former mate never let him off the leash, confined him with tight parameters, and he hated that a woman had that power over him. Slade liked control, to be the man, the devil, and for me, that was what I was getting. He didn't hold anything back for me. Cruel, brutal, and possessive.

"Your old lady never let you talk like that." It was a low blow, even for me, but he got under my skin like no man had ever before, and I wanted to kill him and hump him at the same time. "Never let you be the real you, did she?"

Slade's face went from twisted with rage to shocked in one second flat. He shoved me up against the wall, expelling all the air from my lungs. His hand came around my throat, not choking me, but showing me what he could do if I pushed him too far. An equal part in me rose to the challenge. I wasn't scared. Not in the slightest. Aroused as fuck when the back of his hand skimmed along my waist to the underside of my breast. This was the real him. Passion, power, emotion, flames.

Although my heart scolded me and told me to apologize, I refused because Slade Vincent wasn't the kind of man to apologize for his actions. And I'd be damned if I did either.

"You want to see what I can really do, Aaliyah?" Slade flashed his teeth as he snarled. His grip tightened, and I liked the way his hand enclosed my neck. All the way around. The mate bond flared with my need to both hurt and fuck him.

"You've got nerve, Slade. Coming in here to drink away your dead mate and seek comfort from me after what you put me through." I traced a finger along his cheek, testing him, seeing if he'd bite. He twitched at my touch, but didn't move, holding the line. Conflict rippled beneath the surface of the mate bond, telling me he wanted to both break my finger and suck it at the same time. "Fuck you. Get the hell out of my room." I didn't care if I sounded like a bitch. I knew what he wanted and why.

Aching hunger seared our connection. This turned him on as much as it did me. He liked fire and explosions and laying waste to everything, including my heart. He pinned one hand above my head and ground into me. When he got mad, he lost control of his hold on the mate bond and his emotion engulfed it. And I was going to be the one to push him to it.

"Do it," I goaded. "Hurt me. You've wanted to ever since I took a bullet for you. Worst decision of my life. I thought you were innocent. I was wrong. You're far from innocent."

Slade growled so savagely that my chest rattled from it. "Fuck, Nurse A, you had better be innocent, or I'm going to fucking kill you!"

"Don't call me that!" I wanted to scratch out his beautiful, hard, indigo eyes so they'd never look at me the way they did now. Hungry, both for pleasure and to consume his prey.

"Afraid you'll like it?" He smirked at me again, deploying those damn dimples. My fucking kryptonite.

"Don't flatter yourself, Mr. Vincent." I squirmed against him, but it did no good. He was too powerful, too much a force of nature to move out the way.

He blew air out of his lips, and fuck me, my gaze went there. "Mr. Vincent. The way you say that gets me so hard." He backed that claim up, grinding his growing bulge into my stomach.

Driven mad by him, I scratched at him with my free hand, catching the side of his face, dragging long, red welts down his cheek and jaw. Payback for caging me. His back arched, and he let out a harsh grunt. For that, he tossed the scotch on my bed and pinned my free arm above my head, his long, thick fingers able to close over both wrists. Bucking beneath him, I fought him with everything I had and the flood of desire pooling at my core. This man drove me crazy in more ways than one. One word and he lowered me to a hissing, spitting, jealous beast who wanted to claim her mate and make him forget all about the other.

"I'm going to fuck your brains out and make you pay for that." He lifted me and threw me on the bed. This man got me hotter than a furnace, and I didn't resist him, letting him tear my pajamas off. Fucking tore them with a pop of buttons and shred of my pant legs.

When he had me naked, he parted my legs, crawled over me, and dragged the scotch back. He uncapped the bottle and poured some over my belly, flicking his tongue as he lapped it off my burning skin. My fingers sank through his tuft of hair, yanking it, wanting to tear it out. He grunted and shoved me back, delivering more scotch onto my breasts, sucking them as if my nipples bled the stuff. For his finale, he lathered my pussy in alcohol, making it tingle with a mild sting. I yelped as he jammed the whisky into my pussy, lifting my legs and the bottle, making it trickle inside me. Humming to himself, he let me go, and I bounced to the bed. Oh god, the sweet burn. Like the stretch of a huge cock inside me. Head buried between my thighs, he drank from my pussy, in between driving me to my first orgasm.

I remembered what he'd said before we fucked the first time. He'd make me come three times and every time. Boy, had he delivered. Tonight, he was going to do that to me and more.

"I'm all in," I seductively whispered to him. "I'll let you express all the darkness behind your god." That was what he really wanted. His true motivation for visiting. Slade Vincent didn't just want comfort, solace, and a cozy little chat. He wanted to end the world with me beneath him.

That was all it took to make him break. He paused, his sharp head at the tip of my pussy. "Tell me what you want, Nurse A. I'll give it all to you. All the fire and destruction of my god."

I could barely breathe from the tension crackling between us. "Do it."

That was it. He was a madman unleashed. A beast unrestrained. He crashed into me with no regard for hurting me, and I didn't care because I wanted him balls deep, slamming into me, all his fire, his passion, burning down all the hostility between us.

He fisted my hair so tight, winding it around his hand, yanking it, drawing my head closer, like I was his goddamn dog on his leash. "This is what you get for pushing me."

He could threaten me all he wanted. In that space and time, I had no concern for my safety or life. Only the crash of hips into my ass, the relentless pound of his cock, the harsh breaths in my ear mattered.

"Do it." I tilted my head to the side to let him bite me again. "Go on." I shouldn't have goaded him, but something about him drove me to insanity. To a wild abandon that made me forget about the consequences.

With him, it was all about living in the moment, enjoying it, taking full advantage of it. I'd always been so highly strung, checking doses, double checking, rigid in my nursing, terrified of making a mistake. Terrified that if I lost my career, I'd be sent back to my father's club, crawling for help. And I was too damn proud for that.

I took every beat from Slade, my body skidding across the sheets, him dragging me back for more. He reduced me to a whining, ragged mess, barely able to breathe. My throat dried out from my gargled whimpers. Fingers clawed, I clutched the sheets, unable to hold on as he hurtled me into oblivion faster than a spaceship ride to the moon. I crashed over his cock a second time.

He was my mate, no doubt about it. My body knew it. My soul knew it. My heart knew it. They just had to convince my head. No easy task.

He leaned over me, bracing his arms either side of my head, his mouth to my neck, teeth sinking into my skin, breaking it. I cried out, digging my nails into his shoulder and back as he and his beast claimed me. There was no going back now. Mated together. Unable to be broken even if we wanted to. And I no longer wanted to. He was my wilderness, my darkness, my moonlight. I wanted every bit of it and more.

Back arched, I raised my hips to meet him as my second orgasm hit with more force, and I managed to cry out. Eyes slammed shut, I clutched him tighter, legs clasping his hips, drawing out my pleasure.

He lifted me and repositioned me, straddling him on two knees. I slapped him again, making him grunt and break out into a wicked smile. His hands clamped around my throat, and mine around his. This violent act had turned us into savages. I climbed on top of his waiting legs, thick like logs, and I rode his cock hard.

"Fuck, Slade," I panted, never having experienced anything as wild, brutal, and rough in my life. Sex with him was like the darkness itself. Dangerous and not something to be tempted or toyed with. I played with fire with Slade, lit a damn match in his face, and he'd turned it into an inferno.

This man owned my body like he owned the club, its members, the power of a god. I took the full force of it with every brutal stroke inside me. I wondered if sex with Slade was always going to be this violent and punishing. I'd be walking bow-legged tomorrow, that was a fact. But I welcomed the pain to remind me of this incredible moment.

Fate brought us together in the most unexpected of circumstances and it had no hope of letting us go. It owned us as he dominated my body.

"Get ready for the ride of your life," Slade droned hot in my ear as he brought me to the edge of my third orgasm. Always in threes, just like he promised when we first had sex. The memory distant but so close, glowing in my chest with the fire of our combusting passions.

I screamed out his name, the sound dying in my throat as

his body tightened and he came with a violent explosion inside of me that almost made me black out. Our fight, our sex, our carnal noises were so loud that the other club members were bound to have heard us.

He collapsed on top of me, his breath strained, chest heaving. I ran my hands along his huge arms and back, enjoying his crushing weight on me.

As I came back to myself, I vowed that this was the last time we did that. We'd only come together to work out our frustrations. His loneliness and loss of control with his club and my irritation at being kept captive. This was strictly a second time deal and no more. I'd not let Slade Vincent further into my heart than he already was. He was like a knife that had punctured my organ a quarter of an inch, always trying to sink deeper, but I blocked him.

I couldn't afford to fall for him, or the other Jackals for that matter, with everything up in the air and my father's murderer at large. But every moment I spent with Slade Vincent broke down the barrier between us and let him get a firmer grip on my heart.

CHAPTER 30

Zethan

TRIGGER WARNING: scenes contain memories of child loss and extreme violence (seperate incidents).

MY BIKE always caused a stir when I pulled up here for more than one reason. The rumble of the engine and muffler carried across the slope, through trees and bushes, rattling every bone in this forsaken place.

I killed my engine and dismounted, leaving Castor waiting on his bike. Respectful. Peaceful. The last I wished I could be.

Deathly silence followed as mourners left in a hurry as the big, burly biker thumped through the cemetery in his boots and leather.

Spirits wandering the hallowed grounds took notice and drifted to me, reaching for me, begging for mercy. Mist parted as I brushed through them, my answer always the same.

"Leave me be." I raised a palm at them. "I'm not your master."

Despite the spirits' calls, their Underworld Lords had left them here to dwell forever, for whatever reason. It was not my duty to force them to accept the dead. I ruled my land and they ruled theirs.

Wind tugged my hair as I wandered down the second to last row of headstones, stopping at the thirteenth, shoving my hands into my pocket. Plastic met my touch, and I removed the figurine of the little blue dog with a yellow muzzle and white eyebrows. I crouched beside the headstone, tracing the letters carved into it. *Dylan Stone. Beloved Son.*

Visiting here brought back all the memories, fresh and raw as if they were yesterday. His little heart unable to keep functioning the way his body demanded it. Hospital after hospital visit. Cardiologists unable to find a match for a heart transplant, no matter how much cash I threw at them to fix him.

I leaned on the tombstone to stop from crumpling into a heap. Thick, salty tears dripped down my cheeks as I set the little *Bluey* figurine at the foot of his headstone. Dylan's favorite cartoon. He used to play with his toys all the time and pretend he was the *Blue Heeler*, the main character. I brought one every year to his grave, three years on. The only time I ever visited this fucked place. Some asshole always stole the toys, probably another kid, or some cheapskate bastard swiping it for their children.

"Hi, mate." Cold, solid marble met my fingers as I stroked the headstone with shaking fingers. "Brought you a present." I crushed my eyes shut, my body rocking, my soul unsteady. "Happy seventh birthday, buddy."

Every time I came here, it broke me a little more, my soul forever fractured into thousands of pieces. Twice a year I visited, once for Dylan, the second for my murdered sister, Abigail.

The souls wandering through the cemetery pressed harder upon me to help them. A pressure upon my soul like rope wrapping around my body and squeezing me. Disrespectful pricks never let me grieve alone. Annoyed, I cast them aside with a wave of my fist, banishing them from my presence. Fuck, I had to get out of here before I smashed some stone with my boots. And I could do it with my shifter strength.

Hands stuffed in my leather jacket pockets, I stumbled off the grassy hill, back to my bike. No words were exchanged with Castor as I slid my helmet on. Sorrow and worry hit me through our connection. That was all I needed from him. Tears made the padding inside my helmet rub uncomfortably. I thrashed the fuck out of my bike as I took off, not caring if it grabbed the attention of the highway patrol. Castor could redirect them with a fake callout.

Right now, I needed the wild and free call of the road. The ongoing gray pavement stretched out for miles, taking me to my next destination.

Osiris help the next fucker we planned to visit. The drug dealer who hired the mugger to beat up Aaliyah. Because when I got in one of these moods, there was going to be hell to pay.

***

"Why the fuck did you beat up Aaliyah Heller?" Castor laid another blow to the gut of Gary Young, the scumbag dealer who paid off the junkie to beat up Aaliyah. He groaned and hunched over the chair we'd tied him to in the empty parking garage by the wharf.

I clutched the other figurine in my pocket; the one I kept to remind me of my son. Displayed on my desk back at the club beside a picture frame of Abigail. A constant reminder of what I'd lost. What I fought for and would continue to fight for.

"Was paid to." The scumbag spat blood to his side, and it splattered on the stained concrete. We had taken him to this place below a restaurant by the wharf, packed full of old furniture, decorations, and a dusty car.

For the last twenty minutes, Castor had made mincemeat of his damn ugly mug. Prick already looked like a squashed crab before getting his face beaten in. Crooked nose, lined forehead, squinty dark eyes, slug lips, and a brute face shaped like a troll. Crimson liquid dripped from the various cuts across his face and bleeding nose. Gary held out for longer than most. Crooks usually squealed within the first few punches. The more impressive ones held out for longer. Castor's record was a three-hour torture session that nearly killed him and the man he beat to a pulp.

"By whom?" Another punch to the side of the scumbag's face got the answer we needed.

Gary sighed and lolled his head back. He'd taken a pretty bad beating. Castor broke his nose and cheekbone and almost took out his jaw for what he'd done to Aaliyah.

"His name's Savvy Bill," the scumbag panted. "He organizes hits and beatings for Underworld crime syndicates."

I almost laughed at the nickname. Underworld figures always had the stupidest of names. Some to provoke fear, others to provoke intrigue, the rest plain, old stupid. Savvy Bill sounded like a fucking dumb cartoon character or something.

What I didn't laugh at was getting caught up in the fucking mob. Those bastards were brutal, loyal to family, money, and power. Devoid of morals or compassion, and with no objections to blow out your brains for a price. While the Jackals weren't angels, we didn't kill anyone for the sake of it, and we protected our own, our business, and future.

Armed with a name, I used my magick to cut off Gary's air supply, locking his throat muscles up so he couldn't breathe. I nodded at Castor as the dealer gasped and choked, kicking his legs, making his chair scrape along the concrete and topple over. Time to clear out and for my enforcer to track down Savvy Bill.

"Got an address," Castor said as we slipped out of the basement garage, the salty wind hitting us, ruffling our hair.

Seagulls squawked up ahead, fighting over scraps from a bin behind a wharf-side restaurant. Residents walked dogs along the beach and docks, and tourists took photos of the boats, braving the winter's chill.

Pleased, I smiled and gestured at my brother. "Lead the way."

***

GUNS OPENED fire as we charged into Bill's domain, refusing to address the receptionist or questions of the two security guards stationed outside a hallway. Bullets tore into marble, wood, and metal of the expensive suite out the back of the Sydney Fish Markets. Crappy shots from *'so-called'* goons paid to protect their masters. Still, one grazed my arm and one skimmed Castor's thigh, making his denim stain red and my leather smoke.

Fuck. We'd expected guns and security but weren't sure

of how many to negotiate until we found our target. To save our asses, we might have to use magick, even though I needed to conserve it for our *little chat* with Bill. The guards were packing Kevlar on their chest, and each shot had to strike the neck or head.

"Lock this place down," I ordered Castor.

"Yes, VP." The lights went off and activated the emergency lighting. Security cameras went dead. Precautions to prevent the use of our magick being recorded. Security swipe doors locked and sealed, preventing any escape by the people inside. After we finished, Castor would wipe all traces from the security systems of our visit.

Place stunk like rotting seafood even though they tried to cover it with candles burning at each ornate table.

I unloaded the first clip of my Glock into the two guards' throats, and they slumped to the ground, blood spurting from their necks. Top of my class in the police academy. Rarely missed a shot.

Castor, not so much, his shots hitting wide and off target. Like me, he was a man of law and rules, but his aim shit, his heart on target.

"Losing your touch, Bird Boy," I teased.

"Fuck off," he snorted. "I could take them out if I wanted to."

Nope. Not yet. Save our magick unless absolutely necessary. We didn't know how much we'd need to get to Bill.

I killed the lock on the next door, giving us access to a hallway. Down the hall, we encountered another five gunmen, drawn by the fire in the lobby. My second cartridge unleashed, taking down the front two with bullets to their foreheads. Heavy fire pushed Castor and me into a nearby office. Boots thumped on the marble floor as trained killers came for us.

"Now!" I ordered Castor as we backed away, him taking

cover behind the desk, me using the bookshelf for protection.

We applied a little magick before the men burst into the room. Fire scorched the metal of their weapons, burning their hands and forcing them to gasp and drop them. Without their guns, they only had their hands, batons or knives.

We weren't martial arts fighters by any means, but we could hold our own. As I sprang out to take a shot, a knife flew past me and lodged in the wooden wall panels. The dick came at me with his other knife, and I disarmed him with another academy tactic, the weapon clattering on the bookshelf and stone floor. Before I could untangle myself, he smashed me in the cheek, and I reared back, blinking, eyes watering.

Castor took a few punches to the chest and a baton to the back before I managed to offload more rounds into the armpits and upper torso of two men. One guard gurgled from the puncture to his lung, and he collapsed in seconds. Another clutched the wound in his armpit. I grabbed him by the throat and ejected two rounds into his head. The third guy thumped at me with swinging fists. Castor caught him in a headlock and pumped him with two bullets to the brain.

With that taken care of, we moved deeper, finding a glass-walled conference room, with ten thugs inside. I knew it when I looked at them what they did for a living. My gift let me peer into the soul of a person and see what weighed heavily on their conscience. Each one read differently. Some guilty for murdering their competitors, screwing over others to fight to get to the top, even fucking over their parents or children. Two were remorseful for having mistresses and going to prostitutes every week. The second to the last man was ashamed of his kink for bestiality. Dirty fucker.

When I first met Aaliyah, I'd used my gift on her, and

found her heart heavy with grief. But like Alaric, I found I couldn't read her entirely either.

My sight zoned in on the last man, Bill, his heart as black and dead as mine. No compassion or remorse for what he'd done. Pure lust for greed and power. The only thing that burdened his tarnished soul was that he hadn't made moves in the Underworld sooner to climb the fucking ladder.

We replaced the empty clips before marching into the conference room. Then I used my magick to disengage the lock and enter.

Men in sleek, expensive business suits that cost more than my weekly cop wage tried to hide their shady upbringings, history, and deeds. Fine cloth, thick gold chains or bracelets, and bulletproof cars didn't give them prestige or integrity. These were the lowest of the low, bottom of the barrel-type fuckers. As authentic as the crooked cops placed in the force to serve their Freemason masters. Plants to protect the politicians, lawyers, judges, and officials involved in pedophilia activities and cover-ups. Detectives who refused to investigate their buddies, destroying evidence, whacking witnesses, and destroying their businesses, reputations, and livelihoods. Once the Jackals dealt with the shit surrounding us, I'd go after them, too.

More security guards posted in each corner came at us to protect their bosses. I unhinged and dropped a gaudy chandelier on the head of one man, and he stumbled but didn't go down or drop his weapon. I took care of that with a shot to his fingers, blowing three of them off. Castor blew open the dick's throat, and I hmphed, impressed. The rest I dealt with by single shots to their foreheads. Blood splattered all over the table, the fancy fuckers' fine suits and the thick, woolen carpet.

"Sorry to interrupt your meeting." I shoved my gun in its holster and clapped my hands together as I moved into the room to the head of the table, right to the man we wanted to see.

Castor whistled as he ran his finger along the long, polished wood table with an ornate glass top. He glanced at me, and I gave the command, a single nod, and he carried out the order. One by one, he put a bullet in the brains of the gang members, showing Bill we weren't playing. He fucked with our business, harmed our mate, and was potentially in bed with our enemy. We wouldn't let that slide. Even if he was innocent, so what? One less mobster for the cops to deal with.

I shoved a dick out of the seat, let him thump on the floor, and sat down, hands clasped. "Savvy Bill, right?" The man remained calm, silent. "Paid a visit to a friend of yours. Gary Young." Recognition flickered in his dark eyes. "He said you hired him to beat up a woman. We want to know who engaged your services for that."

He coughed a harsh, wet cough, full of mucous that made my Underworld spidey senses sit up and take notice. Illness. Long time coming. He took a sip of his tall black coffee before addressing me. "I haven't been in the business this long by divulging my clients' details."

Answer I expected. I shrugged. His loss. I had ways of making this psychopath speak. My Underworld eyes performed a scan of his body, showing his death, the cause, and date. Lung cancer. Smoking really *did* kill.

"Here's how it's gonna go." I threw my boots up onto his table, earning an outraged glare. "You've got a nasty cancer there. Bronchial carcinoma. Malignant. I estimate you've got about three months to live."

Bill or whatever the fuck his name was—I could have searched his soul but didn't care to—loosened his tie.

With a twist of my hand, I sped up the cancer growth, metastasizing it, giving him a little insight into the excruciating pain he'd suffer when dying. "This is what it will be like when you die. Agony. Hell. Loneliness."

The bastard moaned and clutched his chest. "Make it stop."

"Oh, I can do that." I smiled, squeezing my palm, tightening the stranglehold of the cancer fibers on his lung, making him choke and wheeze. "For two answers. One—the name of your client. And two—did you steal a truck containing our drug shipment?"

The man yanked off his tie, scratching at his shirt, desperately ripping the buttons off. His bare chest exposed the dark, almost black veins and mass beneath his skin, invisible to all but me.

"Cure me and I'll give it to you," he wheezed, barely able to breathe through the sticky, thick mess in his chest.

Fuck, no. Never. I didn't tempt fate. Knew better than to mess with that. The Fates in Hades' pantheon could clip my fate string if I dared ... if I belonged to the Greek pantheon. Still, I wouldn't test the gods or their limits. Sometimes a detective had to resort to dirty tactics to get the offender, and I wasn't above that.

I wound back Bill's symptoms to the state they were when we met. The trick worked and he gasped, eyes bright with alarm, fingers clawed in his skin. "Thank you." He smoothed his now scruffy hair. "Which woman are you enquiring about?"

"Aaliyah Heller," I growled.

Bill shifted uncomfortably. "I don't know who was behind that job. An anonymous package turned up at my reception. Cash with a note requesting I assault the woman and steal your shipment."

Paid fucking goons with no club and mysterious connections. Just like the mysterious riders who chased Castor and Aaliyah.

I leveled the prick with a hard glare. "Did you send the riders against our club yesterday?"

Bill offered a stiff nod. "They were my men."

I glanced at Castor, silently checking if he had any more information on this, but he shook his head. Fuck. Another dead lead. Whoever was behind this bullshit knew how to get around Thoth's power to trace everything. They were onto us. Onto our godly powers. Were prepared. Always one fucking step ahead of us.

I jabbed a finger at Bill's polished table. "This will be the last time you interfere with our club."

"I haven't been paid for further actions," Bill replied.

Perfect. We were safe. For the moment, at least. Until the prick behind this emerged from the shadows.

Another twist of my hand dialed his cancer symptoms back to critical, and I watched him die in his chair, face gripped in agony, lungs failing, mouth agape to take in nothing.

"Grab his phone and get the data," I told Castor. "Assess this dirty mutt."

CHAPTER 31

Aaliyah

Arguing in Slade's office drew my attention from the Isis book Castor had loaned me. A heated discussion with snippets of words. Something about a shootout. Panic shot down my bond and propelled me off the bed. Someone was injured and needed my attention. Had the Jackals had a run-in? Did Danny come for me again, and they defended their turf?

For once, Alaric wasn't stationed outside my room, and I padded in my socks to Slade's door, listening.

"She deserves to know." Zethan. Rule and order.

"It's club business." Slade. Hot and raging.

"Someone is after her too, and she deserves to know." Castor. Cool and calm.

"Dirty mutt." Alaric. Suspicious and unforgiving.

"Show her some mercy, Slade." Zethan again.

My heartbeat sped up at him defending me and I had to control it, so they didn't detect me through our connection. I was still hurt at Zethan playing me. Hadn't answered his messages the last two nights, despite Slade's plea not to break his heart. *Fuck that shit.* We weren't lovers. Weren't even friends, only brought together by a curse and gods. And now, we were fucking even on the betrayal front.

As I listened in, I felt a new area of my power blossom, the struggle of heartbeats, the leak of blood, rush of immune cells to defend the gashes.

Thank the goddess.

The panic from moments ago spiraled and I had to check myself for worrying about these four men that crashed into my life. Every day my feelings built for them despite me not wanting or inviting it, and that frightened me. That wasn't the curse or my insane hormones talking, either. Each man had managed to capture a little of my heart, and I hated that they'd made me feel that way. Hated that I admired, respected, and was attracted to parts of my captors. Feelings I refused to act on. Well ... besides hot, violent sex with Slade. Not that I was counting ... because that shit was not happening again.

"We need to trust her and she us." Castor. Rhyme and reason. "Share this with her, and maybe she'll be more forthcoming."

My heart bounced around with joy. Finally, I wasn't *Aaliyah the Traitor*, I was Aaliyah ... hmmm. Family? Mate? Not sure about the title ... yet. Fuck, why was I thinking like that when I wanted to stay mad at them? I was a confused, twisted mess, like a ball of twine a cat played with.

"Fuck." I imagined Slade, elbows on his desk, scratching his fingers through his Mohican top hair. A sexy image. One I shouldn't pay attention to. "You assholes both tag-team me. Wear me down."

"You love it, bitch." I couldn't help but giggle into my hand at Zethan's reply. I could totally picture him and Castor working away at Slade to convince him. Logic and rationale ruled their mind. Emotions ruled Slade's. He relied on them both to lead the Jackals and he knew it. Without them, he'd be burning down every single club in Australia and getting the Jackals killed.

Slade sighed. "Come in, Aaliyah, and quit your eavesdropping."

Shit. Breath froze in my throat, and my fingers curled at my side. They knew I was there the whole time and let me listen. Was this another test? How many would they put me through to ascertain my loyalty and allegiance? I loved my family, my mother and father, but all love between Danny and me had been severed with no hope of repair.

Alaric snapped open the door, greeting me with his classic scowl and standing aside. Didn't do myself any favors there.

"Heard you arguing, and I thought someone was injured." I played with my fingers at my stomach as I came to stand in front of the president's desk beside Castor, letting Zethan shift a few paces away. Alaric stood behind me like a solid wall between the door and me.

Slade's eyes were red, his almond complexion pale, cheeks drawn. At the sight of me, his cheeks flushed with a slight pink. Memories from last night flooded to the surface of both our bonds. He ran his fingers down the fading pink scratches I'd made on his face. Fuck, I'd let myself lose control and hurt him when I'd made an oath to treat and heal. Ashamed of my actions, I didn't meet his gaze.

Instead, I concentrated on examining them all, searching for wounds. Castor's jeans were stained red from a gash to his thigh. Zethan had a hole in his leather jacket, and I felt the pump of blood beneath it, his body fighting to close the wound, preventing infection. For Alaric and Slade, I found nothing besides the first's efforts to heal his lung.

"You're hurt." I went to Castor first, assessing his wound, a bullet graze, right over the top of his femoral artery.

"It's just a scratch." Typical tough guy response. Left alone and untreated, this could get infected. Not taking that chance. Especially after he stood up for me.

"You're lucky this wasn't deeper." Grateful for his comments, I placed both hands over it. I ordered the skin and fat to repair, the blood to replenish, any infection to be cleared by the body.

He cupped his bloody hand to my face, rubbing a thumb over my cheek. I blushed, suddenly shy that he displayed affection in front of his brothers when he'd previously gone to efforts to hide it. "Thank you."

With Castor repaired, I smiled and looked at Zethan. We couldn't touch or be close for long, so I'd have to make it quick. Hesitantly, I crept toward him, testing to see if he wanted me to approach. He let me, and I pressed my palms over the hole, not needing him to slide off his jacket. The injury told me everything I needed to know. Deeper than Castor's, cutting into his bicep, making it difficult for him to lift his arm or steer his bike. Onset of cramps hit, and he winced as I restored his wound, calling on the same skills as I'd used on Castor. His took a little longer, and we both hunched, me struggling to finish from the pain. I pushed through it and closed the wound, rebuilt and sealed the flesh torn open.

Appreciative for what I'd done, without asking, without negotiation, Zethan and Castor opened their mate bond and allowed me in. This was them. Every part of them. Shared without hesitation or misgivings. Wholly. No hiding. No secrets. They wanted me here. A sign they trusted me. After all the back and forth, they finally believed me and my story. From everything they'd gathered, through conversations, my reactions, my behavior, they didn't consider me a traitor.

Taken aback, my hand went to my chest, and I scratched my fingernails over it.

Through Slade allowing me into their inner sanctuary, he too demonstrated an element of confidence in me. Overwhelmed, I almost broke down and cried. Defending myself had been exhausting. Proving myself grueling when I didn't need to prove anything besides being in the wrong place at the wrong damn time.

Hell, even Alaric damn well softened at my swell of emotion. I sensed the gooey mess of his heart as the soft romantic in him bypassed the hard, bitter, jagged edges of his suspicion and lack of trust.

"Zethan and Castor came back from an investigation." I stiffened at Slade's words, putting an end to the emotion. He still wasn't entirely sold on me, but he was slowly coming around, just like Alaric. "They tracked down the man hired to mug you, got a name, found an Underworld figure responsible for taking out hits on people."

"Who hired him?" I cut in before he could get it out. My entire body rocked on the edge of a dark chasm. One wrong move, the edge would collapse, and an avalanche would take me down with it.

Slade scraped at his beard. "We don't know. The person paid in cash and a note with details on the job. Phone records Castor pulled from the man coordinating the attacks showed that whoever's behind this knows of our operations."

I bristled all over. They called me here for another fucking interrogation. "And you think it's me?"

Castor set a hand on my arm. "Calm down, Aaliyah. No one's accusing you of anything."

I relaxed a little. But a week of accusations, threats, and worrying for my life left me defensive and testy. Wary, I shrugged him off. "Then why am I here?"

Slade sighed. "We think that whoever's behind the hits

knows we're avatars and what we can do. They're hiding, every move untraceable back to them to conceal their identity."

I huffed out a nervous laugh. "Danny's not that fucking smart."

"No, he's a dumb cunt." Slade's massive hands cupped his hips. "But he ambushed us at our distributor's warehouse, so he's mixed up in this somehow."

Suspicions finally confirmed, my body iced over. Everyone was a pawn in his chess game. Someone to use for his own gain. Psychopath. Any belief that Slade killed my father burned away like the last of the wick in a candle. Any last affection I held for my brother evaporated, lost to the past.

The edge of the chasm caved in and down I fell. Amid the darkness, rough fingers scratched my arms and legs, trying to grab me. Hidden enemies wishing to secure my power. Debris thundered on the ground, and I knew I was gone and closed my eyes. I hit the ground with a thud, losing my breath, unable to see a thing. Lost and frightened, I scrambled to my knees, groping for anything to get me out of here and lead me back to sanity and stability. Strong hands pulled me from the darkness, back into the light, a pearly moonlight. Castor. Grave. Concerned. Protective.

"Aaliyah?" his distant voice called to me like a lighthouse beacon, leading me to shore. "Aaliyah?"

I blinked and shook away the vision. Warm hands stroked me, chasing away the frigid darkness that had settled into my bones. Castor's. Each brush brought me back to the room, back to him, back to them. Processing the news of my brother's wickedness, his mysterious involvement in this shit, I swiped my nose and the single tear that dropped. I clasped my hand in Castor's, squeezing tightly, holding onto his safety and the ease he pumped into me.

Longing torched stronger through his end of the bond. Issuing a possessive growl, he clutched me tighter, tugging me closer, setting his other hand on my shoulder.

The bond between the five of us hardened like steel, every thought from the avatars a silent oath of protection and devotion. I tapped into the mate bond, at the faint hints trickling through. The longing, urgent need, and protective instincts rising to the surface of the connection. Slade and Alaric had done a complete reversal on their rejection of me. All four of them wanted to protect me and regard me as theirs. Reluctance tugged at Alaric's end, telling me he wasn't quite ready to forgive, but he was willing, and that was all that mattered.

Finally, I understood why the gods had paired us as mates. They'd never stop fighting to protect and save me. Destroy every threat to their club, to me, steamroll any obstacle in their way, including my brother. They needed me as much as I needed them. For survival, comfort, support, companionship, and lastly, love. Each man had his demons, some known, others to be revealed, just as I had demons to exorcise. Together, we would banish them. Together, we were stronger, united, and dangerous. Danny would pay for what he did to me, to my father, to the Wolves and the Jackals. The day of reckoning quickly approached and I welcomed it. And whoever else aided my brother would be burned to ash once Slade found them.

Slade studied me with a cautious gaze. "Whoever your cunt of a brother is working for also hired this same fucker to steal a truck full of our product, costing us a mil. Chopped our delivery man to pieces." I cupped a hand over my mouth to hold the vomit back. "We're going to start with Danny first. Hit him where it hurts for killing our family and fucking with us." The strained way he said that told me he wanted to unleash a tirade of fouler curse words but held back for me.

Who would have imagined Slade a gentleman?

The link tightened with his uncertainty to reveal more information, a slight mistrust still lingering. I didn't bite or bark at him for it. Didn't blame him. As president of the Jackals, he bore responsibility for the safety of his men, and he'd always be suspicious and untrusting of his enemies. But he'd given me some of his faith, a part of his heart, and trusted me not to break it. Keeping it safe would be my ultimate test. If I broke it again, that was it for us, and my heart cried out at the possibility.

Yes, *the bitch* was slowly chipping away at my resistance and convincing me to trust these men with my life, my protection, and sanctuary. Besides Jerry and my mother, I didn't have anyone else in the MC world to trust. The Jackals wouldn't let me near the former.

My mind went back to Slade's comment. It was official. The Jackals were striking back. War had come between them and the Wolves, and not for the reason I initially believed. Danny deserved everything he got, and I doubted Slade would be merciful when it came to ending my brother and those that followed his rule. I felt numb about the destruction of my father's legacy, a club he started with Jerry for fun, to ride cross country, growing into a team of fifteen men.

Castor twitched from my iron grip cutting off his circulation. "What will you do?" My voice trembled with fear of Slade's answer.

"I can't tell you any more details, other than we need your help for a certain task." His link shrank back like a wary animal trying to hide from a predator entering its territory. Slade didn't fear me, he just didn't want to tell me. I hadn't earned that level of trust yet. We were at the beginning again, and I was fine with that, so long as we didn't stay there permanently.

"Is it risky? Could I get shot again?" Questions I needed answered before I considered agreeing.

Slade scratched at his beard again, his indigo eyes blazing with revenge, his rugged face regaining some of its handsome quality. "Possibly. I can't promise there won't be a risk." Cute. He worried for me. Wanted me safe. Funny thing was, I wanted him and the rest of them safe, too.

I think I knew where he was going. "You want to take out Danny. Torture him until he confesses his sins ..."

Slade smiled like the devil that he was. "Something like that, Nurse A." The nickname caused smoky tendrils to bleed along our attachment and wrap around it. My body lit awake at the contact, and my spine straightened, my core pulsing with need and wild abandon. I hadn't forgotten the way he'd punished my body, brought me to unimaginable pleasure and pain. Everywhere ached from what he did to me last night. My lips were tender and bruised from his brutal kisses. My neck and shoulders burning from his hard bites and teeth indents.

The jury was still out on my decision. I needed more evidence before I committed to anything. "What do you need me to do?"

"This weekend, we're going to the *Summernat Rally* in Canberra." Slade twisted a fist in one palm. "We need neutral territory to get up close to the Wolves. Assess them."

July. Bikers. *Summernat Rally* in the Australian Capital. Where the clubs came together for races, new bikes, alcohol, concerts and lots of women. No way for either club to attack each other. Slade could question Danny all he liked, but I doubted he'd get answers. Smart. The president wasn't just all smoke and fire.

I rubbed my temples. "Why do you want to meet him there?"

Slade leaned back in his chair, and it creaked under his massive bulk and size. "The Wolves' club and businesses are protected by dark magick. We believe they're using it as protection. Which means we're certain Danny knows we're avatars, and I need Castor to get close to take a better look."

What the absolute fuck? I dropped Castor's hand and rubbed my left with my right thumb. Danny didn't believe in fantasy or magick, he was as straight-laced as they came. Add twisted, cruel, and all kinds of perverted.

I had one more question before I gave them my acceptance, even though I knew their feelings on the matter. The mate bond left me all kinds of tangled, and I needed to hear it from their lips. From Slade's lips, since he represented the other three. "And you trust me not to escape or gangrene your dicks so I can switch sides?"

Castor snorted. Alaric rolled his shoulders.

Zethan covered his eyes, his shoulders shaking from his chuckle. "Fuck, Castor, what have you been teaching her?"

"I gave her a few books." Castor grinned at me.

Slade glared at him and matched my body language, displaying his massive biceps and forearms, which could crush me with all the god power backing him. "We'll see which side you choose, Nurse A."

The fact that he used my nickname told me he knew the side I'd pick. Theirs. Always. And I hated myself for it. Hated that I'd fallen victim to the mate bond and let it manipulate me and made me see my enemy in a different light. As bad men with honor and a code. Men who'd defend their turf, businesses, lifestyle, club, members, and women.

Besides my growing attachment to the Jackals, I needed to look Danny in the eye and ask him straight up if he killed our father. First time I'd been drugged, my mind heavy and weighed down by the sedative. Second time he dodged the question. He wouldn't escape a third.

"I want to go too," I admitted. "Look Danny in the eye and ask him if he murdered my father. He can't hurt me anymore when he's done the worst to me." I tugged at my sweater. "Torn my heart out. Shot me. Whatever he tries to do will be a fucking tickle compared to that."

The men were silent, gazes pinned on me, riding through the pain rolling in my chest, their own losses spilling into the mix, heightening the agony.

I righted myself and steeled for a battle with Slade over my next demand. Because Aaliyah Heller didn't give in so easily. Not without a fight. My fate might be sealed: a life with the Jackals and working for the gods. But that didn't mean I couldn't help those I loved. "I'll go on one condition."

Slade growled savagely, making his desk quake and rattle on the floor. Zethan groaned and slapped his forehead, preparing for another argument. Alaric stiffened, unsure of what I wanted to demand. Castor smirked and winked, proud of me, the whisper of *my little dark sorceress* resonating along our attachment like plucked harp strings.

Slade bent his head and buried it in his hands. "What the fuck is it this time?" Testy. Fiery. The big, bad Alpha was in one of his moods. This was bound to turn him into gale-force winds with hail.

I lifted my chin and stood tall. "You release Jerry." My words came out hard, solid as steel, and as unbreakable as diamonds. "You let him prospect for the Jackals. You protect him and his family. Make him one of your own."

Slade's chair rolled along the floor as he shot out of it, and it hit the wall. His body swelled as the lava in his veins reached critical point for release. "You've got to be fucking kidding."

I didn't stop at that. Because my goddess was the queen of

Egypt, and I, her will on Earth, was going to get my way. "You relocate my mother for the meantime until Danny is dealt with."

Slade's mouth rippled with a ferocious growl. "Fuck, you're a pain in my ass."

"I'm a thorn in your side, Mr. Vincent." What? He was just like me, and Set had once ruled over Egypt, by default, from killing his brother. A king, no less. "Your worst fucking nightmare if you say no."

"Don't test me, woman." Hah! The woman tag. He only used it when I really pissed him off. "Why can't we off Danny and install Jerry as president?"

Another good idea. "The men might not take him back if he's snitched on their president."

Slade scrubbed his mouth, thinking.

"What's your answer, Mr. Vincent?" I crooked an eyebrow.

The desk shuddered again, scraping along the polished wooden floors, prompting Zethan to adjust it back into position.

I stepped up into Slade's personal space and stared up into his blazing dark blue eyes. "Save that anger for my brother and his associates."

Slade grabbed me by the back of the neck and brought me close, tilting my head to the side to whisper in my ear. "Woman, you screw me or my club, and I'll kill you."

I smiled as his fingers knotted in my hair. "Threats will get you everywhere, Mr. Vincent." His muscles surged with hunger at his name. I shouldn't have flirted, but I was elated at my victory. Whatever request I threw his way would always be a yes and I knew it.

He gripped my chin and squeezed hard. Possessive. Owning. Greedy. "One day, I'll punish you for willfulness and defiance."

Yes, please, Mr. Vincent! My heart did three cartwheels. Cheap bitch rolled over too easy.

Me on the other hand, I'd always bargain Slade's ass off. "Pleasure doing business with you, Mr. Vincent. In thanks, I'll gladly ride bitch with you to *Summernat*."

Desire quaked through him, and he squeezed his fists to get a grip on it. "You're riding bitch, all right. *And* giving me a goddamn neck massage after this meeting is concluded."

Hmm. Slade Vincent drove a hard bargain too. Seemed I'd met my match. The idea of touching his thick, corded shield of muscles turned me into a pile of hot, gooey mush. Both times he fucked me, I didn't get a chance to explore his body, see how strong and hard he really was. I'd only been pounded and flattened into the tablecloth and mattress like a pancake.

I thrust a hand out and rolled my stiff shoulders. "A massage for me too, and it's settled then."

CHAPTER 32

Castor

D-Day. War initiated. Troops deployed and on the ground. Battle tanks ready to invade. Confronting the Wolves today would determine the outcome of our feud. Everything rested on my shoulders to determine what magick I was up against and how to overcome it. We just had to pray the Wolves would turn up to the *Summernat Rally* and we could get close enough to them for me to do my job. If they were anything like I imagined, they were gutless cowards who wouldn't show their faces. They preferred working from the shadows, hiring or working with intermediaries to undermine our business partnerships, rough up our mate, steal our drugs, and hide behind dirty cops doing their bidding.

Bike engines throbbed around us as riders competed in drag races. Speakers thumped out rock music played by bands on the stage to our left. Exhaust fumes carried in the air, overpowering the scent of beer, bourbon, fast food, and cotton candy. Tires screeched as riders took off in one of many races held throughout the day. Men and women of all shapes and sizes laughed, drank, hollered, made lewd gestures, or plain old showed off. No signs of the Wolves so far.

Wind tossed Aaliyah's hair over her shoulder. That, combined with the sunlight highlighting the blazing aqua determination in her eyes, left me breathless for a second. Wary that we were open and vulnerable, I clutched her hand tighter despite the no gun mandate. Her lush lips abandoned the tight apprehension to curl into a smile just for me. She was the most beautiful woman I'd ever seen. Body like a damn goddess, shapely, small waist, wide hips, meat on her bones and her cleavage ... I wanted to bury my face in it.

Fuck, I had to keep my head in the game, keep my senses on target for the dark, heavy magick clinging to the Wolves.

Yesterday, her astonishment that Zethan and I endorsed her to Slade and her reaction to the news that Danny worked with unseen forces to betray her, convinced me beyond a doubt of her innocence. This past week, I'd assessed her and detected no secrets or lies. A complete open book. She took full responsibility for her part in the situation, which was rare for a person, and it impressed me.

In court, I'd seen all sorts blaming their enemies or abusers for wrongdoings, while taking no liability for getting into the situation. Letting a bully have power over them by not asserting themselves. Suffering in silence at a toxic workplace and not standing up for their rights. Humans were cowards by nature, and didn't want to rock the boat or lose their jobs and livelihood. My little nurse, however, was a fighter, accountable, and most of all, brave. Few of those kinds of people today. Whistleblowers, rebels, revolutionaries.

Aaliyah didn't sense my admiration as she scanned the

crowd, eyes tight, body taut, and apprehensive. Confronting Danny wouldn't be easy. Today would either confirm for her all our suspicions or cloud them further with doubt. Cement in Danny's mind that she was with us, and he wouldn't let her treachery to the family or the Wolves go so easy. I'd brushed my thumb over her hand to show my support.

Years of prosecution experience gave me the ability to sniff out a liar from an honest person ... Aaliyah being the few exceptions that tricked me. We could tell her our assumptions until we were blue in the face, but she had to come to her own conclusion today, and I'd not sway her either way, no matter how much I knew Slade was innocent.

My president crowded Aaliyah on her right side, his body close, a shield to hers. Nothing was getting to his mate or through him. Occasionally, he'd brush her skin on purpose, put his hand on her lower back, and earn a smack for sliding his hand to her ass. They weren't at our level of rapport yet.

Slade took a lot more convincing than Zethan and me. Losing his mother so young and his mate two years ago left him with deep pools of uncertainty about anyone new in his world. Initially, he'd trusted Aaliyah because she was his mate, chosen by the gods, only to be smacked in the face with her dishonesty and deceit. I appreciated his reservations about her allegiance, but I was almost certain she slowly came around to ours.

Doubt fueled by his god since Set never trusted anyone in his family, and vice versa. What did he expect when he sliced his brother to pieces and cut out the eye of his nephew? Asshole lived up to his devilish reputation.

Until a concrete piece of evidence convinced Slade of Aaliyah's innocence, there'd always be distance between them. Once they moved beyond that, he had a lot of apologizing and groveling to do ... probably in the form of make-up sex like the kind they had the other night, roaring, moaning, and growling the damn clubhouse down. I fucking groaned inside my head at having to share her with him ... or the others. Dark Daddy didn't like to share his toys.

Alaric moved in front of us, scouting with his god's eye, scanning for trouble or anything unusual, always our first line of defense. At the first sign of his alarm, I'd be ready to back him up.

Beside me, Zethan's eyes bored into the side of my head like a laser target. Resentment simmered at the fact he couldn't have what he wanted more than anything. To have her so close and out of his grasp was torture, resigning me to work harder on freeing us from the curse holding us hostage. I felt his echo of agreement in the bond. Guilt thread through me for enjoying her touch and rubbing it in his face. I sent him the sensation of holding her hand through the bond so he could enjoy it, but it only made him sour and darken further.

Slade motioned for us to stop, going to order us all a beer at a stand.

"Hello, beautiful." A drunken member of the Fallen Angels MC grabbed her hand and tried to kiss it.

Zethan swatted him away. "Fuck off, she's ours."

The asshole leered at her. "Well, if you want even more dick, you know where to find it, honey."

She huffed and stared past him at the concert up ahead.

I wished we were here under different circumstances, where I could drag her over to the stage, stand behind her, my arms around her neck and waist, swaying to the band.

Heaviness began to build in the atmosphere, like dry, mountainous air with reduced oxygen, and my throat constricted, working harder to draw it in. Ropes of darkness thread across my chest, compressing, aiding my struggle. Invisible claws dragged along my skin, and I bristled. Electricity crackled around us like a mounting storm cell of crushing clouds, thunder, and lightning. The Wolves were close, their dark magick strong and going to give me a hell of a time to break it.

Alaric stiffened and slammed to a stop, holding his arms wide, signaling for us to halt. Hairs on the back of his head rose from his alarm and the magick prickling the air.

Danny limped out of a gap of bikers with the aid of a walking stick. He clutched his side, clearly still in pain from his gunshot wounds. How the fucker managed to move around with five slugs to his back remained a miracle. Ashen faced, he smirked at us, smug as ever. Greasy, jet-black hair stuck to his forehead. Paler eyes similar to Aaliyah's stared back at us. Inky tentacles of dark magick circled his body, keeping him alive yet draining his energy. If old Danny wasn't careful, he'd end up next to his pop.

Five members flanked him, all clearly packing despite the no gun rule.

"Jackals." The word came out full of menace but with little strength. "Thanks for returning my sister. Hand her over."

Slade stepped in front of Aaliyah, blocking Danny's view of her with his hulking size. Hands clasped to his back and shoulder, she peeked around him, using him as a shield.

"Fuck off, Danny. She's ours now." Our president crossed an arm across his body to cup his hand over hers. "My woman now." Uncomfortable at being called that, she shifted, but let him hold her. Slade played his little pissing contest to goad Danny.

Meanwhile, Alaric and I got to work, him scanning the Wolves with Horus' Eye, and me assessing the black magick, testing it with prods of my power. Smoke curled off the Wolves skin in thin, dark tendrils, but they didn't seem to notice.

Sinister demons whispered foul promises in an ancient language that took me a moment to interpret. *The dark ones seek to return to the Earth and the Black King will bring us back to his kingdom.*

What the fuck did that mean?

Throbbing beats pounded in my head, making it hard for me to concentrate. I'd seen magick like this before when someone had written malicious markings on the walls of our previous clubhouse.

Danny snarled, the tick in his face betraying the pain it cost him to do it. "Always knew you were a traitor, Aaliyah. Never standing by your family and running away from us like you thought you were better."

Slade kept the dick busy while I went about our business. "She knows who her family is, and it ain't you, motherfucker. Family don't put their father six feet under for their own gain."

Danny's smug smile widened. "I wouldn't be pointing fingers, Slade. You put plenty of people down, including your old lady."

Slade's muscles flexed, and we all knew what that meant. He wanted to land one on Danny's nose and crunch it. "Shut your fucking mouth."

Fuck. I closed my eyes for a second. The Wolves president could get to Slade through his emotion.

Zethan clamped his hand on Slade's shoulder to bring him back down. A rock of support. Grounding device to channel Slade's lightning rod of rage.

Danny huffed. "We'll see who's guilty of icing my dad. Justice will prevail soon." The matter-of-fact way he spoke suggested insider knowledge, which put me on edge.

Apprehension tightened the mate bond between the five of us. It was only a matter of time before the cops jumped on Slade with new evidence. I had to push that aside and do my job.

Glad for the diversion, I needled harder, investigating the

location of sigils on their skin, the source material used to write them and the language. By the scabs and red, raw skin, they scratched them into their arms with knives. Magick sealed in blood. Powerful shit. Wielded by the dark priests of Egypt and passed through some familiar lines throughout history to modern day and used in satanic rituals to conjure demons to do their bidding. Demonic entities were bound to and protected the Wolves. Old and powerful. I had my work cut out for me to separate them and render these dicks vulnerable.

Thoth strained his memory to recognize the symbols, their meaning, antidote, thinking some familiar, but unable to pinpoint their origin or etymology.

Fuck, this wasn't helping. I scanned my entire memory bank of languages, scriptures, and symbols, and the closest I could get was to Mesopotamia.

We are older than that, one of the demons hissed.

Formidable, another rasped.

Indestructible, the last one croaked. *The Black King will free us once more.*

I poured through the combined library that was mine and Thoth's brain, finding a few references to a dark king in Egyptian times. Monuments to his reign were destroyed, leaving little evidence. Only one king came to mind that fit the possible identity. A heretic Pharaoh named Akhenaton ruled from 1353-1336 BC and changed the religion to worship a singular god from an entire pantheon. Outraged gods sent their avatars to assassinate him and depose him. Poisoned his children, Tutankhamen among them. Installed a new Pharaoh to reinstate the worship of all the gods. Perplexed, I scratched the side of my head, unable to find any reference to him as the Black King. Akhenaton's reign didn't extend as far back as Mesopotamia 1330 BC, leaving me back at square-fucking-one.

I tested the magick's response, applying a spell to dissolve the Wolves' arm markings. Skin burned and sizzled, and all six of them hissed and slapped their palms over their forearms. The dark voices shrieked in agony in my head. My effort wasn't enough to remove the markings, and they darkened into crimson, then black stains on the Wolves' forearms. It would take a hell of a lot more power and a more efficient spell to get rid of it. Materials I didn't have handy.

Aaliyah pushed past Slade to stand beside him. "Did you do it, Danny?"

Danny squeezed his cane tighter, his face as hard and tense as his hand. "Why would I kill Dad?"

Aaliyah stepped closer, and Slade grabbed her wrist, but she wrenched free. "To take over the Wolves."

His men grunted and glanced between the two.

Danny huffed out another laugh. "I can't believe you would say that to me, Aaliyah. Dad was my hero and mentor. He raised me to run this club. Did time for me. I owe him my freedom. Why the fuck would I smoke him?" He sounded half convincing, a good liar at most.

She hesitated for a moment. "Dad never wanted to expand the business the way you have. Porn and snuff films? I thought you were better than that."

Danny bristled at the last one, his secret uncovered.

"Dad would be disgusted if he were still alive." Aaliyah kept digging at him. "You broke Mom's heart. Broke mine. Demoted Jerry. What the fuck were you thinking?"

Awkward postures and suspicious glares from the five Wolves gave me the impression they questioned their loyalty to their new leader from his actions. Fear in their eyes told me they dreaded Danny's temper and cruel, swift retribution. Disagreed with the way he'd demoted Jerry so callously and disrespectfully. MCs only demoted a member for a serious breach of code, not because of a disagreement.

Danny rolled his shoulders, leaning harder on his cane, his mouth twisting into a menacing glare. "Jerry's a fucking old rat and couldn't do what the club demanded of him."

"He's your fucking uncle!" Aaliyah slapped her brother, and he stumbled back, and two of his men caught him. "Show some respect."

"Don't preach to me about respect, Aaliyah." Danny righted himself and jerked away from his holders. "You don't know the things Dad did to me. Things to raise money for the club. Sharing me around." The handle of his cane creaked. "It made me tougher and resilient."

Hold the fucking phone. Say what? Was he hinting at what I thought he was hinting at? Abuse of some kind? No wonder he was a dark bastard.

"No." Aaliyah shook her head, her voice raw, pained, prompting Slade to tighten his grasp on her. "No, he would never hurt you."

"Where the fuck do you think I got the idea for the porn and snuff films?" Danny sneered. "Old Daddy."

"Don't fucking lie!" Aaliyah went to slap him again, but one of his men punched her. Her head snapped back, and I curled both arms around Aaliyah's waist and dragged her away.

Fuck. Slade lost it and smashed the asshole to the ground, thumping him to a pulp. Alaric and Zethan tackled the other Wolves while Danny stumbled backward, the cowardly little worm retreating.

Brave MC men bounded into the fray, yanking the fighting men apart, holding them back, four of them needed to pin Slade.

"Ain't none of that shit here," one man drawled, releasing Zethan. "Git the fuck outta here."

Zethan straightened his cut and swiped a hand through his hair. Unlike the others, he'd come out relatively unscathed, thanks to his officer training teaching him how to tackle brawling men.

"You okay?" He ran a quick knuckle across the red welt on Aaliyah's cheek, and she winced.

Slade growled, kicked, and fought the four men on top of him. Blood trickled from his busted lip. His hair was as wild as his eyes.

"Fine." Her eyes didn't leave the growling, thrashing Slade.

Alaric earned a nice shiner to his eye. He rolled his shoulders when the man holding him shoved him away. First thing, he went to retrieve his president, then he moved to Aaliyah. Brows heavy over his eyes, he set his hand over her swelling bruise. Suspicion or not, he'd fight for his mate.

Touched, she cupped her hand over his, leaning into him, her eyes closing. Her skin and smile fucking glowed from his caress. They still had a chance to repair the damage done to their relationship. It wouldn't be easy, and Aaliyah would make him grovel, but I had hope they'd get there.

When her eyes opened again and landed on me, the relieved smile that broke across her face completed me in a way nothing had before. I couldn't hold down the pleasure rising in my bond despite the shit that went down.

"Git the fuck out before we throw ya' out, Jackals," the man drawled at Slade, breaking me out of my daze. "Don't fucking come back. You're not welcome no more."

Every single muscle in Slade's body swelled as firestorms pumped through him. He jerked his head at us to follow him, and we left with him, marching through the parted crowd of gathered onlookers.

The crackle of magick that snapped through the bond pointed to the damage he'd done. Blasted out every tire of the Wolves' rides. Melted their engines and parts.

Back at our rides, Slade made us huddle for a debrief.

"Castor, what'd you find with the dark magick?" His lip curled as he touched his side from where he'd taken a heavy blow.

"Here." Aaliyah moved to his side and placed a palm on him.

"Don't need it, Nurse A." He claimed her hand, lifted it to his mouth and kissed her fingers. She shivered at the name and smiled as his palm settled over her bruise. "I'll never let him touch you again."

She nodded, her body stiffening with worry, fears rising through the connection over her brother's next move.

Slade didn't take his gaze off her as he barked, "Speak, Bird Boy!"

"They've carved sigils into their forearms." I scraped the back of my neck. "Blood magick is pretty powerful. I don't recognize the sigils. They're older than Thoth's knowledge. Mesopotamian, maybe."

Slade patted the blood on his lips with calloused fingers. "Will we be able to raid their clubhouse or get the women out of his studio?"

I shrugged, unsure. "I can try."

"Try?" Slade leveled me with a severe glare.

"The Wolves' are protected by some ancient and powerful demons, and I don't know what I'm up against. It'll take time to research that."

"Fuck!" Slade scrubbed his jaw, his glare jumping to Alaric. "Tell me you've got better news for me, Hawk Boy."

Cords in Alaric's neck flexed as he braced to deliver bad news. "The magick conceals them. I only got snippets. They're on the move for something this weekend, but I couldn't tell what."

Slade barked out a laugh and slammed his hands together. We didn't get to hear what he had to say. Flashing lights behind us dragged our attention away. I groaned. Three squad cars. Fucking cops. Two men per vehicle busted out, unholstering their guns and aiming at us.

"Hands up," one shouted. "You're under arrest for disorderly conduct."

Fuck me. Conviction for fighting and disorderly conduct could earn us three months imprisonment. Enough to take down and dismantle the club when we couldn't defend it. How fucking convenient. Another play by the Wolves and their mysterious friends?

CHAPTER 33

Aaliyah

CALL BARRY INGRAM. Slade's instruction to contact his lawyer before the cops cuffed him and the three other avatars and hauled their asses to Mitchell Police Station. I fumbled, entering his password into his Blackberry, almost dropped the damn thing.

"Shit, Aaliyah." I tucked my wildly blowing hair over my ears and scanned the gates of the *Summernat* biker rally.

Bikers and their women hooted and had a good time beyond the gates of the event. Panic threaded through me as I stood outside. Alone. Cold. Shivering. Vulnerable. No Jackals for protection anymore. The cops hadn't arrested Danny and the Wolves, which led me to believe this was another strategy by my brother to separate us. I rubbed at my leather jacket-clad arms. Safety was my priority to avoid another kidnapping, possible torture for information and being set to rest six feet under beside my dad.

Here was my chance. Should I run and leave this all behind? Go back to my old life and never think about bikers, mate bonds or the four men paralyzing my thoughts with indecision? Stay and save the Jackals? Repay Zethan and Alaric for defending me when the junkie beat me up? Find out what else the mate bond promised. Uncertainty and a glitching brain made things more difficult. My home wasn't safe when Danny knew where I lived. Only the Jackals could provide me sanctuary. Not when they were locked in a jail cell. The only safe place was the same damn place holding the Jackals.

What if the cops were on the Wolves' payroll? my brain considered.

Run to your mother's, my heart warned.

About as safe as the cop shop. Fuck. I tugged at my hair, trying to streamline my crashing thoughts. One thing at a time. Call Slade's solicitor. Get to safety at the same time. Rescue the Jackals. A million dollars couldn't convince me to seek out my brother or his club.

Shivers stole through my chest as I dialed Barry's number.

Slade must have been on his solicitor's instant answer list as he responded immediately. "Good afternoon Mr. Vincent."

"Hi, I'm calling on behalf of Slade," I bumbled.

"Who is this?" Barry's tone tightened like I pictured the corner of his eyes doing.

"My name's Aaliyah Heller—"

"I'm afraid I can't speak to you," Barry shut me down. "It's a conflict of interest in your father's murder case." Goddess, did everyone know who I was, even though I tried so hard to put that life behind me?

My hand ached from gripping the phone so tight. "Please. Slade told me to call you before he was arrested."

Barry's breath was the only sound on the line. "I'm listening."

I told the solicitor everything that had happened, and I heard him typing something on his end.

"Are you in any immediate danger?"

I scanned the crowd behind me and the carpark in front of me. "I don't know if my brother and his club have left."

"Get in a taxi and go to the local *McDonald's* restaurant," the solicitor advised me. "A public place as busy as that is the safest place to be. Do not move until I come for you."

"Okay." I prayed I'd not be intercepted before a cab could come and collect me. "I'm wearing a black leather jacket, jeans, and boots. Raven hair."

"I'll find you, Ms. Heller." He hung up, and the urgency to get out of here scaled another level.

Before I could dial for a taxi and move away, a heavy hand clamped down on my shoulder and spun me one hundred and eighty degrees. The jolt of it left me reeling for a few seconds.

Fuck. The Wolves found me.

Danny's normally blue eyes were pitch black as if the demons Castor mentioned that were protecting the Wolves were possessing him. Sure explained his behavior of late.

Slushy ice poured through my blood. My gaze went left and right, searching for someone to help. My scream died in my throat along with my voice.

"You're coming with us, Aaliyah." He jerked his head, ordering his men to make me go with them. "To teach you true fucking loyalty."

Urgency hammered down my spine. "Like hell I am." I rolled my arm out of the dick's grip. Going with them was a one-way trip and I didn't plan on being buried beside my father.

Danny squeezed his cane, the throb of his temple vein

telling me he lost patience and fast. "Removing the Jackals was a necessary evil, Aaliyah. They wasted Dad, and this was payback. Phase two of destroying the Jackals commenced today."

"Phase two?" Whatever Danny had in store couldn't be good. "What the fuck did you do, Danny?" So he was behind this. Pulling the strings or working in concert with somebody else remained unanswered.

He smiled like a damn cheetah about to descend on its prey. "What they deserved."

"What the fuck does that mean?" I didn't get an answer as two of his men seized my arm and dragged me forward. My pulse leapt as did my magick. "Get the fuck off me."

Spikes of golden light emerged from me and struck the two men. Black smoke steamed as my magick battled the one protecting them. I hit them again, and this time, a golden snake wound around their wrists and bit into them. The cobra from Isis' queen crown.

Goddess. I'd never done that before. What other powers were hidden within me? If I survived this and somehow got back to the Jackals' clubhouse, I was finishing the book Castor gave to me.

"Oh, fuck!" The five Wolves accompanying my brother hunched over, clutching their stomachs, their asses stuttering farts as their bowels violently exploded into their jeans.

Oops. My power gave them the runs. Seemed I didn't just have healing powers. Castor was right.

Danny's mouth curled into a vicious snarl. "Get her."

His remaining men grabbed me, and I let them all have the same treatment as the others. Danny collapsed to the ground with his men, stomach cramping, defecating like his minions.

I hurried away, stumbling, almost tripping.

"You're fucking going with them?" Danny croaked behind me. Pitiful. Defeated. Pissed.

I didn't turn around. Instead, I upped the cramps and discharge, and left them with dead legs and severely cramping muscles to ensure they weren't coming after me any time soon.

"You're a traitorous whore, Aaliyah!" my brother's screams pumped my legs and arms harder, and I put as much distance between us as I could.

Anger made my muscles twitch with the urge to slap him again. No, punch him. I couldn't believe he called me that. The same words he used to insult me when his men kidnapped me, sedated me, and threw me in the middle of an ambush. Danny was acting like a madman taking on the Jackals. A war he wouldn't win against four … no, five avatars.

"You're a murderer!" I shouted back, shaking so hard I was surprised I didn't turn into the damn *Hulk*.

I bumped into bikes and cars as I stumbled through the parking lot to wait at the edge of the *Mitchell Exhibition Grounds*, dialing a taxi and waiting for it.

Four hours, three cokes and a freshly opened packet of cookies later, Barry Ingram arrived at the *McDonald's*. He sat opposite me, dressed in a suit, vest, trench coat, scarf, and hat.

"I'm glad to meet you, Ms. Heller." He extended a hand, and I shook it, absorbing his warmth to ward off the chill in my body. "Glad you're safe."

I offered him a cookie, but he waved me away. "Thanks for coming right away." Slade obviously paid good money for the client-solicitor privilege provided by Barry. "My brother is behind the Jackals' lock up,"

Barry didn't give much away. Typical solicitor. They kept their opinions to themselves and provided advice only.

"*Someone* is behind the false evidence being planted against my client." He eyed me as if he assessed me the way Castor and Alaric had. "The fact that you were with them tells me you think so too, Ms. Heller."

It was good to know that he thought Slade innocent too. But not good that he looked at me like I was the guilty party. I guess as Slade's solicitor, Barry was paid to defend the Jackals' interests.

All I could do was nod and rub at my arms again. "Danny tried to apprehend me after we spoke on the phone."

Barry took off his hat to expose a thick mop of dark brown hair and put it on the table between us. "We can take out an Apprehended Violence Order on him if you believe you are unsafe."

I snorted. My brother didn't give a shit about a legal piece of paper, but Barry had to go through the motions. Maybe we could get Danny locked up if he breached the AVO. "I'll think about it when I get back to the club."

"You intend to stay with the Jackals then?" A question that knocked the air out of me. "Is that wise with the ongoing murder investigation?"

Sure as hell seemed safer to stay with them than by myself and be at the mercy of my loose cannon of a brother. I didn't feel safe with my brother attacking the Jackals or me. What kind of life would I have lying in my own bed, wide awake, with a damn kitchen knife under my pillow, waiting for Danny to strike? A week ago, I didn't feel safe with the Jackals either, and any moment could have spelled my last one. A lot had changed in such a small space of time.

At first, I didn't believe in fated mates and fought the mate bond tugging on our strings like we were puppets, forcing us to like each other. Captive and helpless, I decided to ride out the wave, let the Jackals deal with Danny and Castor break the curse between us. Up until yesterday, everything had been pretend, the tricks of gods and a curse. All that changed when the Jackals trusted me enough to include me as part of their team. As much as I wanted to leave all that behind, I couldn't. My father's murderer remained at large. All signs pointed to Danny, but I needed evidence. Concrete damn proof before I put five bullets in his brain and ended him.

Hell, that wasn't the half of it. I also missed Slade's flirty banter, Castor's witty teases, Zethan's agonized longing looks... heck, even Alaric's glares that softened at the first hint of my pain, like it had before he was arrested. The scariest part of all this, the part that stole the most of my breath, was that I didn't think it was the bond talking.

"Yeah, I guess I am." I played with the corner of my mouth, the icy fear inside me warming and subsiding.

My thoughts wandered to the cute stethoscope or cow pajamas from Castor, text message exchanges with Zethan, goddess, the hot night with Slade... and Castor... to the way Alaric swept me out of the clubhouse when it all got too much to deal with. Things with the Jackals had certainly gone from hostile to bearable to comfortable. Fuck, thinking about them, my mouth curled into a smile. A goddamn dreamy smile. I actually wanted to go back with them. Wanted to stay with them. For the near future, at least. Until my brother and father's murderer were dealt with.

The way the avatars responded to me after Danny's men hit me solidified their feelings for me. We were mates whether we liked it or accepted it. Time would tell where that would lead. My heart certainly had herself set on the sexy and mysterious Castor and the dark and haunted Zethan. She couldn't resist the rugged bear Slade, or the damaged Alaric, sweet, and considerate when I was on his good side.

"They'll protect you, Ms. Heller." Barry went on with his

business as he checked the time on his watch. "I've made some calls on my way down here, and I've posted bond for Slade and his men."

Wow, that would cost the Jackals on their next legal services bill. Something I wasn't sure if Slade could afford since Danny had ripped them off one million dollars.

The cookie tasted like dirt as I crunched on it. Nerves in my stomach hadn't stopped burbling since I got here, so I put food and sugar in it to shut it up.

Barry scanned the patrons inside the restaurant as if he were a private investigator. "Slade and his team will be free at 3PM."

I let out a relieved breath, and my shoulders lowered after several hours of hiking them to my neck. "Thank God." I wanted to go back to the clubhouse and have a hot shower to soak away the cold gripping my body. "Thank you for helping us, Barry."

"The Jackals are one of my biggest clients." The solicitor smiled. Of course, they were. Money talked. "Let me drive you down to the station."

CHAPTER 34

Aaliyah

"Fancy seeing you here, Nurse A." Slade's first comment as the two officers behind him begrudgingly released him and handed him his watch and wallet. Backed by that irresistible dimple of his, surprise mixed with pleasure charged along the connection at me pulling through for him when he expected me to leave them behind. Frustration bubbled beneath his skin, but he was unharmed and out, and that was all that mattered. We were back to the nickname. The man swung from one extreme to the other like a pendulum. Hard to keep up with sometimes.

I smiled at the giddy surge in my chest at seeing him.

"I'm getting the impression you *can't* stay away. I think you *like* us." He nudged me gently with his huge elbow.

I bumped him back, needy to touch him "Yeah, you're all right."

"Devilishly handsome too, so I hear." He wagged his eyebrows.

This damn mate bond really gave away too much. Castor ought to show me how to tone it down, so I didn't give these guys massive egos.

Slade and I gazed at each other for a long, electric moment, silently communicating everything. Gratitude, relief, comfort. As long as I stayed locked in his gaze, with him, I was safe.

The rest of the guys arrived, shaking me out of my daze, and I hit Slade on the arm to shut him up. Glares heavy, brows drawn hard, jaws tight, they looked pissed as they collected their possessions. Not the last they'd hear of their arrest. Castor shot me a knowing, proud wink, like he'd expected me to come through for them.

"Not as handsome as me." Zethan gave my cheek a quick kiss. "Thank you for saving our asses." My cheek burned and I cupped it, wanting to enclose the heat in me forever. It fluttered for a few moments before fading, leaving me disappointed and craving more. So much more.

"Don't thank me, thank Barry." I pointed at the waiting solicitor to my right. "Actually, thank Barry with lots of dollar bills." I grinned cheekily, mentally estimating the cost of the Jackals' bill to bail them out and cover Barry's trip down to Canberra to get his clients out.

Castor threw his arm over my shoulder, and an electric pulse raced through me. "Come to ride bitch with me?"

Hell, yeah. After today I needed to snuggle up to someone for warmth and comfort, and he was my man for that. More than that, I ached to touch him, sink into the grounding and sense of safety he provided.

After discovering my infiltration, he never made me feel like a guilty defendant on trial or a burden to bear because of the god's orders. Castor and Zethan didn't trust me but gave me the benefit of the doubt. Innocent until proven guilty. That meant a lot to me. Said a lot about the two of them. Analytical, intelligent, sifting through the pieces rather than making instant judgments, hasty and reactionary decisions. I hated that I felt like I had to prove myself to Slade and Alaric when I just wanted answers like they did.

Alaric reluctantly came over to offer me a solitary nod. Good enough thanks for me. After Danny's man hit me, he showed me more affection, but his warmth came and went like planes at an airport tarmac. I wondered if after almost five hours to think about it, whether he regretted clasping a traitor's face. The bond said otherwise, conveying his heartfelt appreciation and the murmur of acknowledgment that he'd been wrong about me. Trust with him was even harder won and harder maintained, and I wanted to understand why he struggled with it.

Slade moved outside to speak with his solicitor for a few moments.

Castor's arms locked around me, and I nuzzled into his wide chest, inhaling his sweet and spicy scent. "I'm glad to see you." My end of the link purred like a damn bike engine. His fingers thread through my hair, and he pulled my face back to look into my eyes. "Barry said Danny tried to take you again."

Nope. Not going there. Aggravating the avatars further with that story would prompt Slade to charge into the Wolves' clubhouse with an earthquake magnitude of ten.

"I'm okay." I rubbed Castor's hand. He wouldn't ever let me get scared when we were together. "I gave them some dysentery and got away."

"You made them shit their pants?" He laughed. Sexy and dark, I loved the resonance of his voice. All of it made me puddle at his feet and my whole body respond to him. "That's my dark goddess!" His face switched to serious in an instant.

"But I'm a little disappointed you didn't gangrene their dicks off!"

"Hey!" I hit him in the arm, a smile bursting over my face. "It was self-defense and not exactly planned."

"When we get back, I'm going to teach you some tricks." I perked up at his offer, dying to learn more about my magick. Everything between the Jackals and me changed so quickly that I almost lost my head.

"Deal." I smiled and buried my face in his chest.

Being with him, the four of them, was like nothing I'd ever experienced before. They'd bored under my skin, their behavior causing me to rethink my feelings and attitude towards them. My admiration and respect increasing with each minute spent with them. Oh, and fucking fall a little. For once, it was all me, not the mate bond tricking me into believing a flood of fake emotions. They meant something to me and treated me like a partner rather than a duty to the gods. Whatever happened with Danny, I was in for one hell of a ride with the Jackals, and I doubted I'd let go.

Zethan's longing stretched through the bond, his need to press my back, surround me, warm me, hold me. I sent him the same wish back of my hope to one day. Of a little tease of dick pics and hellhound cock. His end of the line tripped with a happier beat, and I smiled.

Alaric watched us. Silent. Observant. Still. A hawk on the hunt. I wasn't sure what to do with him or how to make him trust me and lose some of that unfriendliness. It would take time with him. He'd shown little pieces of his heart, defending my honor against the Wolves, as well as stroking my face. He cared, he just fought it, and that was all I could ask for. I was lucky to get that from a man so damaged and haunted by his past.

Slade whistled at us from outside, and we made our way

to the front of the police station. "Barry's gonna give us a ride back to our bikes. Get in."

Everyone piled in the back of the solicitor's *Audi* 4WD, Zethan in the passenger seat, Castor wrestling Slade to share the rear with me, leaving Alaric to take the trunk seat.

Slade stopped me before I could climb in. "Nurse A?" He clasped my hand and squeezed. "I owe you for that." He choked on the words. Thanking people and saying sorry didn't come easy to the Alpha. The tiny gesture from him sent a desperate ache through my body.

"You sure do," I said it with a tease, but was partially serious, too.

"You could have left us." His head bobbed as he stared at the ground. "But you didn't." The Jackals seemed like the smarter choice. Lesser of two evils. And I was starting to follow my heart instead of my head. Similar to Alaric, still wary, not one hundred percent sold, but getting there.

I waited with bated breath, tipping my head to hear Slade's next words, dancing on my damn tiptoes to stretch up to him.

"I'm starting to see where your allegiance lay all along." His comment stunned me into silence for a few moments.

"That sounds awfully like a sorry, Mr. Vincent." Okay. I couldn't resist teasing the Jackals' president. It was our thing, and I loved it.

His gaze shot up at his name, and he smiled. Dimples on display, bright like the damn sun, blinding me. He didn't answer with words, scooping me into his arms, tight, burning hot, and hard. Just like his kiss. And boy, did I fall into it. Every second turning more possessive, needy, hotter. Our tongues locked, teasing, playing, his kiss a branding more than sensual. This time when one hand supported my back and the other roamed lower to my ass, I let him stay there, and he cupped my globed cheek in his massive palm. I squeaked into his mouth and deepened the kiss.

Castor cheered at us from the back, making me pull back to giggle. Zethan soured again. Alaric looked away, uncomfortable.

Slade's hand shifted from my ass to my face. "Keep that up, and I might just make you another sandwich."

I giggled at his promising and tempting offer. But it wasn't a *Slade and Aaliyah moment* without our banter. "Nah. Don't want to spend the night in the toilet again."

He laughed, let me go, caught my hand, and dragged me to the Audi. "That's a shame, Nurse A. I'd have you coming just from feeding you salami."

Promises, promises. And Slade Vincent delivered.

CHAPTER 35

Slade

Today was the fucking day I found the rat in my club. The dirty, good-for-nothing scumbag who betrayed my brothers and me. Alaric had observed a rider without a cut meeting with Danny Heller and overheard them mention that the Pharaoh had ceased production. Information that only one of my men knew. Unless we had a blabbermouth in the club. A leak I'd permanently fucking seal.

My fire-packed gaze roved over my three brothers and Aaliyah seated in the church meeting room where we gathered to discuss the next step. Alaric had his usual stiff drink ready, gulping it down. Zethan didn't drink on duty. Ever. Castor had a few sips, and Aaliyah kept swallowing down hers to dull her bundling nerves.

I made her sit close to my side to put my hand on her lap, feel her with me, settling me. Whenever my hand roamed up her thigh, she'd push my hand back to her knee.

The woman was as unforgiving and merciless as me. Although she'd let me kiss her and squeeze her ass days ago after getting us bail, she hadn't let me touch her since. Until today.

Sharing part of myself and letting her into my world got us closer, but I'd have to work hard to win her back to my side. Fucking grovel on my knees, beg, cook for her, buy her fucking flowers and chocolate. A headache stung my forehead just thinking about the effort I'd have to put in. How much hell she'd drag me through. I was an asshole and deserved it. For now, I enjoyed holding onto her, throwing side glares at Castor at getting to hold her hand and settle it higher than mine.

Slade damn Vincent didn't wait for anything. Liz had made me go slow too, forcing me to pull out every trick I had to win her over. Fuck. I rubbed my jaw, mentally preparing for my battle on the heart front. I'd change for Aaliyah, show her what she meant to me, fucking work more than I ever had before. She wouldn't be easy to convince or win over like Liz had been.

Frustrated, I growled impatiently at Alaric, "Find anything?" After carefully assessing and scanning every club member with his god's eye, I wanted to know what his observations concluded.

"I cleared Brix after my initial scan, but two members are still concerning me," Alaric reported. "Jaxx and Benny." The names were like a rake down my spine.

Fucking Jaxx. Dumb prick couldn't perform a scope of a warehouse if his life depended on it. I'd chewed him a new asshole about it, punished him with night duty at the club for a month, and he'd sulked for days afterward, avoiding me, grunting and glaring at me. Alaric's surveillance on the three of them hadn't let up since he reported his initial suspicions of them.

Two names. Two suspects. A basic trap to catch the dirty fucker of a mole.

"We've got two names and three dummy trucks loaded with a mock Pharaoh shipment." I leaned back and threw back my finger of whiskey. I'd still send Brix out on the false mission just to be sure and clear his name. "Each team will be given a different delivery address and route, and we'll split up and follow two of them."

I knew which truck I had my money on. Which truck I'd be closely tailing. Zethan and Alaric were on one truck. Castor, Aaliyah, and me on the other.

Aaliyah glanced at me and smiled, part appreciation for letting her in on club business and part cunning. Crafty, just like her goddess. Isis knew how to trick and trap the gods to get her damn way. Tricked Set many times, but he'd wizened up to her calculating ways, and didn't fall for them so easily. Neither did I. But that wicked little smile lighting up her face made my balls tighten with a deep ache to fuck her.

Later. Bigger shit to deal with at the moment. Once Danny Heller, his pups, and the fuckers they worked with were put down, we could rut all day, every day until we had our damn fill.

"Castor?" I shifted my focus to him, wanting an update on the dark magick sigils carved into Danny and his men.

Thoth's avatar had taken Aaliyah into his office for the past few days, teaching her magick, using her research skills to scour his magick tomes. I swear to the gods, he better have a damn answer for me. Otherwise, I was potentially sending good men into a trap.

Castor twisted his tumbler, admiring the brown liquid. "Aaliyah and I found something we think will work to weaken the demon's power and the magick protecting the Wolves." Listen to them, working as a damn team. Avatars of two gods of magick.

"Thank fuck." I slid my crystal glass across the counter, hinting at Alaric to refill it, and he did. "Anyone got anything else to raise before I call church?"

We'd already gone over the plan in thorough detail three times so everyone understood their role. Nobody said anything.

"All right, bring them in," I said. "Church is in session."

"Stay safe, I'll see you soon," Aaliyah said softly, her body tensing up with worry.

We were bringing her along with us in case of injury, but we had to keep her as far away from Danny and his men as possible. We'd already dealt with the Bathurst Police. Every cop van or vehicle, except those out on patrol or attending a site, had flat tires. Twenty in the fleet. We'd take out any more we encountered. They weren't getting in our way this fucking time.

Alaric went outside to summon everyone, and Aaliyah politely excused herself. I slapped her round ass before she snuck away from me. I'd need that to get me through the next phase of my plan.

My men poured into the room, and I took a deep breath before delivering the plans. After church, I'd take each team aside to advise them of their route and destination and send them on their damn way before they had the chance to report to other brothers where they were going. Before they had the chance to suspect something was up.

***

AALIYAH SQUEEZED mine and Castor's hands as she sat beside us in the back of the truck. I gave her a reassuring press of her hand before standing, taking guard duty through the port hole in the truck's rear through to the windscreen and road ahead. Two riders led the truck and two were trailing it. Jaxx, Tank, Kill Bill, and Slim.

Pitch black road extended for miles along the National Park and farmland located on the *Bells Line of Road* behind Lithgow. Headlights illuminated the winding road, the guard rails, the trees and shrubs within the national park. My jackal eyes served as night vision to pierce further in the darkness beyond the reach of the truck's headlights. Bugs, ground-dwelling creatures, and hunting birds foraged and flittered amid the forest. Smooth sailing so far.

When we hit *The Devil's Wilderness*, south of Bilpin, I detected a change in the air. Movement against the wind direction. Shapes cutting through the midnight fog settled over the course. Approaching bikes. Set controlled the weather, allowing me to detect these subtle changes in atmosphere.

Eager to finish this bullshit with the Wolves and their associates, I grabbed my radio and patched through a message to Zethan and Alaric on an alternative route. "Incoming. Eight bikes."

I glanced at Castor and Aaliyah. They lay on the floor to protect her from bullet fire that might penetrate the truck cabin. We'd only hired a small truck for this. No point in paying for a larger one if it took a hit.

"All quiet here," Alaric radioed back. I'd ordered him to remain human as scouting in his hawk form left Zethan open and vulnerable. We weren't losing anyone today if I could help it.

Just as I'd expected. "Keep watch."

The change in air current caused by the bikes got stronger, harder as they pushed against the thick fog wrapping around them. With my power, I made it thicker, heavier, colder, strangling them and the bikes, like higher altitude air.

Their motors struggled at the reduced air intake and cold. Anything to make it more difficult for them and easier for us.

"Get ready," I growled.

Yellow headlights pierced the fog about a half mile ahead. Eight bikes wove around the windy terrain as did we. Vibrations from their engines made the hairs on my arms and neck stand sharp to attention like drawn swords. Time for Danny fucking Heller and his friends to die once and for all. I'd cut off his head and burn his body, so he had no chance of coming back from the damn dead.

At the front of the truck, Jaxx and Tank motioned at the driver signals for incoming traffic. The truck slowed, navigated the sharp bends carefully, steadying the cabin and keeping me on my feet. When it emerged from the curve, four bikes were parked across the road, blocking us from going further. Jaxx and Tank slid their rides sideways to avoid colliding with them, pulling up hard, tires burning. The truck came to a sharp screech, and I slammed my shoulder and forehead into the wall. Another ambush. Totally Heller's and his friends' style. And now I confirmed the identity of my mole and traitor.

Aliyah and Castor were still on the floor but slid across it and righted themselves.

"You good?" I asked Aaliyah.

"Fine." She braced herself on two hands before Castor pushed her back to lie flat on the floor.

"They were waiting around the bend," I growled, returning to the porthole, scanning the road. "Remember what I said, Aaliyah. Do not come out of here until I give the signal." We had a signal we'd call if we needed her to heal us or help us escape.

"What if you die?" Our eyes locked, and a surge of fierce protectiveness overcame me. I didn't plan on dying.

"You call Zethan, and he will come through the portal," I

reminded her of the escape plans she must follow if Castor and I went down.

Two of the four bikers alighted their rides to approach Jaxx and Tank. One produced a gun and shot Tank in the helmet and he dropped to the ground. My gut shrank and receded to my spine. That dirty motherfucker Jaxx remained alive and shook the hand of the shooter.

Chaos swarmed in my blood, desperate for release, to wind around the necks of those men and cut off their air. Soon. Very soon. I needed Danny Heller to pull up first. Solid proof he was behind this.

I snatched my radio and warned Slim and Kill Bill. "Stay put. Ambush. Tank is down."

"Fuck. Yes, President," Kill Bill whispered, and I heard a safety click and release.

More engines roared behind the truck, and I spun around, blind to what approached from our backs. Gunfire erupted and bullets pinged at the metal doors. My men swore, and their boots thudded as they ducked for cover.

Fuck, the Wolves and buddies had us pinned and surrounded.

"Stay down!" I shouted at Aaliyah, tossing her one of my spare weapons. "Castor, with me."

With him at my side, I removed my guns, one in each hand, and threw open the rear doors with my magick. Castor deflected fire our way while I picked off the riders, one by one, and in the chaos and confusion, they stopped firing at my men and aimed at us. Too late. I downed five of them before they realized and backed away, disappearing in the forest where they'd lay in wait.

Fuckers were drawing us out into the open. No problem. My night vision was even better than my day vision, and I was happy to go for a walk among the trees. Maybe even shift and tear a throat or two out. I tasted the blood on my tongue, and my jackal swelled beneath my skin to sink its teeth into flesh. It had been too long since I'd shifted into my animal's skin, and he was ready and raring to go.

"Deal with them, then we go after the cunts out front," I told Castor, jumping to the pavement below. Slim and Kill Bill were backed up against their rides for protection. "Guard the truck and take out anyone who comes around back, including Jaxx, the fucking traitorous mole."

"Yes, President," they both replied, Kill Bill with a menacing curl of his mouth and Slim a flicker of betrayal behind his eyes.

I moved into the underbrush, out of the line of illumination from the truck and bikes, light on my feet despite my massive size. About one hundred yards in, I stripped and nodded at Castor. "Wait behind the tree for any men that try to get back on their bikes and take 'em out."

Castor nodded and moved into place. In that position, he was also close enough to guard Aaliyah if any of those fuckers tried to enter the truck's cargo area. Nothing was getting to her.

Satisfied with my plan on the go, I shifted, able to move silent and predatory in my jackal skin. They'd never hear me fucking coming. Hundreds of scents flooded my system once I'd transitioned. Damp, winter forest floor, leaves, dirt, moisture. Nocturnal animals scurrying and eating their meals. Coppery scent of bugs and blood from an injured rider. Sap, bark, and eucalyptus from the trees. I searched among all the scents for the riders. Leather, oil, fuel, grease, and smoke. Locked onto them, I pursued them deeper, leaving Castor behind.

Within a minute, I tracked them huddled at various locations. Behind boulders, trees, and groves in the forest floor. Perfect spots for me to bring them down singularly. I attacked the closest one, launching onto his back, scratching through his leather in a few scrapes, clamping down hard on his nape. Startled, he dropped his gun, and tried to crawl away. But I was too big, too strong, and bit out his neck, right to the bone. When he slumped to the ground, I licked at his blood and nudged him onto his back, tearing out the front too. Not a fucking Wolf. Another unidentified rider.

Fuck. I'd deal with that later.

The other men shit their pants at the animalistic grunts and whines of my jackal as it feasted on more of them, called out, asking what the fuck was that. Two tried to return to their bikes. Relishing my hunter mode, I played on it, getting another rider behind the tree, taking him quick and efficient. Panicked, they all tried to run, and I stalked the remaining two as they fled. The first was an easy catch, and I got him by the balls while he thumped me in the head, but I didn't let go. I tore off his cock and swallowed it down, going in for the kill next as he fell to his knees. The next—the last—I dragged along the ground by his boot. He struggled to round on me and shoot me. A bullet fired, and I ducked, dodging it. Livid that he dared shoot at me, I leapt onto his back, biting into his arm, tearing it from the elbow in one hard jerk. His gun went off, and I flinched at the proximity to my face, dropping his hand. I finished him off by eating out his throat, then his face, licking at my lips when I was done.

Blood always fueled my chaotic rage and the strength of my beast. Muscles rippled with each step back to the truck. Erupting guns called me back faster, and I threw on my clothes and boots, using magick to finish the deed.

Back at the truck, Kill Bill and Slim defended the cargo as six riders approached down one end. I took down a few before they realized my location and targeted me. Rapid fire pinged off bark, stone, and the guardrail as I hid behind it for shelter.

Riders overwhelmed Kill Bill and Slim and they retreated

from the cargo to save their asses. Fuckers allowed six riders to pour around the sides of the truck. Two flew out from a blast of Castor's magick as they attempted to climb into the back. Discharges from my cowardly men hit another two. Pops went off as the last two got inside.

Fear ripped into my heart at Aaliyah's scream. More rounds echoed, and I had no idea if she'd hit anyone or if they got her. Claws and fangs extended as my jackal took notice, snarling, dripping saliva.

Footfalls thudded as more men rounded on the truck. I clipped off as many as I could before needing to reload. Bullets snapped in my direction, forcing me lower. The crunch of my new clip echoed hard in my hand bones. Danny brought more men. Another club? Guns for hire? Whoever they were, we were overwhelmed and needed backup. My plan to trap them turned around onto me.

I snatched up my radio and called through to Alaric and Zethan. "Get your asses here, now!"

CHAPTER 36

$\mathcal{A}$laric

WHEN THE CALL CAME, Zethan pulled open an Underworld portal, transporting us to our brothers. Crossfire pinged above our heads, near our ears, grazing my arm. Shots came from every direction, front, side, and behind us. Forced to the ground, we rolled and took stock of our surroundings. Slade trapped in the forest, trying to fight his way out. Gunmen closing in around Kill Bill and Slim. Castor defending Aaliyah in the truck. Correction. Aaliyah kicking ass in the truck. Damn woman was a good shot, letting off round after round, knocking down the men coming at them. Twenty to fifty or so men. A damn platoon!

A gunman in leather and no cut descended on us. Zethan pushed him back with three shots right to the heart and he went down for the count. More came at us from every direction. Zethan and Castor reported that the underworld crime figure they killed told them they had no more actions planned against us, so who the fuck was responsible for this ambush?

"Fuck!" I let off a couple of rounds into the chest of an approaching gunman. "Where the fuck are they all coming from?"

Bullets and orange fire tore up the night. Memories of serving overseas flooded my senses. Adrenaline and aching muscles. Sweat dripped in my eyes. Raw panic made my heart thunder in my ears, drowning out everything. I couldn't hear or see a damn thing, escaping my captors my only thought. Enemies pursued me through the desert as I fled. Almost passing out from weakness after no exercise for three months.

A heavy hand landed on my shoulder. "Alaric?" I punched the threat, and someone grunted. Two hands gripped me, one around the neck, the other my chest. "Calm down."

Stones scraped as I kicked my legs. The grip around my throat tightened. Cold breath fanned along my neck and my body numbed.

"Alaric, it's just me." Zethan, squeezing me, grip tight, like a swaddle wrapped over a baby, calming me. Seized muscles prevented me from moving. Terror gripped my lungs. "I stilled you with my death breath."

Thank fuck.

I blinked away the memories and terror and came to. Nighttime. Middle of winter. Thick fog blanket. Darkness lit by truck and bike headlights. Gunfire going off all around us. My brother, Zethan, held me by the chest. I patted the top of my head, my eye, searching for sweat or blood. Not real. Not there anymore. Safe from *him*. Tricks my therapists had taught me to come down from a PTSD episode.

"Fuck, where am I?" I asked Zethan, my memory affected.

"The Wolves ambushed our truck," Zethan reminded me, legs curled around me, rocking me like a damn baby.

My brothers were in danger. I need to get my shit together or one day I was accidentally going to hurt one of them.

I concentrated, recalling our plants to trap for Danny and his associates. To do my job, I had to pull my shit together. Situations like this set me off too easily. Nothing I did helped me avoid it.

"Fuck, sorry, VP," I panted.

Zethan pressed the side of his face to the top of my head. "Don't worry about it. Can you hold it together? They need our help."

I risked a glance at the hell surrounding us. Kill Bill taking a bullet to his shoulder. Slim in a fistfight with a gunman. Slade torching four attackers, trapping them in the forests. Dead bodies everywhere. No Castor and Aaliyah. Dark dread coiled inside me. Where the fuck was my mate?

If I could have moved, I would have held up my palms in a placating gesture. "I … I think so."

Zethan slowly released me, keeping his hands low, close in case he needed to subdue me again. He sucked in his breath and recalled the death breath on me. Heaviness, stillness, and icy cold lifted from my muscles and I tested my legs and arms.

"Get your fucking ass up there and rescue our damn president and woman," Zethan ordered me.

"Yes, sir." I stripped quick and shifted into my hawk form, taking flight, peering down over the scene.

Twenty or so armed men surrounded the truck at the front and back, crouching, shooting, inching closer to the back of the truck. My brothers had killed about ten of them. Bikes were parked on the road and in the forest. Riders had waited for the truck and set a trap to stop and intercept them. Venturing further out, I scoped for more men but found none. I returned, swooped low, scanning the leather jackets and bikes for any discernible logos. Nothing. Hired guns. Not a single Wolf in sight. Who the fuck were these guys? Savvy Bill's men? The mystery was pissing me off. Then I faltered at my final finding. Jaxx amid the dark men, blasting his brothers. Damn dirty traitor.

I sent the intel through the mate bond. Tremors rippled through the link, an earthquake about to tear apart the damn mountain. Boulders were going to tumble and crush every hired gunman. Leave Jaxx for Slade to deal with. Slow torture and agony.

Within seconds, I got another order from my president. *Distraction. Save Aaliyah. Wound Jaxx but leave him to me.*

Shock steamrolled through me for a few moments. We'd never been able to communicate with words before through our link. Only emotion and memory. Fear, or maybe it was Aaliyah, strengthened our connection enough for telepathic interaction. Fucking incredible, whatever it was.

Roger that, President, I replied, hoping he heard it. *Count on me.*

I'd do whatever it took to save my brothers and mate. Even if it meant taking another bullet or laying down my life in service to them. That was what I'd been trained to do. Sky god, Horus, protected his people from above, watching over them in his hawk form. I could do the same on land or air.

Pumped full of determination, I swooped down, jumping from gunman to gunman, scratching at the faces and ears, creating shock and havoc among them. Gun barrels tipped up with fright and shots went off. I dodged several near misses. Men bumped into each other in the confusion, and some stumbled over. A shot went off accidentally and wounded one of the enemies.

"What the fuck was that?" one shouted, crouching low, cupping his face.

"It's a fucking bird or something!" another replied, gaze scanning the skies.

Right, he was. These moves always caused confusion among enemies. I couldn't afford for him to let the rest of the enemy know about my presence, so I came at him from another angle. Sharp talons sliced at his neck, making him scream and drop his weapon. I landed on his head and pecked at his eyes, swallowing down the gelatinous flesh in several gulps. Tasted like harder jelly and salt. He howled and batted at me, drawing attention to us. Fuck, I had to act quick. Blood and heart pumping hard, I slashed at his hands until he could no longer hold his weapon.

Confusion broke out between the men at my unprecedented and strange attack. The distraction was enough for my brothers to emerge from their trapped positions to return fire. A bullet hit the man I clung to in the shoulder, and he went down hard.

I flew free and went after Jaxx. A couple of circles over the scene led me right to him. Headed for the truck cargo. Shrieking, I dove for him. He lunged out of the way and inside the rear. I circled back and by the time I reached his location, he had Aaliyah's wrist in his grasp, and he swung back his palm and slapped her. Her gun fell to the ground, clattering. She reeled from the blow and stumbled back, hitting the wall.

Fucker wouldn't live for striking my mate's face. I dove at him again, slashing at his face, cutting right through his left eye. Now we were truly blood brothers. Shrieks pierced above the gunfire as Jaxx thumped a hand over his bleeding eye and scanned his proximity. Wings working overtime, I came at him from behind, taking a chunk out of the bastard's ear, hot liquid spurting all over my feathers. He screamed, slapped a hand over the gouge and dropped his gun. But I wasn't finished. He'd hurt my mate. Betrayed his brothers.

Aided our enemy. Punishing him as best I could without killing him—leaving that to Slade—I got Jaxx down the left side of his face with a deep gash that cut right to his cheekbone.

Before I flew away to assist my VP and president, a projectile tore through my wing, and I screeched and fell to the ground. Rolled on my side, I caught two men jumping into the back of the cabin.

Forgive me, president. Forgive me, my mate.

"No!" Aaliyah crawled to me on her knees, picked me up and cradled me to her breast. Bruises across her left cheek made her eye swell up and redden. Thank fuck she wasn't shot. "Alaric."

"Move, bitch." One man jabbed his gun at her, but she refused to budge.

"Kill them both," Jaxx gurgled from the corner, a bloody fucking mess. Rivulets of crimson liquid poured from his wounds, eyes and dripped into his open mouth, staining his teeth. I'd given him enough pain to make him shuffle and shift uncomfortably.

The two assailants went down as bullets tore into their backs. Blood stained their shirts for the milliseconds they remained standing before toppling to the wooden floor.

Castor climbed back into the cargo area in two leaping steps up the ladder. He knocked out Jaxx, and shoved him into the corner. The traitorous bastard crashed to his knees.

Castor fell beside Aaliyah. "You safe?"

"Fine." She crushed my body to hers. "But Alaric is hurt. Cover me while I heal him, please."

"You got it, dark sorceress." Castor took position by the entrance, using boxes to shield himself and us.

"Good work, Hawk Boy," Slade told me through the bond. *"We've got them. They're retreating."*

Thank fuck. *"Don't let 'em get away. Kill every last one of them."*

Set's dark, maniacal laughter echoed down the bond. The god of Chaos and War savored the bloodshed. Drank up the confusion, fear, and violence like only a dark, bloody god could.

Pain burned down my left wing, and I wriggled in Aaliyah's hold.

"Sorry, this is going to hurt like hell." She set me down, leaned over me, stretching out my wing.

Startled, my hawk bit her with a quick nip to tell her it hurt. I ordered it to stop but the animal within me raked its feet through the air to scratch anything at the pain, barely missing her arm. Fuck, I couldn't control it, the animalistic side of me in charge and panicked. I panicked even more at the increased gunfire and confused shouts bleating into the night.

"Shit, sorry." Worry creased her brow as she let go of my wing and stroked my body. "Just calm down."

Firm pressure settled over my chest, holding me down, back flat to the ground. Warm tingles cascaded through my wing and body as she injected healing magick into me. It felt even better the second time around. Magical, cooling the heat within my wing. Inflammation pooled at the site to defend the cut from bacteria. Clots formed over the site, blood vessels closing up, ceasing the bleeding. Tissue strands repaired, weaving together as if sewn by a seamstress. Broken feathers regrew and stretched out as new. Fuck, Aaliyah was incredible. Powerful. Formidable. Stronger than Liz had ever been. Her force thrummed in my veins, the effect going to my head, making me giddy and delirious. My body buzzed as it changed back into my human form, naked as the day I entered this world, dirty from writhing on the wet ground and dusty floor.

Castor glanced over his shoulder. "You look better."

Better than better. Fucking amazing. Never felt anything like it before. Rejuvenated. Powerful. Like I could take on the gods themselves.

Aaliyah steadied me, one hand on my blood-stained shoulder, the other on my back. "How do you feel? Did I get the whole wound?" She wobbled a bit from her effort, and I clutched her back.

Castor returned his attention to the dying battle outside.

I clutched my head, riding the high from her damn potent power. "Amazing. Like I've been given fucking painkillers."

"What?" she chuckled, putting a bloody finger to my eye, and I flinched, leaning away. "Let me check your pupils."

I brushed her hand away. "I don't like anyone touching me there."

She offered an apologetic smile, then squinted, stretching her neck forward, studying my eyes. "You don't look high."

Yeah, I was. Drunk on her fucking crazy power. And I didn't want it to end.

A final bullet cracked the night, and a man groaned and thudded on the ground. I flinched again at the sound. It reminded me of the men *he* killed in the cells opposite me. Innocent men. Dead men.

"Good shot, VP!" Slade shouted. "Slim, Kill Bill, Castor, check for wounded and end 'em!"

Castor emerged from the truck's cargo area to assist my brothers.

"Zethan, deal with the bodies," Slade ordered.

"Alaric?" Aaliyah's arm cradled my shoulder, but I recoiled and gasped.

"Don't!" I held up two palms, struggling to get air into my lungs.

"It's okay." Aaliyah spoke slow, soft, hypnotic, and I took

notice. "I'm here. Look at me. Only me. It's safe. They're all gone. Your arm is fine."

The lock on my throat dissolved, and I sucked in a few long breaths. Her hand stroked over my back, injecting more calming power, her touch soothing beyond anything I could imagine. This was the peace I'd been searching for. My mind, body, and soul craved it. The key to releasing me from the captivity of my demons.

"Thank you," I breathed out, gaze bolted to hers.

The back of her hand reached out to stroke my face. Startled by the sudden motion, I leaned back. She pulled away, knowing what I needed. Not to be touched, just to feel safe. Away from *him* and *his* hold over my mind until I shook him away and came back to myself.

"I'm here with you, Alaric," she whispered. "You're not there anymore."

She didn't know where *there* was. Where I was kept. What they did to me. Things she didn't need to know. Period. I hated that *he* still had a hold over me. That my demons clutched my ankles and tried to drag me to hell at every waking moment. That the bottle failed to drown out their dark, cruel whispers, promising me death. Burying my feelings under a sea of alcohol was easier than addressing my fears and nightmares. Maybe I'd not need that anymore with *her* with me.

Aaliyah moved cautiously from the cargo to go and grab my clothes and return them to me. Wide-eyed, she studied my scarred chest and arms. Scars branded my mind as well as my body. Wounds I wanted to be free of. Free of the weight holding me captive. Liberated from the nightmares and torment.

Her eyes welled, and her lips quivered. "What did they do to you?" The dry scratchiness of her voice made me tense.

Shaky fingers reached for me, and this time I let her trace

a scar. I needed her touch to silence the demons, to ward off the anxiety piercing my gut, soothe my tortured soul. Thunder quaked through me at the contact, a combination of trepidation and elation. I wanted her hands all over my body. A hollow ache set off at my groin. My mate touched me, and there was nothing like it.

The Jackals had finally uncovered their mole, and it wasn't Aaliyah Heller. Time and time again, she'd proven her loyalty to her cause... find her father's murderer and seek justice for him. Confirmed her pure and true allegiance to her family. Danny or the Wolves weren't included in that equation.

Fuck, I'd been wrong about her. So very fucking wrong. I'd let what happened to me cloud my judgment and immediately accused her of being a traitor. Default settings were hard to rewire. An apology didn't seem to cut it after what I'd said to her. Dog. Asshole. Bastard. I could think of a hundred more names to call myself for how I'd treated my mate. Hurt her with cold glares. Cut her down with bitter words and rejection. Burned her integrity with false accusations.

Dad taught me to be the bigger man. Admit when I was wrong. Take accountability and be honorable. So that was what I would do.

"Aaliyah." Swallowing the hard lump of cement in my throat scraped and burned. "I was wrong about you. Really wrong. I know there's nothing I can do to take that back. But ..." She stared at me like my apology meant the world to her. "Can we just ..." I couldn't get the words out.

"Fresh start?" Her smile rounded the apples of her cheeks.

I returned the smile. "Fresh start."

A first step. One in the *right* direction. At least I could sleep well tonight knowing I had one less burden poking at my conscience. But I had a long way to go to redeem myself to my mate ... if she'd accept me as hers.

CHAPTER 37

*Z*ethan

AUTHOR WARNING: violent torture

BONE CRUNCHED as Castor gave it his all. Blood splattered across the floor, his face and his shirt. Third bone Castor had cracked this session. Not the last, once he was finished with the rat. Jaxx groaned, his head lolled to one side. Fitting punishment for that dirty, lying, traitorous prick. He was lucky Slade hadn't taken the honors for his punishment. Every single bone in Jaxx's body would be shattered. His throat torn out. Eyes and tongue removed and burned.

Castor rubbed at the rings digging into his fingers from using his knuckle dusters. "Tell us who those riders were."

"Fuck off. I'll take it to my grave." Jaxx spat blood at his feet, earning another hit to his cheek. A loud crack indicated a broken tooth, and he spat that out too on the dusty stone floor. "They'll come for me when the shipment isn't delivered. Fucking kill you cunts."

"Really?" Slade rounded on him, grabbing his hair, pulling so tight I heard his fucking scalp tear. "Who's that, asshole?"

Jaxx chuckled and glanced up through swollen, scratched eyes that Alaric's hawk made a damn mess of. Rebellious. Mocking. Hiding his little secrets like he thought himself better than us. He glanced over at the two chained Wolves, looking worse for wear, their bruises fading, but their eyes carrying the horror of their torture. Signs of what was to come for him if he didn't speak quickly.

I wanted to know how damn long Jaxx had been communicating with our enemies. What other club business that prick had betrayed so we could change it before more shit came our way.

Slade clamped a hand over Jaxx's jaw and lifted it. "I'm going to fucking kill you, resurrect you, and do it all over again if you don't start speaking." A threat he would deliver a thousand times over.

Jaxx laughed in his face, and Slade lifted his boot, kicked the traitor's chest, pushing the chair over. His skull and back thumped on the concrete. My president could be heavy handed, cruel, brutal, and extremely violent when it called for it. He and his god lived for that shit. It was sport to them.

Me, on the other hand, didn't enjoy it, and I'd seen my fair share of deadly accidents, murders, and grisly fucking deaths to last me a lifetime. But as VP and King of the damn Underworld, I had to stay for this part.

Slade put his boot on Jaxx's chair leg, flexed his knee, lifting Jaxx back up to a seated position with ease. The chair rattled as it slammed down on the floor. Large, tattooed hands came down on both of Jaxx's knees, squeezing, crushing bone. I'd never heard a scream fucking like it before. It spluttered out as Jaxx gasped for air over the horrendous pain shredding his body.

"Ready to talk yet?" Slade slapped the side of Jaxx's face three times.

Out of respect for his president, Castor retreated to the makeshift desk in the corner, leaning on it and taking off his beating apparatus.

"Go to hell!" Jaxx grit his teeth.

"Right where I belong." Slade smiled. Cunning. Fierce. Vicious. He was truly at home when he brought out his inner devil. The darkness of his god.

My president grabbed Jaxx by the throat, crushed his windpipe, then lifted him, chair and all, off the ground. One swift movement cast the traitor and chair across the room. Bricks crunched at the impact. Rib, spine, and skull bones cracked as they broke. I winced as my powers scanned for damage. Brain and head injury. Collapsed lungs. Three broken vertebrae. Comatose and he wouldn't last long.

Slade crouched down, checking the traitor's pulse. Low and losing strength. "Do it," he grunted at me.

Underworld magick brought Jaxx back to life, and he gasped, his eyes flinging open, widening at us. Something I could only do if death occurred within a limited timeframe. Resurrection couldn't bring him back properly, only a shadow of himself. Enough to torture until we got our answers. He'd sure as shit feel the pain of breaking limbs and bones. From there, he'd last an hour, tops, then turn into a goddamn zombie and decay. Aaliyah and Isis were the ones who could fully bring someone back from the dead. But she wasn't ready yet, her magick still developing.

"What the fuck you do to me?" Jaxx rasped.

Slade slapped him on the back of the head. "Brought you back to life, you motherfucker."

"No, you didn't." Jaxx laughed again. "I passed out."

"Fairy tales, fucker," Slade growled. "Again."

I deployed the death choke hold and deprived the prick of air. I waited until his heart stopped, then his brain, before Slade's impatience got the better of him. His fist crashed down on our prisoner's head, ending him.

"Hurry the fuck up!" Slade barked at me, gesturing at the three gunmen we'd taken from the ambush. Pulses low, losing blood, weak breathing, they teetered on the edge of life as well. "We've got more cunts to question!"

Grazes over his body needed medical attention. Treatment he'd refuse until he dealt with club business and protected his men.

I sighed and reversed the death, bringing Jaxx back all over again.

He gasped, horrified, eyes wide again, mouth agape. "What the fuck?"

Chains rattled as the Wolves and other unknown prisoners shrank back in horror. They closed their eyes, breath catching in their throat or making shocked bleats.

Jaxx couldn't deny it any longer, either, and wriggled, shuffling his chair away. "Fucking stay away from me, you freak!"

"Freak? I'm more than a fucking freak. I'm a god, motherfucker." Chair legs scraped on the ground as Slade dragged it to sit backward on it in front of Jaxx. "Wanna tell me what you know? Cause we can keep doing this all day. Extend your pain and suffering."

Jaxx's terrified, swollen eyes darted to all the prisoners, to me, Castor, and our president. "What do you want to know?"

"Now we're fucking talking." Slade smiled like a jackal that had caught a bunny. "Who the fuck have you been snitching to, motherfucker?"

Jaxx's vitals went down, his heart and brain declining, lungs straining as the magick calling his body back to life weakened. I needed Aaliyah and Isis to stabilize him, but Slade wouldn't allow it. We still had business with him once our investigation concluded. Next up: make an example of him to the club. Punish him in front of all the members to remind them of their loyalty in case they contemplated switching sides or betraying us.

"I met with Danny Heller three times," Jaxx started.

Fuck, I knew it. All this time we'd suspected Aaliyah as the mole leaking our secrets to her brother when it had been one of our own. The cop in me said the circumstances didn't look good for her. Fingers pointed to her. But investigating the facts and collecting new evidence had cleared her as chief suspect and alerted us to another candidate. Jaxx. Fucking brother of ten years. Lying, traitorous prick.

Alaric hung out with Aaliyah upstairs, having a drink and relaxing. We didn't want her to see the dark side of an MC. From her six years involved with the Wolves, she'd know of its existence, but how much, I wasn't sure. If she ran from that life into a career of healing, I'd say she loathed the torture and retribution aspect of a club.

We kept Alaric away from this shit as it triggered his PTSD. I was worried about him after his episode, hitting him the instant we'd arrived through the portal to help our brothers. His symptoms were getting worse, more frequent, and he was drinking a hell of a lot more than normal. Especially after what he witnessed in the Wolves damn porno snuff studio. He needed help. Serious fucking help. The kind our brotherhood couldn't offer. And I couldn't risk putting him on guard duty at the shelter if he had another episode.

"Who were those cunts that ambushed us?" Slade growled, fire and fury fighting to get free of his body.

"Third party," Jaxx said. "Don't know. Think Danny organized them."

Danny Heller, the dirty prick, wanted his hands clean. Fucking coward. Hundreds more descriptions hit me.

"Why?" The weight of Slade's arms made the chair creak. "Why is he hiding like a fucking pussy?"

"Danny told me he wants nothing to point to the Wolves." Jaxx shuddered as pain sliced through him. "I don't know why. We had to communicate in code. Then we went dark. No text, calls, nothing. Everything shared in person at arranged times according to handwritten letters delivered by his buddies."

The chair creaked again as Slade's massive form leaned forward. "Did Danny steal our shipment?"

"I think so." Jaxx swallowed hard, his heart straining to keep him alive.

"His heart's failing," I warned.

Slade gave me the back of his hand. Wait. A little more.

"I told him where he could collect it," Jaxx rasped, moaning as his heart gave out, thumping harder to pump the blood as his body declined.

"Joey's death's on you, motherfucker." Slade got out of the chair, crossed to Jaxx, grabbing him by the hair, his restraints falling away. "Upstairs, now!"

Silently, desolate, Castor and I marched behind our leader as he dragged the weak Jaxx up the stairs.

Everyone had been called to the club after the ambush, including those sent with the dummy trucks, and they waited in the recreation room. Dirt-stained faces from the ambushed mission knew what was coming. Weary, concerned eyes fell to the bloodied man Slade practically carried. Brother no more. Backs stiffened, jaws tightened as every Jackal knew what was about to happen.

Aaliyah sat with Alaric on the couch, their knees facing each other. He carried a bottle of whisky and she a glass. Jealousy stabbed me that he got to sit with her, so close, legs practically touching. Sharing a goddamn drink. But then I was glad for their mutual comfort. After his episode, he needed her, and she him, because no matter how many times we came up against adversity, it didn't get easier.

"Church, now!" Slade barked, and he dragged Jaxx in behind him.

All the Jackals gathered in the room. No one sat down. Silence clung to the huddle like a python choking us all. Aaliyah clutched Alaric's hand as they slid inside the room, and my jealousy went up another notch, wishing to slip my hand in hers and replace the tumbler she clutched. Some of my brothers stared at her.

"What's she doing here?" one whispered. "She's not a member."

Disgruntled murmurs swept through the room.

Slade shut them the hell down. "'Cause I said so, fuckwits!"

They bent their heads, submitting to their president's will.

At the lectern, Slade stood tall, deadly, removing his pistol, about to do his duty. "Let me remind everyone of what you signed on for," Slade bellowed, jerking Jaxx's head back, exposing his neck. "Truth, loyalty, and brotherhood."

Everyone nodded. These were the men who took their oath seriously.

Slade lifted his Glock to Jaxx's head. "Jaxx broke the code he swore an oath to. Three times he fed intel to the Wolves, including providing locations of our shipments of Pharaoh. He personally is responsible for Joey's and Tank's death."

Angry, outraged mutters swept through church.

"Fucking be done with 'im," Kill Bill clutched his scratched and bullet ridden arm that Aaliyah patched up.

"Kill the rat bastard!" Slim shouted. "We lost Tank because of this."

Our damn mechanic. A good man. Loyal. Hard-working. Steadfast. Jaxx would damn well pay for that with his life. Tank signed up for this life, and he knew the risks. Everyone knew them. Jaxx signed his death warrant the moment he chose the enemy over his brothers. Didn't make the loss any easier. Shittier, more like it.

Every Jackal lowered his head, showing respect for our fallen brother.

After giving them a moment to grieve Tank, Slade held a groaning Jaxx out in front of his body, ready to deliver his final message. "Do you have anything to say for yourself, you cunt?"

Jaxx's eyelids fluttered as he struggled to keep his eyes open. "Slade Vincent killed my brother, Mac."

Answers at last. Our president had nothing to do with Mac's death.

Slade's grip tightened. "Mac was an idiot. He took ice on a mission after I ordered him not to touch the stuff. His death is on him, not me."

"Every death is on you, President," Jaxx snarled back at him, and my insides iced over, knowing he spoke the truth. After this, Slade would retreat to his office and drink himself away in guilt.

He recovered quickly and shook Jaxx to shut him the fuck up. "Any last words, asshole?"

"You're all going to die." Jaxx smiled through bloodied teeth. "You don't know what you're up against."

Before he could frighten the men further, Slade sent Alaric and me a mental image of what he wanted to do to Jaxx. Fuck. Dark shit. I ripped off the edge of my flannel shirt and brought it over to my president. Alaric brought him the bottle of scotch and poured it all over the rag. Slade stuffed it down Jaxx's throat, deep, but not enough to choke him, leaving some outside his mouth. Alaric looked away from the horror about to unfold, but Aaliyah refused to look away. Holding onto the back of Jaxx's head, Slade removed my lighter and set the rag alight, and flames swept toward his face. The traitor choked and screamed against the fire consuming the insides of his mouth.

Set and Slade relished the fucking display of horror, cruelty, and torture.

Jackals shifted uncomfortably, lowering their eyes, twitching at every tortured, cruel scream. No one liked to see a brother be punished or executed. Guns were quick and put someone out of their misery. But fire? That burned, consumed, agonized. I remembered my accident, when the road tore me to shreds, the flames tearing through my skin, the pain and heat like a wildfire. Taking pity on them and on Jaxx, I produced my weapon, putting two bullets in his brain, ending his suffering. I shoved Jaxx's body to the floor, and Slade fucking smiled at the thud.

Stunned, thick, cold silence choked the room. Exactly the response Slade hoped for. Now everyone knew what was in store for them if they fucked over their brothers and deceived us.

"No one fucks with the Jackals or me," he reminded everyone before dismissing us all. "Got it?"

When Slade Vincent made a point, he really hit fucking home.

CHAPTER 38

Aaliyah

"Aaliyah," Slade growled at me as everyone departed the execution.

I threw back my whisky because I knew whatever Slade wanted to say would be heavy and I needed something to lighten it. Drown the images of Jaxx's death scorched into my memory.

When the last man left the room, Zethan closed the door and ushered me to move to stand with the Jackals' president.

"Yes, Slade?" My voice came out hard and thick. I needed sleep. Not sure if I would get a wink tonight after what I'd seen and been through.

The damn ambush. Shot at multiple times. Lucky to dodge a bullet. Slapped in the face. Fearing for my life. Slade shifting into a jackal and mutilating bikers. Alaric's PTSD episode. Zethan taking care of the bodies, transporting them to the Underworld to feed his crocodiles. Ending with wiping Kill Bill's, Slim's, and the truck driver's mind of any indication of shifters or godly action. Goddess.

Alaric poured me another drink as if he anticipated I'd need it. Hell, I did under the heated, demanding, expectant gaze of Slade. A hot, hollow, greedy ache started between my thighs that morphed into a pulse of fire at his voice.

"I want you to stay here," he said, "with us. But it's your choice. You go and we can't promise to protect you."

Fuck. I rocked on my feet. Not from the alcohol, sleep deprivation or the deep, anxious pit in my stomach since the firefight erupted. But from Slade Vincent's kindness. He wasn't the sort of man to defy. The type of man to give someone a choice. Especially after he bulldozed me into agreeing to a date.

"I ... I ..." Lost for words, I rubbed at my tight forehead, easing some of the tension gripping it.

"Nurse A. Lost for words?" Slade whistled and glanced at the others with a sexy, wicked grin. "Wonders never cease."

I hit him in the arm, and his jackal growled, low and deep in his chest, feeding the need pulsing at my core.

"What do you say, Aaliyah?" he pressed, an edge of desperation darkening his words. "Do you want to stay here where we can protect you? Until this shit is over?" Then he hit me with another bomb. "Or will you stay as our medic and woman?"

"Fuck, that's a loaded question, Slade." I paced along the window, clutching my tumbler tight to my buzzing chest, damn well vibrating with the anticipation along the mate bond from the four men desperate for my reply.

"Not as loaded as my dick is to fuck you all night," he growled back at me. "*Old lady.*" Such a Slade thing to say.

The other men except Zethan sniggered at his comment.

A hot blush stung my cheeks. Goddess, the man certainly knew how to stun me into silence. No, thanks. Not interested after tonight's events, and probably for at least a year after that.

Slade Vincent might be my godly mate, might have wormed into my heart, softened me with his rough, devilish charm. But he had a lot of things to apologize for. His men stealing me away from my life, under his orders. Mistrusting me and holding me captive against my will. Forcing the mate bond and all its manipulative emotion on me. Tricking me into sleeping with him. Twice, no less! Giving me the best damn orgasms in my life and leaving me to compare every other man after him. The worst of it, though, was threatening to kill me if I was guilty. Asshole could settle in for the longest dry spell of his damn life because I wasn't going there.

"Kind of inappropriate, Slade," I bit back, putting him in his place. But Slade Vincent never said anything appropriate. Damn devil. "And the only action you're seeing for a long time is with your hand."

Zethan's mouth parted, and Castor gave his classic, proud smirk. Alaric bent his head, a little embarrassed by the crudeness of the conversation.

Slade whistled and grinned, impressed with my comeback. "At least my hands will be warm and waiting for *my woman*."

I shook my head at him. He couldn't help himself. Couldn't stop goading me into taking his bait every time. I shouldn't fall for it, but I did. He had a way of getting under my skin in a good and damn bad way. I ignored his obvious and unwelcome attention. Didn't want to encourage him.

For putting me through hell, I'd make him prepare me a thousand damn salami and cheese sandwiches. Buy me a wardrobe of new clothes. Surprise me with flowers, chocolates, cards, and serenades. By the time I was done with him, I'd bring Slade fucking Vincent to his knees, crawling, begging, apologizing. A place I bet he'd never been before. I'd have him crawling through burning coals and flames. If he wanted me, he'd have to work hard for it, prove it, win my heart and trust ... because he never had it in the first place. He took what he wanted, when he wanted it, playing on my confused emotions and lust. I'd not let him win again so easily. Wouldn't fall at his feet because of his hot dimples, rugged good looks, ridiculous muscles, and possessive, smoldering gazes. *Hell, no.* We might be off to a start with his admission of wrongdoing, but it would take a hell of a lot more to convince me we were mates. Until then, he was just a man who kept me alive and safe.

"I'll stay with you." My voice came out like steel. Unwavering and firm. "Until the mess with my brother is dealt with and a new leader is appointed to the Wolves. Jerry, perhaps, if you won't let him prospect for the Jackals?" I left no room for negotiation in my tone.

"I've already let Jerry out," Slade growled back at me, his irritation growing that I didn't fall at his feet and worship him for the god he thought he was. "He's free to move around the club. Got his own bed, for fuck's sake." Good.

"If I come on board as your medic ... even temporarily," I said, enunciating every word clearly. "I want my own space, my own bathroom."

"Fine, take my room." Slade sighed, fishing in his pocket, removing a key and tossing it on the table.

I wasn't done yet. "Not at the clubhouse!"

He challenged my determined stare with a withering one of his own. "We can't protect you if we put you up in your own place."

Nice try, but not backing down, buddy.

"So put me up in one of your places." My eyes went to Castor. He was the safest bet. No curse to harm us physically.

No PTSD to strangle me. No damn hot and spicy mate bond to confuse me and let me slip up and fuck Slade.

"No." Slade's answer came instantly and backed with fire.

"Then I'm leaving." I crossed my arms. "And you'll never see me again."

"Fucking blackmail!" Slade snatched the whisky bottle off Alaric, popped the cap and swallowed half of it to drench his raging temper. He wiped the liquid dripping down his chin, and goddess, I imagined licking it off. "You're one hell of a negotiator, Nurse A." *Ahh.* Still using the nickname. He couldn't be too cranky then. "Cunning, smart, and whip-like in your determination."

Ohh, a compliment. I glowed at it and smiled. The win dangled in my grasp.

"You can stay with Castor," Slade grunted with defeat, and my insides warmed with victory. "I need the room for my men, anyway."

Nice attempt to cover that up. "Pleasure doing business with you, Mr. Vincent." I strode out of the room with a triumphant stride.

"Yeah, and my balls always get crushed when you do!"

Hah! Maybe he shouldn't be so pig-headed, demanding, and pushy.

"Good night, all," I called out, swinging open the door, waiting for Castor. "Have a good night with your hand, Mr. Vincent."

***

CASTOR'S SHOULDERS shook from his deep, delicious chuckle that rumbled through every cell in my body. "I still can't stop laughing at how hard you pushed Slade." Three days later he still found amusement in it. "You owned his ass. I thought you getting him to make you a sandwich was impressive. But you took it to the next level." He emphasized with his hands.

Delight chased through me. I liked the way Castor laughed. The things it did to my body.

He brought me to Thoth's library. Back in time two thousand freaking years! I reclined in the ancient Egyptian chaise lounge, carved with lion's heads at one end and tails at the opposite, cradling a book in my lap.

"Slade needed a lesson in humility."

From reading the books Castor loaned me, I discovered Set was arrogant, haughty, thought himself better than the other gods. Fit to rule even though he was unpopular, dark, destructive, acting out of jealousy and spite, and not in the best interests of the ancient Egyptians. Slade showed himself to be a fair and strong leader, but a little hot-headed, quick to judge, and he definitely followed in his god's footsteps in terms of burning bridges. He needed to learn the art of tact, deliberation, and wisdom. Qualities possessed by Zethan and Castor's gods. If Slade could learn that, he'd be a formidable leader, and he wouldn't need to rely on Castor and Zethan's diplomacy and discernment.

"He's a good guy at heart," Castor defended his president. "If you let him show you."

Not yet. I wasn't in a forgiving kind of mood. I'd never had to work so hard to defend my integrity and honor, and to a man who sold drugs and guns, of all people! Talk about hypocrisy.

"Stop trying to convince me with your insight!" I picked up a date from the table beside me and threw it at Castor.

He caught it, tossed it in his mouth, and smiled as he chewed it. Sexy. I'd never wanted anything more than being that date, crushed under his teeth, worked into jelly on his tongue. Thinking about him biting and sucking me scorched my body all over.

I had to look at the walls of the library to calm down. At the statues of the Egyptian gods along the wall. Animal heads, shendyt skirts, scepters, ankhs, crowns, scrolls. Sculptures, frescoes, hieroglyphs, and carvings in the limestone. Obelisks springing up along the colonnaded hall. Columns painted with reeds and flowers at the top. Large sphinx statues guarding the library's entrance. Scribes working to translate and transcribe scrolls, storing, and preserving them. Palm trees growing almost to the damn ceiling. The ceiling! All the knowledge contained in this building, humming like the gods themselves.

Intrigued by the beauty and splendor, I went out to the balcony to admire the view below. A river traipsing along the western face of the great library. At the huge statue of Thoth holding a book in one hand and a scepter in the other. Wisdom and power ... or magick, as Castor told me. Lush gardens grew plants lost to history, some still in use today, and the sneaky ingredients Castor told me the Jackals used in their drugs.

"Where are you going?" Castor came up behind me, locking his arms around my waist. "I think I found something."

"Really?" I glanced over my shoulder at him, finding him smiling. "What?"

"Reference to a dark king." He squeezed me tighter and nuzzled into my neck, brushing his lips against my burning flesh. "Which I have to check in a few more tomes before I'm solid on anything.

Castor mentioned something about sensing demons protecting Danny and the Wolves at the *Summernat* biker rally.

"Sounds promising." I clasped his arms. Strong, solid, and warm.

His hips swayed right, moving mine with his, and I swung to the gentle, rocking motion like a reed touched by the wind.

"When are you going to teach me more magick?" I leaned my head deeper into his compact chest.

"We can continue now if you like." His voice held a teasing, light edge that made me want to turn and look at him. But he held me firm. "No, you don't. Stay right there."

I fell under the spell of his command. My ass pressed into his thighs, his cock digging into my back, hardening by the second. I liked the feel of him wrapped around me. Velvet over muscle. Hot need echoed down the mate bond.

"How will I learn magick when I'm hot, bothered, and distracted?" Desire raged through me. I was one touch away from spinning around and losing control.

He tipped my head back. Heat blazed in his gaze, hungry for me. "I wasn't talking about that kind of magick."

CHAPTER 39

Aaliyah

CASTOR LEANED DOWN OVER ME, our mouths locking, tongues playing, sweeping, twirling. His arm came around my waist tighter, holding my back to his chest. The hunger in his kisses intensified, doing all sorts of things to my insides, and making the throb between my legs work deeper. At each delicate, teasing sweep of his tongue, I arched against him and groaned.

"What kind of magick is this?" I panted.

The tension in my body was ready to break apart into thousands of pieces if I didn't have him. He flirted with me, commanded me to touch myself, and left me high and dry for more. Now I needed him. All of him.

He branded me with a fierce, scorching kiss that told me everything he wanted to do. Cock like rigid steel at my back, I ground against him, sliding my hand between us, gripping him, caressing him, making him moan into my mouth. I remembered the last time I'd stroked his length on the back of the bike. Delicious need swelled higher.

"I'm so fucking hard, my dick is going to snap off if I don't fuck you," he murmured into my ear.

"So, fuck me." Shocks pulsed through my body at my challenge. I wanted to cast off my clothes and sit on the balcony so he could take me. But he was content with his firm caress on my mouth. One thing was clear: Castor worked on his schedule, not mine.

"Patience, dark sorceress." My name was part groan, part tease, and I almost screamed. "You'll get it when I'm ready."

Fuucckk.

Shivers wracked his body as I worked his length as best I could at the awkward angle before he lowered himself to rub between the globes of my ass. His hands ran along my arms, shoulders, and neck, before settling on my breasts. I needed skin on skin, and I wriggled in his touch. Anticipating my needs, his hands slipped under my shirt, cupping my breasts, squeezing. Growing more vocal, I showed him what I liked.

"Good, girl," Castor whispered, hot and seductive in my ear, and I practically came apart at the rich base of it. "Tell me what you need."

"That," I ground out, covering his hands, making him knead harder. Squirming against him, I was going crazy, desperate for his hot length between the slick opening between my thighs. I pushed one of his hands lower down along my stomach.

"You want my cock?" He nipped at my neck, then pressed his hot tongue on the spots to chase away the sting.

"Yes." Fuck, he had me impatient and begging.

"Sorry to disappoint, but you're going to have to wait." I groaned at his torturous taunt. He was going to drag my pleasure out for his enjoyment.

My aching whimpers fueled him to unbutton my jeans

for better access. I bucked when he slowly crawled along my skin, inch by fucking painful inch, in time to every kiss along my shoulder and nape.

"Dark Daddy won't give you what you want until you're a good girl."

"What do I have to do?"

"Everything I tell you to."

Shudders wrenched my body at his command. My heart and body willing, able, and fucking eager. I wanted to touch him back, but I held my breath, waiting for his command. His hand melted my pussy, parting my lips with two fingers, giving access to one. I stopped breathing altogether, hanging for his touch, which he denied me, stroking the curl of my sex instead. At my frustrated groan, he pulled back to slap my ass, hard and with warning, making it abundantly clear that he was in charge, and I had no say whatsoever. Thrills trickled through me at his dominance and demand for my submission. I'd never been an obedient lover before. This was a whole new level of new and exciting, and I trembled, swallowing my groan of need, letting him take over.

"Good girl." His low and throaty whisper filled me with promises of reward.

Burning fingertips traced teasing circles on one nipple and compensated me with a single stroke of my swollen clit. Turned on as all hell, that one touch sent jittery shocks through my body, and I twitched and groaned when they struck my pussy. My hardened nipples could cut glass like damn diamonds. If he didn't touch me again, I'd shatter beneath him. Urgency raged within him at my pulsing, thick need, and he could barely contain himself. A cry wrenched from my throat at the second reward of two long, firm strokes to my clit. Urged onward by my pleasure, he didn't stop his relentless drill of my bud, bringing me to my first orgasm. Knees buckling, I panted, holding onto his jeans to steady myself.

"That's a good girl." He stroked my hair with one hand, then lifted his dripping finger to his lips, tasting me. Then he made me taste myself, and I sucked his finger deep and hard, and his body quaked. Every erotic move brought us one step closer to his cock inside me. "I'm going to taste you again."

My fingers dug into his denim tighter. "No, I can barely stand."

"You don't need to stand." He came to face me, lifting me into his arms, and I shakily wrapped my legs around his hips.

We kissed all the way to his private quarters in the library, and he didn't even look up, as if he knew the way blindfolded. Brilliant golds, reds, greens, and blues of the mural above his bed made me squint. He threw me on the huge, grand bed, and I bounced. Goddess, this thing could probably fit me and all four of my …. Nope, not falling in that trap. I shook off that thought.

Surprise, surprise, gold sheets draped the mattress, no blankets needed in the heat. Everything in this library was gold, even the bed frame and bedside drawers. The ancient Egyptians sure loved their gold. I didn't get a chance to admire the room further when Castor removed my clothing with one flick of his wrist. Naked and a little shy, I covered my breasts. Nothing he hadn't seen before from bathing me, but not up close and certainly not under that steaming gaze of his.

One scoop had me in his arms again, his mouth locked to my left nipple, sucking it hard, biting in between. My head fell back from the tingles spreading through my body like concentric waves in water disturbed by a stone. Without taking his mouth away from my nipple, he moved us to the wall, shoving me against it, grinding his stiff, bobbing length against my clit. Vibrations danced along my sensitive, dusky flesh as he moaned his pleasure into it. He let go of me to jerk something off the wall, a contraption mounted on it that looked like an inversion table for stretching.

"What are you doing?" I twitched my arms as he tried to secure me to the device.

"What does it look like?" Castor locked my left arm in place, and I rattled my binding, staring at him, demanding he free me.

"Castor?" My heart hammered. "I'm not sure about this. Whatever *this* is."

"I won't hurt you." His promise thundered through the bond with reassurance.

"But you're gonna fuck me in some weird, freaky position?"

He chuckled. Deep and throaty. Resounding in my core. "Slade might be able to make you come three times, but you'll never forget my fucking."

Wow. Promises. Hope he delivered.

Books flashed in my mind. Medical books. Psychology books. Sexual practices in cultures and the art of sex. Goddess, what hadn't he read? He wanted to try out some moves from one of the books. His last mate hadn't been accommodating or experimental and he thought I might be.

"Do I have your permission to pleasure you?" I almost giggled at the way he said that. Reverent. Courteous. He never asked my permission for anything, like Slade in that regard, but more considerate and caring.

I stared into his heated, eager gaze, digging deeper into his yearning to experiment and satisfy the scientist in him that came from his god. He wanted this so much. Was never able to explore it. This would be a gift to him.

"Yes, you can pleasure me," I whispered, shaking in anticipation. "But if I want to stop, promise me you will?"

He grinned, sexy and mysterious as always. "You won't want to stop."

"I'm serious."

"So am I."

"Castor?"

"I promise."

I nodded my approval, and he took my right arm and secured me in place.

He captured my legs, one by one, strapping them in. "Ready?"

As always, my heart screamed yes, and my head bombarded me with reasons to object. Before I could voice any of it, he spun the device, holding me upside down.

My world pivoted, and I took a few moments to breathe and work through the dizziness. "You're going to make the blood rush to my head," I panted. "And I'll pass out."

"Trust me," he crooned, making his clothes disappear, denying me the opportunity to strip and explore that gorgeous, firm body of his. "With what I'm going to do to you, all your blood will flow to your pussy."

Excited and nervous at the same time, I licked my lips, waiting for the next step. I hope he didn't keep me inverted for too long.

Steel on the machine creaked as he hitched it lower to the ground. When he had me where he wanted, he sank to his knees, grabbed my thighs and buried his face between my legs. His tongue grazed along my clit in merciless motions, up and down, circles, sucks, licks, driving my pleasure scaling. My pussy slid apart at every swipe, and I cried out, hollow and aching, desperate to be filled. Pulses of orgasm flirted at the edges of my core as he buried his tongue inside me, tasting every drop, leaving no place untouched. My nails dug into my palms, because that was all I had to hold on to when I wanted to fist his hair. Stuttered whimpers encouraged him on, and he didn't stop until my body shattered over his tongue. Muscles in my thighs locked up as the pleasure crested through me a second time.

The man didn't even give me time to breathe, hoisting the contraption higher, twisting it slightly, so my feet faced his direction, and I could see the floor. Alarmed at the unexpected motion, I shrieked. But not as much as when he sank his bobbing, solid length inside me, deep and hard.

"Oh, fuck." My body jolted with surprise at the unusual angle of his cock hitting my g-spot hard, rubbing it exactly where I needed it.

"That's it, baby, good girl," Castor soothed, plunging in and out in a steady beat. "Take Dark Daddy's dick deeper."

I bit my lip as his girth and length stretched me, testing my limits. *Fucking hell.* He's fucking me upside down. While I'm tied at a weird angle. Every drive into me shook the device, and I worried it wouldn't hold my weight.

"It'll hold." At his assurance, I relaxed my muscles, allowing him to sink deeper. My core locked him in position, desperate to keep him there forever.

My throat quickly dried and went hoarse from all the moaning as he pounded me harder, faster, driving me straight to delirium.

"That's not the best bit, dark sorceress." I groaned at his gravelly use of my name. At his promise of more. Because his cock completely filled me up and drove me to unreached heights, and I wasn't sure how much more I could take before I split apart again.

Something exploded in my pussy, fibers extending in all directions, caressing every part of me. My eyes exploded wide. Fingernails bit into my palms. Teeth broke the skin on my lips, and I bled. "Oh, God!"

Castor gripped my thighs harder, leaving marks on my

skin that would stay for days. "Ibis shifters have soft spurs to pleasure and grip onto their mate."

"Fuucckk!" I almost spilled over from the stroke of hundreds of strands of his delicious bottlebrush cock grazing every nerve ending, making my body go up in flames. I'd never felt anything like this angle, this upside-down penetration, these goddamn soft spurs delivering pleasure a thousandfold.

My head swam in a mindless haze of pleasure. I didn't want this to end, but an orgasm teased at the edges, and I was about to tip over. On his next thrust, I shuddered all over, screaming his name, holding on for dear life in case I rattled this damn contraption off the wall from how hard I shook.

"That's it, baby, quake all over me." Castor pounded me harder, milking out even more pleasure. Right when I thought I couldn't take any more, his body locked tight, his spurs retreated, and his cock quaked, spurting deep inside of me. Pain split down my shoulder blades, and I arched my back.

Fuck, what the hell was going on? This was supposed to be good. I think Castor made me pull a muscle or something.

I lost control of reality and I think I passed out. Something scratched along my back as if Castor tickled me with a feather, and I murmured at him, unable to form words to tell him to stop. Wind beat at me as if I was fanned with palm leaves or something. My knees rested on the floor. The contraption I'd been in moments ago was broken, the straps snapped, the metal twisted.

Castor's back was pressed to the mattress. Eyes wide, he studied me, a combination of curious, scientific, and shocked.

A relentless itch pestered my shoulder, and I scratched at it. "What?" My fingers came into contact with something soft, feathery, and really long. "What the fuck?" I glanced over my shoulders at the gold, blue, green, and red feathers. Wings. I had fucking wings.

"I guess we figured out how to make you shift." Castor crawled over to me, running his fingers over my beautiful but unwanted wings. He admired them like a true scientist, stroking at first, then plucking them, testing their strength.

"Not funny!" I pulled back. "I'm not your damn science experiment." Annoyed, I flicked my shoulders, trying to get them to fold away. Nope. "How do I put these things away?"

Castor shrugged and grinned. Devious. Dark. Sexy. "Since they emerged at the point of your orgasm, we could try fucking again ..."

Enjoyed this novel? **Leave me a review on Amazon or Goodreads and let me know what you thought.**

Keep reading **for an exclusive preview of the *BRUTAL MATES* or grab it here.**

Preorder **the next book in my mythology and gods series connected to Jackals' Wrath MC - Married to the Mafia.**

Catch up with avatars from the Greek Pantheon where it all started, in Battlefield Love (Operation Cupid #1).
Wounded heroes/heroine discover hidden powers in this sexy tale about a sassy and disillusioned phone-sex worker inheriting the powers of Eros.

Love grumpy heroes and fated mates?
In Operation Hades the cold-hearted Lord of the Dead meets

his match! An original, steamy, addictive Hades and Persephone retelling.

Wounded heroes, shifters and secret supernatural organizations clash in Life's a Witch (Guild of Guardians). Supernatural hunters capture the deadliest of criminal monsters in this delicious slow burn enemies to lovers with plenty of HOT m/m.

Witches and wizards, steamy slow burn paranormal academy romance collides in Darkfire (Nightfire Academy), with twists, turns, protective guardians, student teacher relations and the cutest, fiercest owl gargoyle you'll ever meet!

JACKALS' WRATH MC WORLD REFERENCES

Below is a list of names used throughout this series.

Aaliyah Heller - Avatar of Isis.

Alaric Hawke - Jackal's Wrath MC Road Captain & Avatar of Horus.

Avatar - a human embodied with the power and characteristics of their patron god i.e. Set is the devil of the Egyptian pantheon and his avatar Slade is made of sin.

Bagman - a person who receives payoffs.

Castor Redding - Jackal's Wrath MC Enforcer & Avatar of Thoth.

Church - Official MC meeting.

Cut - MC member's vest.

Duat - the Egyptian Underworld.

Horus - hawk-headed god of the Sky. God to Alaric.

Isis - Goddess of Healing, Fertility and Magic and consort to Osiris (wife). Goddess to Aaliyah.

Little snack - pay off or bribe.

Osiris - God of the Underworld and consort (husband) of Isis. Zethan's God.

Patch - Club logo emblem worn on an MC cut.

Pharaoh - drug made exclusively by Jackals' Wrath MC.

Set - Jackal-headed god of Chaos, Destruction, the Dessert. Slade's God.

Slade Vincent - Jackal's Wrath Vice President & Avatar of of Set.

Stunt man - fall guy set up to pin petty crime on to divert police attention when conveying a shipment.

Thoth - Ibis-headed god of Writing, Science & Magic. Castor's god.

Zethan Stone - Jackal's Wrath MC Vice President & Avatar of Osiris.

EXCLUSIVE PREVIEW OF BRUTAL MATES

1. Aaliyah

IT STARTED WITH BLOOD, and it would end with blood. War launched between the Jackals and Wolves, an ambush on a drug shipment the first act of aggression. Casualties fell on both sides, me being one of them, my brother another. I survived, thanks to scrappy backyard surgery from the Jackal's doctor. My dick of a brother pushed through four bullet wounds, thanks to the help of demons and dark magick.

Edgy from thinking about my brother, I gripped Castor's waist tighter from my bitch-position on his bike. His warmth soaked into me, steering away my fears and the chill crawling through me.

Mysterious players entered the fray with the Jackals, paid for by a shadowy enemy, muddying the waters and confusing the avatars. My allies defeated one threat, staging a fake drug delivery, capturing three hostages, and executing a traitor.

Cleared of guilt, I earned the Jackal's trust, and agreed to remain with them until all threats were neutralized. I didn't know how long that would be or if I'd even want to go home after all this. My life felt insignificant without the avatars in it. But there was still that niggling doubt, the voice inside me that persuaded me to leave them behind, that they were more trouble than they were worth. I'd already lost two people I loved through biker clubs. Adopted my daughter out to shield her from that life.

Blind to our enemy, the Jackals and I were vulnerable to more attacks and couldn't mount an offensive strategy to curb their efforts. In the meantime, the avatars focused on defending their club from ongoing threats and continued their hunt for the real enemy. I hoped this would finally lead to the identity of my father's murderer, because only then would I be able to repay the blood taken from me.

The gods led us to this moment, and they would see us through to the end, whether we lived or died. There'd always be another human to take over as their avatars. Trapped by the curse for thousands of years, the gods were getting edgy and impatient for freedom, and they placed enormous responsibility and trust in Slade, Zethan, Castor, Alaric, and me to break the curse binding us together. Castor bore the brunt of that responsibility, but now that I was here, I could help ease that burden and contribute to his research. I was backed by a goddess of magick, after all.

Castor's bike roared louder as it rolled into his garage, where he parked it and killed the engine. I reluctantly released my grasp of his stomach when he kicked the stand down, and I dismounted.

The trench coat concealing my awkwardly folded wings got caught on his footpeg, jerked off my shoulders, and fell to the stained pavement. Wings that refused to tuck into my damn back no matter how much sex I had with Castor. Squeaks accompanied the garage door's descent, and my eyes shot to the neighboring properties across the road.

"Shit." I bent down to scoop up the coat and threw it over my shoulders.

Castor gave me his signature secretive smile as the door creaked shut. He extended a bruised hand, marked from enforcing his fists on the captives.

"Here, dark sorceress." That deep and rich timbre knocked me on my ass with what little balance I possessed.

Goddess. This dark, enigmatic criminal should be charged for doing such things to my body and making me puddle at his feet. My heart punched my mind in the throat and shut that bitch up.

I accepted his hand, and he hefted me to my feet, steadying me as I rocked against his firm chest. Extra weight from my vivid new appendages put me off balance, and I felt like a waddling pregnant woman. The fabric of my coat caught on my wing, scraping it, and I wriggled, trying to shake it loose. Never accept a dare from Castor to shift. The last two days I was stuck with these heavy-ass things.

Castor unclipped my helmet for me and brushed stray hair over my ear. Blood flowed in a heated rush to parts that demanded to be touched.

Paranoid, I asked, "Do you think your neighbors saw me?"

His devastating eyes roamed over me ravenously. "Mrs. Beatrix at number twenty-one is a nosey neighbor. Very disapproving of a *dirty biker* living opposite her." His impish smirk teased me.

I slapped at him. "Shut up. I'm serious."

He chuckled, and my bond went taut with need. "To her credit, she's the best guard dog I've got. Calls her best friend around the corner to gossip if anyone comes snooping." He tapped his head. "And I hear every word of it."

"Aren't you lucky?" I squinted my eyes and gave him a mock smile for teasing me. "Jim at number six is stoned all the time. Smurf, the little Chihuahua at number three, barks at anything. And Mr. Balfor at number four is deaf. None of them can be relied on to protect my apartment. Thieves broke in and stole my laptop and TV."

"I can help you with that." Castor grinned, tapping his head again.

"*Please*. My laptop has my graduation photos and some of my dad's last birthday party." The thought had me going silent for a moment.

"Consider it done." Castor's knuckles skimmed along my arm.

What he'd said snapped back into my head. I paused, hesitant to take another step after his answer. "Wait. Are you shitting me? Has anyone come snooping?"

"A few cops showed up after your dad died," he admitted. "One tried to plant a gun in my back garden."

What the fuck? Dirty-assed cops. Was there anyone decent in the police force these days?

"I took care of it and warned the others. The cops didn't get far after that, especially when they obtained warrants and searched our houses." He scrubbed his scruffy jaw, stubbled from all the research we'd been doing in the Great Library of Thoth. Oh, and all the sex had kept him too busy for man care. "I wasn't fast enough to save Slade."

Heat in my body dissipated in an instant. I caught Castor's hand, drawing it from his face, clasping it tightly. "We'll find evidence to exonerate him."

Castor's expression remained unsure, and he scratched the outside of his hand with his thumb. "C'mon, dark sorceress. Let's go inside." He dragged me to the door, tugged it open and gestured for me to go first.

A couple of days ago, I bargained Slade's ass to move out of the rough and ready clubhouse and stay in better comfort. I proposed Castor's place as the most ideal, simply because I couldn't trust myself not ending up in the Jackal's president's bed if I stayed with him. Zethan was scratched off the list because of the curse, and I didn't want to risk being choked if I bedded at Alaric's house. Reluctantly, Slade agreed to let me stay with Castor. At last, I could finally get some privacy and freedom from guards following me around all the time. Escape from the constant smell of oil, fuel, grease, alcohol, and sweaty asses of thirty noisy men.

Castor's reluctance nagged at the bond. He liked his space and didn't want me to crowd it, yet I just invited myself into his life and felt awful for giving him no choice. Ever since, a part of him felt distant, a little cold, and detached, like he hid something from me again. Every time we took two steps forward, we seemed to take another back. It made me doubt that he or the rest of the avatars were right for me. I didn't want to be privy to every emotion, and I sure as hell didn't want to know they kept things from me. Bikers weren't exactly loyal to their women, and the club came first. I sure as shit wasn't settling for second best again.

Still, I owed Castor thanks for being a good sport. "Thanks for letting me stay with you. I know I put you on the spot the other day with Slade."

Castor's arm came around my back, drawing me flat to his chest, and a pleased shiver played down my spine. "You're my woman. Your home is with me." The possessive edge to his voice warmed me from head to toe.

Despite reassuring me, smudges on his end of the bond concealed something. I wanted to know what it was but didn't want to pry. He'd tell me when he was ready. If it was another woman, I'd barbeque his ass, because I was not sharing, nor was I letting him go down the path of my father or brother with having a mistress.

Keen for some banter to lighten up his mystery, I stretched up and seductively whispered in his ear, "You might regret saying that when I decorate your sofa or bed with pink cushions." I finished with a playful bite to his lobe, feeding more blood to my southern borders.

"Oh, no you don't." He lifted me over his shoulder to carry me caveman-style inside, and I giggled.

Pain lanced down my wings as they caught on the doorframe, canceling any arousal. Shit, those things were annoying. Two damn days. Itchy as hell and right where I couldn't reach, aching between my shoulder blades. The weight pulled on my muscles, straining them to the point of a constant backache. Made sleeping very difficult.

"Fuck. Sorry, dark sorceress." Castor gently returned me to my feet, rubbing the edges of my wings, dulling the pain.

I groaned and leaned my head back. "Keep doing that and make it up to me, you brute." My nipples hardened at his dark chuckle.

Castor forced me to shuffle sideways, edging me inside his foyer, his hands never leaving my shoulders. Once inside, he took my hand, grabbed the suitcase Zethan had dropped off earlier today in his van, and led me along his hallway.

I wasn't sure what to expect as my boots tapped on the polished oak floors. Messy like his clubhouse desk, packed with books, whisky glasses, and magical items? Smelling like herbs, candle wax, and incense? Completely the opposite. Freakishly neat and clean. Stormy gray walls contrasting with lighter ones. A movie poster from the seventies and weird art on his wall. A guitar and speaker beside his leather sofa. Minibar in the corner of his living room. A motorcycle wheel mounted to his wall. Massive TV on a wooden stand.

Two plush recliners that I wanted to drop into and snuggle. An everyday bachelor pad. At least it wasn't filled with weird sex swings, poles or toys ... although, I bet his bedroom was. Dark Daddy must be into toy play.

We moved into his kitchen, where he deposited my suitcase full of the clothes he brought me. Antique furniture, including a dining table, bookshelves, and wine cabinet featured in the dining room.

"It's nice," I admired.

"Nice?" Castor teased, wrapping his arms around me, enveloping me in his radiant warmth. His hands settled at the curve of my back in a comforting pressure. He pulled an alluring, exciting hunger from me, which my heart demanded I explore, but my mind warned me of the consequences.

"Nice for an enforcer," I joked. "Although, I expected whips and chains." A reference to his weird sex contraption on the wall of his bedroom at Thoth's library, where he strapped me in and fucked me upside down.

He chuckled, breathing hot and heavy in my ear. "That's just for the bedroom. And you wouldn't have the heart for it."

I nudged him with my ass, playfully teasing, hoping he'd lift me on the counter and take me to alleviate the dark need his touch sparked. "You got a red room, huh? A dungeon downstairs too?"

I didn't really know what that was, but my friends at the hospital told me about a patient who came in with a sex toy stuck up her vaginal cavity from some Dom and sub play. Red rooms, BDSM, whips, and chains were the topics of conversation at the water cooler for the next few days. Learned *a lot* from those chats.

Castor was into his Dark Daddy and dominance play, so I assumed he might be into that too. I was eager to explore. Whips ... maybe not. A light spank? *Hell, yeah.*

He scratched the back of his neck. "I wanted to wait a month or so before introducing you to that."

I snorted and smacked him for joking with me. "Good one!"

"I'm serious." *Fuck.* He led me to a wall on the far side and jerked his head at it. "Open it, dark sorceress."

I quirked an eyebrow. "Open what? It's a wall?"

"Panic room," he corrected, and my stomach sank. "I want you to hide down here if anything ever happens. If your brother ever tracks you here. We've all got a basement for protection. Perk of the job."

Tricky Castor always had a ploy up his sleeve. Bikers should always be prepared for their enemies. *Goddess.* Nowhere felt safe anymore, not even with the Jackals. But I was safest with the avatars, four incredibly powerful servants of the gods.

Eager to practice my skills, I summoned the detection magick he taught me to use, seeking out any spells on the wall. Wards beneath my fingertips tingled on my skin.

"Aten," I whispered the Sun god's name, calling upon his light to illuminate the concealed hieroglyphs. Dark symbols of birds, snakes, eyes, and people glowed golden, crackled, and burned red into the wall.

"Good," Castor crooned over my shoulder, and shivers wracked my body. "Now remove the wards."

I swept my vertical hands outwards. "Teti."

Fire razed the wards, and they sizzled and spat embers. Ash fluttered to the floor, vanishing before it burned the wood. An outline of a door formed, gaining clarity, forming a heavy, wooden frame with an iron handle.

Castor massaged my shoulders and kissed the sensitive skin behind my ears. "Good girl."

His magick unlocked the basement door and cast it open

with a stubborn groan, telling me it hadn't been opened in a while. Hand clasped in mine, he took me downstairs for a tour. Another snap of power flicked the lights on, producing a hard, red blush. Musty and stale air encouraged me to sneeze. This place hadn't seen fresh air in goddess knows how long.

At the bottom of the steps, my wings shot outward at the sight in front of me. An antique four-poster bed made of solid damn wood with a mattress sheathed in red satin. How the fuck did he even get that thing down here? Never mind. Magick, probably. A gold stand with various kinky-looking devices dangling on it; feathers, tassels, collars, handcuffs, wrist bands, silk ties, red ropes, and blindfolds. I swallowed at the long leather rods that looked like horse whips. Ten blinks later, my eyes jumped to the dark, leather-studded sofa with a side table covered in crystal glasses and decanters filled with colored alcohol. A rod on the wall with more dangling items I didn't recognize or want to know what the heck they were used for.

"I thought you said this was a panic room." I tried to make light of it, but it came out nervous and stuttered.

"It serves multiple purposes," he explained, magick curling from his finger to summon a compartment from the wall packed with guns and knives.

Fuck me, I shouldn't have joked about the dungeon. He really owned a red room that doubled as a defense pit. All this was a little intimidating.

I swallowed at the thick, nervous lump in my throat. After the BDSM water cooler chats, I bought some erotic fiction books to cure my ignorance. Talk about eyes being opened from those. Some of the kink aroused me, like the control Castor demonstrated, or the gentle tying up, blindfolding, and elimination of senses to heighten pleasure. But I drew the line at having my mouth bound, my body contorted into weird-ass positions, tied up by shibari rope or forced to wear and do humiliating actions.

Wow. Castor really threw me in the deep end. Uncomfortable with the daunting number of toys, I turned to look at him. "Maybe I should stay with Slade."

ABOUT THE AUTHOR

USA Today bestselling author Skyler writes unforgettable paranormal romance with complicated and haunted heroes and the strong heroines they claim.

Skyler resides in Australia, where most of her books are based. Be warned: she'll have you laughing from her wicked humor, crying, and throwing your kindle in the space of a chapter. Sometimes she has to send her alter ego *Evil Skyler* to the naughty corner for torturing her heroes.

When she's not plotting her next story or the demise of her villains, Skyler can be found searching for her partner's ever-moving chocolate stash, snuggled with her fur babies, never following a recipe properly, and making up her own pilates moves… because where's the fun in following the rules? Learn more about her at https://skylerandra.com

SKYLER'S OTHER BOOKS

Are you curious to read the other novels by me?

MYTHOLOGY & GODS UNIVERSE

OPERATION CUPID
Completed reverse harem mythology romance

1. Battlefield Love
2. Quicksilver Love
3. Awakened Love

Cupid's Surrender - Operation Cupid boxset with bonus Valentine's short story Stupid Cupid

HADES' REDEMPTION
Completed fated mates romance

1. Lady of the Underworld
2. Lord of the Underworld
3. Rulers of the Underworld
4. Return to the Underworld

JACKALS' WRATH MC
Completed paranormal motorcycle club romance

0.5 Prophecy of the Gods - prequel exclusive to newsletter subscribers

1. Cursed Mates
2. Merciless Mates
3. Brutal Mates
4. Broken Mates
5. Sinful Mates
6. Festive Mates
7. Vengeful Mates

BLOOD DEBT KINGPIN
Paranormal mafia arranged marriage romance

0.5 Falling for the Mafia (prequel) - coming 2023 (newsletter exclusive)
1. Married to the Mafia - coming 2023
2. Betrayed by the Mafia - coming 2023

More gods series planned! Stay tuned.

WOLF MOON REJECTED
　　M/F Rejected Mates

1. Heartless Wolf - coming 2023

GUILD UNIVERSE - PARANORMAL ROMANCE

NIGHTFIRE ACADEMY
Adult paranormal academy reverse harem romance

1. Darkfire
2. Wildfire
3. Crossfire
3.5 Hearthfire - available by signing up to my newsletter http://eepurl.com/dCOqkL
4. Hellfire

Nightfire Academy Box Set (Books 1 - 4)

GUILD OF GUARDIANS
Paranormal reverse harem romance with m/m

0.5 Witch Hunt (prequel novella)
1. Life's a Witch
2. Hindsight's a Witch
3. Witch Please
4. Karma's a Witch
5. Son of a Witch - coming 2023

FAIRYTALE RETELLINGS:

WINTER QUEEN series
Heart of Frost - a M/F Snow Queen retelling with a snow leopard shifter

DARK REFLECTIONS series
Born into Darkness - a Reverse Harem Snow White retelling with panthers

STANDALONE REVERSE HAREMS

Charmed- an Aladdin retelling
Claimed- a Little Mermaid retelling

FALLEN STARLIGHTS - Shared World series
Orion (Galaxy Huntress) Fallen Starlights series
reverse harem paranormal romantic comedy with a werewolf, vampire, and demon

STALKY STALK LINKS

Become a darkling and join my readers group Skyler's Den of Darkness for exclusive content, latest news, and giveaways.

Sign up to my newsletter here
https://skylerandra.com/index.php/newslettersignup/

Watch my Tiktok videos skylerandraauthor

Stalk me on the Gram skylerandraauthor

Check out my Youtube vids, including book trailers and me reading chapters or sample audiobook chapters: https://www.youtube.com/channel/UC-MQvzm8R8MQEWVX2xd4v2g

For notifications on my latest releases, follow me on:
   Amazon https://www.amazon.com/Skyler-Andra/e/B00JQTFBRI
   Goodreads: https://www.goodreads.com/author/show/8170388.Skyler_Andra
   Bookbub: https://www.bookbub.com/profile/skyler-andra

You're a true stalker if you're following me on all ;)

Printed in Great Britain
by Amazon